# MEGHAN QUINN

# MY *Best* FRIEND'S EX

Published by Hot-Lanta Publishing
Copyright 2017
Cover design by Meghan Quinn
Photo credit: Neil Danvers
Model: Devin Paisley
Formatting by CP Smith

www.authormeghanquinn.com

# MY *Best* FRIEND'S EX

# Chapter One

EMMA

"Just stick it in. Stop stalling and get it over with."

"I can't."

"Emma, it's not going to go in itself."

I twist my hands in front of me and say, "Maybe it will."

Logan gives me a pointed look. "Catheters don't insert themselves. Just do it."

"But"—I bite the inside of my cheek and look behind me at Mr. Freeland—"it's so wrinkly."

Logan runs his hand over his face and exhales. "He's old. It's not the first ancient dick you've seen."

I swallow hard and lean forward. "It's the first ancient dick I've seen wearing a turtleneck."

"A turtle—" Logan, my best guy friend and fellow nursing student pauses and tilts his head. "He's not circumcised?"

"No. And I'm not sure how to handle it. Do I just go in there, pull the turtleneck down, and resume business?"

"I think so." Logan thinks about it for a second and asks, "Should I ask Dr. Thompkins?"

"No," I say quickly. "We don't want him judging us on our inability to handle a wrinkly old penis with a flap. We can do this."

"Why do you keep saying words like we and us? This is your patient; you've been assigned to him. There is no we or us in this scenario."

I cross my arms over my chest and stare at my friend. "There was no we and us when little eight-year-old Donovan came in with a nail sticking out of his kneecap. And when you couldn't stop dry heaving, I stepped in."

"That was different. It was a nail in a kneecap. Nails should never be stuck in kneecaps," he stresses. "This is just an old man's dick. You've done this a million times. You're just being lazy."

My eyebrows shoot up. "Lazy? You're calling me lazy?"

He cringes. "Bad choice of words. Not lazy per se, more . . ." He thinks for a second and then shakes his head. "No, you're being lazy. What are you going to do when we aren't working together anymore? Ask someone else to play with the turtleneck?"

*Absolutely.*

Logan and I have known each other since our first year in nursing school. Both wide-eyed and scared shitless from the amount of crap we had to clean during our first clinical, we stuck together. Now we're in our fourth year, just around the corner from graduating, and he's still by my side, but now he's no longer helping me, but pushing me to be better. He's been quite aggressive in his approach this year, and I know it's because when we graduate we'll most likely go our separate ways.

"Today isn't a good day for me." I pause and twist my long brown hair between my fingers.

"Yeah, why's that?" There is a smirk on his lips. He's calling my bullshit.

"Uh, period." I nod my head, liking this idea. "Yeah. Got the period. Not only do I shed my uterine walls during this three to five day stint of living hell, but I also become very unpredictable. You never know what I'll end up doing." I clasp my index finger and thumb together and start making jabby motions. "See, very unpredictable."

With his giant man-fist, Logan palms my hand, halting all jabbing. "First of all, don't try to scare me with your shedding uterus. You fail to remember I had to assist a doctor in removing a double-tampon pileup from Vagina Veronica my second year. I've been conditioned by female menstruation since then. And second of all, do you really think your little erratic jabs will deter me? I kick-box for a hobby against men twice your size."

Damn it, I forgot both those things.

I cross my arms over my chest and look him up and down. "You're annoying, you know that?"

"Just looking out for my girl. Now, go in there, say hi to Mr. Freeland, and get the job done."

Huffing out my frustration, I walk toward Mr. Freeland's room just as my phone rings. "Oh, I have to get that," I say rather desperately, appreciating the surprise distraction.

"You don't have to—"

I hold up my finger. "I'm on the phone." I catch his smirk as I turn around and answer the call. "Hello?"

"Emma? It's Adalyn." Even though I'm thankful for the distraction, it's rare for my roommate to call during the day when I'm on clinical.

"Hey, what's up?"

"Um, you might want to come home." The wariness in her voice sends prickles of fear up my back.

"Is everything okay?" Logan gives me a *get-real* look, probably assuming I'm making up this entire phone call.

"Not really, just come home as quickly as you can."

"Okay." Confused, I hang up and look at Logan. "That was Adalyn. I need to get home now."

Sitting back on his heels, Logan starts to slow clap for me. "Wow, well played, Em. Didn't think you had such trickery in your back pocket but you proved me wrong."

"I'm not kidding. I didn't make this up."

"Awfully convenient." His mouth twists.

"How on earth could I have asked Adalyn to call me? I've been with you this whole time."

Logan thinks about it for a second and then says, "Telepathically. Women always sync together when they get their periods. I wouldn't be surprised if one uterus shouted to the other an SOS."

I roll my eyes and head toward the locker room; our shift is almost over so this is perfect timing. "And here I thought you were different than other guys, Logan. Can you please just do the catheter? Adalyn sounded really nervous."

"This is such crap." He points at me and says, "How do I know you're not lying?"

"Come with me then if you don't believe me. Of course, *after* you do the catheter. I'll grab your things for you."

He rolls his eyes and heads into Mr. Freeland's room. Thank God! Logan is so much more adept at catheters than I am anyway, so he would be more gentle, just what Mr. Freeland needs. I take my time tying up loose ends for us, grab our stuff, and meet him in the lobby. He's shaking his head at me as he approaches. "You're lucky I like you."

I give him a quick side hug. "Thank you."

Together, we ride the city bus to the stop near the townhouse I've been sharing with Adalyn since the beginning of this year. Logan teases me, accusing me of making something up to get out of touching Mr. Freeland's penis. Naturally, I deny every accusation while feeling very lucky I was able to avoid the touching of old dick today.

That is until I show up at our little house.

When we walk up to the duplex, Adalyn is sitting on the steps, a paper in her hand. What is going on? Adalyn *doesn't* sit outside. She's afraid of the sun, not really, but she's usually in the house, her nose buried in a book, preparing for our upcoming nursing exams.

"Adalyn, is everything okay?" I close the space between us just as she holds up the piece of paper in her hand.

"We're being evicted."

"What?" I shout as I take the paper. Logan hovers over my shoulder, reading the notice at the same time. At least he knows I wasn't lying now.

It takes me a few tries to process the words on the bright red paper. "We're being evicted," I whisper in shock. "How can that be? We've been paying our rent on time. We haven't done anything to the property that would get us evicted. We forgot trash day that one time, but I don't think that would be cause for eviction."

From over my shoulder, Logan points at a sentence and says, "Your landlord hasn't been paying the mortgage. You have one week to find a new place."

"A week?" How did I miss that? I scan the paper again, but nothing is making sense. "So because our landlord is an irresponsible idiot, we get punished? How is that fair?"

Logan pulls me into a hug, taking the paper from me to read some more. "Life isn't fair, sweetheart. Banks don't care about the people living in the house, they just care about the bottom line."

I snuggle into his warmth. "But a week? That seems short to me."

"Yeah, how can we possibly find a place to stay in a week in the middle of the semester? All the student housing is full by now," Adalyn adds.

"There is a buyer already interested in the space," Logan says. "The bank is probably opting for a short sale in the hopes to get the money off their hands."

"Can't we talk to the bank? Maybe they want to rent it to us."

Logan shakes his head. "Sorry, sweetheart, banks aren't really into the landlord business." He hands the paper back to Adalyn. "You two need to start searching for another place to stay because in a week, you won't be living here anymore."

Adalyn lies back on the porch, the warm winter's day not affecting her need to retreat back inside. "This is crap."

"Who can I send a nasty gram to?" I ask, my mind already starting to type out the letter. It would start with something like, "You piece of crap, son of a bitch asshole . . ." Yeah, that sounds about right.

"You can send one to me," Logan jokes as he releases me and sits down on the porch next to Adalyn.

"That's not helpful." I run my hands over my face and think. "I don't have time to search for a new place right now. I have clinicals all week, and I have to study. Plus, I have volunteering hours at the animal shelter. I can't cancel on them again."

"You can stay with me until you find a place," Logan suggests.

I put my hand on my hip, ready to disagree. "You live in a three-bedroom apartment with six men. You sleep in bunk beds. I'm not staying with you."

He shrugs. "Don't judge my living situation. Rent is cheap as fuck." It's true, he pays two hundred dollars a month for everything. EVERYTHING. It's not fair. Although, I don't think I would ever shack up with that many people in such a small space.

"Ugh." I sit on the sidewalk, not minding the cold cement against my scrub-covered ass. "Looks like I'll be staying up late, looking for a place."

"You're good at stuff like this, Em; you'll find a place. I have no doubt about it." Logan winks at me.

I can't help but agree with him. I'm good at *stuff like this*, but for others, not for me. I've always been the nurturing one in my group of friends, making sure everyone is taken care of. But when it comes to me, when it comes to putting me first, I'm freaking terrible at it. I'm more likely to buy a cup of coffee for a friend so they can stay awake in class than for me. Perhaps it's a major flaw that I never do anything for me.

But hey, I guess that will make me a good nurse, right? Always taking care of others?

# Chapter Two

## TUCKER

"Jameson!"

My last name rings through the bare bones of the house I've been working on for the past month. It's my first managing project, and I can already feel my boss breathing down my neck about the timeline and when we're supposed to finish.

Rolling up the house plans, I turn to see Julius, the beer-belly dickhead, my boss, waddling toward me. It *should* be comical watching the veins popping angrily in his neck. *Should.*

Fuck, this isn't going to be good.

"Why the hell are we spending an extra two thousand dollars on an outside electrician when we have one in-house?"

Julius Parsnip. Yup, that's his name. I've been working for him since I was a teenager. Think of your worst nightmare when it comes to a contractor and multiply it by ten. That's Julius. He has zero credibility when it comes to his business, and the only reason he keeps getting hired for job after job is because of the people—like me—holding his company together.

Julius is one of those managers who sits back, drinks beers, and dabbles in plans every once in a while, making a big fucking deal about things when the mood strikes him.

Looks like it's one of those moments.

"Manny is on paternity leave," I answer, keeping my voice calm. Julius has no idea about his day-to-day operations, so his lack of knowledge regarding Manny doesn't surprise me.

"Fucking fathers," he mutters to himself and shakes his head. Boss of the year right here. "You could have waited for him to come back."

I put my hands in my pockets, trying to calm the flex in my chest, the tension building in my shoulders. "Not possible. If I'd waited for Manny, the entire timeline would have been thrown off, and we would be behind. I had counters coming in and the wiring had to be done before I installed them. I didn't have a choice."

Fuming now, his face looking like an ugly shade of purple, he spits at me, "These are things you need to bring to my attention. I could have thrown Danny in there to do them."

"Danny is still an apprentice, and that goes against code."

"Fuck the code. We'd have Manny sign off on it."

I run my hand over my face, knowing I won't get anywhere with this man, so I concede, my jaw tight as I say, "Yeah, next time I'll check with you."

"Fucking right you will. Just because you're managing projects now doesn't mean you manage the entire company. All decisions must be run through me." He wobbles on his feet as he points at himself, the smell of booze now making its way to me. Yup, all decisions must go through the alcoholic. Smart, so fucking smart. "You're lucky I don't take this out of your paycheck."

I try not to laugh at that comment because last time Julius tried to charge a project manager for something "gone wrong," HR backed up the employee, ensuring Julius understood how that was *not* possible.

But hey, empty threats are one of the cornerstones of the perfect manager, right?

Not wanting to indulge in more conversation with this man, especially since he's drunk and stumbling over his own two feet, I ask, "Was there anything else you wanted to talk about?"

Standing tall, well as tall as he can—I still tower over him with my six-foot-three height—he says, "No, that's it. Check with me before you do something like that again. Got it?"

I tap my head and say with sarcasm, which I know he won't pick up on, "Locked and loaded, boss man."

"Good." Turning around, he trips over a two-by-four that he kicks out of his way once he gains balance and strides toward the management trailer. The house we're building is in an entire housing development, new for the area but in high demand.

When the trailer door slams shut, I sigh in frustration and remove my hard hat, running my hand through my hair, lightly pulling on the strands. Fuck, if this wasn't such a damn good opportunity and well-paying job, I would quit. It would be cool to not have to deal with that dickhead anymore, but jobs don't come easy in this area, especially jobs like mine. Upstate New York is a tough place to find work, and I'm not about to fine-tune my résumé.

I work hard. I've never been a slacker, and even though I may have to work with idiots like Julius, I tell myself repeatedly that it's not forever. One day, I *will* be a Julius . . . just not with the alcoholic tendencies and beer belly.

I look at my Fossil watch with the black face and dark leather wristband. Great. It's well past quitting time. I walk to my truck, toss my hard hat in the bed, pop open the tailgate, and snag the cooler I keep there for days like this. I don't drink at the worksite, but I'm not opposed to having a Mountain Dew after work with a Little Debbie snack.

And neither are my guys . . .

Racer and Smalls both stride over to me, their tool-belts now in their hands, their hard hats under their arms, sweat coating their hair even though it's still winter.

"Please tell me you have Swiss Rolls today," Racer calls out just as he sits next to me on the tailgate. Smalls steps on the tire, hoists his body over the side, and sits on the ledge.

I hold out a box of Oatmeal Creme Pies and shrug my shoulders. "Creamy pies, sorry."

"Even fucking better." Racer grabs the box from me, rips it open, and tosses a few pies in our direction. We can take down a box easily in one sitting without even trying, and the best thing about it, we can get away with the calories because we burn five times as much during the day.

With a mouthful of Oatmeal Pie, Racer says, "Saw Julius over here. Did he forget where he put his bottle cap remover?"

It's not a secret that Julius is known for one thing—getting drunk in his trailer—so Racer's question is understandable. Also, Racer, Smalls, and I have been working together for years now, so we don't beat around the bush about things.

"Bitching about paying an electrician." I pop an entire Oatmeal Pie in my mouth and chew.

Smalls chuckles behind me, his broad frame shadowing me from the lights. This man is anything but small, more like Thor's bigger brother. "Dickhead already forgot about Manny being on paternity leave? Sounds about right."

"It's frightening that he owns the top construction company in the area when he's so fucking clueless."

Racer opens a Mountain Dew, the crack of the can echoing through the night. Everyone else has gone home for the night, but since we are the three bachelors of the company, we tend to stay later and hang out, or finish up any projects that might need a little extra in making the promised timeline. We don't mind because we have nothing pressing calling our names, and we would rather hang out than sit alone at home like a bunch of dickheads.

"Not for long," Racer says, a wiggle to his brows.

Fucking Racer. He's convinced the three of us are going to break off and start our own construction business. We would be damn good at it, but stability is good for me right now; it's the only fucking thing I have. After everything I lost just over a year ago, I'm not ready to venture out on our own yet. I'm comfortable with sticking to slaving for the man. Someone else can own the responsibility of running a business for now. I'm only twenty-four. My time will come.

"Still caught up on starting our own thing?" I ask. "Dude, you realize how unrealistic that is, right?"

"The fuck it is. We have the talent, the business skills, the contacts, and the men who would follow us in a heartbeat. You're just scared."

"Damn right, I'm scared." I lean back on the truck bed, my hands propping me up. "Julius might be a drunk, but he's a nasty drunk. You don't think he wouldn't be out to get us if we left and started our own thing? He would bad-mouth us around town, never giving us the chance to stand on our own fucking feet."

And that's the truth. I've known the man for about a decade, I've seen the shade he throws people's way when he doesn't like them. I've seen him destroy other contractors, fucking with their job sites, paying off workers to mess up a project, paying city officials to earn bids. He has no moral compass, and if I become his competition, there is no doubt in my mind he would set out to destroy me.

But fuck . . . to have my own company with my two buddies? That would be living the dream.

"I'm not giving up." Racer opens another Oatmeal Pie. "One day. We'll be sitting in our own pimped out trailer, looking over plans together, making our own goddamn decisions over electricians and showering our employees with Little Debbie snacks. Hell, that curly headed broad, Debbie, will be our sponsor. Our company could be called Debbie's Dicks."

"Orrrrrrr something else," Smalls chimes in. "Something catchy like . . ." he pauses and then snaps his finger, "Tight Squeeze Construction."

"What the hell is wrong with you?" I ask, slightly disgusted with the suggestion.

"Three Erectors," Racer says with a laugh.

"Butt-Swell Builders."

"Log Jam."

"Proud Penises."

"Manufacturing Man-ginas."

Looking at Racer now, I deadpan, "Yes, let's fucking call ourselves the Manufacturing Man-ginas and get a logo with three men wearing hard hats and sporting massive moose knuckles, because if that doesn't say credible construction, I don't know what does." I shake my head at my idiot friends.

They're both silent for a second before Racer calls over to Smalls, "Hey, at least he's considering the idea of us going off on our own."

For fuck's sake.

I hop off the tailgate and stretch my hands above my head. Turning to my friends, I say, "I'm going home so get the fuck off my truck. I'll see you two tomorrow."

They both scatter, chugging the rest of their Mountain Dews and putting their cans in the recycling bag I keep in the back of my truck.

"Think about it," Racer calls out, backing up as he talks to me. "Man-ginas could be a good way to brand our company. Man-gina stress balls for prospective new customers, doesn't get much better than that."

I hop in my truck without a response, shaking my head at my overenthusiastic friend. No way in fuck would I give away man-gina stress balls. No one wants that.

The drive from the job site to my house is short; I don't live very far away. At times I wish I did. It's not because I enjoy driving with my window down, feeling the winter air hit me in the face, but because I hate being at my house. Correction. I hate being at my house *alone*.

I hate every second of its emptiness, of what it represents, of why I bought it in the first place. It's a reminder of my past I wish I could forget. I wish I could let go.

I turn right onto my street and pull into the driveway. When I cut the engine, I stare at the small Cape Cod with its brick chimney and mint-green vinyl siding. The windows are dark, showing no sign of living inside because I don't bother leaving a light on for myself—there's no point. My routine is simple: I get home and head straight to my bedroom after I brush my teeth and take a leak. I don't bother with dinner—not when I eat a box of Little Debbie snacks—I don't hang out in the living room because there's no furniture. The house is empty apart from my bedroom, the only place that doesn't cripple me with nausea.

Sighing, I pull the keys from the ignition of my truck, stuff my wallet and phone in my pockets, and go to the side door that connects to the kitchen. Knowing the place like the back of my hand, there's no need to flip on any lights as I navigate through the hollow walls toward the only bathroom between the two downstairs bedrooms.

After ten hours on the job site, my body screams for a hot shower. I strip out of my dark green Henley and plaster-covered jeans and turn on the shower to a scalding temperature, glad to burn my skin like I do every night to try to rid of the crawling sensation I feel every time I walk into this godforsaken house.

Leaning on the bathroom counter, I look in the mirror as the shower heats up. Battered and tired eyes stare back at me. I look older than my twenty-four years. I *feel* fucking older than my twenty-four years. With the life experiences I have under my belt, the disappointments, the losses I've lived through, I feel like I'm in my mid-thirties. *What's the phrase? Life sucks and then you die?*

Steam billows through the top of the shower. I step past the plain curtain and welcome the heat against my body. The water pelts my back, so hot it almost feels cold, just how I like it. I hiss between my teeth, letting the water run down my back to where it pools at my feet before draining away. If only it took my sorrow with it.

Fourteen months ago, I bought this house for a very specific reason: to start a family with my pregnant girlfriend. I wanted to provide for her, to prove I could be the man she needed, convince her that I was the man she could rely on. Be the involved and caring father I knew I could be. I was happy, fucking ecstatic; my girl was pregnant with my baby. Yeah, we had our problems. Our relationship was off and on for a while, but I believed deep in my fucking soul we were meant to be together, that we were made for one another.

But the world had other plans.

The day after I signed the papers for this house, I got the call. My girl had woken up to blood, blood fucking everywhere.

Sadie miscarried. Lost *our* baby. I'd never felt such devastation in my life. Some might say I was too young to realize the impact that had on my future, but fuck them. I've had to grow up pretty quickly in my life, and I've been adulting longer than some actual adults. I know what loss is, and that night, holding Sadie's hand in the hospital while they told us we'd lost the baby, *that* was loss. That was devastation. Crippling.

But nothing prepared me for the cataclysmic damage that would happen next. Nothing prepared me for seeing the girl of my dreams pull away mentally and physically. Nothing prepared me for the day I learned she was seeing someone else. And nothing prepared me for Sadie moving on and living her life with another fucking man.

I didn't just lose my baby. No, I lost my girl too. *And fuck if I was ready for that.*

She said we were growing apart before we lost the baby, that our relationship was hanging on by a thread, but I refuse to acknowledge that. In my mind, there was always hope for Sadie and me, she just gave up. *On us. On me.*

Now, I live in a house I despise, a house that reminds me of everything I came so close to having. Something I may never hold in my grasp.

It's like constantly coming home to a slideshow of devastation on replay. I fucking hate everything about this house. It represents loss. Darkness.

On a heavy sigh, I finish washing my body, turn off the shower, and towel off. Silence greets me as I sit on my bed, my head in my hands, trying to ease the tension building in the pit of my stomach.

So much fucking silence. Silence, a wife and baby should have smothered. Silence, a family—*my family*—would have filled, but is now possessed by a lonely, bitter fuck.

Me.

Tucker Jameson.

I couldn't despise myself more.

# Chapter Three

## EMMA

"Three old-fashioneds, heavy on the booze," I call out to the bartender. I take a seat at the bar in The House of Reardon, a bar we frequent when we don't want to be caught up in the college life in downtown Binghamton and just want a peaceful drink.

"Three?" Logan asks. He strips off his jacket and hangs it on the back of his chair.

"Adalyn is going to meet us here."

"I thought she had to babysit her niece tonight."

"Niece got the flu. Adalyn wanted nothing to do with that and I don't blame her, especially since we already have to be around a disease pit on a daily basis." I pull out my phone and start searching through my emails, hoping and praying for any kind of news on apartments.

"Hey, guys." Adalyn sits next to Logan just as the bartender sets down our drinks. Logan hands the man his card to open a tab. He always insists on paying since he saves mad money on rent, but Adalyn and I never leave the bar without slipping cash in his pocket. He never mentions it, so either he pretends we never pay him or he is beyond clueless and thinks his pocket grows money.

"Hey, Adalyn," I mumble, not looking up from my phone. Rejection after rejection email hits me. "Ugh." I black out my phone and rest it on the bar. "I'm never going to find a place. It's official. I'm going to be homeless. Any luck on your end?" I ask Adalyn. We split up inquiries to help each other out with our workloads.

Adalyn shakes her head, but there is something in her eyes that says otherwise. I've known Adalyn for a while now, so I know when she's lying because she does this thing with her lips where she presses them up toward her nose. Rather odd quirk actually.

"What aren't you telling me?"

Adalyn takes a sip of her drink and then sets it back down on the bar. She holds her glass with both hands and stares at the liquid as she speaks. "I haven't found anywhere for us to live." She swallows hard. "But my sister offered me space in her basement for the rest of the semester." Apology is written all over her face as she turns to me. "If there was more room, I would say you could stay with me, Emma, but the room is already the size of a closet and if it wasn't free, I would turn her down so we could find a place together but . . . it's free."

My heart falls to the sticky floor of the bar. Great. Adalyn has a place to live and honestly, I can't even be mad at her. If I had the same opportunity, I would be saying yes before I could even blink in surprise from the offer.

"I'm sorry," she says. "I'm going to help you find a place though, I promise."

"It's okay." I sigh and lean back in my chair. "You don't need to apologize, Adalyn. That's one hell of an opportunity. You can save so much money until we graduate. I would be mad at you if you didn't take it."

"But what are you going to do?" Adalyn asks.

"I'll figure something out." I take a sip of my old-fashioned. Whenever I drink with my friends back home, I have one drink, often because I'm too concerned with making sure none of them accidentally trip and fall into the bonfire. When I'm with my college friends, I drink. And tonight I plan on drinking, and drinking a lot.

Logan nudges me with his shoulder. "The offer still stands to room with me."

"And shack up in your bunk with you?"

"Wouldn't be the first time we shared." This time he wiggles his eyebrows and a blush creeps over my cheeks.

No, it wouldn't be the first time. Oh, Emma and Logan sitting in a tree, right? No. Well, sort of, but no.

We went out for drinks after our very first semester finals and ended up getting wasted, a little too wasted. Since his place is walking distance from the bars, we crashed in his bed, the top bunk. We made out for quite some time, fondled each other, but then passed out due to intoxication. I woke up that morning with his flaccid penis in my hand and his bottom lip stuck to my nipple.

Not my best night, or best morning for that matter. After an extremely awkward morning, we came to the conclusion such copious amounts of liquid should never be consumed together because we didn't want to ruin the friendship we had. We've made out on a few occasions after that—what can I say? He's a great kisser—but never took it any further. Nothing is quite like waking up with a limp penis in hand to ruin any romantic vibes. This past year though, strictly platonic, just the way I like it with my Logan.

Turning toward Logan, I say, "As much fun as it was sharing a tiny bed with you on top of crusty sheets—"

"They were not fucking crusty. Retract that statement. I

don't want people thinking I'm some jizzing asshole who never changes his sheets. Fuck me if I don't use fabric softener. I think it's a waste of money."

A laugh pops out of me. He can be so damn sensitive sometimes. "Anyway, you have one bathroom between all six of you. It would never work."

"We can fit you in the shower schedule. How do you feel about midnight showers?"

"Not favorable." I laugh and take another sip of my drink, welcoming the burn of the alcohol down the back of my throat.

"Hey, Emma," Adalyn whispers, leaning forward and looking over my shoulder.

"What?" I mimic her approach.

She nods behind me. "That guy over there keeps staring at you."

Lifting up, both Logan and I say at the same time, "What guy?"

"Don't look . . . ugh," Adalyn groans when we both turn to see who she's talking about.

Sitting in the corner of the bar, a short glass of what I know is whiskey in front of him, his shoulders slouched, but his gaze fixed on me, is the one and only hometown heartbreaker from where I grew up: Tucker Jameson.

When we make eye contact his head tilts to the side, and he smirks. Right there, that look—a slight smolder in his eyes, the broad set of his shoulders, muscles in his chest no man his age should have, and the scruff that lines his strong jaw—that is the look that broke many hearts.

Two years older than me, he was in a tumultuous relationship with one of my best friends, Sadie. For years they were on again, off again, pushing each other's buttons until it all fell apart. It caused a ripple in our little inner circle as we were forced to choose sides. I was never a fan of their relationship, knowing the kind of strain it put on both of them, but once it was over, I focused my attention on my best friend. It took time and patience, but she needed to move on with her life.

I can still see the hollow look in Sadie's eyes after she lost the baby, after she dropped out of Cornell University to be a mom. Life as she knew it was flipped upside down and then taken away from her. Smilly, our other best friend, had to pick up the pieces and luckily, we didn't have to glue her back together; Andrew, her boyfriend, did that.

I grew up in a small town, a town where everyone knew everyone. There were ninety-five kids in my graduating class, so *small* is an understatement. But with a small town, comes strong bonds. To this day, four years after we went our separate ways from high school, we still get together during the summer and hang out, party, reminisce on all the good times, and create some new ones too. But this last year Tucker was MIA, and now that he's only a few feet away, I can't help but think about what he's been doing all these months. Has he recovered from his relationship with Sadie?

Guilt consumes me as the back of my neck starts to flame from my neglect. *Should I have offered more support to Tucker?*

"Do you know him?" Logan asks, whispering next to my ear.

I nod. "I do." I pick up my glass and hop off my bar stool. "I grew up with him."

"Damn," Adalyn says from behind me. "I wish I grew up with him. Hell, I wish he would grow up inside me right now."

"Self-respect, Adalyn," Logan chastises. "Christ."

"Be back." With drink in hand, I walk over to Tucker, who turns on his stool, one arm still resting on the bar, the other gripping the back of his chair. He watches me walk toward him, and I realize it's the way he's always watched women walk toward him: with unbridled attention. It would be intimidating if I didn't know the boy Tucker once was.

"Never would I have imagined seeing your tiny ass in a place like this. I thought college girls like you hung out downtown," he says in greeting, that smirk turning into a full smile now. He runs his hand through the side of his already unruly hair, giving him some amazing sex appeal. It's really unfair how some men can grow hotter and hotter by the minute.

I pop my hip to the side and say, "I'm almost a graduate. I have to start expanding my bar options. Downtown is so last year."

Like second nature, I open up my arms and pull him into a hug, which he returns, bringing me into his familiar arms. Since Sadie is one of my best friends, I've spent a lot of time with Tucker, a lot of time talking him down when he and Sadie would get in a fight, and a lot of the time lecturing him on how to handle Sadie, who also dealt with her fair share of childhood drama.

"It's good to see you. Where've you been? I didn't see you at Smilly's for her Christmas gathering. You missed out on dirty Pictionary." Smilly is the queen of the group. She throws the parties whereas I watch over the parties, ready to spring into action when needed.

"Wasn't my scene." He shrugs and then takes a sip of his drink.

*Wasn't his scene?* Translation: he didn't want to see Sadie with her new boyfriend, who everyone loves. Hell, Tucker even liked Andrew before he knew Andrew was dating Sadie. It's hard not to like the guy. And I would never say this to Tucker, but Andrew is perfect for Sadie. He has shown her joy, contentment, and the softer side of life, qualities from a man she needed . . . desperately. Not that Tucker couldn't give her those things, but it was as if they were stuck and couldn't find their way out of the quicksand sucking them both in.

Tucker has always been somewhat serious and somber, as if he carries the burdens of many on his broad shoulders. He hid this from most, but I spent a lot of time on the outside, watching my friends hurt each other, time after time. Looking at him now, he still seems somber and serious, but also . . . melancholy. When he smiled in greeting, it almost looked as though he doesn't do that as often as he used to. Smile, that is.

Knowing that diving into the reasons he avoided the group at Christmas would be a tad cruel, I say, "Well, we missed you. It's never the same without you."

"Maybe next time." It's a generic response, one I don't think he means. I'm not sure we'll ever see Tucker at another party, and that makes me sad.

"How's life? How's the job?"

He nods. "Good. I'm a project manager, which has its good and bad days." He glances over at Adalyn and Logan and nods, "Boyfriend?"

I laugh as I look back at Logan and shake my head. "No, just a friend."

"Huh." He takes a sip of his drink and then looks at me with a tilt of his head. "The way he's staring at you, you could have fooled me."

"Just friends." I pause and then ask, "Want to meet them? You're just sitting over here by yourself, might be nice to have some company."

"How do you know I'm not waiting for someone?" he asks, a smirk on his handsome face.

"Are you?"

"Nah." He chuckles and stands from his chair. With his arm wrapped around me, he walks me back to my friends.

When I approach, Adalyn's eyes look like they're about to

pop out of their sockets. It's a natural reaction when in Tucker's presence. He's gorgeous with his dark blond, messy hair that's trimmed shorter on the sides and thick on top, his five o'clock shadow, light blue eyes, and unforgiving, hardworking muscles. But Logan doesn't look as thrilled with the addition to our little get-together.

"You guys, this is my friend, Tucker. We grew up together; he knows far too many secrets about me from middle school that will horrify you, and if he wants to keep his balls intact, he will keep those stories to himself."

Leaning over to shake hands with Adalyn and Logan, Tucker quickly winks at me and says, "We'll see." He turns his attention to my friends, pulling from his outgoing personality that never seems to fail him, and shakes their hands. "Tucker, nice to meet you. It's rare I get to meet people outside our little friend circle, especially friends of Emma's. Whenever I see this girl"—he wraps his arm back around my shoulder and squeezes me tight—"she's either butterfly stitching someone's head or patting down their ass with Neosporin. I'm glad I caught her without her first-aid kit tied around her waist and instead with a drink in her hand."

"You've never seen her drink?" Adalyn asks and then says, "Oh, I'm Adalyn by the way."

"Ugh, I'm the worst," I reply. "Tucker, this is Adalyn and Logan. Sorry."

He nods at them and says, "I've seen Emma drink, but I've never seen her drunk." He smiles down at me. "She always took care of us." The sentiment is sweet. I know my friends from back home appreciate me, but it's always nice to hear on occasion.

"You've never seen Emma drunk?" Adalyn asks. "Wow, that's surprising since I feel like I see drunk Emma more than sober Emma."

"Seriously?" Tucker's eyes shoot up to his hairline.

"No." I playfully swat at Adalyn. "She's lying. I don't drink that much. But when I have time off and need to relax, I might throw back a few old-fashioneds."

"And shots of whiskey," Logan adds, tipping his drink into his mouth.

"Well, fuck, I've never seen this side of Emma." Tucker rubs the back of his neck, his gaze fixed on me. "Next party, you're getting your ass wasted. No excuses."

"That's if you show up." I'm joking, but there is a layer of darkness that blankets his expression, and it makes me sad. Tucker is different than most guys. He masks his demons and always tries to put on a good show for everyone around him, which he's doing right now.

My question is, why is he drinking tonight? Alone. Does he do this often? I've been so consumed with my life I've neglected catching up with my friends. How long has he been going to bars by himself? Is this something I need to be concerned about? My need to know—*to care*—kicks in, but not here. He's not an open book when it comes to his life, especially in front of people he doesn't know very well.

Two fingers push against the wrinkle in my brow. I look up to Tucker who pulls away. "What's with the worried face?"

"She has no place to live," Adalyn answers before I can even formulate a response. "We were evicted from our place a few days ago and have to be out in two days."

"Adalyn," I chastise, not wanting Tucker to know about my woes. I'm the girl who always has everything together, the friend who can see ten steps ahead.

"You don't have a place to live?" Tucker asks, concern in his voice.

Squeezing my eyes together for a brief second, I turn to him and say, "Eh, I've got it handled. Just waiting to hear back from a few places, that's all."

"They all said no." *Come on, Adalyn!* What is she drinking over there, truth serum?

"It's all right, she has a place to stay," Logan says, nudging me with his shoulder.

Leaning over the bar to see me, Adalyn says, "There is no way you're going to share a three-bedroom apartment with six men."

"Six men?" Tucker raises an eyebrow at me. "I could see five, but six?" His teasing lightens the irritated mood moving through me.

"It's temporary until we can figure something out." Logan grips my hand to let me know he's serious. "You can have my bunk and I'll take the couch. It's better than having no place to go."

"Are you sure?" I ask. "It seems like a lot of people for a small place. I don't think I can do that to you . . . or me."

"It's not a big deal. Tyler and Travis are never home and if they are, you don't see them very often and the other guys, well, they think you're cool."

"They'll make you do their laundry and cook them food," Adalyn points out.

"Not true. We know how to cook dinner and do laundry. Just the other night we made a five-gallon pot of Kraft Mac and Cheese. We even fried some of it."

"And the kitchen almost caught on fire." Adalyn snickers to herself.

"Last fucking time I tell you anything." Logan's scowl is washed away when he turns toward me. "Seriously, we can make it work, Em."

"You can stay with me." We all turn to look at Tucker, who

is leaning back in his chair, his glass dangling in his hand and his head tilted toward the floor, his eyes the only thing pointed in our direction.

"What?" The bewilderment in my voice doesn't go unnoticed. "I . . . do you . . . where do you even live?" Caught off guard, yup, that would be the perfect way to describe how I'm feeling.

"I have a house in Hillcrest. Probably a ten-minute drive to campus."

"You have a house?" When did this happen? How did I not know? Am I a bad friend for not knowing? Does everyone else know?

"Yeah." He shifts in his chair, drawing back just slightly. He clears his throat and adds, "There are some things I need to fix in it, but it has a spare bedroom."

"You're serious." Live with Tucker Jameson?

"Yeah." He shrugs and then looks at his watch. Standing from his chair, he dresses into his black leather jacket, which fits him like a glove, and lays a twenty on the bar top. "You have my number, think about it." He nods at Logan and Adalyn, pops the collar of his jacket to avoid windburn, and says, "Nice meeting you."

Then takes off.

All three of us turn back to our drinks and stare at the counter, trying to recover from the Tucker whirlwind that just blew through.

"Holy shit, he's hot," Adalyn mumbles while gulping down the rest of her drink. "If it were me, I would be asking him for his address right now."

"Em, I know you were friends growing up, but you didn't even know he had a house. You can't be that close to the guy." He sounds irritated.

I hate to say *not that close*, because we used to be. Seeing him in the bar tonight, *on his own*, actually makes me sick to my stomach, thinking he's been grieving so . . . alone.

"We used to be close; our entire group of friends were close, but this past year, we've all been trying to look for jobs and graduate. When his ex-girlfriend moved on, he stopped hanging around because I think it was too hard on him. I don't have much downtime and when I do, it's spent with you guys." I take a sip from my drink. "God, I'm an ass, I should have checked on him more. I really don't know what he's been doing for the past year. I'm such a bad friend."

"No, you're not." Logan pulls me into his chest and kisses the top of my head. "You've been consumed with earning your RN degree. You know friendship is a two-way street, right? It goes both ways. He could have reached out to you as well."

I shake my head. "That's not the kind of guy Tucker is. Plus, I'm best friends with his ex, Sadie. He wouldn't have reached out to me for that sole reason." Not to mention, he was undoubtedly aware that I'd never been a true supporter of him and Sadie together.

"You can reach out now," Adalyn suggests. "Reach out and stroke his penis." She laughs hysterically at herself, makes a lewd gesture, and taps the bar for another drink. Oh, Adalyn.

"I don't know." I sigh, unsure what to do. "On one hand, it's a place to live, which I don't have in two days, but on the other hand, it's my best friend's ex-boyfriend. Even though we're friends, would that be weird?"

"Yes."

"No."

Logan and Adalyn talk over each other, defending their stances. Much help they are. *Should I consider this? Or is that crazy?* I still have some time. I can find a place. It's Binghamton, New York, there has to be apartments somewhere.

# Chapter Four

## TUCKER

"Where are the tiles?" I look around the room and don't see anything. "Jared, where the fuck are the tiles for the bathroom?"

"On the wall," Jared answers, looking slightly terrified.

On the wall? I walk into the bathroom and sure as shit, there they are, being spaced out and placed on the wall. Fuck, I'm losing it.

"Uh, yeah. Sorry about that." I run my hand over my jaw and stare down at my clipboard, trying to figure out what the hell I'm supposed to be doing.

I'm off. It feels like my entire equilibrium is out of whack, like my world is tilting on its fucking axis, and I have nothing to grip on to.

There is only one reason why: Emma Marks.

When I went into The House of Reardon last night to grab a drink, I was looking for solitude, to drown myself in a few glasses of whiskey and get lost in thought, any kind of thought that didn't involve Sadie, the baby, or the mausoleum I call my home.

And then Emma walks in with her friends. From a distance, I observed her, how carefree she was, never once fussing over the people surrounding her. She was different, and it threw me for a loop. I've known Emma for quite some time, sweet girl with a heart of gold. When she said she wanted to go to nursing school, everyone praised her. She was born to be a nurse, so fucking caring toward others. But the Emma I saw last night joking around with her friends wasn't *that* Emma.

Last night, curious as hell, I wanted to know more about *this* Emma Marks, which is why I joined her friends. And I met college Emma, a beautiful, carefree girl who looks like she loves to have fun. *Not* hometown Emma, whose role is to clean up and sort through everyone's issues. But then her friend hit me with Emma's dilemma and before I could stop myself, I offered her a place to stay. *What. The. Hell?*

It's not that I don't have the space, I do, but I don't want her to see that space. I avoid seeing the space myself. If I could sell it without losing money, I would. I haven't had it long enough, or finished the necessary improvements, to avoid it becoming both a shitty investment and a giant waste of the money I'd saved since I can remember. When I get the chance, I spend my weekends working on the house, intending to flip it myself for a profit, but with my long days during the week, and being the only person to work on the house, it's taking me way fucking longer than I want.

But maybe she found a place. Maybe I'm twisting a nut for no damn reason. I can only fucking hope.

A strong hand grips my shoulder and pulls me out of my flashbacks. "Couldn't find the tile, huh?" Racer asks, humor strong in his voice.

"Fuck off."

"Heard you've been a hot mess today," Racer pushes. I start down the stairs of the house we're working on and head to my truck for lunch. "Heard you were searching for your hammer for five minutes until you realized it was still attached to your hip."

"It wasn't five fucking minutes," I grumble.

I fish out my lunch and bring it over to a stack of wood where I take a seat, setting my hat down next to me. Racer joins me, his lunch pail in hand as well. When he sits down, he removes his hat and runs his hand through his thick and sweaty hair.

"What was it then? Two minutes?"

"A few seconds. Christ." I unzip my lunch and Racer immediately starts sifting through it as if we're in grade school sitting in the cafeteria.

"Dude, what's that shit? Salad?" He fingers the lettuce I have in a bag.

"It's lettuce for my tacos."

"Tacos?" Racer eyes my lunch again and then his. "Want to trade?" *Yeah, we are in grade school.*

Being that Racer is one of my closest friends, I know the ins and outs of his life, and I would bet a thousand dollars on what he has in his lunch box right now. It's always the same thing: two bologna sandwiches with mustard, a Coke Zero, and grapes. There is no way I'm trading in my tacos for bologna.

"Never. I never want to trade."

"Suit yourself." He unzips one of his sandwiches and takes a big bite out of it. He's a man-child. "Is Julius on your back again today? Is that why it took you an hour to find your hammer today?"

"An hour?" I quirk a quizzical brow in his direction. "It went from five minutes to an hour. That's quite the fucking leap."

He holds up his hands. "Hey, I'm just repeating what's being thrown around by the guys."

"Dickheads will be getting pay cuts. All of them." I start to put together my tacos when I answer Racer. "Just saw an old friend last night." I have no clue why seeing Emma is throwing me off though.

"An old friend, huh? Was it Sadie?"

Racer and Smalls are not blind to what I went through the last couple years; *they* were the ones I leaned on when it felt like I had no one else. They were there when Sadie told me she was pregnant, they were there when I bought my house, when Sadie lost the baby, and when she met someone else. They were the ones who picked me up when I was a distanced motherfucker.

So Racer's question doesn't surprise me.

I shake my head. "Not Sadie. One of her best friends I grew up with actually."

"Yeah? Is she hot?" Horny fucking bastard.

"Emma?" I ask, thinking about the question. "Uh . . . I never really thought about her that way. She's always been the mom of the group somehow."

"Moms can be hot. Moms also need a little dick tickling every now and then."

"She's not really a mom, asshole." I shove the rest of one of my tacos in my mouth and chew.

"Doesn't matter, even a pretend mom gets me going. Do you think she would wear an apron for me?"

"What?" I shake my head.

"You're going to introduce me, right?" Racer's eagerness is starting to grate my nerves.

"How did this conversation turn into a hookup for you?"

He shrugs his shoulder and takes another bite out of his second sandwich. Talking with his mouth full, he says, "I like to put my name in the running before it's even an option. Being proactive and all."

"You're not going out with her. You're a dick when it comes to girls, I won't subject Emma to that."

"That's not true," Racer says, defending himself. "I'm not a dick, I just know what I want right now."

"Spread legs and commitment free, I know." Racer is like a brother to me, but he's an asshole.

He bends his head back and finishes his drink before saying, "Enough about me. Why does Emma have you out of fucking sorts? You don't like her, do you?"

"No," I answer quickly. "I guess seeing a blast from the past is fucking with my brain." I rub the back of my neck and look over to Racer. "I, uh, I kind of offered her a place to stay."

Racer pops a grape in his mouth as his brows pull together. "You what?"

A long groan flows from the pit of my stomach out past my lips. I lean back on the wood and look up into the gray cloudy sky of Binghamton. "It happened so fucking fast. I was caught off guard seeing her, she invited me to talk to her friends, she was so different than the Emma I grew up with, like really fucking different, and her friend mentioned Emma was being evicted in two days and had nowhere to go. I offered my house before I could stop myself."

"Dude, you don't ever have anyone over. Hell, I've never been over to your place and you've had it for over a year."

"I know. I don't know what the fuck I was thinking."

"What did she say?" The joking tone in Racer's voice has vanished and in its place a growing sense of concern.

"That she would think about it. She hasn't texted me or anything, so I'm thinking it's going to be a no. Last night it sounded like she had to be out of the place by tomorrow. Thought I would've heard from her by now."

"Tomorrow? And she hasn't texted you yet? I bet she found a place. Although"—Racer sits up—"a little heads-up on her end would be fucking polite. A quick text so you don't have to sit around with your dick in a twist."

"She might be in class or doing her nursing stuff, whatever that entails."

"She's a nurse?" Racer smacks my arm. "Dude, you have to hook us up now. You know I've always had a nurse fantasy. Those little red crosses pasted over her nipples and that's it, boner heaven. Come on, introduce me."

"No, never going to fucking happen. She's not one of your bimbos. She's a long-term kind of girl. She looks for guys who want to get married and have babies."

"Fuck." Racer shivers. "Marriage is terrifying. Commitment and seeing each other poop, no fucking thank you."

I knew that would scare him off. And it's the truth. Emma has always been the girl who wants the white picket fence, the loving husband, and the beautifully smart children.

I look at my watch. Ten more minutes before I have to get back to work.

"Are you heading to Reardon tonight?" Racer asks, shortening the name of our favorite bar.

I'm about to answer when my phone beeps in my pocket. A sinking feeling starts to crawl up my spine. Not many people text me, and the people who do are on the same job site as me, one of them sitting right next to me.

When I pull my phone from my pocket, Racer leans over and looks at the screen with me. Since I have it set on privacy mode, you can only see who the text is from, no preview. Clear as day, Emma's name appears.

"Huh, maybe she's polite after all," Racer says, slicing some of the tension from my shoulders.

That's exactly what it is. She's saying thank you, but I found a place. It's the kind of person Emma is. She'd tell me the outcome of her decision. Hell, I wouldn't be surprised if she sent me an e-card to say thank you.

Swallowing hard, I open the message and let the words sink in.

***Emma: What's your address? I hope the offer still stands.***

Fuuuuuck . . .

"Oh shit." Racer claps me on the back. "Make sure you go halfsies on toilet paper and toothpaste."

# Chapter Five

## EMMA

*It's Binghamton, New York, there has to be apartments available.*

So wrong.

So incredibly wrong.

There is nothing.

That is why I'm sitting in a small U-Haul truck, staring at a charming house with a brick chimney gracing the front, while Logan jabbers in my ear about how he could still make room in his place. As nervous and uneasy as I feel right now, I don't think I could stay at Logan's, even though he would try to make it as comfortable as possible.

"This place seems pretty far from campus." Logan looks around, assessing the area. "Nice neighborhood though."

"It's not far. It's actually a quick jump onto the highway straight to campus, and the hospital is close too."

"Em, are you sure about this? You haven't seen him in a year. He could be—"

I place my hand on Logan's arm and turn toward him in the truck. "Logan, what's the real issue? Why don't you want me to live here?"

He links his hand with mine and plays with the connection as he looks down at it. "I don't know this guy, Emma. What if . . ." Logan pauses and takes a deep breath. "What if he tries to drive some kind of wedge between us? You're one of my very best friends, Em. This is our last semester. I want to spend as much time with you as I possibly can, and I don't want some dickhead I don't know trying to ruin that. I don't want to lose us."

Immediately my heart crumbles into pieces from his confession. I cup his face and say, "Logan, that could never happen. Tucker is not that kind of guy. I promise."

He lets out a long breath and asks, "Are you sure you don't want to stay with me? We've shared a bed before, I'm not opposed to doing it again."

"Nice try." I lean over and kiss his cheek. "Nothing is going to happen to our friendship. I care about you way too much. These last few months are important to me. I want to spend as much time with you and Adalyn as I can before our lives turn from practice to a reality."

"So I can come over and broody eyes isn't going to kick me out?"

"Broody eyes?" I laugh out loud, tilting my head back. "He does not have broody eyes."

"Please, he has the whole broody eyes thing down. I saw how he was looking at you from across the bar. It's how he won Adalyn over so quickly. She was practically licking the bar counter while you were talking to him."

"She was not." I laugh some more over how ridiculous Logan sounds. "He is not going to stop you from hanging out with me. I promise. He's a pretty cool guy, Logan. You two might actually really get along. Give him a chance. He's had a bit of a rough year or so. Once he gets to know you, you two will get along swimmingly."

"Swimmingly?" He quirks his lip to the side. "Not sure about that, but whatever.'"

"Thank you." I pull the keys from the ignition and say, "Come on, let's unload the five boxes I have so I can get to studying."

"Always opening the books. That's my girl." Trustworthy Logan, I adore the guy. He's always there for me when I need him.

I step out into the chilly Saturday afternoon air and quickly zip up my jacket. The weather has been decent all week but the day I have to move, it's scattered flurries and nipple-tightening cold.

Before I head to the back of the truck, I take in the sweet and quaint neighborhood. All the houses resemble the Cape Cod style but differ from one another in their own right. All are very well kept, making it seem like the perfect little place to live, a neighborhood I would never have pictured Tucker living in. Seems almost odd, like a family belongs here . . .

Oh my God.

A family.

My heart feels like it's falling out of my chest as my brain starts connecting the dots. This house, this neighborhood, it's meant for a family, a family Tucker planned on having. The family he lost. My breathing starts to pick up, my throat closing in, just as Tucker pops out of the side door, hands tucked in his pockets as he approaches, a small smile on his face.

"Need some help?"

I push back the tears that want to fall for my friend and nod, knowing words won't form right now.

Tucker starts to walk past me to the back of the truck when he stops right in front of me and lifts my chin so I'm forced to make eye contact. *Please don't see my sorrow; please don't see the pain I feel for your loss.*

"What's wrong?" he asks, way too perceptive.

"Uh, nothing. Just chilly." I sniff.

He studies me, looking between my eyes, searching for answers. The intensity is almost too intense. I can't let it break my walls or disintegrate me under his light touch.

"Is everything okay over there?" Logan calls from behind the truck, pulling both our gazes to him.

I shake Tucker off and nod as I head back to the truck to start unloading. "Just cold, that's all."

Not buying it, Logan whispers, "Did he fucking say something to you?"

"What?" I ask, surprised. "No, of course not. I just . . ." I lean forward and say, "I thought of something, I'll tell you later."

"Promise?"

"Promise."

Putting on a bright smile, even though it feels like there is a battle of emotions warring inside me, I start unloading, watching Tucker lift two boxes at a time, Logan following right behind him. Thankful for two strong men helping me, I lift a sitting chair my grandma gave me that I repurposed and follow them both into the house. We walk through the front where I'm greeted by a white fireplace off to the right, brilliantly beautiful oak wood floors, and a spacious living room that's connected to a dining room by a sweet archway. The thick moldings and antique knobs give the house vintage character, making it more than charming. But with all its little bits and pieces of character, it's lacking one big thing: furniture. There is absolutely no furniture in the house, nothing hung, not even a knickknack above the fireplace. Not that Tucker is a knickknack kind of guy, but a picture frame would have at least added some hominess to the space.

"Tucker, your house is so cute."

"Thanks. Back here." He leads us past the dining room that connects to the kitchen and a staircase leading to what I'm going to assume is the master bedroom, and off to the left, a small hallway. We veer off to the right and into a bedroom that is spacious, much more spacious than I expected. There are two large windows that span almost the height of the wall and the beautiful floors continue into the bedroom as well. The walls are a neutral grey, a nice calming tone, and the room right next to mine is a bathroom. The space couldn't be more perfect.

"This is my room?" I take it all in. "Wow, I feel a little spoiled."

Logan nods his head, and it almost sounds like it pains him to say, "It's nice."

"Thanks." Tucker sets the boxes down and says, "Unfortunately, there is one bathroom so we will have to share, so I hope that's not a problem."

"Not a problem at all. Just knock before you walk in." I wink, which brings a light smile to Tucker's lips.

"Kitchen is around the corner; make yourself at home in there, pretty much everywhere." He pulls on the back of his neck, his bicep flexing in the process and the strain in in his jaw concerns me. "Uh, I just ask one thing of you."

"If you're going to suggest walking around naked on Mondays and Wednesdays, I'm going to have to decline." I joke but my humor barely reaches his eyes.

Instead of returning the humor, he says, "The room across from yours . . . it's off limits. Please don't go in there, don't ask to go in there, don't even ask me about it, just leave it alone." He shifts in place, his eyes fixed on the floor beneath us. "Everything else in the house is yours to play around with, do whatever, set up yoga classes in the living room for all I care, please just don't talk about the room across from yours, okay?"

"Okay." I nod vigorously, wanting to convey to him he can trust me.

"Okay," he repeats, letting out a pent-up breath. "Uh, I'll go get some more boxes. You can start unpacking if you want so you don't have to go out in the cold."

He steps away, just as Logan calls out, "Right behind you." When Tucker is out of earshot, he leans in and whispers, "What the fuck was that about? What's in that room?"

I have a pretty damn good idea, but I'm not about to talk about it because the mere thought of what exists behind that door breaks my heart. *And it's abundantly clear it still breaks Tucker's heart too.*

"Nothing bad. I'm sure just something he doesn't want to talk about right now. Go get some more boxes and stay away from my underwear."

He scoffs. "You think so low of me, Emma. It burns my soul." He holds his chest in mock hurt.

Rolling my eyes, I push him toward the door as he laughs and walks out to the truck to help Tucker, leaving me in my new space. Not a bad place at all to spend my last semester in college. I'm already half in love with the little house. Tucker chose so well. As much as I know Tucker and Sadie weren't right for each other, seeing this very vivid manifestation of his commitment to Sadie, my heart breaks a little more. I didn't grow up in a house like this, and just in these few moments, I feel myself growing attached. I can't help but wonder if it's because of the powerful gesture behind its purchase though.

But that's nothing I have to worry about now. I have a warm, lovely place to stay. The unease in my heart about living with Tucker starts to unravel as realization sets in. I have my own space for the next few months, a comfortable space with an old friend. An old friend I desperately want to reconnect with because even though I'm here to study, I want to know how he ticks and learn everything I missed out on this past year.

• • •

"How's it going in here?" Tucker stands at the doorway, his hand gripping the top of the molding, his shirt lifting just high enough that I get a peek of his boxer briefs.

"Good." I scan my bedroom and chuckle. There are boxes, books, clothes, and pictures scattered all over the space. "It looks like a giant mess right now but I know what I'm doing."

"I sure hope so, because your floor looks like a nightmare."

I wave a hand of dismissal at him. "Controlled chaos, that's all it is. But, I finally figured out where to put my furniture. What do you think?"

He takes in my setup and nods. "Looks legit to me, but what do I know? My furniture consists of a bed and a TV upstairs."

"I've noticed." Biting my bottom lip, I contemplate asking him about the non-existent furniture. Will he get offended? Only one way to find out. "I really like what you've done with the place. Keeping it very light on the furniture, great idea."

He chuckles, his chest rising with the sound slipping from his mouth. "Yeah, I haven't really gotten around to decorating. Sorry about that."

"No need to apologize. I'm so grateful for you offering your house to me. I would be happy sitting on cardboard boxes if I had to. I'm just glad there is a roof over my head right now."

His brow creases, irritation masking the smirk on his face. "If you were in trouble, you should have called me, Emma. You know I would have helped you out."

Ashamed, I look down at the clothes in my hand. "I never would have called you, Tucker."

"Why the hell not?" He steps into the room, his irritated presence making the room feel smaller. Squatting before me, he forces me to look at him.

His unruly hair looks like he's been running his hands through it all night, and his eyes, they're bloodshot in the corners, like he's still carrying the weight of the world on his shoulders.

Unable to lie to him, especially when he only speaks the truth, I say, "Because, I haven't really heard from you in a while. I didn't think it would be appropriate to call you up and ask for a place to live. Plus, I uh, I didn't know you had a house. I honestly had no idea where you lived."

Still squatting in front of me, he searches my eyes. I feel intimidated under his watchful eye as if there is a certain way for me to react, but I have no clue what it is.

Standing, he reaches out to me, his hand extended for me and says, "Fair enough. I guess it's time we reconnect. Come on, I ordered pizza."

Smiling brightly, I grab his hand and allow him to help me to my feet. He starts to head to the kitchen when I stop him and point to a box by the door. "That's kitchen stuff, you interested?"

He scans the box and then smirks at me. "I don't know. Do you have a bottle opener in there?"

"One in the shape of a lobster."

Chuckling, he picks up the box and says, "This I have to see."

He leads us to the kitchen where there is a pizza box on the counter and a six-pack of Angry Orchard. I eye the alcoholic beverage and give him a questioning look.

"Seemed like a chick drink you would enjoy and I would tolerate."

When he sets the kitchen box down, I dig through it quickly, find my lobster bottle opener, and snag two bottles from the six-pack. I pop them open and hand him one. "For the record, I'm a whiskey girl if you want to drink with me."

"Whiskey, huh?" A lazy smile spreads across his face. "Damn, Emma, I never would have guessed. You've always been the girl drinking lemonade with a touch of vodka at parties."

"I've ventured out in college. It's hard to drink heavy alcohol when I have to deal with you hooligans blowing crap up and severing limbs."

"I don't remember limbs being severed, but you didn't always have to be the one to take care of all the drunk idiots. You could have had fun too, Emma."

"I did." I flip open the lid of the pizza and grab a slice. Grease drips off it, just like every other New York-style pizza as I fold it length-wise and bring it to my mouth. "I've just had a little bit more fun in college."

Before he grabs a piece of pizza, he steps forward, encroaching on my space and places his hands on my hips, his fingers igniting a wave of heat in my body.

*What the?*

Before I can ask what he's doing and get too distracted by the delicious smell of his cologne, he lifts me up on the counter and then steps toward the pizza box to grab a slice for himself. He sits on the counter across from me and says, "Now that you're living under my roof, I demand that you have fun these last few months of college. No more of this *taking care of people* shit. We are all grown-ups, if we decide to sit in a pile of poison ivy, that's our own damn fault."

I laugh out loud, thinking back to the party last summer where Amy sat in poison ivy and I spent the night with her bare ass in my face as I tried to dab it with itching lotion.

Continuing, he adds, "I'm serious. You have a few months before you have to start acting responsibly. Might as well let loose these last couple of months, right?"

"I have been letting loose."

"Yeah, but I want to see it, not just hear about it." He winks and takes another bite of his pizza. No wonder Sadie had such an off-again on-again relationship with this man. He oozes sex appeal with just one simple wink.

"It's nothing special, you know. Me drunk and all." I pick at the cheese on my slice, feeling a little nervous around him, a feeling I've never felt before. All because one wink? *Get a grip, Emma!*

He shakes his head and takes a sip of the Angry Orchard he bought for us, wincing as he swallows. "I'm not just talking about getting drunk, I want to see you loosen up." He takes another bite and holds up his finger while he chews. Once he swallows, he says, "I've known you for a long time, Emma, and every time I've seen you, you were either playing nurse for our dumbass friends, or your nose was stuck in a book, studying—"

"For good reason. You don't want a nurse treating you who has no idea what she's doing, now do you?" *Does he think I'm boring? Gosh, I hope not.*

"I really don't." He chuckles. "But that being said, I have a rule for this household."

"Yeah? Is it buy furniture so we don't have to sit on counters?"

Chuckling, he shakes his head. "Didn't you see the last issue of uh . . ." He scratches the back of his neck and looks up at me through his eyelashes, boyish charm written all over his face. "Shit, I don't know any decorating magazines, there goes my joke."

"Oh, does Playboy not offer interior decorating ideas? Is it really just about the articles?"

He nods and points his bottle at me right before he brings it to his lips. "That and the tits, Emma. You can't forget the tits."

I roll my eyes. "I wouldn't know. I've never looked at one."

"Seriously?"

I nod. "Seriously. Why would I? I don't want to diddle myself to bare-breasted women."

The strain in his neck is evident as he swallows hard from my comment. He clears his throat and asks, "Do you diddle yourself?"

"Do you think that's an appropriate question to ask your friend?"

He studies me, his intense once-over drawing a line from my toes to my eyes, causing a shiver to run up my spine. "Fuck yeah, it's an appropriate question."

"Fine, do you self-mutilate?"

"Yes," he says without skipping a beat. "Come on, that was a toss-up question. Every guy does and if he tells you otherwise, he's a liar who probably does it twice a day."

"Twice a day? Doesn't that hurt after a while?"

Tucker laughs and hops off the counter to grab another slice of pizza. When he stands next to me, I catch a second whiff of his cologne . . . what is that heavenly smell? A little sweet, a little woodsy, with a huge dose of pheromones . . .

"Babe, if you're using any kind of lubricant, you can rub one out as many times as you want."

*Babe?* God, that's cute coming from him.

"Yeah? What's your record for one day of masturbation?"

*Did. I. Just. Ask. Tucker. Jameson. How. Many. Times. A. Day. He. Masturbates?*

*Emma!*

"Like how many times?" He bites his slice but doesn't retreat back to his counter; noooo, *he* stands next to me, his broad frame making me feel tiny.

Answering his question, I nod.

"Hmm, all-time record?" He calculates in his head, a smirk on his face. "I would have to say about thirty."

"Thirty?" I nearly choke on my drink as I spit out the number. "How on earth could you get hard thirty times in one day?"

He's laughing now. His hand is wrapped around his waist as he bends over. That gives me a great view of his back muscles flexing with every bout of laughter. The sound is deep, earthquake-esque, shaking my entire body to its core.

"You're stupid." Mature, I know. I hop off the counter and carry my drink and another slice of pizza toward my bedroom. I don't make it past the kitchen doorway before Tucker is wrapping his strong arm around my waist, halting me in my progress. I freeze from his hold, and goosebumps spread like a curtain of arousal as his low laugh filters through my ear. His heat surrounds me, capturing me.

"Don't be like that. Remember, loosen up."

I turn on him, our bodies only a few inches a part, and I hold back the catch in my breath, not wanting to show him how much he's affecting me right now. I'm tired, that's what this is all about. I'm just tired. *And it's been QUITE a long time since I've had sex.*

"Fine, you want me to loosen up?"

He nods, putting some more distance between us to grab his drink that he's clearly only drinking to quench his thirst, not because he's loving the appley taste. "I do, that's why I'm setting the rule that once a week, you have to put down the books and do something fun."

"Oh, is that how this is going to work?" I tease. "Your house, your rules?"

"Damn right." He smirks over his drink.

"Do I have any say in the matter?"

He shakes his head and then a slow, drawn-out smile starts to spread across his face. Uh oh, something is brewing in that handsome head of his, and I'm not actually convinced I'll handle whatever he's coming up with.

*Shit.*

# Chapter Six

## TUCKER

"Grab a pen and a pad of paper," I say to Emma as I bring the pizza box into the dining room along with our six-pack of gross cider.

"Should I be nervous? You're not going to make up some kind of weird blood pact where we have to eat the eye of a squid and share a tentacle *Lady and the Tramp* style, are you?"

"What?" I laugh and shake my head. "No, just get the pen and paper. Christ, woman."

She disappears into her room where she shuffles around all her belongings and fumbles over boxes. I consider going in to help her but once the thought passes through my mind, she's already coming back into the dining room.

She eyes the pizza box on the floor and asks, "Are we doing the whole picnic thing?"

"Yeah, call it adventurous. Now sit that little ass of yours down." I pat the hardwood floor next to me.

She holds up a finger and says, "One second." Once again, she disappears into her room but quickly reappears with two throw pillows in hand. She tosses one at me, which I catch with ease. "Don't want your ass to get sore from not having a chair."

"Considerate." I lift to the side and sit down on the fluffy cushion, welcoming the barrier between the hardwood floors and said ass. *Even if it is on a fluffy,* girly *cushion. God, are those tassels?*

With pizza box between us, Emma sits down, placing the pad of paper on her lap and readies her pen. "Okay, what are we doing? Playing hangman? I just want to warn you, I'm really good. I once used the phrase chocolate hostage."

"What the hell is chocolate hostage?"

A light pink blush creeps over her cheeks as she looks down at her paper and mindlessly doodles on the side. It's cute.

"It's nurse slang for someone who's having difficulty passing stools."

For fuck's sake.

I shake my head, tying to rid the image that seems to be sticking in my mind. "That's fucking disgusting. Do you really say that?"

She shrugs. "It's fun having your own language. Makes some of the dark parts of the job not so heavy. It can lighten the mood at times."

"I get that." I swallow hard. "But please, keep your nurse slang to yourself. Chocolate hostage is going to burn my brain for a while."

"Are you picturing an old man?"

I nod. "Who's sitting on a bed pan." I shiver. "Fuck, okay, change of subject. Thanks for ruining my appetite by the way."

"Anytime." I glance over at her to catch the smile on her face. It's . . . it's beautiful. So genuine, so fucking happy. I haven't been on the receiving end of a smile like that in a while. "Do I have pizza on my face?" she asks, interrupting my thoughts. Quickly she wipes the back of her hand over her cheeks and lips. "Did I get it?" Fuck. *I was staring? At Emma?*

Clearing my throat, I nod. "Yup, just a little bit of sauce," I lie, trying to cover up my ass. Once again her cheeks stain in pink. I like seeing her blush, it's so goddamn sweet. "Okay, uh, let's make a list of rules for the house. I think it only makes sense given our first rule, you have to let loose once a night every week up until graduation."

Shifting on her pillow, she seems to be getting in position when she says, "Oh, this is a good idea." Like a goof, she cracks her knuckles, presses the tip of the pen to her tongue, and starts writing on the pad of paper.

### *Tucker and Emma's House Rules for Living Together.*

"Long title," I comment as she writes out the first rule.

"I want to be thorough." She lets out a long breath once she writes down the first rule and then says, "Rule number two, all rent will be paid on the first of the month."

She goes to write when I snag the pad from her grasp, a small protest slips from her lips. "Hey, I was writing."

"No way are you paying rent. That won't be a rule, and we aren't making administrative rules either. We don't need to say shit like don't walk around the house naked and clean up after yourself. We're smart enough to show common courtesy to one another."

She ignores my statement and says, "I'm paying rent."

"No, you're not," I counter.

"Yes, I am." The lift to her chin says she's being serious.

"Fine." When I succumb, she does a little fist pump in the air. "Rent is due at the first of the month. I accept cash only."

"Cash? Okay. I'll have to stop by the bank, but there is one near the hospital. I could make that work."

"Good. I won't negotiate on the amount. Sorry, a guy has to make a living too."

"Fair enough. I wouldn't dream of negotiating. You did kind

of save me from either sleeping in a creepy hotel, or living with six other men in a three-bedroom apartment, or shacking it up on Homeless Lane, so the least I can do is respect your rent amount."

"Glad to hear it. Rent is one dollar a month. Have it on the counter in an envelope, Mr. Jameson marked on the front. When it comes to rent, I would like to keep things official."

"Tucker." There is protest in her voice. "I'm not going to give you just one dollar."

"I'm sorry, but didn't you just say you would respect your rent amount?"

Her face twists in frustration. "Ugh, fine. One dollar. But if I buy you a couch, I'm not going to be sorry about it."

"Buy me a couch and get your ass spanked," I warn.

There's that fucking blush again. Shit, this may be too much fun.

"I thought there was an unspoken no-sex rule in the common-courtesy-to-one-another bundle."

I lean back against the wall and peer over at her. "Funny that your mind went straight to sex when I mentioned spanking. I was just speaking of pure discipline, but now you've intrigued me. Rule number two—"

"We're not having sex," she quickly says before I can even put the pen to paper.

A light chuckle floats out of me. "Having sex wasn't going to be a rule. Settle down, Emma. Rule number two is one night a week, we talk sex."

"What?" Her brow pinches together. "Why would we do that?"

"It's healthy. Plus, you're a nurse, you have to have some good stories about people coming to the hospital for some sex act gone wrong."

That smile of hers returns. "Sex gone wrong really picked up after *Fifty Shades of Grey* came out. Those first two weeks after the movie were quite enthralling."

"Fuck, I bet." I laugh. "Since I've made two rules, it's your turn to make one. But I have the option to veto if it's lame."

She scoffs. "Thanks for the vote of confidence. Jeeze."

"Listen, you were going to write down rent as being a rule. Can you blame me for claiming a veto card?"

"Fair enough." She brings her knees to her chest and leans on them as she looks out to the empty living room. "One night a week, we cook dinner together. This way we are forced to eat healthy at least once a week, and it will force me to step away from my books for a second. Also, can we make a stipulation that rules can be bundled together?"

"Yes to both." I jot down her rules and put an asterisk at the top of the paper noting rules can be bundled together.

"Question, do we have to enforce the sock rule? You know, if you have a lady friend over, you leave a sock on the door so I don't disturb you?"

"No." I shake my head, keeping my eyes on the paper in front of me. "You don't have to worry about that. Not really a ladies' man." *But what about Emma* . . . I glance at her and ask, "Are you going to be putting socks on the doorknob?"

Looking flustered from my bold question, she says, "Oh, gosh no. It's been so long for me. You don't have to worry about Mr. Donkey Dick coming in here and drilling me while you're trying to catch a little shut-eye. Nope, nope, nope, the sex doesn't happen very often for me. Nope. No . . . no sex here."

"Okay." I chuckle and try to focus on the rules, but what the fuck? *It's been so long for me. Sex doesn't happen very often for me.* Are the guys at her college fucking blind?

Exactly how long? Fuck, I want to know, but it's not my

business, so I bite my tongue and take a few deep breaths, warning myself from getting too personal with Emma. She's clearly flustered, and I don't want to embarrass her more by diving deep into her lack of sex. Not that I have much room to speak.

"Well, this is awkward," Emma states, twisting her hands on her lap.

"Nah, it's cool." I clear my throat and say, "We already talked about this, but rule number four is don't go in the other spare room."

"That's a given, you don't have to write it down." She places her hand on my arm. "Please trust me, I won't go in there."

I let out a long breath. "Yeah, okay." Wanting to lighten the mood, I say, "Rule number four, we might not have to worry about it given our recent confession of apparently both being celibate motherfuckers, but this is important. If at any point in time the butter leaves the kitchen, for any uh, reason"—I wiggle my eyebrows at her—"the butter is not to be returned to the kitchen."

Her pause in reaction throws me for a second before she throws her head back and laughs. "I don't even want to know how you've been scarred in the past by misplaced butter."

"Yeah, you really don't." I put a period at the end of the rule and then say, "One more rule, five seems like a respectable number. Your turn, Em."

"Hmm, I want to make it a good one, but I'm not going to lie, it's going to be hard to follow up the butter rule."

"Give it your best shot," I say with humor in my voice.

"We're good on stuff like dishes and toilet paper reloading and putting the seat down?"

"Yeah, common-sense shit doesn't count."

"And returned butter isn't common sense."

I lean forward and whisper, "You would be fucking surprised."

The shiver that shakes her whole body . . . "Gross. I really don't want to know what happened. You keep that tidbit to yourself."

"All right, but if you ever get the urge to know . . ."

"You'll be the first I come to." Shivering again, she rests her head against the wall, her neck stretching to a long length, showing off the smooth column of skin. For some odd reason, I have the urge to lean over and take in her scent, to see if she smells as sweet as she acts.

*What the hell, man?* This is Emma. Jesus, this hard cider must be getting to my head. Cheap girly shit of a drink.

"Oh, I got it," Emma says, moving her head back to a neutral position. "Music Mondays. We get to pick a song for that week. We can rotate weeks. And we should write down the songs we pick. Who knows, we could have one hell of a playlist by the time I graduate."

"Good rule. I'll fucking school you in music selection, just a fair warning."

"No way. Weren't you listening to EMO back in high school?"

I pull my gaze from the pad where I'm writing to say, "People change, babe, I have good taste now. Just you wait." I finish up writing down the rule and ask, "Who gets to pick first?"

"Rock, paper, scissors?"

"That works." We get into position and clang our hands against our open palms and both say rock, paper, scissors. My paper covers her rock, making me the victor. "That's fucking right, I go first. And since I won, I think whoever's in charge of Music Monday is in charge of the rest of the rules that week. That way we don't get confused. Deal?"

I hold my hand out to her, which she stares at for a second before gripping it and shaking. "Deal."

"That a girl." I look down at my watch, my eyes feeling tired as I take in the time. "Fuck, I'm spent. I'm going to head up to bed. Are you all set? Do you need anything?"

"I'm good." We both stand. She gathers the pizza box and drinks and sticks them in the bare-bones fridge. Shit, I need to buy groceries.

Wanting to make it official, I rip the rules off the pad of paper, reach into the junk drawer in the kitchen and take a piece of duct tape from the roll I keep handy. I put the paper against the wall in the kitchen where we can both easily see it and tape it down.

I bring Emma close to my body by wrapping my arm around her and say, "It's official. We're roomies." It feels like I'm having an out-of-body experience with my arm around Emma. I don't do this, this touchy-feely bullshit, and yet, here I am, being a considerate motherfucker with Emma.

"I guess so."

"Don't forget to pay your rent. I'm not opposed to evicting." I give her a wink before taking off upstairs. "Have a good night, Emma. I'm glad you're here."

"Me too." I hear her whispered response. My chest swells with pride. For the first time since I've lived in this house, I don't feel so fucking lonely. Maybe having Emma stay with me was a good idea after all.

### *Tucker and Emma's House Rules for Living Together*

*Once a week, Emma has to put down the books and do something fun, let the wind flap in her tits. Enjoyment of chosen activity is a must. \*Edited to add all activities involving heights, holding snakes, or porcelain dolls aren't considered enjoyment for Emma. Do not try to include them.*

*One night a week, Emma and Tucker talk about sex, all the*

*sex, penises and vaginas, vaginas and penises. The good, the bad, and the dirty. Condoms are encouraged to be used as hand puppets for educational purposes.*

*One night a week, Emma and Tucker cook dinner together, something healthy that doesn't involve pizza, tacos, or beer. One veggie is required in the meal, but it can't be iceberg lettuce (it's just water) nor a potato.*

*If the butter is removed from the kitchen, the butter is not allowed back in the kitchen. Respect the butter, respect your roomies, and keep genitals away from butter tub, even if said genitals can't believe it's not butter.*

*Music Mondays. DJ Hot Cock, aka Tucker, and DJ Jazzy Nurse Tits, aka Emma, take turns picking a song for the week. DJ Hot Cock will ultimately school DJ Jazzy Nurse Tits in what's good music. \*Edited to add, DJ Jazzy Nurse Tits is not happy with her DJ name. \*\*Edited to add, DJ Hot Cock is very pleased with his DJ name.*

# Chapter Seven

## EMMA

Bacon.

Yes, I lift my head some more, my nostril leading the way. That is bacon.

The position of my bed allows me to easily pull back the curtain covering one of my floor-to-ceiling windows and take a look outside. Still dark. What time is it?

I roll my dream-filled body to the side, recollecting the night I spent eating lemon-cherry filled cookies with Greg Kinnear—he's hot in his own right—and press the home button on my phone to light up the screen.

Six fifteen. In the morning. I groan and flop my head back on my pillow. Why is it so early? I start to drift back to sleep when my traitorous nose sends SOS signals to my stomach about the bacon-filled air floating under my door. Being the little bitch my stomach is, she betrays me in the nastiest way and grumbles loudly, churning in on herself, begging for a slice of bacon.

"Ugh, stupid freaking bacon smell." I roll to a sitting position on my bed and wipe my eyes, trying to convince them that this early morning hour is okay, that they will make it through the wee hours we usually don't see. *No college student should be awake at six fifteen.*

Taking a second to stretch, I arch my back and let a few bones crack before I step into my slippers and make my way to my door. Yesterday I organized my room and set everything up for the new week, which I was happy about because trying to study surrounded by a pile of boxes isn't ideal. It's not like there's a comfortable common space in the living room where I could study. So my hard work yesterday was key.

Since the house was built in the 1920s, the mornings during the winter apparently are chilly, that's why I'm leaving my room in a pink and green matching pajama set. Well, who am I kidding? I wear matching pajama sets all the time. I find them to be whimsically fun.

When I open my door, the sound of eggs in a frying pan and fresh brewed coffee hit me head-on, as well as the sweet, smoky smell of bacon, of course. I push my hair away from my face and head to the kitchen where lights are blazing, burning my retinas.

"Hell," I mutter, covering my face from the fluorescent lighting of the kitchen.

"Morning," Tucker's deep voice rattles off the cabinets. It's his morning voice, deeper, throatier—if that makes sense—and I hate to admit it, because he's just my friend, but sexier.

Once my pupils adjust to the light, I take Tucker in. He's standing in front of the stove, rubber spatula in hand, wearing a white long-sleeved Henley, the top two buttons undone, a pair of worn jeans with a few paint stains on them, and tan work boots. Sweet Jesus, he makes construction look good. Strap a tool belt around his hips and stick him in front of a camera for the benefit of all womankind.

"Morning," I say in reply, using the counter to help hold up my tired body. "You're up early. What time do you have to go into work?"

"Around seven thirty. I like to get an early start before the boys come in." He looks me up and down, a small smile at the corner of his lips. "You look good." He motions around his head with his hand. "I really like what you did with your hair."

I turn toward the window in the kitchen and check out my reflection. Sure enough, my long brown hair looks like a lion's mane poofed out and framing my face with an abundance of volume. Beautiful.

There is no use in taming it, so I leave my hair as is and turn back toward Tucker. "Not many people can get this kind of height while sleeping." I pretend to fluff my hair.

"Impressive." He chuckles and then points to the coffee maker with the spatula. "Coffee is done, mugs are above in the cabinet. Grab me a cup, will ya? Eggs will be done shortly, bacon is warming in the oven."

I do as directed, thinking it's kind of cute how he's including me in on his little morning breakfast. "I didn't even know you had eggs. I was expecting to hit up Dunkin' Donuts or Tim Horton's this morning."

He turns off the stove and reaches for two plates from the dish rack. "I went to Walmart this morning. Picked up a few things."

"This morning?" I pour two cups of coffee and turn toward him. "What time did you wake up?"

"Four thirty," he answers casually. "Got a quick run in, did some weights, took a shower, and then went to Walmart." He fills our plates with bacon and eggs and then nods toward the dining room, plates and silverware in hand. "I have a surprise."

I follow him to the dining room where he flips on the light and reveals a table and chairs.

"You got a table." I chuckle, loving that it's a fold-out card table with matching chairs. Anything is better than the floor.

"And placemats," he adds, as he lifts two plastic placemats

from one of the chairs. "The options were bleak so I went with dinosaurs for me and Trolls for you. Given the look of your morning hair, Trolls was the right choice." *Clever bastard.* He sets them on the table and then puts our plates on top of them.

God, it's too freaking cute. Chuckling, I take a seat and hand him his coffee. "Look at you getting all domestic. I never thought you would be a placemat kind of man, so I stand corrected."

He rests a napkin on his legs, which are spread drastically, almost the length of the table and leans over to fork some eggs into his mouth. "Didn't want our food to damage the plastic of this high-class table." I love his humor; it reminds me of all the good times we had, before the end of his relationship with Sadie.

"Smart man, you want this table to last."

"Of course, you don't see fine furniture like this in houses anymore. Everything has to be so sturdy. What ever happened to rickety furniture and living through a meal with the threat of your food possibly kissing the floor at any point in time?"

"The horror," I joke.

He looks up at me. Some of his hair is still wet from his shower. Pointing his fork at me he says, "Are you ready to be schooled?"

"Schooled on what?" I take a bite of bacon and my stomach jumps in excitement for finally rewarding it for waking up early. All right, I will admit it, getting out of bed was a smart idea.

"It's Monday, babe. DJ Hot Cock has his song picked and ready to show you what real music is."

"When was my music taste ever questioned? I like good music."

"We'll see." He reaches into his pocket and pulls out his phone. I watch as he flips through it until he lands on the song he wants to introduce me to. He presses play and sets his phone on the table. The light pickings of a guitar fill the small dining room. I don't recognize the song, but I like the sound of it so far.

Just as I'm settling in to the sweet pickings of a guitar, the distinct voice of Zac Brown chimes in. I've known Tucker for loving EMO growing up, so his choice in a country song is very surprising to me, but when I look up at him, pure hometown country boy sitting across from me, it makes perfect sense.

And then the lyrics hit me. *My Old Man.* Zac sings about his father, hoping he's proud of the man he's become. I'm transported back to a dreary day in Whitney Point, where we grew up, when Sadie called me one Saturday morning. I was getting ready for the day. We were in middle school. Tucker's dad was killed by a head-on collision. He'd only recently reconnected with his dad, and had plans to move in with him to get away from his neglectful mom. Those next few days— and weeks—were a whirlwind of sorrow. Attending his funeral, my first ever funeral, seeing the look of devastation on Tucker's face, wondering what he might be feeling, trying to channel his hurt, it was so much to take on as a teenager.

Glancing up, I take in Tucker's expression. He's lost in the music, in the words, just like me. When the song ends, I lean over and place my hand on his; our eyes meet and there is an unspoken understanding between us. I don't have to say anything about his dad, about the tragedy he experienced so many years ago. We all felt his loss. It's all said between this silent exchange.

Clearing his throat, he asks, "What did you think?"

I take a moment to answer. "I think your taste in music has drastically changed. You actually impressed me with your selection."

"Yeah?" A slow smile spreads across his face. "Told you, DJ Hot Cock knows what he's doing." He looks down at his watch and cringes. "I have to get going. Think you can handle the dishes? I cook, you clean?" Good God, he eats fast. Shovels it right in there, doesn't he?

It's obvious he's trying to lighten the mood with his jokes, and I'll let him get away with it because there isn't enough time to get into why he chose that song, why he wanted to share it with me. "If I knew I was going to have to clean, I would have gotten up earlier to make you breakfast."

"Ha, yeah right. You barely dragged your carcass out of bed this morning. Nice try though, babe."

He stands from his folding chair, which is entirely too small for his commanding body, and pockets his phone. "Off to classes today?"

"Yup, all day, then clinicals, then studying. That's my life."

"All right, have a good day."

"You, too. Thanks for breakfast."

He walks out the side door to the driveway. In the distance, I hear him say, "You're welcome," but it's drowned out by the shutting of the door.

I look around the dining room and assess the space. The emptiness. It's . . . consuming. It really is a cute house, but the man needs to decorate. I pick up our plates and mugs and do the dishes quickly before I head to the bathroom. I spend most of my time in my bedroom because honestly, it still feels weird staying in Tucker's house. Maybe it's the bare palette on the walls or the echo of each step that reverberates when you walk around the house, or the sterile feeling I get when I step outside of my bedroom. It might be a while before it feels like home.

Maybe with my short time here, I can help Tucker transform this shell of a house into a loving home for him. That is . . . if he will let me.

· · ·

"Hand me another slice."

I quickly take count of the slices in the pizza box. "You realize you've eaten over half this pizza, right? We were supposed to split it fifty-fifty."

A charming smile, those light blue eyes, and scruffy hair. It's hard to stay mad at this man, or even pretend to be. Instead of waiting for me, Logan picks up his own piece of pizza and takes a large bite. While chewing, he replies, "You weren't going to eat it anyway, so why bitch about it?"

"Uh, leftovers."

He pauses for a brief second and then nods. "Oh right, I didn't think about leftovers." He holds out the pizza he just took a bite of and asks, "Want me to wrap it up in some foil for you for tomorrow?"

"No." I giggle. "Finish it. But next time we get pizza, I'm taking one of your slices."

"Fair enough, but can we make it a small slice? This guy likes to fucking eat." Which is true and crazy at the same time because I've seen Logan with his shirt off and his muscles don't make it look like he loves to eat, more like workout.

"We'll have to see." I lean back and assess the mess of my bedroom. Pizza box, soda cans, paper plates, studying materials, Logan sitting on my bed. Yup, it's a typical night for me. "Why do we always end up making a mess at my place?"

"Because, if we went to my apartment, you wouldn't have even tasted one pepperoni before the entire pizza was swiped by my roommates."

"Don't they have manners?"

"Not really. Matt, I think, is the only one who has some semblance of decency for others, but that's because he's been dating someone recently who doesn't put up with untamed college men."

"Matt has a girlfriend? Since when?"

"Few months. He just told us, so before you get all hot on me about not telling you, just know, I only recently found out." Logan knows me too well. I've been dying to see his roommates find someone special but so far it's been a lost cause.

"That's right. You better keep me updated on the gossip in your apartment. It's the only real gossip I get other than what's floating around my circle of friends, but when they're back at school, it's quiet. Summer, on the other hand, that's a different story."

"Don't worry, sweetheart, I'll keep you in the circle. I know your goal for everyone is to find love, start a family, and live happily ever after."

"Isn't that the goal for everyone?" I ask, shocked that it wouldn't be.

My friends know me. I'm a girl who believes in family, in surrounding yourself with love. Ever since I can remember, I've dreamt of starting a family one day, being a working mom, having a supportive husband, a partner in life, one to share the good and bad with. I'm still looking for that man, and maybe once I get my feet wet in my career, I can start focusing on finding my forever. For now, I'm content with my friends, studying, looking toward graduation, and finding a job.

"Not everyone wants a family. There are people out there who are content being by themselves." Logan looks down at his books and plays with the pencil in his hand.

I shove his shoulder playfully. "Don't act like you're one of those people."

A smirk on his face, with his head still down, his eyes look up at me. "My time is up for a family. I let the good one get away." The way he's gazing at me leads me to believe is talking about our tiny fling. Heat fills my cheeks from the mention of our brief fooling around.

"Don't be awkward." I laugh, tossing a pillow at him.

His laughter fills the room as well, easing the tension that was starting to take over. Friends, that's all Logan is to me, and that's all he'll ever be.

There is a light knock at the door that is almost covered up by our laughter. Calling out over Logan, I answer, "Come in."

The door cracks open just enough for Tucker to show his face. He seems concerned until he looks around and spots Logan. For a brief moment, his brows pinch together in what seems like anger until his face turns into a mask devoid of emotion. Finding me in the sea of books, pizza, and soda cans, he quickly smiles and says, "Uh, just wanted to let you know I'm home. Wasn't sure if you had dinner, but seems like you did. I'll let you guys get back to what you're doing."

He goes to shut the door when I stop him. "Hey, wait, you don't have to go right away. We're taking a break. Come in for a second."

Looking uneasy, his hand gripping the doorframe tightly, he swings the door open to show off his now filthy work outfit. The once white Henley that clung to his muscles is now decorated in dust and mud. His jeans seem to have the same collection of muck on them, and the boots he wore this morning are nowhere to be seen and neither are his socks. There he is, standing in dirty, form-fitting clothes, bare feet, and *that* is doing things to my insides I haven't experienced in a long time.

They're just bare feet, Emma, get hold of yourself.

But . . .

There is something to be said about a man in jeans, wearing nothing on his feet. Why is it so hot? Why does it make me want to take my bra off and throw it at him, only to attempt my very own helicopter with my breasts? Titty-copter on the loose!

Clearing my throat, trying to rid the image of me flapping my tits around in Tucker's face, I say, "You remember Logan, right?"

Tucker nods at Logan and says, "Yeah, what's up, man?"

"Not much." Like the nice guy Logan is, he holds the pizza box up and asks, "Would you like a slice?"

That's my pizza he's offering, but I'll let it slide since it's Tucker.

"I'm good. I, uh, I have a peanut butter sandwich calling my name."

Well, that's sad. I should have thought ahead and asked Tucker if he wanted to join us for dinner. Now I feel like an asshole.

"I'm sorry. I should have text you we were going to have pizza."

He waves me off. "Nah, you do your thing, Emma. You don't have to worry about me." He inhales a deep breath and takes one last look at my room and taps the doorway. "All right, I'll let you two get back to the books. I'm heading upstairs for the night. See you later. Logan, good to see you, man."

"You too."

Tucker shuts the door, leaving me once again with Logan, but this time it feels awkward. I'm not used to accounting for another person since Adalyn was always doing her own thing when we lived together. I never thought about asking Tucker if he wanted to join us. Such a dick move.

Twisting my hands in my lap, I say, "God, I feel bad. I should have called or text him about dinner."

"He doesn't seem torn up about it," Logan answers, now flipping through the book in front of him.

"You're a guy, you don't notice things like I do."

"Hey, I'm perceptive," Logan replies.

I stare at the door, wondering what's going through Tucker's mind, why he briefly had a look of anger in his eyes. Was he mad I invited Logan over without his permission? Is that something I need to do? Ask for permission to have someone over to his house? I never even considered it.

Shit.

I know he said we're adults and decent human beings who don't need roommate rules, but I feel like I need a basic outline of the rules for his house, especially since he's letting me live here for a dollar a month. I want to make sure that if I can't pay Tucker for giving me a place to live, I'm at least making sure I'm not making him uncomfortable.

# Chapter Eight

I don't like him. Nope. Not one fucking bit.

Logan.

What a . . .

Fuck, I can't call him a douche because he really hasn't been a douche. I can't call him an asshole because it doesn't seem like he possess asshole type-qualities nor does he seem like a dickhead, asshat, scrotum face, or tool bag. But there is something, something I don't like about him. I can't fucking place it, but I will.

*No, Logan, I don't want your fucking leftover pizza.* And hey, who fucking wears a polo shirt to study? And your laugh? Fucking irritating.

I wish I could have worn earphones while showering because I kept hearing his deep chuckle come from Emma's room and with every laugh my skin crawled. What the fuck is so funny about studying? It's nursing shit; nothing should be funny about nursing shit. I don't want my nurse laughing while tending to me. All his laughter tells me is he's going to be one fucked-up male version of Nurse Ratched at this rate.

Congrats, buddy. You belong in a psycho-thriller with Jack

Nicholson.

Shaking thoughts of Logan out of my mind, I remove my towel, letting the rest of my body air dry as I pick out a pair of boxer briefs and some comfy sweatpants. Standing naked in my room, I run both hands through my hair and stare down at my peanut butter sandwich. The same thing I have almost every night if I'm not full from Little Debbie snacks, but this time, it makes me feel more pathetic than usual.

She has company. She has her own fucking life. I realized this after a few days of living with her. This isn't a surprise, and yet, when I was driving home, for some fucked-up reason, I kept thinking about what *we* could have for dinner. The thought of not being lonely at night appealed to me.

When I pulled into my driveway and saw a car parked by the front yard, I knew Emma wasn't alone. And I shouldn't fucking care. I don't have a claim on her, she's living in my house for a few months. That's it.

But breakfast has been . . . fuck. It's been nice to not be alone. To not sit in an empty house, the echoing of my every movement filling in the silence, reminding me of the shitty way my life has turned out. But tonight I made a mistake. I got ahead of myself. I pumped myself up for dinner, not eating alone, when I know I shouldn't have.

Christ.

She's here until she graduates. That's it. Not to fill the empty void of my house. Of my life. She's not . . . she's not someone who will ever fill the gaping hole of Sadie's spurning.

With a fresh perspective on my living situation, I step into my boxer briefs and sweatpants and flop on my bed, where I lean back on my pillows and place my plate of depressing dinner on my stomach and then one hand behind my head. I turn on the TV, which hangs on the opposite wall of my bed, and go straight to

ESPN to watch some hockey. Racer's friend, Hayden Holmes, who I met a few months ago, is now playing for the pro-team, the Philadelphia Brawlers. He just made it big, so following his career has been fun. I like rooting for the newbie, but knowing him makes it that much sweeter.

Relaxing into my bed, I take a bite out of my sandwich and listen to the announcers prep viewers for the game, running over stats for both teams and the key players to watch. Since Hayden is the center for the Brawlers, his face is plastered across the screen, and unlike all the other players, he's actually smiling in his picture, but that's Hayden. The guy's full of life.

Reaching for my phone, I shoot a text to Racer.

***Tucker: The announcers seem to be jacking off over your boy's stats.***

Two more bites and my sandwich is done. Shit, I should have made another one. Normally I'd go downstairs, but with Logan down there, laughing like a fucking nimrod, I won't.

My phone beeps back with Racer's reply.

***Racer: That text made me sound a little gay, but shit, with the salary Hayden is getting paid, I'd be gay for him.***

I chuckle to myself and take a sip of my water.

***Tucker: Why doesn't that surprise me?***

***Racer: Maybe because I'm sick of working fucking side jobs to pay for my damn house on top of the workload I'm already doing.***

Fucking Julius. I've been trying to get him to give Racer a raise for a few months now but he won't budge, even though Racer is putting in extra work around the job site. Julius is a stingy bastard.

***Tucker: I'm working on him.***

***Racer: I know. In the meantime, I'm working my way through Vestal Hills—Richville—feeling like Kurt Russell in***

*Overboard, fixing rich bitches' closets. Good times.*

*Tucker: Still doing that on the weekends?*

*Racer: Yeah, if the strip clubs weren't one step away from handing out STDs when you walk in the door, I might consider taking my pants off for the ladies, but my dick is my best friend, and I don't want him to get any kind of venereal shit up his pee hole. What kind of friend would that be?*

Fucking Racer and his dick. The man worships it. Pretty sure he writes a thank-you note to it every night, two if he gets laid.

*Tucker: Life isn't always about your dick, man.*

*Racer: Life is my dick.*

*Tucker: Did I mention I'm not friends with douche bags?*

*Racer: You're too far into this relationship to drop me now.*

The game starts and Hayden immediately takes control of the puck, breezing through the opponents, passing to his teammates, and making the game seem so easy, when in fact I know it's not. Racer and I shoot the shit the entire time, talking about the game, about work, and about the bitchy women he's been working for on the weekends. It's a normal night for me, a night I'm settling into after my earlier unrealistic expectations.

My eyes start to drift shut as I hear the distinct sound of someone creeping up the stairs. Lazily, I look over to see Emma reach the top step and knock on the wall. Since there's no door to my bedroom, it's just a big open space.

"Come in."

Wearing a matching blue pajama set with little pink hearts scattered over the fabric, hair tied up on the top of her head, and her face devoid of makeup, Emma approaches, hands twisting together in front of her.

When she spots me, her eyes temporarily go wide as they scan my naked chest. Normally I wouldn't care about a girl seeing me without my shirt on, but I don't want to make Emma feel uncomfortable. Although, from the way she's looking at me, the heat passing over her eyes, I would say she's less than uncomfortable.

I sit up on the edge of my bed, facing her, hands braced on the mattress beneath me and say, "Hey Emma, everything okay?"

She takes another step forward and nods. "Yeah, I, um, I wanted to say sorry about earlier."

My brow pinches together in question. "Sorry about what?"

With her fingers, she starts to twist the bottom of her pajama shirt. It's kind of cute how nervous she is. I've never seen this side of Emma. She's always been very confident, never scared. Do I scare her? I sure as hell hope not.

"I should have asked if it was okay if Logan came over. It was inconsiderate of me. And then I got pizza without asking if you wanted any. That was real shitty too. So basically, I'm a terrible roommate and I suck, and if you want to try to twist my nipple off as punishment, please do so. I accept the punishment."

She shifts from foot to foot while glancing up at me, her face looking so regretful, it's almost comical.

Fucking Emma.

Not saying a word, I stand and close the distance between us. Before she can react, I pull her into my chest and wrap my arms around her. For a second, she stands stiff as a rod until she slowly melts into my embrace and wraps her arms around me, her head gently pressing against my chest.

"No need to apologize, babe. This house is yours too. Do what you want in it. You don't have to ask me permission to have a friend over, and don't feel like you have to include me in on anything. You do your thing, and if our paths cross, great." I pull away for a second and lift her chin, those brilliant eyes staring up at me. I can't help it; I add, "And twisting your nipple wouldn't be punishment, it would be sweet gratification. Quote me on that."

Surprised, maybe a little shocked, her mouth forms an O as I pull away and head back to my bed where I pat the other side for her to sit on. "Come on, have a seat."

"But," her voice is shaky as she continues, "what if I want our paths to cross? I want to spend time with you, too, Tucker. I've missed you."

My lips twitch to the side, and I start to feel brighter, or something. Something I haven't felt for a long time. "I missed you too, Emma, but I don't want you to feel obligated to include me. I'm used to doing things on my own. Don't let me get in the way."

"You're not, I promise. I'd like to include you, unless you don't want to hang out." She puts her hand to her head in distress. "Oh God, I didn't even think about the fact that maybe you don't want to hang out with me, that I'm actually encroaching on your space. I'm a dumbass."

"Emma, get your ass over here, now." My voice is stern, commanding, and without skipping a beat, she does as she's told and sits next to me on the bed. I force her to look me in the eyes. "I'm not going to repeat myself when I say, I want you here. I'm glad you're here, and I'm looking forward to spending more time with an old friend I lost touch with. Got it?"

She nods, a smile playing on her lips.

"Good. Now"—I shift on the bed and turn the TV down—"are you ready for our sex talk for the week? Might as well check off another rule for the week."

"Sex talk, now?"

"Yeah, now." I stand from the bed and go to the little attic closet right next to the stair landing and open the door. I reach for the box that hasn't been touched in quite a long time and grab the first magazine from the top. Before I turn around, I swipe my hand over the top to give it a quick dusting and then walk back to my bed, sit next to Emma, and hand her the magazine.

"Playboy?" I rest my head against the wall and take in her innocent shock. It's fucking cute.

"It's time you looked at one, don't you think?"

"How does this coincide with talking about sex?"

I chuckle. "Babe, there are sex tips and shit in there. It really isn't just about the bare breasts. Go on, open the old girl up. Let's see some tits."

"I can't believe you're making me look at a nudey magazine." She starts flipping through the pages as she talks. "Guys are so weird that they subscribe to . . . oh wow, she has some nice areolas." She brings the magazine closer to her face for a more detailed glance, which causes me to laugh out loud, the kind of laugh I haven't laughed in a very long time. "What's so funny? Look at her areolas, they seem so perfect for her breasts." She lifts the magazine for me to see.

Still chuckling, I nod. "Very nice tits."

"Then why are you laughing?"

"Because. Most people who look at a Playboy don't immediately compliment the areolas on a woman."

"I don't see why not. This woman sitting in a soda shop, wearing nothing but a cut-off apron, deserves the praise. It's a very bold outfit for a public place."

"Fucking hell." I chuckle some more. "You're not going to be one of those people who tries to make sense of every picture and what the girl is doing, are you?"

"I don't know what that means, but what I do know is this woman is super bendy. How . . .?" Emma sets the magazine down, open to the page she's looking at, and gets on all fours on my bed.

Oh. Fuck.

She starts popping her backside in the air, her pert, little ass shaking before me and asks, "How is she doing that? Am I bending like her?"

I swallow hard, really fucking hard, as I glance at the picture Emma is trying to recreate on my bed and then back at her. Her shirt is starting to move up her back, exposing a small patch of skin. "Uh . . ." No fucking words, none. All thought has quickly disappeared as the blood in my body starts to pool uncomfortably in my crotch.

Fuck, do not have a boner right now.

"I don't understand how she can bend her back like that. She really has to drop her stomach, but I don't know how that's accomplished."

This is fucking torture. She continues to stick her ass in the air, her shirt really starting to ride high now. I know if I fucking glanced down, if I really took a look, I might be able to see her breasts from the way her shirt is dropping in the front, but I keep my eyes trained on her ass instead. It's the lesser of the two evils. Although, fuck, all I want to do is spank it.

Christ. Where is this coming from? *The girl is in a matching pajama set for fuck's sake, and she's your goddamn friend.* Note to self: get laid soon because my mind is starting to go crazy from lack of sex.

"Oh well." She sits back up on the bed, as if she didn't just put me through the guillotine. "Oh, look at this girl. She looks nice. She has a great butt, but look at those melons." Emma puts her hand over her mouth and giggles while looking at me. On a whisper, she says, "They're huge. Like two tetherballs dangling from her chest."

Well, there goes tetherball for me. I'll never be able to look at them the same anymore, but I hate to admit it, Emma has a point. Her boobs are huge. Very ill-proportioned for her body.

"She does know how to pose though. I wonder if I posed like her if my boobs would seem bigger."

Just when I thought I was out of the danger zone, Emma faces me, kneeling on my bed, legs spread, she leans forward and with her upper arms, she squeezes her breasts together in my direction. The buttons that are undone at the top of her shirt give me a flash of cleavage as she looks down at herself. I really shouldn't be looking down her shirt, I should seriously look away, *but fuck me*. I can't seem to train my eyes to look away.

*I'm a guy and there are boobs facing me.*

"Maybe they look bigger."

Emma has curves. She doesn't have the biggest boobs I've ever seen, but they are big enough to fill the dresses she wears, and that ass? Let's just say I might have seen it in a new light tonight.

Glancing up at me, she asks, "I wonder what guys do to enhance the look of their penis. I mean. You can't pump up your pelvis and look natural at the same time. We can lean forward and squish our boobs together and voilà, mega tits. But what is there for mega dick? Lifting your scrotum up to the air?"

Chuckling, I shake my head and say, "Erections, babe. Erections make dicks bigger."

*And* I'm trying to hide my fucking aching cock right now.

She tilts her head to the side and gives me a pointed look. "I know erections make dicks look bigger. But what if your dick isn't that big?"

"Then you're not posing for a camera, that's for damn sure."

"Aw." She pouts her lips. "Poor petite penises. Their dreams of being a dick model forever vanished. It's like models; you can't be one unless you're taller than five eight. There is discrimination everywhere. Maybe I should start a small-dick magazine, to help all the little shrimpies get a shot at glory."

"No one is going to want that magazine, babe. Sorry to say."

"Well, I would look at it."

"Yeah?" I raise an eyebrow at her. "You would look at dicks so small that you would have to use a pair of chopsticks to sift through the pubes to get to it?"

"They are not that small. And no pubes allowed. If I have to keep things pretty, so do men."

I sit back again. For obvious reasons, my legs propped up and I rest my arms on my knees. *She keeps things pretty down there. Perhaps I should re-evaluate this rule. Sex talk with Emma may be dangerous.* "Keeping things straightened up down there, Emma? In case you happen to have that one-night stand?"

She shifts on the bed and flips through the pages. "You never know when you're going to find a pretty meatus you can't turn your vagina away from."

"What the fuck is a meatus?" The urge to puke in my mouth is strong.

"You don't know what a meatus is? You have a penis, don't you?"

"Last time I checked."

"Do you not know the anatomy of your own dick?" Her voice sounds exasperated, as if I really should know the technical terms of every part of my penis. Sorry, but I know everything I need to know.

"I know what needs to be known. Balls, taint, dick, pee hole. What else do I really need to be aware of?"

She rolls her eyes and, with one hand, forms what I'm going to assume is a penis by sticking two fingers out and curling the others into her palm to represent balls. Clever. With her other hand, she points to her hand, laying out the parts of the penis. "This is the scrotum . . ."

I put her hand down to stop her. "I don't need a lesson on

cock, babe."

She huffs from my dismissal. "Seems like you do if you don't know what the meatus is."

Challenging her, I say, "Go to the mall, query every man and woman who pass by and ask them if they know what the meatus on a man is. I can guarantee you no one will know."

"Ugh, the education in this country." She folds her arms over her chest indignantly and sticks her chin in the air. "For your information, the meatus is part of the urethra. I hope you keep yours clean."

"Christ." I run my hand over my face.

"Hey, you wanted to talk about sex tonight. This is your doing."

"We're not talking about sex, we're talking about fucking pee holes on a man. Can we at least talk about nipples or something? Jesus, Emma."

She starts flipping through the pages of the Playboy rapidly and says, "Ugh, men. They always have to go back to the breasts. Heaven forbid a woman gets to talk about what entices her."

"All right, what entices you? Besides a good meatus, that conversation is fucking over."

"What do you mean? What can get me to strip my clothes down?"

I laugh from Emma's words. For some reason, I can't quite see her as a girl who strips down. In my mind, she's shy in the bedroom—sweet, innocent—but then again, I'm learning a lot more about Emma here. Maybe she's a little wild, different from what I presume.

"Yeah. What turns you on, Emma?"

Her posture switches from confident to modest in seconds. She quickly brings her knees to her chest and wraps her arms around her shins to keep her legs close to her body. She rests her chin on her knees and avoids all eye contact with me while she speaks. "What turns me on? Hmm, besides the obvious meatus?" She giggles.

"No more fucking meatus. Christ, woman."

"Fine. All right, what turns me on." She thinks for a second and I know immediately when she comes up with her answer because her pretty cheeks stain pink with embarrassment. It's fucking adorable. "The kiss."

"The kiss? Explain."

She quirks her lips to the side, a picture of innocence and joy on her face. "The kiss. How can I describe it? It's the defining moment of any new beginning. It can either make or break what's to happen next." She sighs and looks off to the side. "It's all about the pressure of his lips, the passion in the way he holds me, and the confidence in his body language. It should be soft, delicate, but also passionate, as if my lips are the only thing holding him up. Nothing sloppy, nothing too demanding, just the right amount of yearning that won't scare me away. It should sweep me up into a dreamland where I forget everything around us, where I'm captured between two strong hands and one set of perfectly attentive lips. The kiss, the kiss is everything, Tucker."

Silence falls between us as I think about her words.

Fuck.

Why do I want to kiss her now? Why do I want to prove myself to her, to see if my kiss would be everything *she* wanted? This is Emma, my friend, someone I've cared about my whole life, not someone I've wanted romantically. The only person I've ever wanted, tasted, is Sadie. But fuck, that ship has sailed, even though I'm still not in a place in my life where I want to say goodbye. I still feel bitter. And fuck me if I still don't want her . . .

"It's stupid, I know." Emma cuts through my thoughts and

shrugs. "I'm a dreamer."

Shaking all thoughts of Sadie out of my head, I focus on Emma and clear my throat. "It's not stupid. It's sexy."

"Sexy?" Her nose scrunches cutely.

"Yeah, sexy. You know what you want. That's hot."

She stares at me for a few brief seconds before her hand covers her mouth, and she starts to giggle.

Fucking giggle.

What's so damn funny about me saying that's sexy?

Growing a little irritated, I ask, "Why the hell are you laughing?"

She waves her hand in front of her face, trying to ward off the giggles. When she composes herself, she says, "I'm sorry. It's just . . ." She bites her lip and looks up at me through her eyelashes. "Tucker Jameson just said that something *I* said was sexy."

"So?" Why am I not getting this?

"Oh, come on." She gives me a pointed look. "You're the hometown heartbreaker."

"The what?"

She clenches her knees even closer to her body as her cheeks blush. Her blue eyes search me over, making me feel exposed, as if I really should know what she's talking about. Honestly, I have no clue.

"Figures." She smiles. "You were so wrapped up in Sadie, you had no idea how many hearts you were breaking with every kiss you gave her. You were *the* boy, Tucker. Every girl wanted you to look their way, to give them a second of your time, to . . ." she swallows hard and continues, "to be swept up into your world."

I grab the back of my neck uncomfortably. "That's, uh . . ." Fuck, what does someone say to that? "That's interesting." I cringe inwardly.

Emma chuckles and shakes her head. "You're so oblivious. You always have been. And it never made sense why you thought you weren't good enough for Sadie."

"Clearly, I wasn't." My voice is forlorn, pensive almost.

Emma scoots closer and puts her hand on mine, causing me to look her in the eyes. "You were good enough to be with her, Tucker. You just weren't right for her."

Seems to be the common opinion among our group of friends, besides me. Not for one fucking minute did I think I wasn't right for Sadie. In fact, I thought I was the perfect fit for her. We'd been through hell and back together. Up until she met her boyfriend, Andrew, there was nothing I didn't know about her; there was nothing she kept hidden from me.

Irritation consumes me, my patience growing thin quickly with every memory of Sadie that passes through my mind.

"I don't believe that," I answer honestly, my voice stern and to the point. "Sadie was the love of my life. Is . . . she is the love of my life." I run my hand over my face and try to calm my racing heart.

"Tucker, I didn't mean to—"

"You know what, it's getting late," I snap. "I think we should call it a night." I snag the magazine from my bed and toss it to the side, putting an end to our "sex talk."

"Oh . . . okay." Emma shifts off the bed, her voice weak. "I didn't mean to offend you, Tucker."

Consider me fucking offended.

"It's fine. I'll catch you later, Emma." And just like that, I shut down, tucking myself into bed and letting her show herself out of my bedroom.

There are two things I don't want to talk about, ever: my mom and Sadie. Both topics cause me pain, self-hatred, and make me question every aspect of my desperately pathetic and shitty life.

As she slowly leaves my room, I turn on my side away from her and her "opinion," still fuming from thoughts of Sadie, of everyone's doubt in our relationship. Of fucking Sadie's doubt in our relationship. She didn't even give me a second chance to prove to her that I'm the man she needs. Not a boy, but the MAN she fucking needs.

*No, Emma, you're wrong.*

*I wasn't good enough.*

*I wasn't good enough for Sadie to stay.*

# Chapter Nine

## EMMA

Have you ever said something you wish you could take back the moment it comes out of your mouth? I'm sure you have. I'm sure there has been a time in your life where you say something stupid, something that changes the course of a relationship, something so out of character that you start sweating. And not just underarm kind of sweat, but the type of sweat that coats the back of your neck, your upper lip, and every crevice of your body.

Regret immediately hits you hard in the chest and all you can do is sit back and chastise yourself while apologizing profusely to whomever you offended. And they can say it's fine, they can act like everything is hunky-dory, that life is still the same, but it's not. Do you know why? Because those words you uttered are out there in the universe, sitting there like a giant purple set of man balls, unshaven, in the room. This isn't pink-elephant-in-the-room status. We're talking nasty, uneven, purple, hairy man balls, tickling you under the chin with its pubes. It's there, exposed, reminding you every day of the one sentence you should have kept to yourself.

*You just weren't right for her.*

Those . . . how many words are there . . . four, five, six. Those six little words changed everything in my living arrangement. It's been a week, and I can count on one hand the amount of words Tucker's said to me despite trying to reach him. I've tried. I try every damn day to include him in conversation, but he's short, terse, and uninterested. *Somber. Hiding.*

Note to self: he doesn't like to talk about Sadie. Got it.

And you know what? Even though I regret saying those words out loud, I still believe them. I actually didn't like them together at all, because even though they had some really good times, their bad times outweighed the good . . . easily. Their relationship was volatile. I can remember some of the arguments they would get into at parties, how they would scream at each other and verbally hurt one another. Some nights they ended on a good note, some nights I wound up driving Sadie back to my place.

Unfortunately for me, I was privy to all their fights and most often, what soured between them on that particular occasion. They were two broken kids, seeking comfort from the wrong outlet. I can't even recall how often I sat with Sadie in my arms, crying over the boy, wishing he could move past his troubled relationship with his mom and stop projecting that relationship onto theirs. Granted, they were in high school, and it seems Tucker has done some growing since then, but never once did I sit back and think, these two were meant to be with each other. In some respects, it felt like a small-town relationship of convenience. You know, too hard to break up because you'll see them every day.

I always thought they were pulling each other down rather than lifting each other up.

But I guess my opinion on the matter doesn't count. What do I know? I was only there for Sadie through the trials and tribulations of the Tucker and Sadie melodrama. I know nothing.

Absolutely nothing . . .

Do you hear the sarcasm? Gah! So frustrating.

I'm shaking with irritation now. He really shouldn't be mad at me. It's not fair. I was just being a friend, telling him like it is, and I even tried to do it in a sensitive way. Last time I do that.

Yes, that's my bratty thirteen-year-old self popping in for a visit. Just let her fester for a few seconds.

"Stupid men," I mutter as I wrap my robe around my waist and head to the kitchen for coffee, no longer feeling sorry, more in the mood to kick some crotches.

I'm not surprised when I enter the kitchen and see Tucker hovering over the stove making himself eggs. Unlike our previous mornings when we had breakfast together, he only makes eggs for one now. Typical spiteful man. I get it. *You're giving me the cold shoulder. No need to rub your fluffy scrambled eggs and crispy bacon in my face.*

Prick.

My sorry*s* are long gone now, forget the regret. I'm a girl without coffee and yummy eggs and *with* a roommate who is acting like a dick. Beware of what's going to happen next.

I reach for a mug in the cabinet but come up empty. I look over at the sink and see the one I used yesterday morning . . . dirty. Brain is starting to boil.

Honestly. Who only has two fucking mugs?

On the verge of losing it, I slam the cabinet shut with more force than necessary and huff toward the sink. "You should really get more mugs. Two is ridiculous; you're a grown-up, Tucker; it's called owning things," I snap at him. And the mature award goes to me, the girl with the morning hair and ragey eyes.

I turn on the faucet and start washing my mug. It's not even a pretty mug. It's from his construction company. It's your basic white mug with a blue logo on it. Hideous. Where's the Disney princess mugs? The boob mugs? The lick-my-dick mugs?

"Ugly construction company mug," I mutter as I rinse it out.

When I turn to fill it up, I catch a glimpse of Tucker, his back still toward me, pushing eggs around on his pan. Did he even hear me? Does he even care about dinnerware? Why is he being a giant jerk and not talking?

"You know, it's polite to talk to your roommate." I fill my mug up with coffee and turn toward him. "You're being rude by not even saying good morning." He doesn't say anything, causing my bitch pants to be pulled on one leg at a time. Things are about to go downhill quickly. "Okay, so you're just going to hover over your stupid yummy-tasting eggs and not say anything? That's just fiiiiinnnnne." My arms open wide as I say the word, and I can feel the crazy starting to take over. This is what happens when someone gives me the silent treatment. I lose my shit. "Just stand there in your holey jeans and, and, your, well, you're not wearing a hard hat now, but if you were, just stand there in your stupid holey jeans and hard hat eating your bacon and jerking yourself off to your morning eggs while drinking out of your one-of-two coffee mugs." I give him the thumbs up, exaggerated of course, really making sure he can see it. "Real cool, Tucker. You're sooooo cool. Don't mind me." Walking over to the cabinet, I bump him into the stove as I reach for a granola bar. I hold it up to him, making sure he can see that my Chewy Bar is what I'll be eating for breakfast. "I have my Chewy Bar and, you know what? My Chewy Bar is a better friend than you are; at least it lets me eat him." Eh . . . I pause. Not what I wanted to say. I shake my head. "I don't want to eat you, that would be weird. Shit, forget I said that." To myself I say, "I was on such a roll." Getting back to my rant, I poke Tucker in the shoulder, which garners his attention. At last. His face is devoid of any emotion as I continue my mini tirade. I hold up my Chewy Bar and coffee and say, "I'm taking this to my room and, you know what? I'll have a hell of a better time staring at my walls than listening to you heavy breathe over your scrambled eggs. Yeah, you breathe heavy." He doesn't, but it's the only insult I can come up with. "Blow your nose every once in a while, it might stop you from sounding like a barge coming into dock."

Satisfied, I start to leave but then realize I forgot something. I turn to him once more and say, "And for your information, it's polite to keep your condoms in your nightstand, not the medicine cabinet, unless you want me to start tossing my tampons around like fireworks, popping them in your face. Is that what you want, Tucker? Tampon fireworks? Because don't test me, I will make it happen. I will make it rain period products." Walking off, I shout, "Feminine hygiene will be your worst nightmare, son!"

I slam my door shut and smile to myself. Job well done.

● ● ●

"Oh God, I was such an idiot this morning." I slouch in a booth at the student union and place my tray of food in front of me on the table. I ordered my favorite orange chicken from my favorite quick-order place in the food court but now it's not looking so appetizing. I've spent my entire day at school. This will be my second meal in the union because I can't bear to go home. Not after my embarrassing morning rant.

Tampon fireworks? Come on, Emma!

Adalyn sits across from me and starts to open her straw, tearing the paper off at the end and expertly working the plastic through the opening, saving the tube of paper so she can tie it in a knot, like she always does.

"Oh, you were an idiot? This is exciting. What did you do?"

Adalyn takes a sip of her Dr. Pepper, orange soda combination—gross—and leans forward.

Before telling her what happened, I ask, "Was I a bad roommate?"

"No. If you were a bad roommate, do you really think I would have roomed with you for so long? Why do you ask?" Adalyn is always to the point, and I like that about her.

"I feel like I'm a pretty considerate person. I mean, I didn't put mint on your pillows or anything, but I made sure to make things as comfortable as possible between us, right?"

Adalyn picks up her wrap and looks at me, a knowing glint in her eye. "Uh oh, trouble in roommate paradise? How is that possible? You're rooming with a genuine, bona fide, certified, personified piece of man meat. What could be wrong with rooming with the epitome of all men? I mean, his smirk alone should make you feel complete at night."

I haven't seen that smirk in days.

I tug on my ponytail and shift in my seat. "I said something stupid the other night. I meant it, but I shouldn't have said it to him, and now he barely says anything to me. We're just co-existing, not actually living together."

"What did you say?"

Groaning, I poke my fork at a piece of chicken and put it in my mouth. I talk and chew at the same time; it's Adalyn, she doesn't care. "I mentioned his ex-girlfriend who is one of my best friends."

"Who?" Adalyn is really getting into the conversation.

"Sadie, you met her."

"Oh yeah, she has the hot, nerdy boyfriend with the glasses. God, I wish she would use him as a feather against my body."

Slightly weird, but it's Adalyn. "Yeah, that's her. Tucker and Sadie were childhood sweethearts. Our group of friends always thought they'd get married one day."

"Huh, what happened?"

I think back to the day Sadie called me in tears, unsure of what to do, her future in the balance. "They were always rocky, especially when Sadie went to college at Cornell, but it wasn't until she got pregnant that everything went spiraling."

"Sadie was pregnant?"

I nod and take another bite of chicken. "Yeah, she lost the baby a few weeks later which changed everything, even our friend dynamic. Their relationship combusted, and we were all kind of forced to choose sides. They didn't make us, but it felt like we had to. Tucker, being two years older than us, easily slipped out of the scene, and that's why I didn't see him for so long."

"That's kind of sad."

"It is." My gut starts to churn as I think about the turn of events Tucker had to face. He lost his baby, his love, and his support system. He lost everything, and here I am, rubbing it in his face that Sadie wasn't the person for him. God, I'm such a freaking asshole.

"What did you say that made him so mad?"

I swallow hard, thinking back to the other night. The devastated look on his face, the way he shut down so quickly, and then dismissed me, after we were having such a good night. I really should have kept my mouth shut. "I told him Sadie wasn't right for him."

"That doesn't seem so bad." I love that Adalyn tries to ease the tension in my heart.

"It is when she was everything he ever wanted." Leaning forward, I place my hand on the table and say, "Adalyn, he was, and I guess still is, so in love with her. He worshipped the ground she walked on. Yes, they had their fights, but even when they fought, you could still see the passion in his eyes for her. When they weren't together, he was miserable, and when they were together, he was happy. She literally could make or break him with a few words."

"So why wasn't she right for him?"

Good question. He might have loved her, but I think he was in love with the comfort of Sadie, the ease she gave him. "I don't think they were ever truly in love. They were at each other's sides for some of the worst times in their life. They were each other's backbones for so long. They knew the ins and outs of each other. They both grew up in unhealthy environments, mostly caused by their moms, who left heavy scars on their childhoods. They bonded over the misfortune, but sometimes two broken souls can't fix each other. In their case, that was true."

"It makes me sad. But I get it. The Sadie you speak of is not the same Sadie I know. She seems so happy, so content in life."

I nod. "That's the new Sadie. Andrew brings out the fun-loving side of her. The Sadie I love and adore, but for a while, before Andrew, she was bitter, liked to be alone, and would drink a lot. For a few months, she literally had nothing going for her. It wasn't until Andrew came along that she rose from her ashes and became the brilliantly vibrant woman she is now."

"I bet that is a bitter pill for Tucker to swallow."

Leave it to Adalyn to smack me in the face with logic. Tucker must be in so much pain, seeing Sadie happy with someone else. And there I was, bringing up the past and then throwing threats of feminine products in his face. What kind of friend does that? Once again, I feel like I've failed him.

I slouch even more in my booth. "Ever seen what a troll wart looks like?"

Adalyn tilts her head in confusion. "What?"

I point to myself. "That's me, a freaking troll wart. No." I shake my head. "I don't even deserve the distinction of being a wart on a troll's body. I'm the rotten, crusted-over, split toenail on a Bergen. A BERGEN."

My voice elevates, which causes Adalyn to try to tamp down my anger by using her hands to bring down the noise. "Your Troll references are frightening sometimes. That movie is for children."

"But it's sooo good. Snub of the century during the award season." Upset, I push my tray to the side, not feeling the Chinese food. "I'm such a horrible person, Adalyn. I was so mean to him. I told him to act like an adult."

"What?" Adalyn is actually surprised by this. "Why would you say that? Did he burp in your face and ask you to tell him what he had for dinner?"

"Ew, no. Gross, Adalyn. Has anyone ever done that to you?"

Leveling out her arms along the table, she gives me a knowing look. "Emma, I grew up with seven, yes, seven brothers. There wasn't a night that went by that I didn't get burp faced."

"I don't know how you're still alive now."

Looking off to the abyss, she nods. "I can't believe they're still alive, actually. After the night they cut my hair, drunk as shit, they should be kissing my feet that their dicks are still intact." She shakes her head and glances my way. "But that isn't what we're talking about right now. I want to know why you told Tucker, the beautifully damaged man, he needs to grow up."

"It's so stupid. I really think I lost my mind from his silence." I'm just not used to people dealing with problems like that. With Adalyn, we simply cleared the air and moved on. *Aren't guys meant to do that?*

Adalyn doesn't let me get away with anything. "Spill it."

"I told him to grow up because he only has two mugs in his house. Two mugs, Adalyn. How is that even possible? I mean, when I was in middle school I think I had more mugs than he does now. He's a grown man and has two mugs; it's just unheard of." I try to defend myself but even on my ears my words sound hollow.

"Oh, Emma." Adalyn shakes her head in disappointment. "You fucked up."

"Yeah, I fucked up big time." I don't need Adalyn telling me the kind of sorry excuse of a friend I am, I can see it plain as day. *Tampon fireworks, ughhh.*

I don't even bother finishing my meal. I pack it up in a to-go box, and say my goodbyes to Adalyn, who asks me on my way out to sneak a picture of Tucker naked for her. Nope, that's never going to happen.

The drive home from campus is miserable. Usually I take this alone time to decompress, to blast my music and enjoy the little drive home before I have to start studying, but this trip is full of replaying the conversation I had with Tucker this morning over and over in my head.

Yes, he's been ignoring me; well, not ignoring, just quiet. And yes, that was annoying, but did I really have to criticize him? The man who took me in. The only one of our friends who'd bought their own house. *Gah. He probably hates me now.*

The more I think about it, the more I feel sick to my stomach. He's had it hard. And then there's his house, the room he won't let me go into, and the empty place he comes home to every night. It's desolate and empty. There has to be a reason he feels no urgency to make it a home, why he doesn't even bother to furnish the rooms. He's content with how it is, and that makes me even more sorry for the way I behaved. *He* didn't deserve my judgment or criticism.

When I pull into the driveway, I spot Tucker's truck parked off to the side. He doesn't bother parking in the driveway any more since he usually leaves before me in the morning. I should be the one parking on the side of the road, not him. The guilt keeps piling on.

Because he's the nice guy he is, the outdoor light is on, giving me visibility to the side of the house. He's always considerate.

See that wheelbarrow behind me? You can start shoveling all the guilt in there.

When I open the side door, I notice immediately how quiet the house is. Usually I can hear the faint sound of Tucker's TV coming from his bedroom, but I hear nothing. I check my watch and notice it's only a little past eight. He must have an extremely early morning if he's already asleep.

The house is dark besides one light above the sink, illuminating the kitchen and spotlighting a set of mugs on the countertop. My heart seizes in my chest. *Oh, what has he done?*

Stacked up like a pyramid is a set of seven teal mugs, one for each day of the week, labeled appropriately in cute cursive. Sticking out below them is a note. With trepidation, I set my backpack on the counter and pick up the note, my hand shaking uncontrollably. I quickly unfold it and read Tucker's signature chicken-scratch handwriting.

*Emma,*

*Sorry about the mug situation. It's only been me, so I never thought of having more. Saw these at Target, thought you would like them. Now you have one for every day of the week.*

*Tucker*

Tears start to fall down my cheeks from the thoughtful gesture. Here I am, barging in on his space and acting like a total priss, calling him names, and he does something like this. Forget the wheelbarrow of guilt; I need a dump truck.

I hold the note close to my heart and walk toward my bedroom when, from the corner of my eye, something bright catches my attention. In the dining room, on the card table, is a bouquet of flowers with another note tucked under the vase. It feels impossible to breathe as I step forward to read it.

*Emma,*

*Thought you might like a little color in the house. Ever since I've known you, having a home and a family has meant everything to you. I'm sorry this place isn't more like a home. I hope this helps.*

*Tucker*

"Oh my God." My cheeks are stained with sorrow, with regret, with remorse for everything I said to him. How can he be so nice when I'm the one who should be apologizing?

I press the other note to my chest and go to my bedroom where I grab a set of pajamas and go through my nighttime routine.

When I reach the bathroom, I feel as though someone punched me in the gut and knocked all the wind out of me. Instead of the plain shower curtain encasing the tub, a white curtain with pink flamingos scattered across the fabric hangs from the railing. On the floor, a matching pink rug. Hanging on the towel hooks are pink, fluffy oversized towels, and on the back of the toilet is a pink flamingo wearing sunglasses holding a margarita glass. A snort of a laugh pops out of me, along with more tears. When I face the mirror, I'm greeted with a note taped to the glass. This one doesn't need to be unfolded.

*Emma,*

*Saw the flamingo shower curtain and went a little crazy. I'm not thrilled about the pink, but fuck, the towels are soft. Also, the medicine cabinet is cleared out and there is a special decorative box next to the toilet for any personal things you need to put in there. Sorry I didn't think of it beforehand.*

*Tucker*

And that does me in. I break down, right there on the flamingo-attacked bathroom. I hold my pajamas in my hands and cry, hating myself. He went through all this . . . for me. He got pink towels for me. He got a tampon box for me.

Peeling myself off the floor, I quickly get ready for bed while thoughts of Tucker swarm through my mind. When I reach for my toothbrush in the medicine cabinet, I immediately notice the absence of his condoms and in place of them, a note.

**Emma,**

**Didn't mean to make you uncomfortable. Sorry, Em. I hope you can forgive me.**

**Tucker**

That does it. I can't go to bed without talking to him. I don't care if he's asleep. I quickly brush my teeth, wipe the tears off my cheeks, and deposit my clothes in my room. When I reach the stairs that lead up to his room, I try to tamp down the twisting and churning feeling in my stomach by taking deep breaths. Tucker doesn't want an emotional wreck barging in on him. *Be cool, Emma.*

Feeling marginally composed, I take the steps one at a time, the creak of them sounding loud within the silent house. If he wasn't awake, he's awake now.

When I reach the top stair, I peek over to his bed where he's resting with one hand behind his head, his night table lamp providing the only light in the room and a hardcover book in his hand. I start toward him and that's when he looks my way.

In the dim light, his book casts a shadow over his bare chest, his ruffled hair barely visible, and those soulful eyes of his breaking me in half.

I don't even get a word out before I start breaking down again. Fat ugly tears cascade down my cheeks like a waterfall of despair.

With purpose, Tucker places a bookmark in his book, sets it on the nightstand, and then scoots back on the bed, opening the comforter up for me. With a slight nod of his head, he calls me over. I spare no time in accepting his invitation. I join him in bed where I snuggle into his chest and hug him. I hug him hard, feeling comforted by the way his heart pounds against my cheek.

"I'm sorry," I sob, my tears staining his chest.

"I know, babe."

Babe.

That one little word unravels the knots forming in my stomach. The anger I expected to hear from him is nowhere to be found, and instead, all I feel is his arm, pulling me closer.

"I was so mean to you this morning and then you go and do all these nice things for me. I don't deserve them. You should have left boxes in my room instead and told me to pack up."

"Nah, you're not getting rid of me that easily."

I sit up and look at him. There's a light smirk on his face. How can he be so casual about this when I feel like total shit?

"Tucker, I'm serious. I was so mean to you, so inconsiderate. You need to tell me you're mad at me, say something mean back to me."

He shakes his head. "That's not how this works, babe. We got in a little fight. I was a dick to you too. You caught me off guard, said some things I didn't want to hear, and I cut you out. I'm just as much to blame. So let's just call it a truce and start over. I'm sorry for being a dick."

"You weren't a dick. You were upset, and I acted like a jerk. I'm sorry." I shake my head. "I really didn't mean it when I said I would shoot off tampon fireworks in your face. I would never do that. I don't even know how to turn a tampon into a firework."

He chuckles. "Really wasn't nervous about the tampon

fireworks." He pulls me back down to his chest where I rest my head.

"You got me coffee mugs," I say, not really knowing what else to say.

"I did. Got the impression this morning that the construction coffee mug wasn't your style."

"They're just fine. I was only upset about you not talking to me and I lashed out, inappropriately. I don't handle the cold shoulder very well. If you couldn't tell."

"Noted." He sighs. "But for the record, I wasn't giving you the cold shoulder."

"You didn't talk to me for a few days."

I feel him shrug under me. "Nothing to say."

"You couldn't even say good morning? Or how about a little heads-up about trash day, or maybe a little nod in my direction that you were calling it a night."

He pauses and then says, "Okay, maybe I was giving you a bit of the cold shoulder, but not intentionally."

"I knew it." Playfully, I pinch his side.

"Watch it." He pushes my hand away.

I sigh into his chest and squeeze him again, making sure to let him know how happy I am that we're talking again. "I don't want us to fight again. I've been miserable without my friend. It makes for a very uncomfortable living environment."

"Ah, you're saying that because you want my eggs."

"You can't just cook your eggs and not make me any. It's so unfair. And just so you know, that Chewy Bar did nothing for my appetite."

"Shocking," he says sarcastically. "The way you were parading it around my face, I would have sworn it was the breakfast of your dreams."

"Not so much." Happy Tucker is talking to me again, but,

feeling a little awkward lying in his bed with him, I sit up and say, "Well, I guess, I'll let you get back to your book." I turn to get out of his bed when he wraps his arm around my waist and pulls my back to his chest. With his arm wrapped tightly around my stomach, he spoons me from behind.

Tucker *is spooning me.*

"Don't go." His voice is quiet, almost desperate sounding. In all the years I've known him, I don't think I've ever encountered vulnerable Tucker. He's always been so tough and rugged, a man's man. So, instead of going downstairs to my books, I lean forward slightly, turn off Tucker's light, and rest my head on his pillow, giving in to his unexpected request.

Taking a deep breath, trying *not* to enjoy the feeling of Tucker's strong arm enveloping me, I say, "Thank you for everything, Tucker. You really didn't have to get all those things. You could have seriously asked me to leave. I deserved it."

His head is right next to mine, and his breath tickles my skin when he says, "I wanted to, Emma."

"Okay . . ."

"I do request one thing." There is determination in his voice, all joking set aside.

"What's that?"

He takes a deep breath and says, "Rule number six. Sadie and my mom are off limits when it comes to conversation topics. Okay?"

Without skipping a beat, I say, "That's fair. I'm sorry I brought Sadie up the other night, I just felt—"

"Emma." He squeezes me. "Off limits, okay? We're not talking about it."

I guess not. "Okay."

"Thank you." He pulls me tighter to his chest, his grip never loosening.

"Uh, are we spooning right now?"

"Yeah." He's so casual about it, as if all friends do this. "Got a problem with that, babe?"

"Uh, no. Just wanted to make sure you knew what was happening."

"I'm well aware. It's okay to spoon, Emma. Sometimes human touch is all you need to heal wounds. We opened some wounds between us this past week, and I want to heal them." He takes a second and then adds, "I don't want there to be any beef between us. I lost your friendship once already. I don't want to lose it again."

I try to turn around to face him, but he holds me in place. "Tucker, you're not going to lose my friendship, I promise." And surprisingly, I relax into his embrace.

*Sometimes human touch is all you need to heal wounds.* He's right. He's healing mine now.

He kisses the top of my head, and I feel his warmth spreading through me. "I'm holding you to that, babe." *I'm holding him to that too.*

# Chapter Ten

*Emma: I really don't think making pizza classifies as making dinner. We need to choose something that challenges us.*

*Tucker: Pizza is challenging when made drunk. Pick up lots of booze; it will be a fun game.*

*Emma: We are not cooking drunk, you're just asking to set your house on fire, and then where would that put us? Looking at Playboys together under a bridge while sharing a sleeping bag for shelter.*

*Tucker: That doesn't sound exciting to you?*

*Emma: Not even in the slightest.*

*Tucker: Fine, no pizza. How about goulash? That's simple and doesn't require having to be drunk.*

*Emma: Can we have garlic bread with it?*

*Tucker: I would be pissed if you came home without it.*

*Emma: Will you judge me if I eat half of the loaf?*

*Tucker: Will you judge me if I lick the sauce jar clean?*

*Emma: I think we just established a judgment-free zone. Can you attest to this?*

*Tucker: Attested.*

*Emma: Good. We shall convene at six. Bring your cooking*

*pants.*

I pocket my phone and direct my attention back at the plans in front of me. Thankfully we were able to get the basic structures of the homes we've been working on completed before the cold weather rolled in. Now into the thick of things, we're making sure plumbing and wiring are carefully installed. It's tedious work, but luckily we have a system, and once those are completed, we can start hammering away on floors, walls, moldings, and all the fun aesthetic stuff homeowners like to fawn over.

A strong arm claps me on the back, and I turn to see Racer and Smalls walk up behind me. "Drywall is up on the second floor." Racer runs his hand through his hair, spiking up the mussed-up strands.

"Patched and primed?" I ask.

"Patched. Not primed yet. We ran out of primer."

"Mark didn't order more?"

Racer shakes his head and turns to Smalls. "You don't have any extra from the Waverly house, do you?"

Smalls removes a cloth from the back of his pocket and wipes down his face. "No, we used every last drop."

Grunting to myself, I shoot a text to Mark to get his ass on the primer. How the hell does a construction company run out of primer? I like having more responsibilities with my job, and I'm not going to lie, I like the paycheck, but it does mean I have to deal with idiots, Mark being one of them. I swear, being a manager of sorts is more handholding than anything. It's like I'm the parent of a bunch of grown-ass boys who should know how to do their jobs.

Once I finish texting Mark, I say, "We should have some soon. We better actually, or I might have to tie Mark on the banister by his nuts." I toss the pencil I've been scribbling with all day on the table in front of me and stretch my neck from side to side.

"How the fuck do we run out of primer?"

Smalls and Racer exchange looks.

"He's not in a good mood," Smalls says, ignoring my question.

"He was in a good mood until he found out about the primer. You have to admit, if this happened two days ago, he would be tossing cinder blocks at innocent workers."

"Cinder block-tosser for sure," Smalls confirms with a nod of his head.

Irritated with their little conversation, I say, "What the hell are you two talking about?"

"Oh, come on, when was the last time we had a Little Debbie date? I haven't suckled on her sugary teet in so damn long because you've been in a bitchy mood." Racer pokes my shoulder.

"Yeah, you've been a real bitch," Smalls tacks on.

Staring between my two friends, I cross my arms over my chest. "I'm the bitch? When you two are crying over not sitting around like a couple of gossiping hens after work and partaking in lard-filled treats?"

They sit there for a second and think over my words. Racer looks up at me and with a straight face says, "They're not all lard-filled. Cosmic Brownies, Nutty Bars, PB Crunch Bars, and Fig Bars are lard free and just as tasty." Racer hops off the table and presses his hand against my arm. "Seriously, dude, do you need to talk to us? Vent a little? What can we do to help?"

Smalls grabs my other shoulder and adds, "What can we do to bring back our Little Debbie dates?"

Christ. I run my hand over my face and step back from the two large men closing in on my space. "I've just been . . ." What have I been? Stressed? Not really. Upset? Not so much. Irritated? Maybe a little. "I've been irritated with things."

"What things?" Racer presses. "Your mom?"

"What? No. Why would you ask about her?"

Racer shrugs timidly. "She's one of your hot-button issues. Didn't know if she was the cause."

"No." I shake my head. "I can't remember the last time I talked to her. This has nothing to do with my mom." My phone buzzes in my pocket and I reach for it, hoping it's Mark telling me when he will have primer back on the job site.

"Then who is this about?"

I open the text message and my irritation grows.

***Emma: Soooo . . . are you opposed to having Logan over for dinner as well? We have some studying to do and I kind of invited him. I hope you're not mad.***

Fucking Logan. That kid. I inwardly roll my eyes. After the rocky days I've had with Emma, I was hoping to have this night with her to repair our friendship. I still feel on edge around her, and a night of joking around, making a meal together, could have helped bandage some of the awkwardness between us. But now . . .

Logan.

Jesus.

"Uh, I'm going to guess your bitchy pants is due to . . ." Racer leans over and looks at my phone, "Emma. Am I right?"

"Who's Emma?" Smalls leans over as well, trying to catch a glimpse of my phone. I swear they're like two nosey little sisters I can't shed.

"Emma is his roommate; I told you about her. The hot nurse we have yet to meet." Turning to me, Racer asks, "When are we going to meet her?"

Knowing they're not going to give up this conversation, I capitulate. "I got in it the other night with Emma. We were having a good time, looking at a Playboy—"

"That's hot," Racer says.

"And I don't even know how it came up, but we started talking about Sadie."

In sync, both Racer and Smalls cringe and say, "Damn."

"Yeah, it didn't go over well, I ended up snapping at her and ending the night abruptly. I then proceeded to evade talking to her for a week, hating every second of it, but I was so damn mad at what she said. And being the not so mentally healthy individual I am, I clearly had no idea how to fix the situation once I went silent on her."

"I'm afraid to hear, but what did she say?" Smalls asks.

I look around the house and notice everyone is focused on their work. "She said I wasn't the right man for Sadie, that we weren't meant to end up together. Honestly, I don't think anyone should have an opinion on the matter beside Sadie and me. It pissed me off that she so easily made such a shitty statement."

Racer and Smalls both exchange glances with each other. It almost seems like they're trying to gain the courage to say something, but I stop them before they ruin our friendship.

"I suggest you keep your opinions to yourself." I let out a long breath and grab the back of my neck.

"Fair enough." Racer shifts in place, his hands slipping in his pockets. "Since your attitude has brightened slightly, I'm going to guess you worked things out?"

"Yeah, for the most part. We both apologized. She cried a lot. And then we fell asleep . . ." She fell asleep quickly. I, on the other hand, soaked in the night with her pressed against me. I would be lying if I said I didn't enjoy the feel of a woman in my arms again, but what I really enjoyed was the feeling of not being alone. There is something to be said about human connection. There was nothing sexual about our night together; it was strictly platonic . . . just two friends—consenting adults— engaged in some solid spooning. Nothing wrong with that.

"Why did you trail off like that?" Smalls asks. "Did you fuck her?"

"No. Jesus, man. We just slept. I don't see Emma like that. She's a friend, that's it." Except when she's trying out poses from Playboy, showing off all her best attributes. Shit, I can still see that perfect little ass of hers up in the air.

"All right, so things are good now with you two, right?" Racer asks. "So why is your brow creased from looking at a text from her?"

I sigh. Dinner with Emma and Logan. Seems like torture. "Because, we were supposed to have a dinner thing tonight, and she's bringing her friend I don't like."

"Her friend?" Smalls wiggles his eyebrows. "A fuck buddy?"

I smack his arm. "What the hell is wrong with you? It's not always about sex." Logan better not be her fuck buddy. She is so much better than him. Granted, I don't know him all that well, but he's a tool. "They're just friends."

"She seems to have a lot of 'friends.'" Racer uses air quotes and it takes all the strength in my body not to pummel him to the floor. These idiots are not helping at all. Usually I welcome their company but, for some reason, talking about Emma with them is not sitting well.

I look at my watch. "Time for you dickheads to get back to work." I snag my clipboard from the table and make my way to the stairs. I'm going to check out their drywall job, maybe fuck it up a bit so they have to redo it. That's the kind of mood I'm in.

"You're so sensitive these days," Racer says as he chases after me, Smalls closing in behind him. "If I didn't know any better, I would say you were developing feelings for this chick."

That makes me stop my ascent. Spinning on my heel, I look down at Racer and Smalls who have shit-eating grins on their faces. Christ.

"I don't have feelings for Emma. I'm just protective, I always have been. She's a good girl and deserves the best, especially after having to put up with all the bullshit our group of friends put her through."

"And her friend she's bringing to dinner doesn't meet your standards?"

"No," I answer flatly and make my way up the rest of the stairs.

Who knows? Logan could be the greatest fucking guy on the planet, but I'm not feeling his vibe. There's something there, I just don't know what it is. Call it friend's intuition. Call it *male* intuition.

Once on the second floor, I examine the drywall job. I know I don't have to, their craftsmanship is impeccable, but I feel like paying back the favor and pushing their buttons, like they're pushing mine.

"Shit patching," I mutter and pretend to write something on my clipboard.

"The fuck it is." Smalls walks up to the wall and starts running his hand over it. Racer stands to the side, reading my bullshit.

With his arms crossed over his chest, he says, "So you don't want to be alone with Emma and her friend. Fair enough, invite us over for dinner to be a buffer."

"Oh, I like dinner," Smalls chimes in.

That actually isn't such a bad idea.

"All right, you can come to dinner." They both fist-pump but I hold up my hand. "On a few conditions: you dickheads bring your own booze."

"Easy," Racer remarks.

"And there will be zero tolerance of you hitting on Emma. She's off limits."

"Well, fuck." Racer lets out a long huff of air. "There goes my hot-nurse fantasy. I was looking to fake an injury tonight."

I point my pen at Racer. "Don't even fucking think about it."

When I walk away, I hear Racer and Smalls high-five and then say, "We finally get to see where he lives."

Shit. I'm going to need more folding chairs.

• • •

"Oh, Tucker. I love what you've done with the place," Racer coos in womanly voice, holding a pack of beer to his chest, acting like an idiot.

"Just get the fuck inside." I grab his shirt and yank him inside. Smalls follows behind him. "You two are late."

"Smalls forgot to put deodorant on. We had to stop at Price Chopper so princess could smell like a ship sailing into bay."

Smalls moves past me and says, "It's actually Swagger Red Zone scent." He lifts his arm in my face and asks, "Want to take a sniff?"

Scrambling with his arm, I push him away and say, "Christ, no. Just get in the fucking house."

I shut the door behind us and turn to see Smalls and Racer both taking in the empty space. "Wow, man. Going for the minimalist look?" He turns to me and gives me a thumbs up. "Nailing it."

I push past both of them and turn around so my voice doesn't carry through the empty house. "They're in Emma's room right now doing a bit of studying. Don't be assholes, don't hit on Emma, and for the love of Christ, don't take off your pants at any point in time."

"We're not fucking untrained dogs about to pull out our wild whizzers and piss all over your walls," Racer protests.

"Speak for yourself." Smalls starts to unbuckle his pants. "I haven't had a good piss on a wall in a long time and these plain

Janes are calling my name."

Giving him the death glare, I whack his hands away from unzipping his jeans. "I'm not fucking kidding. Behave yourselves or else I'm putting you on dumpster duty for the next month."

"Settle down." Racer pats my shoulder, a fucking twinkle in his eyes I don't appreciate. "We're going to be on our best behavior. Now, are you going to give us the grand tour?"

Taking a deep breath, I concede, giving them the nickel tour, scratch that, I give them the penny tour. "Living room, dining room, kitchen is through that door, bathroom is right there along with Emma's room; upstairs is my bedroom and the room off to the left is off limits." Growing serious, my voice lower, I say, "Don't ask to go in there. Got it?"

Either from the tone of my voice, or the look in my eyes, they both nod in understanding. We may give each other a hard time whenever we get the chance but when it matters, we understand one another.

Emma's door opens and she filters out, bringing her girly scent with her. "I thought I heard voices." Adorably she waves and holds her hand out to Racer. "Hi, I'm Emma." Racer gives her a quick once-over before stepping forward to take her hand.

"Racer, nice to meet you, darling." From his term of endearment, Racer winks at me. Fucker. He's always been a big flirt.

Emma turns to Smalls and her eyes widen slightly from his intimidating size. "Emma, it's nice to meet you. I'm Aaron, but everyone calls me Smalls."

She takes his hand and then laughs. "Yeah, because that nickname really suits you." Turning to me, she claps her hands and says, "Are we ready to make some goulash?" *Shit, she is cute.*

"Pasta is cooking as we speak. We just need to brown the

meat and dump the sauce in."

"Lovely. Logan is finishing up on a chapter and then he'll be out here. Boys, make yourselves at home." She gestures to the dining room table that I added a few chairs to and then grabs my hand and leads me to the kitchen.

Whispering under her breath, she leans close to me and says, "That Aaron guy is huge. Does he use his fist as a hammer at work?"

"Only on Fridays." I wink and pull out a skillet for the meat.

"Seriously he's—"

"Do you have a bottle opener?" Smalls asks, making a motion with his hand. "The beer isn't a twisty top."

I pull the bottle opener magnet off the fridge and toss it to Smalls. "Beer shouldn't have twisty tops, dude."

"They're easier," he mumbles and walks out of the kitchen.

Face bright red, Emma buries her head in my back and says, "Oh my God, he almost heard me talking about him. How embarrassing."

I chuckle and put the beef in the skillet. "He wouldn't have cared. Probably would have loved to hear how big you think he is."

"Still, ahh, he's huge."

Pulling her from behind me, I put her in front of the stove with a wooden spoon and lean down to her ear. "If you keep talking about how big Smalls is, you're going to give me a complex."

I start toward the basement door when Emma asks, "Hey, where are you going?"

"To do some bench pressing, lift some weights, bulk up so I can keep up."

Laughing, she pulls me back toward the stove. "Oh stop. You know you're a beefcake."

From behind her, I lean over her shoulder and help her brown the beef, loving how unexpectedly easy it feels with her again. It's all Emma, though. I know I'm a stubborn shit. "Beefcake, huh? I'm going to have to put that on my résumé right next to DJ Hot Cock."

"Oh, Jesus," she mutters and shakes her head.

I step away and open the fridge. "Thirsty? I can offer you a beer or make you a drink."

"Water is fine."

I laugh and shake my head. "Water won't do, Emma. Rule number one."

"Man, you're a stickler with these rules."

"You bet your pretty little ass I am." Her face immediately blushes sending a surge of pride to my chest. Odd, never thought causing Emma to so innocently blush would affect me, but I guess I was wrong. "Now what will it be? Beer or should I make you an old-fashioned?"

Turning away from the meat, she considers her options. "Hmm, let's go with the old-fashioned."

"That's my girl. Two old-fashioneds coming up." Knowing I should be a good person even though I don't want to, I ask, "Do you think Logan will want one as well?"

"Want what?" His voice trails into the kitchen, pulling my gaze to the doorway. He's wearing jeans, a Binghamton University T-shirt, and for some unknown reason, just his presence in this moment with Emma annoys me.

Pushing my feelings aside, I say, "I'm making Emma an old-fashioned. Want one? Or a beer?"

"Ah, no drinking for me. Just water. We still have some studying to do, right, sweetheart?"

*Sweetheart.*

Sounds like fucking rusty gear grinding coming from his mouth.

Answering for Emma, even though I know she should *and can* talk for herself, I say, "Emma is done studying for the night. She promised me one night a week free of studying, just relaxing, and that's tonight."

The look on Logan's face doesn't read happy or even pleased. He glances at Emma who is happily smiling and nodding.

"It's rule number one." She shrugs as if it's common sense that Logan should know this and starts pushing the beef around in the skillet again.

"Uh, okay. I guess I'll take a beer then."

I reach into the fridge and gently toss him a bottle of mine, knowing Racer is not keen on sharing with strangers. "Bottle opener is in the dining room with my buds. Dinner will be ready soon." And with that, I dismiss him.

*And what's really weird? He leaves us.*

Rule number three, Emma and I are supposed to cook a meal together once a week. This isn't a threesome.

I finish making our drinks and give Emma hers. She takes a sip and quietly moans to herself as the liquid slips down her throat. Shit, she sounds so sweet.

"So good and a little strong. What are you trying to do, Tucker? Turn this into a drunken orgy?"

"Fuck, no. Way too much dick out there for that."

She takes another sip from her glass and nods her head. "You're right, it would be a bit of a sausage fest. Although, if I use every part of my body, I could make it work. Three holes and two hands. Hell, I could add one more guy to the mix."

I spit out my drink, literally spit it out spraying the counter and the floor in the process. Whiskey drips from my chin as I look at my *innocent*, sweet friend. "What the ever-living fuck, Emma?"

Her laugh echoes through the kitchen. The sound is so pure

to my ears, the crinkle in her eyes so beautiful, and the stretch of her smile, amusing.

"Oh my God, the look on your face." She wipes joyful tears from under her eyes. "That was fantastic."

Uh, so not fucking fantastic.

"Rule number seven, you're not allowed to joke about orgies and all the holes you have." I run my hand over my face with a towel. "Fuck."

Still laughing, she says, "It seems like these rules are starting to become one-sided."

I toss the towel at her, which she expertly catches. "My house, my rules, babe. Don't forget, I'm still your landlord."

"More like slumlord."

I raise a questioning eyebrow at her. "Excuse me?"

Giggling to herself, she stirs the beef some more and then says, "I think we're ready for the sauce."

"I think your rent just went from one dollar to two after that slumlord comment."

I hand her the opened jars of spaghetti sauce so she can pour it in the skillet. "Pretty sure I can handle the increase, which is an absurd one-hundred percent upcharge in rent by the way."

"Never said I was fair."

I walk over to her, wrap my arm around her shoulders from behind, and kiss the top of her head. As she leans into my side, something about it feels so right. Easy. It feels as though we have been this affectionate for years. *Weird.*

"Hurry up with the sauce. I'm going to put in the garlic bread. I'm starving."

# Chapter Eleven

## EMMA

I feel weird.

Not the kind of weird where I ate something wrong and not the kind of weird where I drank too much.

No, I feel a different kind of weird. A nervous, fluttery kind of weird. The kind of weird you get when an attractive man keeps smiling at you, making you laugh, and stealing touches when he can. The kind of weird you get when your friend is starting to make you feel things you know you shouldn't feel.

And I'm not talking about Logan . . .

It's all Tucker. Tucker freaking Jameson and his sexy side smile. Tucker Jameson and his deep, rumbly laugh. Tucker Jameson and his innocent, friendly touches that make me melt on the spot. To him, those touches are free of any kind of commitment, but to me, they feel like so much more. I want to ask him to stop because I'm worried my mind will get confused. I'm worried that I will fall for my best friend's ex-boyfriend, her former everything and that terrifies me.

No wonder every girl our age fawned over the man; he's magnetic. There's no use denying the pull, because all you want to do when around him is cling to his side. And I'm having a hell of a time trying to detach myself.

Plates cleaned, drinks consumed, I've watched how effortlessly he's engaged both his friends and Logan into conversation, never allowing a dull moment. And the whole time, all I could think of was how different he is from the boy I grew up with. He's a man now, a confident man with experience under his belt, an addicting man you want to surround yourself with. It's confusing. He confuses me.

For so long, I've been on the other side of the fence, listening to Sadie and her side of the relationship. It's been so long since I've spent time with Tucker that I've forgotten who *he* truly is. He was never Sadie's shadow per se, but he was so connected to her, that I wonder if I ever met Tucker the individual. My image has been clouded from the past, but after last night and tonight, the clouds are parting and I think I'm meeting Tucker Jameson the man for the first time. An effervescent man with a sexy smirk, ovary-splitting laugh, and killer eyes.

"Isn't that right, Emma?" Funnily enough, around company, Tucker has referred to me as Emma, not babe.

"Ehh, what?"

"Sixth grade, your first kiss was with a guy who worshipped the black Power Ranger."

"Daniel? Yeah, he was a bit obsessed. But despite his obsession, he tongued me up real nice."

The table erupts. Well, apart from Tucker who gives me a pointed look that causes me to laugh. He wanted me to let loose. This is Emma letting loose. She's a little loose with the lips.

"Daniel sounds like a real winner." Logan tips his bottle in my direction and takes a sip. I'm surprised with how much he's been fitting in with the guys, especially since I hadn't thought they would mesh well together. Tucker and his buddies are rugged men's men, whereas Logan runs the line of more sensitive.

"Oh shit, I could use a good tonguing, especially after sitting on this piece of trash seat all night." Racer shifts and whacks Tucker on the arm. "Dude, splurge a bit and get a fucking couch. What is wrong with you?"

Tucker smiles over his glass, looking more at ease than he has in the last couple days. "I have everything I need in my bedroom."

"I would say let's take this up to your bedroom, but that would quickly divert this little gathering into a glorified sword fight, and I'm not drunk enough to start whipping my willy about."

Smalls turns to Racer and asks, "Would you ever be drunk enough?"

Racer takes a moment to think about it and then shakes his head. "No, but for the right price, I would smack someone with my dick."

Tucker shakes his head. "There is something seriously wrong with you."

"Hey, I'll take money anyway I can get."

"Let's play a game," I say, interrupting the little battle of wits between Tucker and Racer.

"Yeah?" Tucker asks. "What did you have in mind?"

I hold up my finger and stand up, feeling a little shaky in my legs. Thank you, alcohol. "One second please." Quickly, I run to my room, grab a deck of cards and my makeup case along with a little mirror. When I come back into the dining room, all four men give me confused looks.

Sitting back in his chair, arms crossed over his expansive chest, Tucker says, "No, we're not playing that stupid game."

I set my stuff on the table and take a seat. "Come on. I haven't played it in so long."

"No." Tucker stands his ground.

I jut out my bottom lip. "Pleeeease. It will be so much fun."

115

"Yeah, for you."

Racer leans forward. "Uh, am I missing something?"

Playfully staring me down, leaning back in his chair, giving off a casual vibe, Tucker asks, "You want to tell them? Or should I?"

"I will because you'll just ruin it."

He gestures to me, giving me the floor. "By all means, introduce the game."

"Don't mind if I do." I sit tall and clear my throat. "The game is called Beauty Parlor." All three men groan but I tamp them down. "There is one dealer, or beautician if you will, the rest of the players are the clients. We divvy out the cards equally and on the count of three, we flip our cards over. Whoever has a card that is lesser value than the beautician, they have to put on some makeup—"

"No way," Logan says.

"Fuck, no." Smalls sits back in his chair as Tucker gives me a knowing smirk as he takes a sip from his bottle.

"I'll play," Racer chimes in, causing all the men to turn their heads in his direction. "What?" He shrugs. "I'm man enough to put on a little rouge and be okay with it."

"Jesus." Tucker stands and says, "Fine, I'll play, but I'm grabbing another drink." Without even asking, he snags my glass as well for a refill.

"Logan, Smalls, are you still going to sit out?" I ask. They both exchange glances and then let out long pent-up breaths. I'm taking that as a yes. Men. They're so easy. "Yay, okay, we'll draw cards, and whoever has the highest card is the beautician for this round. If you play a higher card than the beautician, you don't have to put makeup on, but you do have to drink. If you flip over a lower card, the beautician tells you what makeup to put on. And this is quick, so no dawdling."

"Do we get to look at our cards?" Racer asks, looking really interested in the game.

"No, it's like war. We just flip over the top card in our pile. Now, in the past, we've played the person to your right gets to apply a swipe of makeup on you if you lose, but for your scrotum's sake, we'll keep the rules to applying your own makeup." The men chuckle and agree with me on my rule change.

Tucker joins us again, handing me my drink as he passes by. "Explain everything to them?"

I nod. "I think they're ready." I hold the cards, fanned out. "Draw a card to see who's the beautician. Eep, this is so exciting."

Tucker picks his card and deadpans, "Yeah, real exciting."

I ignore him and say flip. We all turn our cards over and look around. Immediately it's obvious who the beautician is.

"Yay!" I clap my hands together as all four men groan. "Oh, and for the record, aces count as ones."

Quickly, I shuffle the cards and then divvy them out equally. I don't think I've been this excited in a while. Not only do I get to watch four grown men put on makeup while drinking, but I get to watch *Tucker* put on makeup, the ruggedly handsome man who is nothing but all male. I don't know if this night can get any better.

● ● ●

"Oh, for fuck's sake." Tucker puts his drink on the table and huffs. Looking brilliantly beautiful in a full face of makeup, blue eyeshadow, foundation, and blush, he looks up at me and says, "What will it be this time?"

I try to hold in my giggle but it's almost impossible with how "pretty" Tucker looks. You know how people always say makeup enhances your features? Not on Tucker. He is the ugliest lady I've ever seen. Gathering myself, I point to the blush. "I think you're looking a little pale. You need more."

"Can I get some of the bronzer this time?" Racer hogs the mirror and turns his face from side to side. "I think I need to enhance my cheekbones."

"You definitely need some," Logan agrees. "Make sure to get the apple of your cheek."

"I know I drew a higher card, but I'm feeling a little naked without something on my lips. Maybe I can put on some of that peach gloss Tucker has on?"

"I think apple would look nicer with your complexion," Logan says.

Racer nods. "I'm going to have to go with Logan on this one. The apple for sure."

Tucker stands from his chair, causing it to crash to the floor. "And we're done for the night. You have five minutes to leave this house before I start smashing you on the dick hole with an empty beer bottle."

"My, my, my, no need to get testy just because you're not as pretty as the rest of us." Racer stands and finishes his drink. "Not everyone can pull off a blue eyeshadow, Tuck-man. But you gave it a go, you should be proud of yourself for that."

Grinding his teeth together, he replies, "Get out . . . now."

Glancing at Smalls, Racer says, "I think we should leave."

"I'm right behind you," Logan calls out as he takes off toward my bedroom for his backpack.

Giggling to myself, I start cleaning off the table, packing up all my makeup, making sure to keep the brushes out so I can clean them.

"Thanks for a great night, Emma. I would thank your roomy but he seems to have started pacing the dining room. He looks like a loose cannon." Smalls eyes Tucker who does seem like he's about to lose his shit in seconds.

"Anytime, boys." I wink. "And Racer, you keep working hard on the eyeliner, you'll get it."

Jokingly he crosses his fingers and says, "One day." Gosh, he's cute and very charming. I bet he's someone the girls easily fall for.

We say our goodbyes, and Logan gives me a hug and tells me he will see me tomorrow. Once I shut the door, Tucker walks up behind me and locks up, his breath tickling the hair on the back of my neck. There is no personal space with this man, not that I mind it all that much.

When I turn around and come face to face with him, a snort pops out of me. I cover my mouth and nose quickly, but it's too late, the damage is done. He's even angrier, which just makes me laugh more.

Between giggles, I say, "You're just so pretty."

Slowly, Tucker pins me up against the door, his face coming within inches of mine.

Errr . . .

For a few seconds, he doesn't say anything; he just takes me in, his eyes wandering back and forth between mine, his breath steady, and his body like a wall of armor, holding me in place. "You know, if I wasn't so damn happy to see you smiling, laughing, and having one hell of a time, I would be fucking pissed at you right now for turning that little gathering into a beauty session. But fuck, seeing you relaxed where you're not putting the needs of everyone else above your own, it warms my cold soul." He leans in and kisses me on the forehead. "I fucking like it, babe."

Gulping, I hold my breath, unsure of what to say and definitely how to react.

Before I can reply, he lifts off the door and grabs my hand. "Come on, show me how to get this shit off. We can clean up in the morning."

We head toward the bathroom, my hand feeling miniature in his strong palm, and my stride having to make up for his larger one.

"I don't know how you can wear this shit. It feels like I have mud on my face."

I turn him and pat the counter for him to sit on. But before he sits, he takes off his shirt and tosses it on the floor. "I don't want any of that stuff getting on my clothes."

I swallow . . . hard.

I've seen Tucker with his shirt off since I've moved in, but for some reason, with the recent close proximity we've shared, I feel my body start to heat up. *I was spooned by that chest . . .*

Don't look down. Don't scan his body, and for the love of God, don't reach out and feel each intricate, well-defined ab.

LEAVE HIS BODY ALONE.

I got this. Taking a deep breath, I reach into the medicine cabinet and pull out my makeup wipes. "Here. Take one of these and start wiping."

Together, we wipe our makeup off. And for the first time in an hour, Tucker smiles at me. Playfully, he nudges my side with his foot.

"Look at us, a bunch of ladies taking our makeup off for the night."

That garners a snort out of me, which makes him laugh as well. God, his laugh. It's so rich and velvety that it hits me straight in my core. Hell, that sound could make a feral cat moan out loud.

"We should do this every night together," I joke.

"Or not. Honestly, you shouldn't be wearing makeup anyway. You're pretty without." Cue the rapid beating of my heart. "You really didn't wear a lot of makeup in high school. I liked that about you."

"My mom wasn't too keen on me wearing makeup. Still isn't."

"I agree with your mom." Taking another wipe from the package, Tucker pulls me between his legs and starts swabbing my face clean. He's gentle with each stroke, caressing my cheek with his other hand, giving me one of the most sensual experiences of my life. It's weirdly intimate, a moment I almost feel like we shouldn't be sharing, but a moment I wouldn't trade for anything. *How did we get so comfortable with each other? We were never like this. Never tactile with each other. He was always with . . .*

"Tonight was fun." I close my eyes as he holds my face and wipes off my eyeshadow. "Besides the whole makeup thing."

"Ah, you liked it. Stop trying to be all manly around me."

"I don't have to *try* to be manly, babe." I open my eyes in time to see him wink at me. *Shit.*

Change of subject. "I like Racer and Smalls. Did you meet them on the job?"

"Yeah. We've been working together for a few years now. Over the last two years, they've really been there for me. I would be lost without them."

Tucker tosses the wipe to the side and hops off the counter as I stand still in the small, flamingo-covered bathroom.

*They've really been there for me . . .*

His comment brings back a truckload of guilt I've carried since I *chose a side.* I don't think it was wrong that I looked out for Sadie. She'd been my best friend for over ten years. *I* had seen Tucker as responsible for her pain and heartache. But there are always two sides to every story. Knowing what he had done to embrace Sadie's pregnancy, and a house in this area couldn't be cheap, I wonder if I should have asked someone to reach out to Tucker. He wasn't *guilty* as such. Now, with the blessing of hindsight, I wish I hadn't so easily overlooked how lost Tucker would have been without the woman in his life who had clearly been his everything. *He* pursued her time after time, fight after fight, because he loved her. And that wasn't a crime. But I didn't have that perspective back then. No one did, really. But, considering my cool lack of concern for him and his emotional state, I feel sick.

"Emma, you okay?" He stands behind me, his stature taking up the small space. Every last nerve ending in my body is aware of his presence.

I turn toward him so I'm no longer looking in the mirror and say, "I'm sorry."

His lip quirks to the side in confusion. "Sorry for what? The makeup?"

"No." I shake my head and press my hands against his chest lovingly, hoping I can convey how sorry I am. "I'm sorry for not being there for you, for choosing sides."

Understanding crosses his features. "It's no big deal."

"It is to me." I reach up, and grip his face so he has no other option but to look at me. "I shouldn't have chosen sides—"

Sternly he says, "Rule number six, Emma."

"I know." I let go of him and turn around, my hands braced on the counter, my mind going a mile a minute. Can't he just let me get this off my chest. "But—"

"Rule number six," he grits out, frustrating me more than anything.

Irritated now, I fling the bathroom door open and mutter under my breath about his stupid rules. I make my way into my room and like the "adult" that I am, I slam the door shut.

"Impossible man," I say under my breath. "Can't even let me freaking apologize." I open my dresser drawer and start changing into my pajamas. My pants are the first to go, replaced by a white pair of flannel pants decorated in owls. Removing my shirt, I quickly toss my bra in the hamper and put on one of the camisoles I like to wear under my matching pajama shirts. Digging back in my drawers, I search for the matching top when my door opens.

Startled, I stand tall. Tucker walks in, his hand in his hair. He goes to open his mouth when his eyes travel down my body, stopping a few seconds longer at my chest. His gaze sharpens on me, on my outfit, and the way my camisole rides high and tight on my stomach, showing a few inches of skin. When his eyes meet mine, they're not full of anger, or irritation, or frustration.

No, they're full of heat.

Everything in me freezes and when he takes a step forward, my body ignites, and sweat breaks out all around me. What is he doing?

Nervous and unsure what to do, I pull the first thing I feel out of my drawer and try to cover my hardened nipples that are poking through my thin camisole. His eyes widen for a second before a grin spreads across his face. I look down to see I'm holding my purple lace bra over my chest.

"Goodness." I shake the bra to the side and stand tall. "You're supposed to knock before barging in here."

"Was that on the rule list?" His voice is sultry as he takes another step forward. Yes, *sultry.*

*What the hell is going on here?*

One second he's pissed that I'm breaking his precious rule number six and the next he's closing in on me like a lion to its prey.

"No." I take a step back. "It falls under being a decent adult. Remember that conversation we had? Oh, and do you know what else falls under being a decent adult?" I cross my arms over my chest. Of course, that draws Tucker's attention back to that area. Good grief, his eyes feel like laser beams heating me up from my toes to my ponytail.

Another step, so now he's only a foot away. "What else falls under being a decent adult?"

Not letting his eyes, smirk, or handsome personal-bubble-breaking self affect me, I poke him in the chest, hard. "Allowing someone to apologize even if you don't want to hear it. I get it, no talking about Sadie, noted. But at least let me apologize for being a shitty friend when you needed someone by your side the most."

"Emma—"

"No. You listen here, mister." I try to stand taller but I'm no match for his towering height. "I'm saying I'm sorry and you will accept that apology or I'll . . ."

Errr . . .

What will I do? Kick him in the crotch? Give him a noogie? Purple Nurple to the rescue?

Although they're all viable options I'm not afraid to do, I don't think they'll get the point across.

Leaving no space between us now, he presses his hands on my hips and with his lowered voice, he asks, "Or you'll what?" His breath mixes with mine, the smell of my makeup wipes fills the space between us, and the firm grip he has on my hips is weakening me second by second.

Why is he so touchy? And why the hell do I like it so much?

AND why do I want him to touch me in other places?

*Shit, this is your friend, your best friend's ex. Focus!*

"Or I'll . . ." I look around and finally say, "Move out. Yeah, I'll move out, leaving you without a tenant. Say goodbye to two dollars a month." Crap, I wish I paid him normal rent right about now.

He bites his bottom lip, holding back a smile, and presses me into his body. Okay, I'm not an expert on friendship or anything, but this hold right here, with the way he's looking down at me, like he's about to gobble me up, I don't think this is how friends act. Although, I might be old school. Who knows with my generation? We're always switching up everything. Who knew you could eat chili from a Fritos bag by just dumping it in there? Millennials knew, that's who.

But seriously, why does he look like he's about to kiss me?

Ah, is he going to kiss me?

He can't kiss me, that has to be against the rules, right? It's against girl code at least, that's for damn sure.

"You'd move out if I don't let you apologize?" he whispers in what I can only say is a gravelly voice. I nod, my throat starting to clamp shut. "Well, I can't be losing out on rent." With another smirk, he nods at me. "Go ahead, babe, apologize."

Is this some sort of trick? I don't understand. Is something going to pop out of me if I apologize? Is this a hidden camera show? Punk'd for regular people?

Instead of apologizing, I really want to ask him why he's holding me tightly, and why he's casually licking his lips like I'm his second supper, and why for the love of all pheromones does he smell so freaking good?

"Uh," I clear my throat and try to get my brain to formulate some kind of coherent sentence. "Thank you for this opportunity." Thank you? *You're thanking him right now*? No, don't thank him, you idiot, he didn't just present you with a royal scepter and make you queen of the night. He said you could apologize. Gathering my wits, well, what's left of them, I try to recall how to form words. "On this day, this wintery day . . ." *Why am I making this a speech?*

Wait, is he . . . oh my God, he's making small circles with his thumbs on my skin and wait a second . . . Yup, the results are in, my panties are getting wet. *Christ!* This is not happening. I am *not* becoming aroused by Tucker. No. Way. Not me. Not Emma Marks. Not turned on . . . *oh shit*, that feels so good. It's been way too long . . .

"On this wintery day . . ." he presses, as his hands move up my sides. I swear to the cheese on my pizza last night, if he touches my boobs, there will be no stopping the feral howls that escape my lips.

*Just finish your damn apology and get out of this little touch-and-feel play-by-play you're having with Tucker Jameson.*

"On this wintery day," I continue, "I would like to apologize for not being a good friend when you needed me the most." There, I said it, in one quick swoop, with no inflection in my voice whatsoever, but I said it, and that's all that matters.

"You're sorry, huh?"

I gulp and nod.

"How sorry?"

Oh God, is this one of those questions where a guy asks you a question like, "How horny are you?" And they say, "Horny enough to eat my dick" while pelvic thrusting their jean-clad hammers in your face? Would Tucker ask me to eat his dick? Would I want to eat his dick? Why is relish popping up in my head from the thought of eating Tucker's dick? Relish and celery salt, no, relish, celery salt, mustard and onions. *Mmmm.*

"Relish," I mutter.

His brow pinches together. "What?"

Errr . . . how would he respond if I said relish dick? I'm going to lean on the side of thinking I'm crazy.

"Umm, relish in the moment," I cover with a fist-pump of glory into the air. "I don't apologize often." Sheesh, that was close.

"Uh, okay." Leaning forward again, he asks, "You didn't answer my question, how sorry are you?"

Big moment right here.

Do I say sorry enough to relish your cock and munch down? *Nom. Nom.* Sorry enough to twist your nips if you like that sort of thing? Sorry enough to try my best at an oil painting of him stroking his erection while a parrot sits on his shoulder?

Probably not.

His thumbs continue to stroke my sides, making everything in my brain fuzzy . . . if you haven't noticed already. I look him in the eyes, his gorgeous, smoldering eyes and say, "Very sorry."

"Very sorry?" Okay, here it comes, the lewd question I've been waiting for. The suck-my-cock apology request. I cringe inwardly, waiting as he leans over to my ear, his lips mere millimeters away as he says. "Okay. Then I accept your apology on one condition . . ." Get the ChapStick ready, we're turning into a phallic sucker tonight. "You have to do the dishes for the next week."

Of course he would want his balls massaged too . . . wait. *Dishes?*

"You want me to do the dishes?"

He chuckles and kisses me on the forehead. "Nah, I'm just kidding." He separates himself from me so casually that I feel like falling over from the sudden lack of support. How can he just switch moods like that? As if he wasn't just inches from touching my breasts. "I wouldn't make you do the dishes for a week. Two tops." He winks and heads toward my door. When he turns around, he nods at my body and says, "By the way, don't wear that shirt around the house, please. Your tits look far too tempting. Have a good night, babe."

*My tits look far too tempting? What the what?*

"Wait," I call out, my mind all sorts of confused. "Are we,

uh, are we okay?"

He grips my doorframe and genuinely smiles at me. "Yeah, babe. We're okay. Your apology wasn't necessary, but I appreciate it. That time of our lives is over. I want to move on. I want to focus on the present with you, on our friendship and the time we have before you graduate." He pauses and then says, so freaking thoughtfully, "Asking you to move in was one of the best decisions I've ever made. Having you in my life again means the world to me." With one last look, he bids me good night and quietly shuts my door.

*Friendship. Our friendship.* How can he act so casual when he's burning up a wave of desire inside of me?

I fling myself on my bed, my hands on my heart, feeling the rapid beat of it as I stare up at the ceiling. Why is he the nicest guy ever? And why would I think he would ask me to suck his cock? He's not that kind of douchey. Maybe subconsciously I wanted to suck his dick . . .

No, that can't be it, can it? I'm not a huge dick to the mouth kind of girl.

Oh God, am I crushing on my roommate?

Images flash through my mind.

Tucker shirtless.

Tucker smiling over his morning coffee.

Tucker's deodorant that I've sniffed a few times . . . make that every morning.

Shit, I'm crushing on my roommate.

*I'm crushing on Tucker Jameson.*

This is bad. This is really bad.

# Chapter Twelve

I don't think I've been this enthusiastic in a really long time. And over a piece of furniture. No, scratch that, I'm not necessarily excited about the piece of furniture, more excited about the look on Emma's face when she sees said piece of furniture.

When I heard our local furniture store was having a sale, I went down and took a look at what they had in stock. Lucky for me, I found a dark grey couch that would fit perfectly in my empty living room. The cost was reasonable, the delivery was free, well, besides the beer I owe Racer for helping me bring it into the house, but now, standing in my living room, looking at the piece of furniture, I can't help but wonder if Emma will approve.

I've never picked out a piece of furniture from a store before. I have no decorating style whatsoever, so I picked a color I liked and made sure it was comfortable. The comfortable part was the most important factor. I hate stiff sofas. They're meant to be good enough to sleep on.

Nervously, I pace the living room, occasionally looking out the window every few minutes. It's past eight. She should be home by now. She's never home this late. What the hell is she doing?

I pick up my phone to see if I missed any messages from her but there is nothing. I'm about to call when I see a car pull onto our street and when the headlights flash down the driveway, my stomach flips and my nerves kick into overdrive.

She's home.

*Home.*

Up until now, I haven't considered this place my *home*. How is it that with Emma living here, it actually feels like home to me?

Maybe because she brings a certain light to the dreary dungeon I've created between these walls.

I go to the side door, open it, and stick my head out to greet her. When she sees me, her gorgeous smile lights up her face. That smile, that thick, lush hair, those kind eyes.

*Emma.*

The girl I grew up with, the girl who I'm now sharing a house with, temporarily at least.

"Hey there." She shuts her car door, her nursing books close to her chest and her backpack slung over one shoulder. "Is this a new rule? Must meet roommate at door?"

*Yes, because you came home to me.*

"No." I take her books and backpack from her and step to the side so she can walk inside. "I have something to show you."

Looking a little skeptical, she steps into the kitchen and turns around to face me as she takes off her coat. Underneath, she's wearing her blue nursing scrubs, a pale blue that make her eyes shine. "You have something to show me; should I be scared? It's not a bunch of guys with small dicks for the magazine we talked about, is it?"

I laugh and set her gear on the counter. "No. And if that's something you're expecting me to do for you, find a bunch of mini wieners, you're going to be sadly disappointed. Not my forte, babe."

"Don't know any small dicks?" Her smile practically reaches her ears.

I shake my head. "I know one dick, babe, and it sure as hell isn't small."

Her eyes quickly glance at my crotch, causing a little chuckle to come out of me. Oh Emma, the sweet girl.

"You got some X-ray vision I don't know about?"

"What?" Her eyes snap up. "No, I wasn't . . . there was a fly . . . I . . ." She sighs and then puts her hand on her hip. "I'm going to level with you." Taking a deep breath, she continues, "You can't just say something about having a not-so-small peenie weenie and think I'm not going to glance down."

"Peenie weenie? I sure as fuck didn't say that? What happened to medical terms?"

She waves her hand in front of her face. "I use those all day, so it's nice to not have to be technical. Why? Do you want to talk meatus again?"

"Christ, no." I grab her shoulders and spin her around. Leaning forward, my lips close to her ear, I ask, "Can I trust you to keep your eyes closed, or am I going to have to blindfold you myself?"

Shit, she smells so good. After a long-ass day of school and then working at the hospital, she can still smell like vanilla and honey; how is that possible?

"Blindfold? Tucker, is there some kind of kinky orgy in the other room? I'm not sure I'm okay with more than four nipples in a sex romp."

"Jesus." I chuckle and wrap my arms around her shoulders, hugging her from behind. "No orgy, now will you just close your damn eyes so I can show you?"

"Okay," she breathes out, her chest hitching under my hold.

Moving my hands to her shoulders, I lean over to make sure her eyes are closed and carefully guide her through the house to the living room.

"You're making me nervous. There aren't going to be clowns popping out at me, are there?"

"No clowns, babe. Now stand here." I move around her so I can see her reaction and hold my breath. "Okay, open your eyes."

Her beautiful eyes open, blink a few times, and then fixate on the couch in front of her. For a brief second, I think she's not going to care, but that's quickly washed away when she brings her hands to her mouth in surprise and then jumps up and down.

"You got a couch!"

I nod, pride filling every inch of my body. "I got a couch."

"Oh my God." Quickly she runs over to me and hugs me from the side. "Tucker, you got a couch and it's so stylish." Looking up at me, she asks, "Can I sit on it?"

"Yeah." I chuckle. "That's kind of what it's for."

She claps and hops over into position. Making a big deal of it, she turns toward me, puts her arms out and falls backward into the couch that sucks her into the cushions. She moans and sighs. Damn, I kind of want to hear her make that noise again.

Clearing my throat, I ask, "What do you think?"

Her eyes are closed and her head is tilted back on the cushion. Without looking at me, she pats the couch, calling me to come sit next to her. "Bask in the gloriousness with me, Tucker."

I don't sit on the couch as dramatically as she did, but when I sit down, my shoulder bumps with hers, our proximity on top of each other despite the size of the couch.

"It's so nice." She turns her head toward me. "Are you happy?"

"I am. It's a nice couch. I feel so grown-up." I look around the empty room and smile. "It might be empty in here, but hey, we have a place to sit that's not a counter, folding chair, or bed."

"I can't wait to study on this bad boy. Am I going to have to call dibs? Sign out the couch for the night? Take turns?"

"It's all yours, babe, whenever you want to use it."

Snuggling in close, Emma rests her head on my shoulder. "Oh, Tucker, you spoil me. You're the best landlord ever."

"I try."

Together, we sit, stare at the ceiling, relax. Emma is snuggled into my side, enjoying the couch for what seems like an hour when in fact it's only a few minutes. I feel so comfortable around her, safe, like nothing real can affect us when we're in our little bubble together.

And the weird thing is, I've been looking forward to this moment all day, knowing my couch would be ready for pickup. Fuck, I couldn't wait to get it home and surprise Emma, to see the look of joy on her face. And hell, she did *not* disappoint. Her reaction was just what I was looking for, appreciation, excitement, and a warm smile.

I've also realized something important. I look forward to that smile, to the lightness in her eyes, to her gentle touches. I look forward to her quirky comments, the sound of her heavy books hitting the counter, and to sharing a morning coffee with her when her hair is in disarray and her matching PJs are askew.

And what's really weird is that on a daily basis I want to please her. I want to win her laughter. I *want* to cook with her, watch TV with her, relax with her. I want to engage her, keep her connected to me . . . to my house. *My home.* But the icing on top of this fucked-up friendship is that I can't stop touching her.

Even worse? Every fucking day, I think about what she would look like beneath me, naked, those steel-blue eyes staring at me, her innocence and yearning seeking me. *Me.* The last time I felt anything remotely close to that was when I was with Sadie, which scares the fuck out of me, but also intrigues me.

Hell, she's my roommate, not a potential girlfriend. She's my friend. *Get a fucking grip on your life, Jameson.*

"Hey, I have an idea," Emma says, sitting up, pulling me out of my reverie. She places her hand on my thigh and squeezes tightly. Shit, that feels good. "Let's get in our PJs, grab a deck of cards, and play War. Break in the new couch, what do you say?"

How can I say no when she's practically jumping up and down on the couch in excitement? I'm learning that it's almost impossible to say no to this girl.

"Sounds like a plan."

"Yay." She leans over and wraps me up into a hug before quickly pulling away and skipping off to her room while calling out, "We shall reconvene in five minutes. Get your butt ready, Jameson. Your ass is mine."

If only she knew what I was just thinking about regarding her ass.

• • •

"If I have to tell you to stop looking at your card before you flip it one more time this game is over, got it?"

"Who made you the War police?" Emma grumbles.

"It's not fair," I counter. "We should both see the cards for the first time together."

"Are you going to cry about it a little bit more? I don't think you've shed enough tears on your new couch."

Sassy little mouth.

"You know, I have a perfectly good book waiting on my nightstand for me; I don't mind tossing my cards in the air and leaving you to play by yourself."

Emma sits back. Her legs are crossed on the couch, and she eyes me up and down. "Oh, I get what's happening here."

"What's happening?"

"Mm-hmm, act all innocent in your thin plaid pants and stupid tight-fitting shirt. I'm onto you, Jameson."

"Yeah? What are you onto?"

She waves her finger up and down my body. "You're causing a scene."

"I'm not causing a scene, I just want the card flipping to be fair."

"Oh, you're causing a scene. Classic Tucker Jameson game technique; cause a scene and storm off so no definitive winner can be named."

"What? Are you drunk?"

Leaning forward over the playing area, she points her finger at me and asks, "Are *you* drunk? Is that part of your scene technique? What's going to happen next, you shuck your pants, pee in the corner, and then start running around the house, your hands cupping your dong while you do sumo squats up the stairs?"

"I would never pee in the corner." I shake my head. "If I were to shuck my pants and pee somewhere, it would be in your dresser drawers, just to fuck with you."

"You wouldn't," she playfully seethes.

"Oh, I fucking would. I would pee so hard in your drawers."

"You can't make yourself pee hard, only girls can."

"Untrue." I'm trying very hard not to laugh from this ridiculous conversation. "I just push harder, therefore I pee harder."

"Yeah, more like dribble like a leaky faucet."

"I don't think it's wise for you to question my stream. You have some late nights in the library, you don't want to come home to wet sheets one night, now do you?"

"Are you trying to tell me you want to pee in my bed?" She sets her cards down now and crosses her arms over her purple-pajama-clad chest.

"It's not like it wouldn't already be used to being peed on."

Sitting up on her knees now, looking ready to pounce, she asks, "Are you, Tucker Jameson, calling me a bed-wetter?"

I set my cards down as well, preparing myself for whatever wryly move she's going to make. "I might be; what are you going to do about it?"

Just when I think she's about to answer, she hops off the couch and runs up the stairs to my bedroom. What the fuck? Is she going to pee on my bed to prove a point? And is she going to pee hard? Oh, Jesus.

Stumbling for a second, I gain my balance and charge up the stairs. I turn the corner to my bedroom when—

"Grrrrrrawwwwwwllll!" Emma pops out from a closet with her claws out and a snarly look on her face. Not expecting her to go all psycho bobcat on me, I jump about a foot in the air and let out a less than manly version of a yip, causing Emma to buckle over in laughter. "Oh my God, the look on your face." She tries to impersonate me, her face contorting, making an enormous amount of double chins, hands shaking in the air, and a girly scream coming out of her mouth. When she's done, she laughs some more.

Not amused, I say, "I did not look like that."

"Oh my God, you so did."

Her laughter carries through the small space of my room, the sound a melodic harmony in my ears. And before I can stop myself, I charge toward her, grab her by the waist, and toss her on my bed where I quickly climb on top of her and pin her to the mattress with her hands above her head.

Her laughter fades. Her face grows serious, and I can see the questions running through her eyes. I'm welcomed by one of the most beautiful sights I've ever seen: Emma under me, her chestnut hair fanned out along the comforter, her brilliant eyes searching mine, and her pajama shirt is open at the top, a peek of the swell of her breasts as well.

Her breath starts to pick up as she waits for my next move, a move I'm entirely unsure of as well. The only thing I know right now is how good she feels in my arms, how mesmerizing she smells, a combo of honey and vanilla, and the way her legs are slowly rubbing together, as if she's a cat purring in need.

The air around us becomes thick as I lean my head closer to hers, the tension in the room growing with each passing breath. Bodies pressed together, thoughts of every move I could make with Emma beneath me passes through my mind as I try to gain control of my raging emotions. I fucking want this woman. I want her for her innocence, for her purity, for her friendship, for her kind and caring hands. I want her for human contact, for healing, for the power to forget. *The power to heal?*

I want her for all the wrong reasons, and yet, I can't help but think how right she feels.

When I lean closer, I start to run the tip of my nose up the column of her neck, taking in her scent, and loving the way I can feel her swallow hard. With nerves? Still, almost lifeless, Emma lies beneath me, not making a sound or move. Her breathing is slow yet erratic, waiting, just waiting to see what I'll do next.

When my nose reaches her jaw, I move it toward her ear where my lips barely caress her lobe before I pull away. Her mouth is open, her skin starting to coat in a sheen of sweat. She's so fucking edible, I want to take a bite. I want to nip up and down her body, taste her, see what it's like to not just be friends with this woman, but to cross the line, to find out what it's like to be inside her.

I move my nose to the other side of her face when her breath catches in her throat and she says, her voice shaking with each word, "Uh, if you find that my lymph nodes are swollen in your exploration, please let me know." *For some reason, her request doesn't surprise me all too much.*

Stopping my pursuit, I lift up just enough to see her eyes. "You want me to check your lymph nodes?"

She swallows hard. "Only if you're into that kind of thing. I mean, not that you would really feel them since they're only about half an inch across and you're not a trained professional, but if it seems to be lumpy around there, just give me the old heads-up."

"Uh, do you feel like they're swollen?" She's so fucking nervous, she's shaking like a leaf beneath me, which explains the whole rambling conversation about the lymph nodes. Maybe I've read her wrong this entire time. The glances, the touches, the snuggling, maybe they were all just her way of being friendly.

"Not necessarily, but it's always good to be aware of symptoms before they occur. Staying on top of things is how we stay healthy. You know, catch it before it happens." She sighs and bites on her bottom lip.

Fuck, that's sexy.

"Yeah, I get that." This moment quickly turned awkward.

Looking unsure, she pauses for a second and then asks, "Do you want me to check your lymph nodes?"

Not really, but at this moment, we need a smooth transition from the intimate moment we were just experiencing, to the awkward one we're experiencing now. So, I shrug my shoulders and say, "Why not?"

Reluctantly, I stand from her body and sit down on my bed where I lean my back against the headboard and pat my lap. She eyes me, unsure if she should take the invitation or not.

"I don't bite, babe. If you're going to check out my lymph nodes then you should get a front-row seat, don't you think?"

Christ. I'm flirting with her . . . about checking my lymph nodes. Has it really been that long since I've flirted? And should I really be flirting with Emma? Touching her, imagining her lips on mine, wondering what that damn seductive mouth of hers tastes like? She didn't come to live with me so she can fuck one of her childhood friends; she came here so she had a place to live while she finished up her last year in college. And yet, I want to make it the best semester of her life and if that means I spend my nights deep inside her, making her call my name while that goddamn sweet face looks up at me, then so be it.

Emma shifts in front of me, still unsure until she finally looks in my eyes and says, "Well, if it's for examination purposes, I don't see the harm in it." Carefully she climbs onto my lap, her legs parting and falling on either side of my thighs. She scoots up and settles directly on top of my dick.

Fuck me, control it, dude. *Do not poke her with your dick.* Yeah, it's been so damn long, but stay down and don't get excited.

"Okay, I'm going to touch your neck if that's okay?"

"Sure, nurse. Feel me up." I wink at her, unable to control myself.

Her fingers dance along my skin while she looks me in the eyes. "How come you've never grown a full beard? Like mountain-man style?"

"Not sure I could pull it off, plus those things are high-maintenance. Pretty sure you have to condition it. I barely want to take a five-minute shower these days, let alone stand under the water and let the conditioner in my beard soak in. No fucking thank you."

"Might be worth it, you know."

"Why do you say that?"

She continues to stroke my neck, and I'm not sure if she's touching me to just touch me or if she's actually feeling for swollen nodes. Either way, her soft hands feel so fucking incredible. "Well, if you were interested in dating someone ever again," she pauses and holds up her hand. "Don't worry, I'm not going to break rule number six, but if you were into dating someone again, the dating pool is a tough one now."

"Is that why you don't have a boyfriend? Tough field out there?" Has Emma ever really had a boyfriend? I can't imagine adorable little Emma not having a boyfriend. She's a fucking catch for any lucky bastard.

She shrugs and drops her hands to my chest where she casually plays with my shirt. "No, just haven't found anyone worthy enough of the position." She sighs and continues, "But for you, if you grow a burly beard, your dating chances would grow exponentially."

"Beards on high demand?" Is she part of some secret society for beards? Is that why she's harping on it so much, or is she still in ramble mode?

"I'm not quite sure, but I do know about this dating website that is for women searching for bearded men. My friend Adalyn joined it a little while back. She didn't mesh well with anyone, but she did mention the hot, bearded guys being on high demand in that dating circuit. There are so many dating services now, it's nice to be able to narrow it down to a few specific people, you know?"

"So that's why I should grow a beard, to narrow down my dating circuit?"

She cutely nods. "The dating world is a scary one, the more help you can get, the better."

"Is that right? You think I need help when it comes to dating? I thought I was, according to your words, the hometown heartbreaker. Doesn't that give me any kind of fodder?"

"In your hometown, not in the real world. You're just a fish in the river."

I raise an eyebrow at her. "Is that so? Just a plain-old fish in the water? Nothing special about me at all? Nothing I can offer anyone?" There is a teasing tone to my voice.

She takes her time, giving me a once-over, her hands still clasped onto my shirt. Although every now and then, I feel her fingers exploring my chest. Fucking hell, that feels so good. I wish she'd take the damn shirt off. We're in a very intimate position, something friends usually don't do, but for some reason, both of us are okay with it. "There is one thing you can offer."

"Just one? All right, lay it on me, babe. What is the one attribute I have to offer the dating world?"

She straightens up and pats my chest, as if to say, *"You're a good boy."*

"You know how to make some killer eggs. It's a great skill to have, especially if you date someone who isn't a morning person like myself. Those eggs are a real eye-opener; they get you going in the morning."

I pause for a second, reading her facial expression, the way she playfully speaks to me. It's so fucking . . . adorable. That's the perfect way to describe Emma, adorable.

"Eggs, that's what I have to offer. Eggs. Not a killer ass, or sexy set of abs, or a dick so huge that it will tickle your stomach while impaling you?"

Her laugh hits me straight in the gut, and then her smile, tag-teaming a wave of awakening in my body I'm not ready for. "Sorry to say, but I know nothing about your Happy Harry Hard-

On, so I can't have an opinion about that. Your ass, eh, it's okay, and your abs, well, those are nice."

"Hold up." I grip her hips tightly in place. "You think my ass is, *eh*?"

Smirking evilly, she says, "I mean, have you been missing leg day at the gym?"

My mouth splits open for a second from her joking insult before I scoop her up and start carrying her down the stairs with her over my shoulder. "What are you doing?"

"This evening is over. You can stare at my inadequate ass as I take you to your room. Maybe you will learn a lesson. Skipping leg day. You've lost your fucking mind, girl."

When I reach her bedroom, I toss her on her bed and watch her laugh as she bounces a few times on the mattress from my toss. Pointing at her, a fake sense of seriousness coming from me, I say, "Now, you sit there and think about what you said. Maybe next time you'll think twice about insulting my ass."

"Don't be a little bitch, Tucker." The elation in her face from the insult is overwhelming. Like a fucking punch to the stomach, it's one of the most beautiful things I've ever seen. *She's one of the most beautiful things I've ever seen.*

Playing along, I say, "And for that, no eggs for you tomorrow morning. Looks like you'll be reunited with your old friend, the Chewy Bar."

"You wouldn't."

"It's already done, babe." I give her a wink and say, "See you in the morning."

When I retreat to my room, I wonder if I should go take a cold shower. A long, cold shower. I'm so fucking turned on. Even when she's sassy and faking impertinence, she's sexy. That can't be legal. I can't help but think about the separation between us and how I desperately wish she'd come back to my room. If anything, just for the physical contact. The night we spooned was one of the best nights I've had in a very long time. Now I crave the gentle touch of her hands, the feel of her body tucked against mine, and fuck if I won't be thinking about it all night long.

• • •

*CRASH*

From a dead sleep, I sit up in my bed and look around, blurry eyed, trying to decipher if what I heard was from a dream or if it was in real life. With my heart beating at a rapid pace, I hold my breath and listen closely for any other semblance of a possible break-in. And then it hits me, if someone is breaking in, Emma is on the first floor. "Shit."

I throw the blankets off, grab my baseball bat from next to my bedside table, and take off down the stairs. When I hit the hardwood floors, I quickly look toward Emma's room. The door is open and from my view, she's not in her bed.

What the fuck?

Next option is the bathroom, but when I see the light is off and the door is wide open, I start to panic. With the bat raised, I flip on the dining room light . . .

"Ahhh!" Emma screams when the light switches on, one of her hands going up to block her eyes. My own pupils curse me out at the moment. "What the hell are you doing?" She's rolling on the floor clutching her foot a look of pain crossing her features.

"What am I doing? What the hell are *you* doing?"

When she is finally able to look at me, her eyes do a quick scan of my body before answering and that's when I realize I'm wearing nothing but my Calvin Klein, hip-hugging briefs.

Looking away, she answers, "I left my phone on the couch.

I woke up wondering what time it was and realized I left it out here. I didn't want to wake you, so I tried to make my way through the house with no lights, thinking it couldn't be that hard given the two pieces of furniture we have. I guess not. I flipped over the folding chair."

"Flipped over? Are you okay?"

She nods, still not looking at me. "Pretty sure I broke my toenail. It's throbbing. I'm sure it will be a pretty shade of gross tomorrow morning."

"Here, let me help you." I put down the bat and reach for her when she spins away on her butt.

"I can handle this. Just go back to bed."

"Emma, you're hurt. I'm going to help you. Now, come here." I bend down and scoop her up into my arms and take her to the bathroom where I set her down on the counter. I bring her foot up to my eye for a better look. "Can you bend your toes?"

When she doesn't answer me, I look past her foot to see what's going on. And . . . that's when I catch her staring at my package. Right there, eyes trained on my dick and balls, no hiding it whatsoever. Christ.

"Emma," I say a little louder. "Can you wiggle your toes?"

"Huh?" Lazily she scans my body slowly, all the way to my eyes where she finally meets me.

I hold back the laughter bubbling inside me. "Toes, can you wiggle them?"

She almost seems drunk when she answers, "I have toes."

Your future nurse, ladies and gentleman.

Be terrified.

"Good, babe, but can you wiggle them?"

"Hmm? Oh yeah." She wiggles but cringes at the same time. "I think they're going to be okay, just sore."

I nod. "Well, you have a little cut on your big toe, so let me clean it up and put a Band-Aid on it." When I reach for my first aid kit under the sink, she clears her throat, almost like she's trying to gain the courage to ask me a question.

"Tucker?"

I stand and hold the first aid box in front of her. "Got it." When I see the bewildered expression on her face, I ask, "What's up?"

"You're, uh, you're wearing tighty-whities."

I take in my apparel. "No, I'm not. I'm wearing briefs, and they're black. Tighty-whities are for grandpas with saggy asses and liver spots."

She scans me again, a pull in her brow, "But, they're bikini cut."

I roll my eyes. "They're not fucking bikini cut, whatever the fuck that is. They're regular briefs." I slip my fingers in the waistline and snap the elastic.

"I thought you wore boxer briefs." She's now nibbling on her finger, still scanning my body.

"I do. I wear both. Underwear models wear these all the time. Hell, David Beckham wears these." No idea what her issue is. They keep everything snug; sometimes it's nice to not have your cock turning into a propeller in your pants.

From the way her eyes are eating me whole, for the first time, I feel exposed around her. And if she keeps it up with those sultry eyes, she's going to be feeling just as exposed as I am. That would be when I rip off her clothing.

"Oh. They're um, they're nice." She turns away and stares at her feet.

Not going to work, sweet Emma. I lift her chin so she's forced to make eye contact. "Nice? That's all? They're just nice? I'm standing here, in front of you, being a sexy male nurse for your toe in a pair of very snug briefs and all you have to say is *they're nice*?"

"Wh-what do you want me to say?" She shivers. "That I like your man thigh? That your abs are unfair to look at because they're so well defined? That those things"—she gestures to the V in my waist—"are like valleys headed straight to your penis? That I can clearly see the definition of your dick, including your meatus, and it's . . . it's . . ." She stumbles. "It's thick." She presses her hand against her forehead as her cheeks redden. "Oh God, you have thick dick." Is that a compliment? It almost sounds like a disease, like elephantitus.

"Uh, thank you?"

"Thick dick. You have a thick dick. Of course, you're Mr. Thick Dick, what else would you be? Skinny Minnie Ween-Ween? No, you're thick dick." Her hands are now in her hair, pulling on the strands, acting on the border of insanity and losing her ever-loving mind. Still muttering, she shakes her head and says, "Thick dick in the tight black bikini bottoms."

"They're not . . ." I huff out my frustration. "They're not fucking bikini bottoms. They're normal briefs."

She shakes her head. "Not for thick dick and milky man thighs." Milky? More like manly man thighs. I do squats. She hops off the counter in her fit of insanity and then starts hopping on one leg. "Shit, my toe." Still hopping, she pushes off my chest with her hand and propels herself out of the bathroom.

"Where are you going? Let me fix your foot."

"Nope, nope, nope. I'm good. Just . . . go upstairs and put pants on. No one wants you walking around with your scrotum dangling between your legs." *It does that every fucking day. What's the difference?*

"Well, it's not going to dangle from my ears like earrings, babe. The scrotum is kind of a set thing."

She makes it to her bedroom and slams her door shut. Well . . . fuck. She was the one who woke me up, the one who disturbed my slumber. She's not going to hobble away like that. No way.

Not caring what she's doing on the other side of the door, I fling it open and see her sitting on her bed, rocking back and forth on her hands. "Emma—"

"Tucker, I'm going to stop you right there. It's been a pretty humiliating night for me, with the fall and the staring and the thick-dick mumbling. I would like to just move on from this moment and forget it all happened. I don't want to hash it out with you." She glances up at me and says, "Rule number eight, no mentioning thick dick . . . ever."

"But—"

"Hey, rule number six." She lifts an eyebrow at me to acknowledge what she agreed to when it came to the rule I set.

I grit my teeth and move my jaw back and forth. "Fine. Do you need help with your foot?"

"No." She keeps her eyes trained on the floor, dismissing me.

Fuck me. I *want* to talk about this little encounter, about the oddity of it all, and about those damn wandering eyes of hers that have this thick dick getting thicker by the second. But I'm going to respect her wish and push her in other ways.

She might have dismissed me tonight, but this is far from over.

She's attracted to *me*. She was speechless as she gazed at *my* body. She rambled about my fucking dick. I think she wanted me to kiss her.

*And fuck, did I want to kiss her.*

Hold her.

Touch her.

Lick her.

Devour her.

Fuck her.

But what's surprising and a huge mind fuck?

It seems like my friend Emma wants to fuck me just as badly as I want to fuck her.

# Chapter Thirteen

## EMMA

"Everything feels great here. Emma, come over and feel around for any lumps."

The woman with the bushiest nipples I've ever seen lies on the exam table, in all her glory, tits out, ready to be felt up.

It's woman's health week, and we're shadowing OB-GYNs to determine if it's a field we're interested in. Let's just say, I have no desire to be scooting around vaginas day in and day out. Nope, no interest at all.

"Oh, that's okay." I wave my hand as a dismissal. "I felt the last lady's breasts. You feel one, you feel them all, you know."

"Not even in the slightest," Dr. Tinkle scoffs. Yes, Dr. Mary Ann Tinkle. Might as well call her Dr. Pee Pee and get it over with. Dr. Pee Pee to exam room four, there is an immature urethra waiting for you . . .

"Come over here." Dr. Tinkle turns to Debra and says, "Students can be a little gun-shy when it comes to sexual organs."

Thank you, Dr. Tinkle, for making this that much more uncomfortable.

Holding back my groan, I mechanically stick out my arm from my side and press around Debra's breasts like Dr. Tinkle taught me earlier . . . on her own breasts. And when the nurse walked in her office to let us know her nine o'clock arrived, that didn't make things weird at all, you know, with my hands on Dr. Tinkle's naked breasts and all.

"These seem very soft, no lumps detected." Stepping back, I clap my hands together. "Good job, Debra, on not growing the lumps. Well done, breasts." I give her an awkward thumbs up and keep my distance.

Please, God. Please remove me from my misery.

"Thank you, Emmett," Debra says condescendingly. Total bitch, right?

She's been nasty to me ever since I asked if it was normal for patients to leave their socks on during examinations. It just seemed odd. They're naked beside a thin garment that's open in the front but wearing socks? I mean, at this point, with your cooter winking at everyone, you might as well remove the socks and be done with it.

Dr. Tinkle starts moving things around on her little metal table and scans Debra's chart. Thankfully, the old PAP smear has already been done, so I think we should be finishing up.

"Do the cysts on your uterus still hurt? Has the birth control helped?"

"It seems to be. I haven't been having the side pain like usual."

"That's good, I still want to check things out." Turning to me, Dr. Tinkle says, "Grab a pair of gloves." I quickly snag a pair from the box and try to hand them to her but she shakes her head. "No, those are for you. Put them on." From the table beside her, she grips the lube and pulls the top off. "Hold out your finger."

What the?

In a haze, I do as she says, my finger pointing awkwardly

in the air as if I have vagina lube on it. Oh wait, I do. I have freaking vagina lube on my finger. I thought I skipped the whole tunnel digging, but I guess I was wrong.

"Okay, we're going to do a quick rectal insertion and feel around for cysts. Debra, are you ready?"

Debra nods as I attempt to interpret the word rectal.

"Emma, go ahead and stick your finger in her anus and then press down on her uterus. We are feeling for any large lumps."

Errr . . . anus? Finger in the anus? What?

Before I can process what's happening, Dr. Tinkle is guiding me, finger forward, lube ready, straight toward the spread of Debra's legs. I don't want to be doing this; I don't want my finger up someone's ass, especially Debra's, who seems like she's ready to eat my finger through her rectum. Knowing I *shouldn't* have a grossed-out look on my face—doesn't seem like the right thing—I impersonate a psychotic clown instead: mentally scary smiling eyes fixed on Debra's asshole plunging forward.

The insertion is just as I expected, dreadful beyond belief.

Dr. Tinkle guides my other hand where I press down on Debra's uterus.

"Do you feel anything?" Dr. Tinkle asks.

Besides Debra clenching so damn hard on my finger that I'm starting to lose feeling in it? Not so much.

"Uh, seems okay to me."

She really needs to unclench because the sensation of her butt trying to slice off my finger is completely freaking me out right now. "Debra, I think it might help if you relax a little," I suggest, praying for the throbbing in my finger to stop from lack of circulation.

"How can I relax when you have your finger up my butt and a demonic smile on your face?"

Dr. Tinkle quickly looks at me to see the smile being wiped away from my face.

"Why were you smiling at her?" Dr. Tinkle asks, a little upset.

Finger still in Debra's ass, I look back and forth between the two women, not quite sure how to answer this question. "Uh, I didn't want things to be weird, so I smiled to help Debra feel at ease. You know, good bedside manner and all."

Good save. Buyable for sure.

Dr. Tinkle grips my shoulder and lectures me. "Emma, when we have to do invasive exams on patients, we try to keep a controlled neutral face, especially when the patient is nervous. You never want to make them more uncomfortable." *Controlled neutral face. Right.*

I nod. "Okay, but don't you think we should be having this conversation when my finger isn't up the patient's rectum?"

Debra sits up on her elbows and looks at both Dr. Tinkle and me, her boobs flopping past the "garment" she's wearing. "Dr. Tinkle, I don't care for this nursing student very much, but she has a point. Maybe she can remove her finger, and you guys can have this conversation without me in the room."

Without Dr. Tinkle's permission, I remove my finger—*from the horrible shackles it was bound to*—and hold it by my side, finger still pointed. Turning to Dr. Tinkle, I bow—no idea why, it just happened—and I say, "Thank you for this experience, but I think it's safe to say I won't be investing any more time into the OB-GYN field." Turning to Debra, I curtsey—because why the hell not—only seems fitting with what we just went through together, and I leave the room.

I'm going to have to do some serious extra credit to make up for today. Not to mention, some brain and finger bleaching. I'm tainted for life.

No pun intended.

• • •

"I've never seen anything like it. It was disgusting."

I hold up my hand, willing Adalyn to stop. "I love you, Adalyn, I really do, but if you continue to talk about your patient's neck goiter, I might seriously throw up on you."

I sit back on my bed and take a deep breath. What a rough fucking day. After I ran like hell out of the OB-GYN wing of the hospital, I spent the rest of my afternoon in the cafeteria studying with Logan who would not stop laughing over my finger in the butt misery.

And then there was last night, when I couldn't stop calling Tucker "thick dick." Ugh, why did he have to come downstairs in his tight black briefs that showcased everything he has to offer? I've never been one for briefs on a man, but HOLY HELL Tucker is an exception. It was almost like he was naked standing in front of me, that expansive, muscular chest rippling with every movement he made, those abs contracting when he bent down to look at my foot, and that deep V in his waistline. I was a goner. There was no stopping myself from staring. And there sure as hell was no stopping myself from dreaming about him last night. Oh, the things that passed through my mind. I woke up horny, embarrassed, and on edge. But most importantly, I woke up guilty. Guilty for checking out the one man I should stay away from, the one man who is completely off-limits.

Now Adalyn won't stop talking about the goiter guy, which is frankly disturbing. It's a goiter; it's disgusting, let's not talk about the ins and outs of it. (Pukes in mouth.)

Don't get me wrong, I knew what I was getting into when it came to earning a nursing degree but there are some days I wish I was doing something else, something less disgusting where bodily fluids and human deformities aren't surrounding me.

Perhaps something like accounting instead. Accounting sounds really nice right about now. Safe, easy, a job full of numbers instead of protective gloves and lube.

"Are you still upset about the butt thing?" Adalyn asks.

I wipe both my hands down my face. "I just need a break from anything that has to do with nursing. It's been a rough day."

Adalyn tosses me another fudge-striped cookie—thank you, Keebler, for these delightful treats—and pops another in her mouth. She likes to take the whole cookie down at once where as I like to wear them daintily on my finger like a ring and slowly nibble.

"Sticking a finger up an unwilling asshole does seem like a rough one. So I'm guessing we won't be doing any studying."

I shake my head. "Not so much. My mind is fried." I take a little bite off my cookie and ask, "Anything new with you? Did you ever go on that date with beard-man Bradley? Is that what he called himself on his profile?"

Adalyn giggles and nods. "Oh beard-man. He's quite the charmer online, but in person, kind of a dud. But I will say, his beard was something to marvel at. He must condition it at least twice a day. It looked so soft, like the hair of a pussy . . . cat."

"Why did you have to say it like that?" I shake my head at my friend.

"It's more fun that way. I like to throw you off your game."

"I'm already thrown off." I take another bite and chew while looking up at my ceiling, trying to will the image of Tucker in briefs out of my head. But hell, he is so FUCKING hot. I've always thought Tucker was good-looking, but grown-up Tucker, Tucker with a house, and abs, and pecs, and thick dick—oh my God—that Tucker is a force to be reckoned with.

Adalyn props herself up on my bed and says, "What's throwing you off? Please tell me it's the sexy roommate you

153

have living upstairs. Please tell me you're doing him, and he's knocked your head so hard against the headboard that your brain is a scramble. Please, oh please, tell me that he's had his evil way with you."

I shake my head but keep my eyes trained on the ceiling. "No, nothing has happened between us." Unless you want to count the amount of times I've sat on his lap, or when he's run his nose along my neck and jaw, or how about the amount of times I've stared at his body like a horny teenager licking her One Direction poster—Niall only. It's the accent, ladies, am I right?

"Are you sure? Because when I mentioned Tucker, your face got red."

"It's just hot in here." I wave my hand in front of my face, trying to cool myself down. It really does feel hot in here. Maybe because I'm living in Dante's inferno, lusting after my best friend's ex-boyfriend. Not even her ex-boyfriend, her long-time love for goodness' sake, the person she thought she was going to marry one day. Oh hell . . .

"So you're telling me nothing—"

*Knock knock knock.*

"Hey." Tucker peeks his head in the door and smiles brightly when he sees Adalyn and me. "What's up, Adalyn?"

*Oh look, it's thick dick . . .*

Like the flouncy woman she is, Adalyn twiddles her fingers at Tucker as she flips her hair over her shoulder. "Hi, Tucker."

*He doesn't even have a beard, Adalyn.*

"Just wanted to let you know I'm home, babe. I'm going to take a shower and make some spaghetti. Want some?"

Adalyn snaps her head in my direction from the term of endearment. Act cool, Emma, just act cool. "Uh, sure." Right about now I would eat anything with him if it meant I get to see his mouth work back and forth. That's what it's come to. I'm pathetic.

"Cool. What about you, Adalyn? Are you staying for dinner?"

She looks down at her phone and cringes. "I wish I could, but I should be getting home soon since this one isn't studying anymore tonight."

Tucker raises his brow at me, and Lord help me, my uterus just kicked me in the stomach from how sexy the move was. "No studying, huh? Looks like a night of fun is in our future." He winks, because why wouldn't he, and then shuts the door.

I let out a long breath just as Adalyn hits my leg. "He calls you *babe*? You guys are so fucking."

"Adalyn," I snip at her, trying to shut her the hell up. "He can probably still hear you."

"So, if you're fucking he already knows about it."

Leaning forward, I grit between my teeth. "We're not fucking." Since I share a wall with the bathroom, I can hear the faucet turn on, garnering us a little more privacy. "We're just friends . . ." My words trail off as I think about that for a moment. Just friends. Honestly, I now desperately wish there was more between the two of us.

"Come on, be straight with me."

Knowing she won't leave me alone, I sigh and fall flatter on my bed. "We're not fucking, but sweet Jesus, I wish we were."

"I knew it." Adalyn bounces on her knees with glee.

"It's been torture, Adalyn. He's so hot. I mean, it's obvious he's good-looking and has a nice body under his clothes, but I've seen him with his shirt off, I've felt the way his hands feel on a woman's body. It's addicting. Every time I'm around him I want him to touch me. I want him to slam me against a wall, spread my legs, and make me come until my voice is hoarse." I look over at her and say, "And last night didn't help. I saw him in nothing but a pair of black briefs, and I'm going to be honest, I think I almost came just from the sight of him."

"Oh my God, like Chris Hemsworth good?"

"Yeah, like Chris Hemsworth good, but dare I say, sexier? If that's even possible."

"I didn't think it was possible until I saw Tucker. You lucky girl."

"No." I shake my head. "Not lucky at all, because he's my friend, and he once belonged to my best friend, but all I want to do is rip his pants off, tap his penis and say, 'I have a friend I want you to meet. It's my vagina; want to have a play date?" Adalyn laughs so loud I think she might have rattled my windows. "Do you know how bad it is? How bad I want him?"

"How bad is it?"

"It's so bad that I want to stick my pinky finger in his pee hole and say, 'goochey goo, I want you.'"

Adalyn howls in laughter at my expense, her hand clamping over her stomach. "Oh my God. Please do that. I will give you a hundred dollars just to see you stick your finger in his pee hole."

"Never. I would never ever do that, even though the urge is strong." Taking a deep breath, I sit up and hold one of my throw pillows to my chest. "I just need to focus on the task at hand. School, graduating, and finding a job. That's all. I can do this."

Adalyn starts to gather her items and stands while slinging her bag over her shoulder. "Yeah, good luck with that, Emma. I know if it were me, I would be in that man's bed faster than you can blink. But that's just me."

That is just her. She hasn't had many years of history with the boy Tucker. She didn't watch him drool over her best friend for years, or then watch him mourn when things ended. She didn't know the boy who was so lost and alone when his father died, who desperately needed loving. She didn't see the empty expression in his eyes the day he showed her his house, or experience the elation of watching her expression when he'd spoiled her with coffee mugs and a couch. Yes, I want to have sex with Tucker, but there are strings we're balancing on.

Shrugging, she heads to the door and calls out, "See you tomorrow, sweet cheeks. Try to get some sleep, if you can." She wiggles her eyebrows and takes off.

Get some sleep, ha! The only way I know I'll get any sleep is if I pull out my little vibrating friend, take care of the thick-dick images in my head, and then pop Tylenol PM down the gullet.

I'm abut to change for the night when my phone chimes. I see the name displayed on the front and groan. Just what I need.

**Sadie: Hey girl! I miss you!**

Shit.

Shit, shit, shit.

When was the last time I talked to Sadie? I can't even remember, before I moved in with Tucker, that's for damn sure.

Swallowing hard, I reply.

**Emma: Hey Sadie, I miss you too.**

There, short and simple. Nothing incriminating. Nothing that says, "I know we're best friends and all, but hey, I'm living with your ex-boyfriend, and I can't stop lusting after him, to the point that if I slipped and fell, my mouth landing on his penis, I would probably start sucking."

**Sadie: Can we get together soon. We need to catch up. We haven't talked in so long, I feel like a piece of me is missing.**

Sweat starts to coat my upper lip as guilt rains down on me. What would she think if I told her how I was feeling, if she knew I was dreaming about Tucker. She would hate me, I just know it. Tucker was such a big part of her life and for me to step in her territory, it almost seems unforgiveable.

**Emma: I would love to get together. Just let me know the**

*time and place.*

I really don't want to see her, which is sad because she's one of my favorite people, but I'm not sure how much I can hide from her. She reads me like a book, and she will see right through my wall.

**Sadie: Perfect! I will text you tomorrow about a day. Maybe we can grab coffee.**

**Emma: Sounds great.**

Yeah, sounds great. Not really, but I can't avoid her, she will know something is up.

Tense and uncomfortable more than ever, I change into my favorite deep purple plaid pajama set, tie my hair into a messy bun on the top of my head, and put some lotion on my hands. I can do this. Of course Tucker is gorgeous, but am I so undisciplined I can't live with him in the same house and not think about him? No, I have self-control. I'm an adult for fuck's sake. I can handle my yearning with dignity. I can stop lusting after this man, this man that belongs to someone else.

Puffing my chest out with my head held high, I open my bedroom door just as the bathroom door opens as well. Billowing steam pours out of the doorway, the bright bathroom light reflects off the pink of the flamingos, casting an angelic type haze over Tucker as he walks out into the hallway, dewy, dreamy, and wearing nothing but a low-slung towel. My heart seizes in my chest, my thighs clench together as I take in his damp, messy hair, his freshly shaven face, and the little droplets running down his chest to the edge of his towel that is barely covering thick dick.

"Oh my God," I drawl out. And it isn't until Tucker wickedly grins at me that I realize I said that out loud. Okay, maybe I have ZERO self-control.

"You okay there, babe? You look a little flushed."

I nervously laugh, probably one of the ugliest laughs I've heard come out of my mouth. "Oh yup. You know . . . uh, oh my God," I move my hands around, trying to act casual but not pulling it off at all, "Look at all that steam. Ever heard of a fan?"

Smooth, really, really smooth.

Tucker tilts his head to the side and studies me, one of his hands on the knot of his towel. "If I had the fan on, then how could I have possibly heard what you and Adalyn were talking about?"

And just like that, my face heats up, my ears are in a blaze, and my body feels like lava was just poured all over it.

"You heard us?" I whisper. I don't know why, seems like something I have to whisper, maybe to make it less true.

"Just a little." He takes a step toward me, which causes me to back into the hallway wall. "Something about fucking. What could she possibly be referring to?"

"Guh, you know." I put my finger to my chin trying to look thoughtful. "I can't seem to remember exactly what we were talking about."

"No?" He takes another step closer, the smell of his soap making me feel drunk, hazy, so damn infatuated that it's hard to stand on my own two feet. "So Adalyn didn't ask you if we were fucking?"

Gah! Stupid Adalyn and her big stupid mouth.

Playing dumb, I ask, "Did she? Huh, well Adalyn doesn't seem to have a filter."

He nods and takes one more step closer, now only a foot between us. He places both his hands on either side of my head, framing me in place, giving me the perfect view of his flexing chest. Sweet mother, may I? Just a little touch, a lick of his nipple, maybe a little bob for apples on his penis.

"What did you say?" The rumble of his voice vibrates through my ribcage, sending my libido into overdrive. He smells too damn good, looks too damn good, and sounds too damn good for any girl to have coherent thoughts.

The space between us evaporates as he brings his face inches from mine, making the air feel thick. When he speaks, his breath tickles me, sending me further into a sexual awakening. My entire body throbs with need, with yearning for the irresistible man standing before me.

He enunciates every word when he repeats himself. "What did you say to Adalyn about fucking?"

"Oh yeah, the fucking." I laugh nervously. "I told her we were not doing the fucking."

"Did she believe you?"

Unsure of what's happening, I fidget with the hem of my shirt. Why is he so close? Why does he continue to tempt me like this? Is he trying to drive me crazy?

"She did. You know, we're honest with each other and everything. Kind of like you and me, acting like adults, telling the truth and all. No need for roommate rules or boundaries." I swallow hard.

Boundaries, man, we should have set some of those, because right now, Tucker doesn't understand the common courtesy rule of personal space. I don't think he's ever understood that since I moved in.

"Telling the truth, huh?" He licks his lips and bends his head down, which draws my attention to the towel barely hanging on his hips. My heart rate picks up when his eyes meet mine, those sultry, seductive eyes. "Tell me, Emma, when was the last time you fucked someone?"

Everything inside me is aware of his question, of his presence, of the way my clit is throbbing uncontrollably. In case he can't tell by the flush of my face and the sweat breaking out on my skin, it's been a while.

Continuing to twiddle with my shirt, I answer, "It's been a bit. I can't quite remember."

Tucker nods and brings one of his hands to my face where his thumb runs along my jaw to my mouth. He rubs the pad of his thumb along my bottom lip, tugging it down ever so slightly, his eyes fixed on my mouth.

"And when was the last time you used this mouth for anything other than talking and eating?"

"I . . . I don't remember." My breath hitches on me, causing my words to stutter.

Nodding again, Tucker steps in another inch, the heat of his body starting to warm me from the tip of my toes to the top of my head. "Can I ask you one more question?"

I wish he'd press me against the wall and end this horrible burning need I have for him, but I nod instead.

"What if Adalyn asked you, *do you want to fuck Tucker,* what would you have said?"

His eyes bore into me, slicing me in half. He knows the answer, it has to be written all over my face, displayed in my body language, and in the way I react to his every touch.

Do I tell him? Do I admit my burning crush? Does he even feel the same way? Or is he teasing me, trying to get me to admit something just because he can?

No, that's not the case. Tucker is not like that. He's sweet, caring, considerate, sexy, and irresistible. If I tell him I want to fuck him, what would that do to our relationship? Would it ruin everything we rebuilt over the last few weeks? But what would happen if I didn't tell him? Would the tension grow so thick that I eventually give in and throw myself at him? At least if I tell him now, I could get it over with and we could have an awkward moment and move on.

Taking a deep breath, I face him head-on and answer his question. "If Adalyn asked me if I want to fuck you, I would have told her yes."

Slowly, like the Grinch on Christmas morning, a sexy grin takes over his handsome face. I shake in place, waiting, as if my next breath depends on it. Lazily he takes me in, starting at my feet and meeting me at my eyes, when his perusal stops, he says, "Good to know, babe."

Lifting off the wall, he puts unwanted space between us, and like a cold bucket of water, every ounce of heat building inside me extinguishes when he grips the knot on his towel again and starts to walk away.

He's got to be kidding me right now.

*That's it?*

*Not that I wanted anything to happen . . .*

He's not going to do anything about my little confession? A kiss would have been nice, a little diddle against the wall would have been nice. I would have even taken a vag tap with his index finger. Anything really, but instead, he takes off toward his bedroom, taking the steps two at a time before he's out of my sight.

"What just happened?" I ask myself softly, trying to make sense of it all.

Why the close calls with Tucker, but never anything substantial? Never anything to feed this need to be around him, this need for him to touch me in any way possible. And that little interaction between us only worsened the ache between my legs.

Huffing, I walk into the kitchen and grab a pot to start boiling water. "Jeeze, thanks a lot, jerk."

Unsatisfied, hornier than ever, and frankly irritated, I put the pot on the stovetop and turn it on. Storming around the kitchen, I take out all the ingredients for dinner, which consists of a box of spaghetti and a jar of sauce, and set them on the counter.

I'm just going to say it; men are stupid. Men are stupid and rude. Men are stupid and rude and teasers. They like to tease your fantasies but never really make them come true. I mean, would it really have hurt Tucker to pull my pants down and stick his dick in me just once? I'm not asking for a whole lot here. Just a little dick to vagina friction accompanied by an orgasm for the ages. I've officially lost my mind.

"So stupid." I cross my arms over my chest just as I hear Tucker come down the stairs. Casually, as if he didn't just blow my clit up to epic throbbing proportions, he walks in the kitchen, shirtless, wearing a pair of thin plaid pajama pants with his large hand ruffling through his hair.

"Got the water going?"

Don't show him your anger. Don't let him know how much he affected you. Be cool, Emma, be cool.

"No, thought it would be fun to boil bleach to see what happens," I snap sarcastically, exposing my poor attempt at a bluff. Nope, not cool at all.

Knowing fully well I'm irritated, he swaggers toward me—*yes, swaggers*—his stomach flexing with every movement and with one quick lift, he has me sitting on the counter. Without looking at the stove, he reaches over and turns the burner off, his eyes fixed on me. Parting my legs, he steps between them and positions himself right in front of me. Once again, my heart rate picks up, my body coming alive from its short hiatus.

I swear if he teases me again, he's getting a kick to the balls.

Moving in closer, he places his hands on my thighs and says, "You seem tense, babe."

*Ya think?* At any moment I'm about to combust from the amount of sexual tension running rampant in my body. To say I'm tense is an understatement.

"Oh I'm just fine," I lie.

"Doesn't seem like it." His hands start to move up my thighs to my waist where he grips tightly and presses himself even closer so there is no space between our bodies. "Seems like there's something you want to get off your mind."

"Nope." I shake my head. "I'm just dandy."

"Dandy, huh?" His hands work their way up my arms now, to my shoulders where they land on my neck. Spread over my collarbones, his thumbs rub the column of my neck as his eyes search mine. "Ask me the question."

Confused, I ask, "What?"

His thumbs are now caressing my jaw, his head drawing in close, his lips wet and ready. "Ask me if I want to fuck you."

Oh God, I feel like if he answers the way I want him to, I will orgasm. I'm right there, ready to be pushed over the edge, my clit begging for release.

I take my time and search his eyes, pleading for his answer to be yes. "Tucker"—I pause to take a deep breath—"do you want to fuck me?"

His eyes bounce back and forth over mine, his grip on my face growing tighter. When he speaks, his voice is deep, full of a sensual rumble that takes over every bone and muscle in my body. "I've wanted to fuck you since I saw you at the bar with your friends."

*Hnnnnnnng*

From his little confession, I clench my legs around him, knowing damn certain that I'm wet, aroused, and beyond ready for him.

Shyly, I look at him through my eyelashes and ask, "What's taken you so long then?"

He strokes my cheek, heart in his voice. "You deserve more than just a quick fuck."

I gulp, deciding to throw all my cards on the table. "Sometimes a quick fuck is just what someone needs." Where is this coming from? What happened to all the guilt, all the knowledge coursing through my mind that this is wrong?

I look into his sultry eyes and know it's coming from deep within me. No matter how wrong it might be, I can't help myself. I can't help but egg him on and see how far I can push him, how far he will take this. If he will actually make a move . . .

He shakes his head. "Nah, not with you, Emma. You're the kind of girl you spend the night worshipping."

One of his hands slides to the back of my neck, pulling me closer to him where he rests his forehead on mine.

"If that's the truth, then can I ask you another question?" My breathing isn't the only erratic one. Before me, Tucker seems to be feeling the same kind of tension I'm feeling with every passing touch of his thumbs.

"Ask me," he says, his nose rubbing against mine intimately.

"Do you want to worship my body . . . tonight?"

Not even skipping a beat, he says, "More than you fucking know."

His hand tightens on my jaw, the other one curling around my neck. His mouth opens as his nose grazes my face. Fuck me. Fuck me. Just do it. Just kiss me. I can't take it any longer.

Our breathing quickens, our breath caressing one another as the air around us ceases to exist. With one more pause, Tucker presses his thumb into the back of my neck and then his lips graze mine, teasing me, tantalizing me with what's to come. It's a whisper of a kiss, a brief glimpse of our connection, and when I think he's going to end everything with just that light touch, he presses further but never too hard. He keeps his lips soft, his need in control. It's sexy as hell, to the point that I'm forced to wrap my legs around his waist and clench hard.

Lightly he nips my lips, runs his tongue along them and tastes each corner, as if he's trying to memorize this moment. There is no memorizing for me. It's impossible when I know this moment will be forever engrained in my brain.

Wanting more, I glide my hands tentatively up his chest. He groans from my touch and starts to work my mouth a little faster. When I press my hands over his pecs, he groans louder, and his mouth picks up the pace. I match each kiss with his, our mouths sliding against each other until his tongue parts me, begging for entry. There is no denying his demand. I open my mouth and collide my tongue with his, the force of his kiss taking control. I try to keep up now, matching each thrust, each groan, every lick of his tongue.

This kiss is *everything*.

From the pit of my stomach I know this moment will top every first kiss I'll ever experience. From the way he presses his body into mine, to the hold he has on my neck and face, to the way he equally matches my kisses with his, it's undeniably the most sensual moment of my life, as well as the most misguided judgment of my life.

And just as I settle in for a long night of kitchen make-out time, Tucker removes his mouth from mine, but not before placing a final kiss on my lips. Hazily, I open my eyes to meet his. When I expect to see that charming grin of his, instead, I see a look of uncertainty.

*Uncertainty?*

Uh, not the kind of thing a girl wants to see after experiencing by far the best kiss of her life.

Uneasy, I ask, "What's wrong?"

He steps away from me and grabs the back of his neck while his other hand rests on his hip. God, standing there, looking unsure, he is the sexiest man I've ever seen.

"Tucker?"

With his head still turned down, he looks up at me. "Shit, Emma." *Oh no.* "I lost control . . ."

And there it is, regret. Wow, that was a lot quicker than I imagined it would be. I would have at least given him the night.

I hop off the counter and put on a big smile. "No problem. I get it." I pretend yawn and stretch my arms over my head. "You know, it's getting late, and I'm not really that hungry. I think I'm going to call it an early night." I start to walk away and then turn to him. His eyes? They still look uncertain.

*He wishes he didn't kiss me. Does he want me to leave? Do I just go?*

"Let's just say this never happened, okay? A lapse in judgment. I'll see you in the morning. Night, Tucker."

I make my way to my bedroom, listening intently for him to quickly follow behind me, to tell me he was just kidding, that he actually wants to continue our kitchen make-out session, but he doesn't follow me. Instead, the house fills with an uncomfortable silence, while inside my heart and head, I'm screaming. In frustration, in anger, in humiliation.

Disappointed and more than embarrassed, I shut my bedroom door and go straight to my bed where I bury my head in my pillow.

*Do not cry, Emma. This is not something you cry over. This is merely an experience that ended sooner than you expected.*

Despite my self-talk, my nose starts to sting, the moment in the kitchen playing over and over in my head. Why did he stop? Was I a bad kisser? Was I not what he expected? Did I disappoint the hype he might have had in his head? *Was it because I'm not her and never will be?*

I can't stop the stinging feeling in my nose and before I know it, tears start to leak from the corners of my eyes. The tingling, burning sensation of having Tucker's hands and mouth all over me is quickly washed away by a vat of utter mortification.

There had to be something—

My door opens and without turning around I can feel Tucker's presence. I have my back turned away from him so he can't see the devastation I'm feeling.

"Emma."

I don't think I have the strength for this . . .

# Chapter Fourteen

## TUCKER

*Fuck.*

The grip on the back of my neck is so tense that it almost feels like I'm about to move all of my vertebrae out of place with one swift movement.

*What the hell do I do?*

I kissed her. I fucking kissed Emma Marks. The sweet, compassionate, slightly spicy Emma I grew up with, and I only have myself to blame.

It's been a monumental buildup from the moment I saw her at the bar, to her impersonating Playboy models, to her blatant staring and thick-dick comments, to the way she practically hums with pleasure when I invade her space. Tension, sexual frustration, and yearning built and fucking built until I could no longer resist her.

*I've wanted to fuck you since the moment I saw you at the bar.*

What was I thinking? Hell, I wasn't thinking, I was acting on pure instinct, on desire, on everything I've been holding back since the moment that incredible woman walked back into my life.

And I pushed her. Fuck, did I push her. I wanted to see how

far I could go, how many innocent touches I could get in, how many times I could crowd her space just to catch a glimpse of her scent. *She might think it wasn't fair to her, but it wasn't fair to me either.*

But tonight, seeing her in those matching pajamas, bright-eyed, beautiful, and innocent, fuck, I couldn't hold back. I had to know if she wanted to fuck me. From her body language, the way her eyes would peruse me every chance they got, or the hitch in her breath when I walked by her, I knew there had to be something there, but I had to hear it from her lips, those sweet, plump lips.

Christ.

I run both hands through my hair and glance toward her bedroom. That kiss, fuck, it's still making my body hot. And then like an asshole, I pulled away, unsure of every little nip and press of my lips I gave her.

It's not that I don't want her, that couldn't be further from the truth. But it's hard, giving in to the desire coursing through me when thoughts of Sadie still lurk in the back of my mind, taunting me every goddamn day of my life with what could have been, the future we missed out on, the world we could have created just between the two of us. *The world she didn't want. Doesn't want.*

*Get over it.*

It's the common thought in my mind. Drop it, she's moved on. But how can I drop it when I'm far from moving on? When I don't want to move on? When there is a room right across from Emma's that was designated for the little life we were supposed to bring into this world?

Taking a deep breath, my hands on my hips, I look to the ceiling and try to ease the ache in my chest. I can't worry about Sadie or what could have been. I need to focus on the present and the present isn't looking too special right now. *But it was.*

Flashes of Emma's face plague me as I think about what I said to her. *I lost control . . .*

Yeah, I fucking lost control, but in one of the hottest ways possible, with her lips screaming across mine, full of sweet relief from the fucking incredible tension built between us. And then like the bastard I am, I threw it away.

I need to make this better. Despite my reservations, my baggage, I can't let Emma think she's anything less than perfect.

Storming to her room, I open the door without knocking to find her curled up on her bed, a slight shake in her shoulders.

Fuck. Me.

One word falls past my lips; it's all I can get out.

"Emma."

Keeping her back turned away from me, she refuses to rollover as she says, "I'm tired, Tucker."

Her voice wavers with each word, a mirror image of anguish passing through her. *God, I hurt her.*

Knowing I did this to her . . . again . . . I take a step forward, past the books and pillows on the floor from her study session with Adalyn and tread carefully.

"Emma, please look at me."

"Just go, Tucker. Let's not make something of this, okay?"

Fuck that. Even though I'm battling with relationship demons, there is a comfort within Emma I'm craving, that I need to get lost in, that I desperately want to soak in.

"Turn toward me." It's a demand, not a request, and from the way she slightly shifts on the bed, she hears the seriousness in my voice.

When her wet eyes meet mine, a feeling of utter turmoil hits me straight in the gut. I should have known from the beginning if I was going to pursue this, I was going to have to dive in, not fucking tiptoe my way around whatever electric energy is surrounding us. I did this to her. Once again, I need to fix this. *She* is worth it.

Gently, I place my hand on her wet cheek and brush away the tears coating her beautiful face. "Scoot over."

"Can you just go?" More tears stream down her face, her lip quivering with each word.

"I'm not going to ask again, Emma; scoot over."

Her eyes bounce back and forth while looking at mine before she shifts to the side, making room for me. Taking charge, I lie down next to her and pull her into my chest so she's resting her head on my shoulder and my arm is wrapped around her, playing with the thin fabric of her pajama shirt.

Immediately, I can feel her tears on my bare skin and it breaks me inside.

Taking a deep breath, I say, "I'm temporarily breaking rule number six." I stroke her back with my fingers, hopefully conveying the warmth I feel for her. "I haven't been with anyone other than Sadie. She's been it for me. You know that?" I gruffly clear my throat. "Until *you* walked back into my life." I run my spare hand over my face, nerves tickling my spine. "This is new to me, Emma, being attracted to someone else, and I mean attracted enough where I think about you constantly. For so long, I'd just believed I would end up with Sadie, that we would have a family together, living in this house, growing old together. But I *think* we both know that's not going to happen. No. We both *know* it's not going to happen. So I have to switch gears, and it's been fucking hard. I need to learn to be okay with that, and I think I will."

I take a second to gather my thoughts, gathering strength from Emma who now has her arm wrapped around my stomach. *How does she know how to hold me in a way that comforts me so well?*

"But, I want this, Emma. I want your arms around me, your lips on mine, your body tangled in my sheets, naked next to me. We just have to go slow, despite how much my dick thinks differently. My mind has to catch up." *I want this. I want her.*

Emma draws little circles on my chest as she speaks, "This is new for me too, Tucker. These feelings. I don't think I've been so attracted to anyone before."

"Not even the man-nurse?" I can't help it, I have to ask.

"Man—" Emma pushes up to look at me, the sorrow gone from her eyes. "Are you talking about Logan?"

"Yeah. You're not itching to have him give you a one-on-one checkup?"

Laughter boils up out of Emma's mouth as she shakes her head. "No. I mean we tried at one point, but it never worked out. We're just friends."

"Nah." I shake my head. "You think you're just friends, but he so wants to fuck you."

"No, he doesn't," Emma states in defense with such surety in her voice. It's cute. Women can be clueless about men sometimes.

"Babe, he does. It's all in his eyes."

"You don't know that."

"Like hell I don't. He wants you. I know this because it's the same look in my eyes when you're around."

Swallowing hard, she stares at me for a few seconds before laying her head back on my chest. "Well, that's neither here nor there."

I chuckle and grip her tight. "I'm sorry, babe. I didn't mean to make you feel inadequate or embarrassed. It's just . . . fuck." I wish I knew how to say this right. "When I gave in to the yearning that's been eating me alive over the last few weeks, I lost it, and it scared the ever-living fuck out of me. I don't want to lose you, but fuck me, do I want you."

Her fingers graze across my nipple, the she-devil. "I want you, too, Tucker."

"Are you scared about our friendship? Of what might happen?"

Not answering right away, silence falls between us before she shakes her head against my shoulder. "No, I'm more worried about what Sadie might think."

*Sadie?*

"Why?" *Why the hell does she care what she thinks?*

"Tucker, she's one of my best friends, and I just made out with her ex in the kitchen of the house we're rooming together in. I'm now cuddling with her ex. That's not very best friend like." Her hand pauses on my stomach and then goes to her forehead where she grips it with concern. "Oh God, what is she going to think? She's going to disown me."

"She's not going to disown you. She's in her own little world right now." And isn't that the fucking truth. The last time I talked to her was when I brought her to the house, after she was already committed in her heart to someone else. Since that day, I haven't spoken to her. Hell, I hadn't spoken to anyone from my hometown until Emma came along.

Wanting to pull away from the topic of Sadie, I say, "There's no need to tell her anything because we don't know what the hell we're doing. Yet." There's no need to fuel a possible fire of drama over something we can't even label ourselves.

"I guess so." Emma starts to drag her fingers over my chest again. "Can I ask you something though?"

"Sure."

"What is going on here? What's happening between us? I mean, does the fact that we kissed change anything between us?"

I take a moment to think about her question. She wants to know what's next for us. Are we going to let this be awkward or give in to our yearning?

Knowing the answer right away, I say, "We're still roommates, Emma, there is no changing that, and I want our friendship." *I need our friendship.*

Her fingers stop immediately as she nods. "Okay, yeah. I don't want to lose our friendship."

I kiss the top of her head and add, "That doesn't mean we aren't going to fuck like bunnies all over this house. Just when the time's right, because at some point, my head is going to be between your thighs, and I'm going to love every fucking second of it."

Her breath hitches in her chest as her body relaxes into mine.

When the time is right.

I just need to get my fucking head straight first. *For Emma. For me. For us.*

# Chapter Fifteen

## EMMA

"Oh God. Oh, fuck me," I moan as I twist in bed. "Ahhhh." I sit up and grip my neck, pain coursing through it. The morning sun streams through my window, blinding me enough to let me know it's later than my usual wake-up time. Slight panic picks up in the pit of my stomach until I realize it's the weekend. I don't have classes or scheduled clinicals.

As my anxiety wanes, the pain in my neck becomes noticeable again. Muttering to myself, I swing my legs to the side of the bed. "Stupid muscular man shoulder, putting a kink in my neck." I rub the side, trying to ease the tightening of my muscles where I must have rested the entire night on Tucker.

God, that man. We slept together again. Platonically.

I don't even know what to do with him. He's my friend and still caught up on Sadie. He's also the man I can't stop thinking about, the man that makes one move toward me, and my entire body lights up. And let's not forget the man who told me, straight to my face, that there *will* be fucking between us. Fucking. Tucker Jameson.

I mean . . . how do I even respond to that? What do I say? "Oh sure, yes, please tell me when the fucking will commence."

Do I sit back and wait, to see if it will ever happen? Or do I just decide one night to strip down to nothing, point at my crotch, and say, "Open for business." Maybe I put an additional sign that says, "Tucker welcome here."

I'm so confused. I feel like last night was nice, but the mixed signals confuse me. He wants me, but not yet, but we will be having sex, but he's waiting, but then he sticks his tongue down my throat in the kitchen. I've never met a more indecisive man. It makes me question whether or not he is capable of deciding what to do with us.

Sighing, I stick my feet in my slippers, brush my hair out of my face—another winning morning do—and trudge out to the kitchen where I stop dead in my tracks.

Standing in front of the stove, freshly showered, wearing nothing but a pair of briefs and a spatula in hand, is the man who gave me a kink in my neck. Right now, I couldn't care less about the pain.

With his back toward me, I observe him in his chef element. One of his hands is tucked behind him in the waistband of his briefs, the extensive amount of muscles rippling through him flex and contract with every shift of his feet, and little droplets of water run the length of his back from his still wet hair. I'm enamored . . . once again.

Grown-up Tucker is one fine specimen.

I take a step closer, which causes the floor to creak, and draw Tucker's attention away from the stovetop. When he turns in my direction, a slow, sexy, heart-stopping smirk catches my attention, causing every nerve ending in my body to be on hyper-alert, jumping, jiving, and dancing across my skin with excitement.

"Morning, babe." His voice is gruff, low, still waking up from a good night's sleep. He pats the counter next to the stovetop and motions with his head for me to sit down. Still taking in the sight in front of me, I follow his non-verbal request. Of course, when I go to lift myself on the counter, Tucker does it for me, picking me up at the waist and gently setting me down, all the while, I stare at the way his chest ripples with every movement. His thumb and index finger gently pinch my chin in a loving way as he says, "Didn't think you were going to wake up."

"What time is it?"

"Nine. You took your lovely ass time waking up this morning, but I guess I wouldn't expect anything less from you."

I rub my neck where it's sore and sheepishly reply, "Guess I was tired. I never sleep in this late. Now I feel like the whole day is gone."

"Nah, it's just beginning." He winks at me and turns back to the stove where he tends to his magical eggs. I swear he whispers sweet nothings to make them taste so good. Hell, if I was an egg and Tucker started tantalizing me with his words, I would put on my best egg show as well.

"How did you sleep?" I ask awkwardly, still rubbing my neck.

His head tilts in my direction, a droplet of water from his hair cascading in my direction. "Perfectly." When he sees me rub my neck, his brow pulls together in concern. "What's wrong? Are you okay?"

"Yeah, just have a bit of a kink in my neck. That's all."

Without a word, Tucker puts the lid on the eggs, turns the burner down to low, and places the spatula on the spoon rest—which I'm surprised he even has, given his limited household items. With his finger, he motions for me to spin around. "Face the wall."

Thankful for the depth of the counter and my ability to easily cross my legs, I slide into position just as Tucker comes up behind me. His fingers dance with the collar of my pajama top as he tries to fold it down. From the irritated grunt that comes out of him, the fabric isn't performing in the way he wants, so his hands move toward the front of my shirt where he finds the buttons. Leaning over my shoulders, his breath tickling my skin—sending a wave of goosebumps over my body—he starts to unbutton them, one by one.

*Tucker is undoing my shirt.*

The one and only time I'm not wearing an undershirt or bra. Of course!

"Wh-what are you doing?" I ask nervously, unsure of his next move.

"Just trust me and try to relax," he whispers into my ear, his voice so low, so thick of testosterone that my body immediately ignites into a torch of flames.

All I can do is watch his dexterous fingers undo the buttons of my shirt, carefully never opening the shirt, just unbuttoning until he gets to the two at the bottom, which he doesn't seem to care to touch.

He moves his hands back to my shoulders where he very slowly starts to push the fabric of my shirt down my back so my shoulders are exposed to the morning air. He goes inch by slow inch, his fingers grazing my skin in the process, his head lined up with mine, his lips so close to my face all I want to do is turn and kiss him. I want to kiss him so freaking madly with every ounce of passion that's building in my body.

Expertly, he moves my shirt so my breasts are still covered, but so my back is exposed to him, along with my neck and shoulders.

Quietly, he asks, "Is this the side that hurts?" His lips press gently against my skin, sending a vivid tingling sensation down my spine.

I nod, unable to make any kind of formation of a sentence.

*What hurts?*

*No clue.*

Like a whisper, his lips dance over my skin, starting at the spot behind my ear, down the side of my neck, to the tip of my shoulder, relentlessly making rousing and heady chills spread all over my body. When his lips lift off me, I almost groan in protest but halt my objection when his strong, and very large hands replace his mouth, his thumbs kneading in an upward motion from my trapezius to the base of my skull. Each deep, thought-out stroke from his thumbs melts my body further and further into relaxation until I feel like a puddle on the counter, unable to hold up my own body.

He switches between stroking upward with his thumbs to making small, methodical circles along my strained muscles, sending my mind into a tailspin of lust. He's touching me with his fingers. *Massaging me.* All I want to do his throw myself at him, beg for him to break up the tension that's been billowing in my body ever since I moved in.

"How does that feel?" he whispers.

"Good," I answer, breathlessly.

"Is it hurting because I wouldn't let you move an inch last night?"

"Maybe." *He didn't let me move?*

He presses deeper with his thumbs and brings his mouth to just behind my ear. "I'm sorry, but I would do it again. Having you in my arms, pressed into my body, it helped me forget."

*Forget.*

Two syllables.

It's the large word that created the wall that exists between us. I need to stop existing in this haze of lust. What if he can never let go?

Is that what I want? Sex with Tucker? Yes. But do *I* want

more?

*Maybe I need to get my head together as well.*

There is much to let go, not just forget, but let go. Even from our conversation last night, it's easy to see how tormented he is from losing the baby, from losing Sadie. The hurt in his eyes, the demons that lurk behind his anguished expressions, it's almost like staring into an empty soul. But then somehow, he washes away the emptiness, puts on a charming smile, and is fun-loving, sweet, and sexy as sin. *He wants me. Sort of.*

Which only makes me torn. I'm torn between diving head first into a relationship with a man still mourning the loss of his last relationship, or stepping back, acting only as a friend, patiently helping him when he's ready to open up.

His lips brush across my neck, his fingers now moving down my shoulders where he presses them deep into my muscles. This is not friendship touching; this is *there is something naughty in your future* touching and for the life of me I can't stop it. I want him too much.

"Does that feel better?"

"It does."

"Good." He lifts his fingers from my muscles and spins me around quickly before I can even think what's happening. My top is halfway up my front, not exposing anything but definitely awkward, which he doesn't seem to care about because he keeps his eyes trained on mine as he lowers me to the floor. His hands go to the front of my shirt and he starts to put it back in place. The buttons down the front are all undone except the last two, giving him a view of the middle of my cleavage and stomach.

I watch as his neck strains, his jaw ticking with each passing moment, his eyes still trained on mine until he takes a deep breath and looks down at my chest. Every piece of my body is on fire from the way he takes me in, his teeth nibbling on the side of his mouth, making him look even sexier than I thought possible.

I break out in a sweat, wishing and praying that he removes my top and presses those sexy lips up and down my chest, sucking my nipples into his hot, wet mouth. God, it's all I want. Just a little release, something to ease the ache between my legs.

Slowly, he traces a line from my collarbone down my chest, between my breasts, over my stomach, and stops at the waistline of my pants, causing exploding passion like fireworks on the Fourth of July throughout my body. My breathing's erratic, my chest is moving up and down in rapid succession, and my core is throbbing with need. *Please remove my shirt.*

Looking back at me, his head tilted to the side, he says, "You're so beautiful, Emma." He scans my hair and smiles. "Even with that crazy morning hair of yours. Makes me want to see what other ways I can mess it up."

Leaning forward, his hand goes to my cheek where he holds my head in place before he presses his lips against mine in an open-mouth kiss. His rock-hard body braces me against the counter, his bare chest connecting with my exposed skin, warming me instantly.

Wet, hot passion. His grip on my cheek grows tighter, angling my head to where he wants it, his other hand gripping my hip, pulling me closer. Tentatively, I run my hands up his well-defined chest, trying to memorize every curve and divot my fingers caress.

Sparks of arousal fly between us as his tongue thrusts against mine, tangling, molding, melding together, like we've been doing this for years, like our mouths have known only each other and were meant for one another. A low groan erupts from his chest as he dives in deeper, pressing me farther and farther against the counter. The hand gripping my hip slips inside my open pajama top where the warmth of his palm spreads over my side. He trails his hand north and all I can do is hold my breath and wait for his touch, wait for the connection of his palm to my breast.

*Oh God, please.* I moan in his mouth, my hips starting to rock against his, and I'm greeted by his hardened length, probably one of the most amazing feelings I've ever experienced. I did this to him. *I* turned him on, and that has my libido skyrocketing through the ceiling.

"Fuck, you taste good," Tucker mutters as he moves his mouth across my jaw to my ear and then down my neck. I rest my palms behind me on the counter, bracing for whatever he has in store.

I'm tempted to run my fingers through his hair, guide him to where I desperately need release, but I hold back. I don't want to push him. I want him to want this. *Me. I want him to want me.* When his lips meet my collarbone, he kisses the length of my shoulder. Gently he starts to push my shirt to the side and a part of me wants to cry in relief. *Please keep going, Tucker. I want you. Need you.*

But when he kisses my arm and replaces my shirt, I'm close to breakdown in frustration.

And then his hand inside my shirt retreats.

As does his mouth, followed by his other hand, leaving me cold, turned on, and beyond frustrated. When I think he's going to step away, he doesn't. Instead he looks down at my chest, and the rapid rise and fall of it. His hands lift to my shirt, and he starts to button it up.

I'm not joking when I say my vagina starts to cry, my sensitive nipples as well, pretty much my entire body is weeping for the loss of hope, for the loss of what could have been one epic climax on the kitchen counter.

I must not be good at hiding my disappointment because Tucker says, "Don't look so sad, babe. It will happen."

*Don't look fucking sad? Is he kidding me?* He teases and tantalizes, touches and twists my heart each time he runs his hands over me. He may be confident we'll get there and *fuck like bunnies.* But what if he is wrong? What if he can't let go? I'm horny. I'm angry. I'm turned on. I get that Tucker needs time, but why the fuck does he have to use my body for his desire while he doesn't even know if we'll become a *we*?

Trying to be light about the heady situation surrounding us, I say, "No other guy teases like you. I swear to God, they would have given in by now."

Tucker tilts my chin up after he's finished buttoning my shirt. "I'm not like other guys, Emma."

I step past him and go to the coffee pot and busy myself, my back turned toward him. Of course he's not like other guys; that's an easy assessment just looking at him. He has a type of sex appeal that draws you in, drowns you, and leaves you wanting . . . begging.

I'm scooping the coffee grounds into the filter when Tucker wraps his arms around me and presses his head against mine. "Don't be salty."

I feel his erection press against me, and I can't help it when the words fly out of my mouth. "How can you say that when clearly you have a boner right now? How can I not be salty when you have pushed me way past sexually frustrated? Pretty sure my vagina is a nasty shade of blue by now, Tucker."

He chuckles into my ear. CHUCKLES!

"You're sexually frustrated?" His hands start to snake under my pajama shirt where he plays with the waistband of my pants, his fingers grazing the elastic of my underwear. Once again, my body heats up, my palms go to the counter as I try to hold myself up, my chin dropping to my chest.

His finger dips what feels like a millimeter inside my underwear where he plays with me, caressing my pubic bone but never getting anywhere close where I need him to be.

He slowly pushes his thick cock against me. *Oh God.* His voice trails over my neck as he says, "You're not the only one sexually frustrated, Emma. I want to fuck you more than you know, but not yet."

"Why not?" I practically cry in frustration.

His hands flee from my pants, and he quickly turns me around and pins me against the counter. He moves his hips against mine, his arousal causing my mouth to water. "Because when we fuck, we're going to do it in my bed, where I can spend hours tasting every inch of your body, where I can hear you moan my name with every climax, and where I can watch this beautiful face come apart when I'm buried nine inches deep inside of you."

Gulp.

*Nine inches.*

Oh God.

He leans forward and kisses me ever so lightly on the lips before turning me back around, swatting me on the ass and saying, "Fuck, Emma. I want you." He walks toward the stairs and then looks back over his shoulder, and I have to honestly say, I have just been smoldered with the *Mr. Darcy* look. "Five minutes. Need five minutes. Then you'll make us some coffee while I cook us some new eggs." And just like that, he takes off to this room, leaving me confused, horny, and wanting more and more.

• • •

*Because when we fuck, we're going to do it in my bed, where I can spend hours tasting every inch of your body.*

185

My brain will NOT stop repeating Tucker's words over and over in my head, in that deep, sleepy voice of his, even when Sadie jabbers on about a psychology experiment she's conducting with one of her classmates.

Did he talk to her like that? Did he tell her he wanted to fuck her? Or did he say make love? When they were in bed, did he want to taste every inch of her? Did he make her fall apart like he said he wanted to do to me?

Did they measure his nine inches together?

As my friend talks to me, I can't help but think of all the questions popping up in my head, comparing what I have with Tucker to what Sadie and he had. Of course there really is no comparison. They had love, they had a true, deep-rooted bond. I have . . . infatuation? Curiosity? Loneliness? *Lust?*

No, don't downplay what you have with Tucker. It's definitely not loneliness, although, it isn't anything near what he had with Sadie either. They had years. *Years.*

"I could not stop laughing. It was so funny. I wish you could have seen it." Sadie chuckles, pulling me out of my thoughts. Awkwardly I laugh with her because it seems like the thing to do even though I wasn't paying attention.

I'm such a bad friend. Here I am, daydreaming about Tucker as Sadie sits right in front of me, catching me up on her life. *Oh Emma, you're such an awful person.*

"Gosh, I wish I would have seen it as well," I say, even though I don't know what she's talking about.

Sadie brings her coffee up to her mouth and says, "So tell me about you. What's been going on? I really can't believe we haven't seen each other in a few months. How crazy is that?"

I shrug my shoulders. "Busy schedules and demanding boyfriends." I smile over my coffee, knowing Sadie has been swept up by the beautifully nerdy, sexy, and charming Andrew.

I don't blame her. Our friend Smilly actually tried to set me up with him back when Sadie and Andrew were first working together at Friendly's, the best ice cream parlor EVER! Sadie wanted nothing to do with Andrew, and he was a solid catch. I don't blame Smilly. Andrew and I actually hit it off, but the minute I saw him look at Sadie, I knew. He was infatuated with her. I settled for being friends.

"He's not that demanding . . . only in bed." Sadie winks and then giggles while drinking her coffee.

Hand to heart, if you knew this girl a year and a half ago, you wouldn't have recognized her. She's not the same person. Andrew brought the happiness out of her and helped her smile again. In high school, she was guarded, overprotective of her heart. She could laugh and have fun with the rest of us, and Smilly, Sadie, and I got up to *plenty* of crazy. Tucker made her smile. *And cry. That mixture of joy and sorrow was why I never thought they were right for each other. It was like a restless friction, like a pushmi-pullyu.* But this smile? This . . . lightness? It's like she's been freed from a shackle. As if she has truly found herself. As if she's emerged from a blanket of grief.

Genuinely, I say, "I'm so glad you're happy, Sadie. I really am."

"Thank you. What about you though, are there any men in your life?"

Ha, what a loaded question. Well, let's see, yes, as a matter of fact there is, but it's so beyond complicated that I can't even begin to discuss it, let alone with Sadie. And even if I decided to talk to Sadie about my feelings for Tucker, I would have no clue how to go about it.

I shake my head. "No. Not right now." The lie feels heavy falling off my tongue, but the truth would feel like trudging through quicksand, so I stick with the lie, too scared to see her reaction.

"What about Logan? Still nothing between you two?"

I laugh. "No. Still just friends."

"Friends to lovers maybe?" There's hope in her eyes.

"We've been there. It didn't quite work. It's the reason why I didn't move in with him when he offered. We would never make it work. It's way too awkward. We are way better off as friends."

Sadie's brow pinches together. "Why did he ask you to move in with him?"

Oh shit. Did I say that? It just slipped out.

"Uh." I cringe. "When I was evicted from my place with Adalyn."

"You were evicted? Oh my God, why?"

Crap, this was not the conversation I wanted to have right now, but knowing I won't be able to get out of this, I go for it.

"Our landlord wasn't paying the mortgage. The bank foreclosed on the property and gave us five days to pack up and find another place to live."

"Oh my gosh. Where are you living now? Are you back in Whitney Point?"

Our hometown, where we grew up, where we have the most memories *and* the most heartache, is about half an hour away from campus, an inconvenient commute especially with my schedule. Plus, I love my parents, but living with them again, no thank you. I would end up being forced into playing pinochle with them every Friday night with Roseanne Joanne—my mom's hairdresser—as my partner. And I refuse to have RJ as a partner again; she thinks passing nines is funny.

"No, I'm not in Whitney Point. I'm actually"—I swallow hard and stare down at my coffee—"living with Tucker."

Inwardly I cringe, unable to make eye contact with Sadie.

"Tucker? Tucker Jameson?"

"Mm-hmm." I nod.

"Oh, how did that happen?"

I glance up at Sadie and take her in. She doesn't *seem* mad, so I say, "I was at a bar with Logan and Adalyn, drinking my sorrows away about not being able to find a place when I saw Tucker. He was by himself so I went over to see how he was doing. We got to talking, well, Adalyn actually let her big mouth flap and mentioned my homelessness, which spurred Tucker into offering me a room in his house. It wasn't my first option, it was my only option." I quickly add, "I'm sorry if—"

"Why are you sorry? You needed a place to stay."

"I don't know." Maybe because almost every waking minute of my days are spent daydreaming about your ex-boyfriend's lips on mine. "Just seems a little weird since you and Tucker were together for so long."

"Yeah, but there is nothing between us anymore. And we were all friends before Tucker and I became an item. I'm just glad you're rooming with someone you know rather than a random stranger."

"But . . ." I pause. "It's in the house he bought for you."

Sadie stares down at her coffee. "Yes, but that house was never my home, Em. It was a beautiful gesture, and maybe if I never miscarried, we would have made a lovely home out of it, but that's not how our future rolled out. I can't think of the what-ifs with Tucker. But, I can be grateful that he has a friend like you to lean on, someone to keep him company in that house." As if she's reaching into my soul, Sadie asks, "How's he doing?"

How is Tucker doing? How do I even answer that question? He has his good days and bad days. He doesn't seem to be fully over Sadie, but then again, there are moments of clarity and calm in his eyes that make me think the demons of his relationship with Sadie might be dissipating. *How can he touch me, kiss me, hold me so fully if he's still invested in Sadie? Is that possible? It's so confusing.*

I shrug, not really sure how to answer. "He seems to be doing okay." *He likes to kiss me a lot, and I want to climb him like a tree and meet his nine inches. Oh, and he looks really good in nothing but a pair of briefs, but that's neither here nor there.*

Sadie sighs and leans back in her seat. "I worry about him. Last time I spoke to him was when he showed me the house. He wanted to give us one more chance, but I had already moved on by then, my heart had already fallen for Andrew." Sadie shakes her head. "All I want is for him to find peace, Em. Do you think he has?"

Peace? Ha, not even close. There is no peace in that man, only anguish, maybe a little bit of playfulness, and a whole bunch of pent-up frustration.

I can't help but wonder what he would be like full of peace. Full of happiness. How different would he be? I feel that I've seen glimpses when he's completely focused on me and waiting for my reaction, especially when he teases me. It's hard to imagine, and yet, I want to be the girl who helps him find peace, who helps ease his heartache, the girl who helps turn his house into a home.

And that realization hits me hard, right in the heart. *I want him to meet me at the side door with that smile on his face.* The one that stole my breath as if my arrival *home* was the best thing that had happened in his day.

"Uh, I don't think so," I answer honestly. "But I'm trying to help."

"Glad you're there, Em. He needs a friend to pull him out of the darkness."

A *friend*; why does that word feel like acid on my ears?

Maybe because I don't want to be his friend.

Maybe because I want to *fuck him in every room of his house.*

Maybe because I want breakfasts, weekends, and happiness . . . with him.

Maybe because I want so much more.

# Chapter Sixteen

"Come on, man. It's the one Sunday I have off," Racer complains into the phone. "I don't get many days off and when I do, I want to get wasted with my friends while watching hockey and eating fucking Little Debbie oatmeal patties by the box. Is that too much to ask?"

I button up my jeans and feel them hang off my hips but not enough that require a belt. Shirtless, I bend at the waist and lace up my brown boots.

"Sorry, Racer. I have plans with Emma." I really have no idea if she's available, but I planned a day for us, and I'm hoping she'll put the books down for a day and join me. I'm not ashamed to use my body as a weapon against her, hence the reason I'm waiting to put my shirt on. I think asking her *shirtless* will better my chances. Is it wrong? Yes, on all levels, but am I desperate to get out of this house with her and spend some time together? More than anything.

"Of course you have plans with Emma. When did you two start dating?" His tone is snide. I don't blame him. He really doesn't get many days off, and we've often spent them together, so I can understand his frustration. But there is always Smalls.

"We're not dating. We're just . . ." What are we? On the verge of sexual combustion? Pretty much. At times I wonder why I'm holding back. Whenever I go near her bedroom, I can't help but look at the room opposite hers and think about what I lost. And I really don't want to bring Emma into my bedroom when I still have Sadie on my mind; it wouldn't be fair to her, but it hasn't prevented me from touching and kissing her every chance I get. *But is that fair?*

"Are you going to finish that sentence?"

I blow out a long breath and run my hand over my jaw "Shit, I really don't know. I want her, Racer. I want her so bad, but I can't seem to let the past go."

"Sadie." It's one word but it means everything. *He understands.*

"Yeah."

The whiney-bitch Racer disappears. "Tucker, it's over, and you know I wouldn't just say that. You have to move on, man. Easier said than done, I get that." He sighs and says, "Fuck, fine, have your day with Emma, clear your head, enjoy the moment, but promise me something."

I chuckle. "I didn't know I had to get permission from you."

"You always do. Remember that. Every major life decision goes through me."

"Noted."

"Good. Now that's settled and I'm allowing you to abandon me on my day off, promise me this: you will take this day to actually enjoy yourself, enjoy Emma, and for one day, for twenty-four hours, forget the past and experience the present. Can you do that for me, penis breath?"

Jesus. I chuckle to myself and think about what he's asking me. Twenty-four hours of forgetting everything behind me. Can *I do that?* Hell, I want to try. Maybe I'll finally be able to breathe.

"Twenty-four hours? Easy."

"Better be, especially with Emma at your side. Now hang up before I change my mind."

"Enjoy your day off, don't get too fat from Little Debbie."

"Metabolism of a fucking god, dude. There is no fat on this body."

Such a dickhead. I hang up the phone and snag my black sweater and leather jacket from my closet and head downstairs. Emma's door is closed so I give it a light knock.

"Come in."

I already know she's settled in for studying because her "calming candle" is lit and the scent started to float up the stairs to my bedroom. When I walk in, sure enough, she's parked on her bed, legs crossed, hair over her shoulders and a highlighter in her mouth.

"Hey. What're you doing?" It's a stupid question, because it's obvious, but I want to gather her attention.

When she looks up, her brows pinch together as she takes in my shirtless body. Waving a pen in my direction she asks, "Why aren't you wearing a shirt?"

Not looking to be coy at all, I answer, "Because I have a question to ask you and thought it would be harder for you to say no if I wasn't wearing a shirt."

She snaps her book shut and sets it to the side. "You don't play fair, Jameson."

"Never claimed to." I walk toward her bed and link our hands together, pulling her to her feet. Her eyes search mine as I say, "I want to get out of here for the day and I want your company."

"But I have to study," she replies weakly.

"Not an excuse."

She laughs. "My student debt begs to differ."

"Are you saying no?"

"I'm saying I have to study."

Having zero shame, I place her hands on my chest and say, "But can't you see that I'm asking you with no shirt on?"

"Yeah, and maybe if you took care of me yesterday in the kitchen instead of teasing me, your shirtless tactic might actually work on me. But I see through you, Tucker. You're a ball of tease."

Damn.

Plan B.

I take a step closer and start to move my hands up her back, getting ready to really make a move. I lean my head forward, lips wet, and ready when she palms my face, stopping my pursuit.

Strong-arming me away, she says, "Nice try, but your attempt has been blocked. Now, please excuse me while I get back to my books; at least they give me what I want."

She's playing hard to get. Fair enough, I deserve it.

"Yeah, and what do you want from me?" I link my thumbs in my belt loops, dipping my pants a little lower, it doesn't go unnoticed by her.

She clears her throat and turns toward her books, settling on her bed again. "You know what I want from you."

"Can you be clear? I tend to forget things."

She eyes me for a second and shakes her head. "If you can't remember what I want then there is no hope for us."

I snap my finger and say, "Ah, you know what? I have a faint memory of your hard nipples rubbing against my chest. Does it have anything to do with that? Or the way my cock rubbed against your wet center? Didn't think I noticed? Babe, I could feel your heat through your pajama pants."

Her mouth falls open only to be quickly shut. "You did not."

"I did. And I also heard you last night as you came around your vibrator."

Once again, her mouth falls open, but this time her face blushes an embarrassing shade of red. Caught . . . jill-handed.

"No need to be shy about it, babe. It was hot, so hot that I jacked off to it." I shrug and start to walk toward the door. Instead of teasing her, which only gets a good blush out of her, I try for honesty. "I really just wanted to spend a day with you, away from everything. Just you and me. But I get it, school comes first . . ."

I head out into the hallway when I hear her groan. "Fine, I'll go if I can study in the car."

I peek my head back into her bedroom and give her a big smile. "Deal. We leave in fifteen, babe." I wink and head to the banister to don my shirt. She put up more of a fight than I expected, but hell, that was fun.

Twenty-four hours, I can do this, especially with Emma by my side.

• • •

"I thought you were going to be studying the whole way." I tease Emma, who's had her head turned, looking out the window for the past ten minutes.

Huffing, she turns back to her book and says, "How am I supposed to study when there are so many pretty houses to look at?"

"You're not. So put the book down and enjoy the view. What are you really going to retain in the next few minutes anyway? Sometimes it's a good idea to rest the brain, babe. Have fun with me today, pick up the book tomorrow."

She sighs heavily and caps her highlighter. She sets her book on the floor and says, "You're a bad influence, you know that?"

I link our hands, pressing our palms together. "Nah, I'm good for your studious soul and you know it." I playfully squeeze her hand. "Why doesn't DJ Jazzy Nurse Tits find some good music for us? And when I say good music, I mean it. None of this *One Direction* crap."

"Oh please, you like them."

"I really don't, but thanks for trying. Hook your phone up to my radio and play me the best you've got."

"Hmm, okay."

I glance over at her and I swear her smile stretches as wide as a Cheshire cat. What is she up to?

She takes a few minutes to flip through her phone. "Really taking your time there, aren't you?"

"Just making sure I impress, that's all. Can't have DJ Jazzy Nurse Tits letting you down. Which by the way, I'm still not committed to that name."

"Too bad I am." I squeeze her knee, which causes her to buckle over and laugh. "Fuck, are you ticklish?"

"Badly."

"Huh." I can't help my smile. "Looks like I can have fun with that later."

"Go ahead," she answers nonchalantly. "Hope you like getting kicked in the balls, because that's what's going to happen if you try to tickle me."

"Vicious."

She chuckles and then says, "Ah, found it. Are you ready for this?"

"Lay it on me, babe."

The sound of a single guitar strums through the speakers of my truck and it immediately pulls my attention just as a male, folky type voice matches up with the strum of the guitar. I've never heard the song, and I'm kind of fucking shocked it's on her phone. This doesn't sound like the kind of music she listens to.

The song plays out, little strums, followed by some background piano, it all works. Fucking catchy as hell.

When it ends, Emma turns her body in her seat and says, "What did you think?"

She's practically bouncing on her seat, waiting for my opinion.

Not answering right away, she gets frustrated and pokes my shoulder, causing me to laugh. "Fine. I liked it. You shocked me actually; I didn't think you were going to pick something so soft. Good choice. Who was it?"

Her smile grows even wider. "Niall Horan. The song is called *This Town*."

"Niall Horan. Is he new? I've never heard of him. I like his voice."

"You've heard him before."

"Have I? What song?"

"Any *One Direction* song I've ever played. It's his first solo song." The cackle that follows her confession is actually quite endearing because it's a full-on belly laugh, as if she just caught me with my pants down, willy out, dawning a fucking duck hat on my dick.

When her laughter starts to die down a little, I say, "You think you're so fucking clever, don't you?"

She wipes her eyes. "I do actually. Tucker loves *One Direction*," she singsongs.

"You couldn't be more wrong." I turn into Main Street in Skaneateles, New York, and start searching for parking. "I don't like *One Direction*, but am I starting a little boy-crush on Niall? Well, I'm not going to deny that."

Once again her laughter fills the cab of my truck and I can't help but soak up the beautiful sound, loving this day already . . . even if it's at the expense of my manhood.

• • •

"How cold do you think that water is?"

I have my arms wrapped around Emma's shoulders, her back is to my chest, and I'm holding her tight as I lean my head over her shoulders and take in the expanse of Skaneateles Lake.

"Freezing, babe. There might not be snow on the ground right now, but it's cold."

"Like I would get a black foot if I stepped in it kind of cold?"

"Yeah, black foot-worthy for sure."

"Only one way to find out." She shifts and then nods her head at the lake. "Go ahead, give it a go, you can be my guinea pig."

I squeeze her tighter and kiss the side of her head. It's insane how easily I can be affectionate with her. I don't even give it a second thought. "You're cute, but never going to happen."

"Not even if I asked sweetly?"

I chuckle and shake my head. "Why is dipping a toe in the freezing lake something you even want to do right now?"

She shrugs. "Just interested in the arctic."

That garners a laugh from my belly. "You're interested in the arctic? It's Upstate New York, Emma, not the northern most part of the earth."

"Sometimes it feels like that."

Can't disagree with her on that. Living in Upstate New York is not for the faint-hearted. You have to be ready to fight winter day in and day out and the unpredictability of its cumulative snowfall.

"I would say you should be used to it by now, but I can remember seeing you walk the halls in high school, bundled up from head to toe. You had this red winter hat with a pom-pom on top that almost seemed like it covered your entire head. The only reason I knew it was you under that hat was because you were the only one in the whole school who owned such a ridiculous piece of winter wear."

"Don't you dare speak ill of that hat," she teases. "Scarlet gave me many years of warmth."

"Gave? Do you no longer have the old girl?"

She shakes her head and then rests it against my shoulder. "My cat, Marla Hooch, peed on it and once cat pee hits anything, it's over. There was no saving it."

Laughing, I say, "Oh fuck, I forgot about Marla Hooch. You named her after your favorite player in "A League of Their Own." She would piss on everything. She pissed on my backpack."

"No, she didn't."

"The fuck she didn't. We were all over at your house after school because you, Sadie, and Smilly were selling cookies for Christmas and wanted us to be taste-testers before you went out in public with your product. I went home with a very wet and very foul-smelling backpack. Luckily Saddlemire had a backpack he wasn't using and gave it to me." Thank God for my friends, because I was the kid with nothing. I made a little side money from working under the table for Julius and anything I made went straight to food and clothing for myself since my mom was MIA.

"Oh my gosh, I totally forgot about Birdie's Bakery, our little Christmas cookie scheme."

"I think I can still taste your gingersnaps. It was supposed to be a hint of ginger flavor, not a burn-your-tongue-off flavor."

"Yeah . . ." She chuckles. "We might have added a little too much ginger. Thank goodness you guys were our taste testers.

"Yeah, thank goodness," I deadpan. "How is Marla Hooch; is she still around?"

Emma nods. "She is, wearing a diaper now because she just squats wherever she wants. My mom finds it endearing, taking care of a cat with urine issues."

"Endearing? I can think of a hundred other ways to describe that situation, and none come close to endearing."

"Not into being the cat-pee kid?" Her laughter once again hits me in my soul, lifting me up.

"Never. No one ever wants to be known as the cat-pee kid."

• • •

"Don't wuss out on me, just take a sip."

With lips sealed shut, Emma shakes her head rapidly as she tries to back up but is trapped by her chair.

"It's one of a kind, lass," Phillip the bartender says, a deep brogue in his voice.

"Yeah, it's one of a kind, lass." I mimic and hold the glass in front of her and shake the contents just enough so it doesn't spill out. "When will you ever have another chance to drink this fine flavor of vodka?"

"Never. Not going to happen."

I set the small tumbler on the bar and step closer, invading her space. I place one hand on the bar counter and the other on the back of her seat. With a low, seductive voice, I say, "I dare you."

Her mouth quirks to the side as she slowly shakes her head, her soft, lustrous hair floating from side to side. Fuck, I want to run my hands through it. "I'm not the type of person who can be dared, Tucker. I'm the responsible one, you should know this."

Shit, she's right. She is the responsible one. I need a different approach. "Fair enough. You drink this shot of pickle vodka, and I'll do something you want me to."

That garners her interest. "Anything?"

I lean forward and whisper into her ear, my nose grazing against her soft skin. "Within reason."

201

She scoots forward and tugs on my leather jacket while her eyes look up at mine. "What does within reason mean? What are your limits?"

"It's startling to me that whatever you're thinking might pass someone's limits."

"Just keeping my options open." She wickedly grins.

I study her for a second and then answer, "No public nudity—"

"Well, there goes my idea."

"Funny." I nod at her. "Nothing that involves the freezing lake. Unlike you, I'm not interested in whether or not I can get a black foot. And I refuse to purchase the giant recycled material flamingo you couldn't take your eyes off two stores down."

"But it would be the perfect toilet paper holder," she fake whines and then pouts her bottom lip. I stroke it with my thumb and shake my head.

"Sorry, babe. That flamingo will have to find a home with someone else."

"Fine," she drags out. She folds her arms across her chest, glances around the bar and then her head whips to mine. "Oh, I know."

I don't like that look on her face, the one that says *I have something good to make you do*. Is the pickle vodka really worth it?

"Do I even want to know?" I ask, a little worried that she's going to make me lick the underside of one of the tables. At that point, the answer would be no. The vodka is *not* worth it at all.

"Do you want me to drink that disgusting vodka?"

I look down at the vodka and then back at her. "I really do."

"Good." She smiles and props herself up. "Remember when you went to the bathroom and left me here, at the bar, all alone with no one to talk to?"

"Yesss," I say, unsure of where she's going with this.

"Well, while you were 'pissing' as you so crassly said, I met a very nice woman who seemed to have taken a liking to you."

"Oh yeah?" I buck up. "Hard not to resist such a rugged man like myself."

Emma rolls her eyes and says, "Well, she said she would give anything to rub her face up against a set of abs like yours."

"How does she know I have abs?" I ask, getting an idea of where this conversation is going.

"I confirmed when she asked. I said they were little divots you could get lost in."

"Did you now?" I smugly ask.

"Don't make me get a pin to pop that obnoxiously large head of yours. I was just giving the woman a happy image to consider during her day."

Picturing a little old lady with white curly hair and a pink cane, I look around to find her. "All right, so what's the deal? And where is this woman you speak of?"

Emma rubs her hands together and gets ready to lay it on me. Fuck, she's cute. "She introduced herself as Floats Like a Barge Marge, and she's the dishwasher in the back. So the deal is, I drink this vodka and you let Floats Like a Barge Marge rub her face against your abs for ten seconds."

My eyebrows lift in question. "You're going to let another woman touch me with her face?"

Emma shrugs and takes a look at her nails. "Not like you've claimed me or anything so I have no reason to claim you. Although, if you actually put out yesterday instead of teasing me, your abs might be hearing a different request right about now."

I knowingly nod. "You're going to keep throwing that in my face, aren't you?"

She leans forward and whispers, "Tucker, that was torture, so yeah, I'll keep throwing it in your face."

"You thought that was torture? You have no idea, babe. I can make it way worse."

"Is that a threat?" She leans even more forward so our foreheads are almost touching from my bent position.

"I can make it one."

Looking between my eyes, Emma says, "Don't forget, Tucker. I'm the one with the hot pocket; you just hold the pepperoni. You need my warmth way more than I need your meat."

She leans against her chair and folds her arms again, causing me to throw my head back and laugh. Fuck if that wasn't the truth.

"Playing hard to get now?" I ask with a raised brow. She just stares at her nails. I sigh. "Fine, Floats Like a Barge Marge can rub against my abs."

"Really?" Emma claps her hands excitedly and then lifts off her chair, standing on one of the rungs, and wraps her arms around my neck. Without seeming to take a second to think about it, her lips press against mine briefly before she taps on the bar counter. "Phillip, can you please tell Floats Like a Barge Marge that her dreams have come true?"

He nods, throws his towel over his shoulder, and heads behind the mirrored bar to the back. When Emma turns to me, she smiles brightly, kisses me again but this time, with a little tongue.

Hell, I like that. I like that a whole lot. I start to bring her in even closer when she pushes against my chest to sit back down.

"Hey, I was in the middle of something. Get your ass back up here."

She wiggles her finger at me. "Uh-uh, you have to get those abs ready."

"What do you want me to do? Hop up on the bar and start

doing crunches?"

"Might be nice." She leans her elbow on the bar and props up her chin. "Kind of dreamy actually. Let's see it. Do some sit-ups."

I pull my jacket closed and turn my body slightly away from her. "I'm not some piece of meat you get to parade around. I'm a man with feelings," I tease. "I have emotions and needs. I'm not just on this planet to give in to your every demand."

She laughs, picks up the pickle vodka, downs it one swift swallow, cringes for a second, and then pats her mouth dry with a napkin. "Yeah, we both know that because if you were giving in to my demands, I would have had at least five orgasms by now instead of the one from my vibrator."

Holy fuck, Emma. Never in my life would I have imagined such a sentence coming from her sweet little mouth, but with every day we spend together I see a different side of her that I fucking like. Sassy, smart . . . sexy.

"I told you not to be salty."

"And I told you to fuck me. I guess we both don't listen to each other." She winks and turns toward the kitchen door just as it starts to swing open. Phillip steps out first, holding a towel in his hand, leading the march like he's the front man of a boxing posse.

In the right corner, we have Tucker Jameson, construction worker, and all around sex throb. In the left corner we have . . .

My mind goes blank as Floats Like a Barge Marge steps into view. Turning to the side to fit her shoulders through the doorway, a six-foot-five woman stomps—yes, stomps— toward me wearing a white apron, hairnet, and white knee-high stockings. I gulp as she smiles, revealing a lovely gold shade set of teeth. With one swipe of her paw, this woman can flatline me in a second, and I'm a big fucking dude.

"There he is, the man of my wet dreams," she says in the deepest voice I've ever heard come out of a woman. Step aside, James Earl Jones, we have a new Mufasa in the running. She holds out her foot-long hand and shakes mine. "I'm Floats Like a Barge Marge. And you, my little dumpling are . . ." She releases my hand and squeezes my cheeks together with her man-claw.

Barely able to talk over the clamp she has on my face, with my lips puffed out like a fish, I say, "Tucker. It's a pleasure."

FLAB Marge—Floats Like A Barge, see what I did there— lightly taps my cheek and says, "Oh no, the pleasure is all mine." She rubs her hands together, looks down at my abs, and licks her lips. "I'm ready when you are." She strokes her jaw and oddly winks at me. "And don't worry, dumpling, I shaved this morning for you. This is one fresh face."

Annnnnnd, my penis just shriveled up inside itself.

I glance at Emma who, with tears streaming down her face and her hand over her mouth, is silently laughing. Once again, seeing her so happy has me by the balls. With a sigh, knowing this will make Emma's day, I lift my shirt up, close my eyes, and let Floats Like a Barge Marge do her thing.

● ● ●

"This is my wallpaper for the rest of my life!" Emma hugs her phone to her chest as we walk into another little shop on Main Street, Skaneateles.

"Laugh it up, pretty girl." I shut the door behind us and take in the eclectic store full of house décor, quirky kitchen supplies, and coined tourism gifts.

She bumps my shoulder with hers and shows me her phone once again. It's a picture of me with my shirt up, abs exposed, and a cringe on my face as FLAB Marge rubs her prickly face against my skin. Hands down, the worst ten seconds of my life—

not really, but fuck, it's pretty high up there. I'm scarred for life.

"I'd rather not reminisce on what happened back there." I rub my stomach. "I'm not shitting you, I think she gave me beard burn on my skin."

"She did not." Emma laughs.

"She did. Ever hear of aftershave, Marge?" I pick up a wine stopper that looks like a daisy and then set it back down. Pointless crap, that's what all this shit is.

"Maybe we can pick some up and you can give it to her, you know, as a little thank you for the experience."

"And why the hell would I do that?"

She loops her arm through mine and rests her head on my shoulder. "Because you're a nice guy?"

I kiss the top of her head. "Not that nice, babe. Hate to say it but my time with Floats Like a Barge Marge is over. It was a one-and-done deal. She got hers, I got to see you drink pickle vodka, which you took down like a champ amazingly, and now the moment is over. We're moving on."

"What's Racer's phone number? I want to send this picture to him."

Or we're not moving on . . .

"If you really think I'm going to give you his number, you're delusional."

She snakes her hand around my waist to my coat pocket and fishes around for my phone. I twist away from her and bump into a display of soybean candles, causing a slight clash of the jars against each other.

"Please no horsing around inside," the shop owner calls out, sounding like a grumpy old coot.

Emma, of course, blushes in embarrassment and apologizes while scurrying toward me, trying to hide her face. From behind, I wrap my arms around her and whisper in her ear, "Ooooo, you got in trouble."

Her boney little elbow flies into my stomach as she whispers, "You got in trouble too."

I laugh and grip her tighter, ceasing her little elbowing attempts. "Yeah, but whereas it matters to you when you get in trouble, I couldn't care less."

It's true. Emma has always been the goody two shoes, the compassionate and caring one. I've lived a hardened life and getting in trouble is nothing new to me. It's actually quite fucking endearing to see how someone like Emma cares so much when she's "scolded." Fuck, it makes me want to wrap my entire body around her and protect her, tell her the world isn't coming to an end just because she was lightly reprimanded.

I come to her side and put my arm around her shoulder as we continue to walk around the store. Her hand links with mine so she's holding my arm that's wrapped around her body. She's affectionate, really affectionate actually, and I like it. I've liked that she hasn't shied away when I've kissed her in public today, or that holding my hand has been a must for her while walking around. Stopping us in our tracks just to give me a hug comes so naturally to her, and I really like that.

Growing up, there was no affectionate mom in my life. Mine was neglectful. I would get hugs from friends' parents when I was young, friends, when I got older, but I've never truly experienced the affection Emma dishes out. It's sincere, wanted . . . needed.

"Oh my gosh, look," she gushes as she drags me over to the kitchen area. Retreating from my arms, she slips her hands into a pair of lobster claw oven mitts and holds them up for me to see. "You need these."

Attacking me with the oven mitts, she tries to pinch me but I dodge her while laughing. "Why the hell do I need those? So you can chase me around the house, playing demon lobster mistress?"

She pauses, holds the lobster claw mitt up to her chin and ponders for a second. "I never thought of that, but now you mention it, we are so getting these. I was just thinking you needed oven mitts since you don't have any. But now that you mention this little lobster pinching game, it's a slam-dunk buy for me."

"Slam-dunk buy, huh?"

"Absolutely." She jukes around, trying to pinch me, but I'm too quick for her. When she reaches for my stomach, I yank on her arm and pull her into my chest where I trap her, arms at her side. No pinching is going to get her out of this little cage.

"What are you going to do now? Your little punk claws can't help you here."

"That's what you think." She wiggles in my arms but gets nowhere.

"All you're accomplishing right now is some great friction between us. Face it, Emma, you're trapped."

"That's what you think, but . . . with . . . just . . . urghhh, why are you so strong?"

"I work out every day and also do construction for a living. I've got muscles, babe."

She struggles some more and says in a strained voice, "Yeah, but do you have brains? Hi-ya!" Out of the blue, she stomps on my instep, which frees her from my grasp, sending her into a turning wheel of booklets. The display topples over, and in cute Emma fashion the lobster claw oven mitts go to her mouth in shock. She looks completely horrified.

"Oh my gosh, I'm so sorry."

The shop owner marches toward us, the depths of hell in her eyes as she starts picking up the display Emma knocked over.

"I told you not to horse around. I'm going to have to ask you to vacate the store."

"Oh gosh." Emma starts fumbling around, trying to help the shop owner with the display, but is useless with her lobster hands. "Um, can I just get these items real quick before we leave?" Faster than I've ever seen her, Emma floats around the store and plucks random items from the shelves. She holds them to her chest as she walks over to the counter and plops them down.

I stand aside and chuckle to myself. Guilt purchases. That's what she's doing. She's buying a bunch of shit because she feels guilty. I wouldn't expect anything less.

Annoyed and wanting to get us out of the store as soon as possible, the owner leaves the collapsed display and checks out Emma. When the total comes into view, Emma pulls out her wallet, but I hand the owner my card before Emma can. I wrap an arm around her and kiss the side of her cheek. "I got it, babe. Consider it a little thank you for spending the day with me."

Still slightly embarrassed, she mouths a *thank you* and puts her wallet away.

Disgruntled, the owner packs us up and sends us on our way. I hold on to Emma's hand tightly, while I carry our goodies with the other and lead her outside into the chilly air.

"She was pleasant."

"We destroyed her store. I feel so bad," Emma replies.

"Don't. We just spent over one hundred dollars in her little store. I'm not even sure what the hell we bought."

"Me either," Emma deadpans before looking at me and chuckling. "I was so nervous, I grabbed whatever I saw and blacked out in the process. Shall we look in the bag?"

Two lobster claw oven mitts, an Earthly Embrace soybean candle, garden-patterned cocktail napkins, eleven-bean soup mix, hummingbird feeder mix, and two "wine glasses" made of solo cups and plastic stems later, we're in my truck, hands linked, laughing about the big night we have planned ahead of us with all our new goods.

• • •

"This soup really isn't that bad," Emma says while plugging her nose and bringing her spoon to her mouth. "You just have to avoid breathing when you eat it." *It should have a warning label saying, "Rancid. Do not smell while consuming."*

My bowl of the eleven-bean soup Emma snagged while at the kitchen store rests a foot in front of me, barely touched.

"Yeah, I've heard food critics talk about how NOT smelling the aroma of your food is the way to really enjoy a meal. The more pungent, the better." I grab my very white trash-esque solo cup wine glass and bring it to my lips, trying to get past the Angry Orchard that's inside it. It was, unfortunately, the only booze in the house, and I needed booze to make it through this soup, therefore I had no choice.

Emma sits back in her chair, grabs one of the cocktail napkins we bought, and dabs at her face. "It really is unpleasant soup, isn't it? And what's the crunchy thing in there? I'm all for texture in a meal, but I'm not quite sure what that crunchiness is."

"No fucking clue. I took two bites and was done."

She sighs and then smiles while she lifts up her hand, which is covered in red. "At least we got these bitchin' oven mitts." Lifting up my hand as well, the one that's donning the other oven mitt—she made me—we high-five across the table.

"I can't imagine ever topping such a prestigious buy. Not everyone can be as lucky as us," I say, playing into her delusional purchases. I look over at the soybean candle we have lit and say, "I will admit, that candle smells damn good. It was a risky purchase, buying a candle without taking a sniff test, but your spontaneous purchase paid off."

"So would we say I only had one dud for the day?" She nods at the soup.

I hold up my fingers. "Two, babe. Hummingbird mix?" It's the "centerpiece" of our weird dinner she threw together for us. In her words, she didn't want it to feel left out.

"But it looks so pretty sitting in the middle of this ornate card table." She pulls a Vanna White and shows off the table, motioning her arms around our mishmash of a dinner table.

"So ornate. I really enjoyed seeing warning signs of human digestion on the mix container while I tried to suck down that soup. Made for an appealing atmosphere."

She chuckles, turns the hummingbird mix to see the warning labels and cringes. "Maybe not the best, but," she holds up her finger and says, "I have an idea. Take your drink and oven mitt over to the sofa and I'll meet you there."

"Are things about to get kinky?" I wiggle my eyebrows at her.

"You wish."

She clears the table, which I feel guilty about. There is a need inside me to take care of her, and clearing the dishes, although simple, seems like something I should help out with, but knowing Emma, she would snip at me if I didn't do what I was told. Therefore, I pick my drink up off the table and head over to the sofa. The only light in the room is from the small chandelier in the dining room, but it makes for some great mood lighting.

I press my body against the armrest and lift my legs on the cushions so I'm spanning the length of the entire sofa. I place my oven mitt hand behind my head and wait. When Emma returns, she saunters over to me in her cute heart-covered pajama set with a spoon and a gallon of ice cream.

"Up for a different kind of dinner?"

"I'm always up for dessert for dinner. What flavor?"

"Chocolate chip cookie dough, the best kind."

"Can't argue with you there." I pat my lap. "Have a seat, beautiful."

She raises an eyebrow at me. "You expect me to just sit on your crotch?"

"Normal people call it sitting on a lap, but if you prefer to say crotch, we can lean that way."

"It's your crotch," she replies with indignation before letting out a heavy breath, as if my request is borderline torture. Regardless, she straddles my lap before sitting down, and I didn't miss the little smirk on her face as she did so.

She places the ice cream in front of us and holds out the spoon for me. Not wanting to prolong my dinner much longer, I remove the oven mitt despite her protest, snag the spoon, take a big scoop, and plop it in my mouth.

"Hey, I thought we were wearing the oven mitts."

"It's getting in my way of ice cream time."

I take another bite and relish in the cold, creamy taste of the vanilla base. When I swallow, I notice Emma's eyes trained on my throat, her lips wet from her tongue, and I can't help wondering what's going through that pretty head of hers.

"Want a bite?" I ask her.

She nods and licks her lips again. Despite her sitting on my lap, she's still at eye level with me, which I enjoy because it's like I can see straight into her soul, into her desires. Right now, without a doubt in my mind, Emma isn't just thinking about ice cream.

I scoop some ice cream out with the spoon and feed her a bite. I watch in fascination as her mouth closes around the spoon and sucks the ice cream off with a more powerful force than I was expecting. Hell, this woman surprises me every single day.

Sweet, motherly Emma— the girl I knew in high school and at our parties—is not in the house tonight. When it's just us, there is this electric energy about her. It floats between us. Masked is the girl who holds back the hair of her friends. Disguised is the girl who warns us about using coasters, or the selfless girl who's busying herself cleaning up after others rather than enjoying the moment. Instead, I'm graced with this lively spirit who is sucking me into her little world of sassy imagination. I want to get lost and live on nothing but her smile, her jokes, and her incredibly beautiful charm.

When I pull the spoon from between her lips, I watch her mouth expertly work the ice cream around, and when she swallows, all I can think about is what it would be like to see that sinister mouth wrapped around my cock, taking everything I can give her.

Eyes trained on each other, Emma takes the spoon from me, scoops a ball of ice cream and brings it to my mouth. I don't break eye contact with her; instead I stare into those pools of blue, and open wide, letting her slip the spoon into my mouth. I close around the utensil slowly and pull the ice cream off. Her eyes widen and then turn heady when I lift the spoon vertically and lick the metal. Her spare hand that isn't holding the spoon floats down her neck, her fingertips grazing her long column until they get to her collarbone. *Oh hell. That's sexy. And she has no clue.*

I follow her fingertips with my eyes, watching how they graze tenderly across her skin. I imagine my tongue following the same route. When she starts to plunge her fingers down toward the buttons of her top, the pit of my stomach rumbles to life with heat and my cock starts to strain at the zipper of my jeans.

Expertly one-handed, she undoes the top button of her shirt, and then the second and third. Before she goes on with the fourth, she parts the shirt ever so slightly so I can see the swell of her cleavage. Her hair floats like a fucking cloud over her shoulders, cascading down to where her shirt is open for me. How can I not imagine what she would look like with just her hair covering her breasts? The image in my head makes me even fucking harder.

Not feeling like ice cream any longer, I take the spoon, put it in the carton, and set them on the floor next to the sofa. When my hands are free, I immediately grip Emma's waist and reposition her on my lap so she's a little closer and so her pussy is lined up perfectly with my erection. When I settle her down, she gasps, her eyes widening and her breath uneasy.

I bite my bottom lip and look down at her, nodding at her shirt for her to continue. A small smile slides across her mouth as she starts to unbutton the rest, button by button, deliberately taking her time, which I can appreciate because this girl is worth taking time with.

When she reaches the bottom, she doesn't open her shirt, instead she leaves it so I can only see two inches of her soft skin peeking through. She leans forward and the fabric dips with her as she places her hands on my stomach and slowly works them under my shirt. Her palms feel like fire against my skin, igniting me with a sexual awareness I haven't felt in a very long time. As she moves her hands up my stomach, her fingers inspecting every contour of my abs, she brings my shirt up with her until her hands are on my pecs.

Our breaths are heavy with anticipation, the sparks kindling between us, the built-up tension that's on the brink of detonation. My heart hammers rapidly under the palm of her hand as the air stills between us. Our souls connect in this moment. It's as though we're making a silent vow to one another that our friendship will never be the same, but what resides in our near future has the promise of parallel serendipity beyond anything we've ever experienced.

# Chapter Seventeen

## EMMA

I've realized two things: up until now I've never truly felt alive; I've never known the feeling of what it's like to genuinely have an understanding of breathing, of the feeling of a human's touch, of listening to the sound of a beating heart. But with Tucker, his eyes heavy with yearning for me, I can hear distinctly without question the beat of a human heart. I can feel the air I breathe pass through my lungs and pump through my veins, and the contact of skin against skin has never felt so real, so authentic, so utterly transparent. And secondly, what is about to transpire between Tucker and me will forever change me from the woman I am today. I know the minute he buries himself deep inside me, the familiar colors of this world will change, alter in a way that I will forever see differently. It's inevitable with a man like Tucker Jameson.

And even though I'm scared of this change, of the transformation I'm about to embark on, I wouldn't back down for anything. Not for my friend, not for the protection of my heart, and not for the shelter of the imprinted marrow that runs deep within my bones. Because for the life of me, I can't say no to this beautiful man, to his damaged eyes, to the carved jaw that ticks with his emotions, or the heart that beats quickly under the palm of my hand.

I want him.

*I hope he wants me.*

I want him to alter my life.

*Does he want me to alter his?*

I want him to change the colors of my world into a kaleidoscope of tangible, prickly, all-consuming awareness.

*I hope he wants to be a part of me and my life of color.*

"Emma." His voice is husky, on the verge of breaking.

"Take me upstairs, Tucker." *Please.*

His hands quickly button up the button that rests between my breasts, and then in one swift movement, he scoops me into his arms and takes me upstairs, leaving our little dinner party behind without a second thought.

With each creak of the stairs leading to his bedroom, my heart rate picks up. I'm excited. I've never felt this need, this . . . rightness. What will he feel like inside me? Will he be tender? Will he be rough and demanding? Will he compare me to . . . *her*?

No, I can't think about Sadie right now. I can't begin to think about what they might have had together. As attracted adults learning more about each other, this is different. What is between Tucker and me is different, and I'm going to revel in the disparity.

When he reaches his bed, he relies on the light in the stairway to cast the only brightness in the room, leaving the area dim. To me, it feels romantic.

He places me on the floor in front of him and takes a small step back. Eyes still trained on mine, he reaches over his head to his back where he grabs his shirt and quickly tugs it off. I watch in fascination as each and every one of his chest muscles flex in the process, leaving me panting for a redo.

I've never seen a more gorgeous man in my life. From the messy style of his hair, to the thick scruff on his perfectly defined jaw, to the powerful, corded muscles that twist and twine over his athletic chest, he weakens me at the knees. I'm dizzy with lust.

Still looking me in the eyes, he unbuckles his jeans but leaves them on. I glance down for a second to catch a small trail of trimmed hair that leads to the waistband of his black briefs. I want to lick a path down that trail to what he's hiding beneath those dark wash jeans.

When I return my eyes to his, the smirk on his face almost splits me in half. There's no denying my attraction to him. He probably noticed *that* within the first two weeks we were living together. I've never been good at hiding emotions, most notably it seems when it comes to Tucker and his ruggedly handsome features.

He takes a step forward. I can feel a small shiver down my spine in anticipation of his touch, of his kiss, of his body moving flawlessly on top of mine. The space between us closes as he takes one more step forward. The heat emanating off him envelops me into a ball of desire as his hands unbutton my last button. His fingers trail along the edges of my open shirt, sending goosebumps along my skin and a shot of awareness straight to my sex. I'm so wet, even though he hasn't touched me yet.

"I want you so fucking bad, Emma."

"Take me, Tucker," I say on a whisper, hoping and praying his stalling has nothing to do with second-guessing. Please let him be ready.

He gnaws on his bottom lip for a second before both his hands trail a line over my collarbone until they push the shirt off my shoulders and onto the floor. His eyes are on mine for a brief second before they flick to my breasts. I don't have to look down to know my nipples are hard. I can feel them tingling in awareness, yearning to be touched, sucked, licked. *Yearning for him.*

Tucker slowly takes me in, his eyes not giving him away but from the way he's running his hand over his rough jaw, I can tell he's feeling the same way I am, nervous with a whole bunch of desire.

"Fuck, Emma." His hand glides over his mouth in awe. "You're so goddamn beautiful."

The compliment hits me hard, giving me a boost of confidence I desperately needed.

We *are* a separate entity from our past, from his past.

Leaving me topless without his touch, he hooks his fingers in the waistband of my pajama pants and slips them down my legs, exposing nothing but a red thong that matches the hearts on my pajamas. A low groan travels up his throat as he takes me in. He links our hands together and helps me step out of my pants. I kick them to the side with my shirt so they're out of the way. Releasing one of my hands, he slowly spins me around, stopping me when my back is toward him.

He stops and grips my shoulders tenderly until he slides his hands down my arms, to my ribcage where his fingers barely graze the side of my breasts. I take in a sharp hiss of a breath from the contact, my core heating up with every touch. Slowly, his hands glide down my sides until he reaches my hips. His body presses flush against mine, and his lips find my neck where he lightly kisses me and whispers, "Your ass is so fuckable, baby. I've dreamt of this ass. I've had visions of punishing this little ass, of biting into it, claiming it as mine." His lips dance across the space between my neck and shoulder, sending chills all over my body.

He slips his hands under the thin strap of my thong and pushes it down, leaving me bare to the cool night air.

Behind me, I can feel the roughness of his jeans against my legs, and the sensation of my burning skin against his pants sends a wave of yearning through my body.

Hands still on my hips, he leans his head forward and brings his lips from my shoulder up the column of my neck to my ear where he whispers, "I knew you were gorgeous, Emma, but fuck me, you naked makes me want to worship every inch of your body." He nips at my ear. "Combine that with your heart and your mind? I'm drowning in desperation for you."

Does he know I feel the same? That his heart is just as kind, that his mind turns me on, that his protective instincts make me want to never leave his side?

While he kisses my neck, his tongue peeking out every once in a while, his teeth nipping at my skin, his hands move to the front of my body, his palms spanning over my stomach. His touch is warm, demanding, and all I can do is lean my head back so I'm resting on his shoulder.

"What do you want me to do to you, Emma?" His voice brushes against my skin, making my nipples even harder if possible. His hands go higher to the point where they rest right below my breasts.

Everything inside me is pounding with need, a throbbing craving taking root in my center, vibrating through my bones, reminding me just how turned on I am.

"Everything, Tucker," I gasp when he nips at my neck. There is no doubt that will leave a mark tomorrow.

"Tell me what you want." His lips are right next to my ear again, his teeth tugging on my earlobe. The shy side of me clams up. I've never been approached like this during sex, being asked what I want. It's always just been given to me, sometimes with less finesse than desired.

Helping me out, he whispers, "Tell me, Emma. Do you want my hands plucking these tight nipples of yours? Do you want my thick fingers sliding into your wet cunt only to be followed by my tongue? Do you want me to bend you over this bed and spank that delicious ass of yours until you cry out in pure ecstasy? Or do you want me to spread you across my bed, hands held above your head, while I slowly pulse in and out of you until you can't take the languid strokes of my thick cock inside your tight pussy any longer?"

My breath escapes me, my mind is a whirl of yeses, a mash-up of *please, God, let this happen* and *holy shit I want him to fuck me immediately*. I want to scream yes to everything but I'm speechless, unable to voice my opinion from the ball of need clogging my throat.

"Not going to answer? Fine, baby, but that means I get total control." Within a second, he has me spun around, facing him. My hands fall to his chest for support. His muscles flex under my palms reminding me of the sexy and strong man he's become. He lifts my chin and says, "Don't want to tell me what you want, then you're at my mercy. Can you do that? Give me total control?"

I swallow hard and my voice sounds miles away as I speak. "Is that what you want?"

He shifts in his stance and cups my face with his hands. "I *want* to make you come until you pass out."

I can't help it. I swallow hard again. "I want that too."

"Good."

He doesn't take a second for me to catch my breath before he's laying me down on the bed and parting my legs so he can position himself over me. Still with his jeans undone, his hair slightly askew, and a heated look in his eyes, he places his hands on either side of my head and lowers his mouth to mine where he gently parts my lips with his tongue.

I grant him access, not putting up any sort of a fight. *Why would I? How could I?* I want this. I need this. I will explode without this.

Our mouths meld together, slowly. There is no rush in his movements; it's as if he's imprinting every single flick of our tongues, movement of our mouths, and nibble of our teeth in his brain. I would be lying if I said I wasn't doing the same thing.

There is something about kissing another human, of fusing your mouths together, exploring, that can make or break an experience. From one kiss, I can tell if the man I'm locking lips with is worth the effort, if there's hope for a future between us. The first time Tucker kissed me, I knew I was doomed. But now? I know I'll be ruined for life.

He doesn't mindlessly kiss me as a way to get to the next step. No. There is purpose in each flick of his tongue, of every movement of his mouth, as if he has a blueprint to my arousal and he's following it step by step.

His body barely presses against mine, leaving his lips in charge, making me feel overwhelmed, needy, and so hot for him that I can't control myself. I put my hands on his cheeks and try to pull him closer but fail when he pulls away. Lips swollen, he looks me in the eyes and says, "Hands linked above your head; keep them there until I say you can touch me."

"Tucker . . ."

"You gave me control, baby. Trust me and listen." When he calls me babe, I melt. When he calls me baby, I fall further and further for this man.

I link my hands and raise them above my head, which brings my breasts closer together. He groans when he takes me in, and when I think he's going to return to my mouth for more kissing, he scoots down my body until his head is even with my chest. With his knee propping him up between my legs, he runs his left index finger in circles around my right nipple. He barely touches me, just circling and circling—*madly*—until I can feel my hips start to ride his jean-clad leg looking for release. He lifts his fingers and goes to the other nipple where he does the same kind of torture, burning me from the inside out.

My clit pounds. *I need. Need him so much.*

"God," I gasp, surprising myself. I've never been one to vocalize during sex, but the way Tucker makes me feel, it's hard to keep my mouth shut. "Tucker, touch me."

"I am," he whispers.

"Squeeze me," I say on a moan, my hips really starting to move against his leg.

"Who's in charge, baby?"

"You," I groan, my eyes shut now as his nose starts to skim across my jaw, his breath hot and sweet on my neck.

His fingers continue to circle my nipple as he says, "Good." His voice is firm and just when I think he's going to continue to torture me, he pinches my nipple so hard that my upper body arches in response and a low moan escapes past my kiss-swollen lips. "Fuck, that's sexy," he mumbles, making his way down my neck to my breasts.

He continues to pluck and pull at my nipple while his mouth pays attention to the other, sucking it between his teeth where he nibbles, pressing down with just the right amount of pressure that I think I might just come from his touch alone. His mouth is so hot, so wet on my burning skin, causing a myriad of sensations to roll through my body. My clit pounds, begs, seeks release as his hands and mouth work along my breasts. He's single-minded in his efforts; torture Emma in all the right ways.

Hands above my head, my naked body melting into the

coolness of his comforter, I lose myself as this gorgeous man tongue-fucks my breasts, squeezing them with his hands, occasionally flicking my nipples, making me so aroused that I can't feel anything but the solid, relentless beat that drums between my thighs.

Release.

Need it.

Badly.

I wiggle under him, knowing my efforts will go unnoticed by Tucker who has his own agenda, but I need to make it known that he's driven me to the brink, that I'm there, provoked by his touch, ready, wet, and waiting.

"Tucker," I breathe out heavily. "I'm so wet." The words feel foreign coming from me, in such a sensual moment, but they also feel right, like I was meant to save them for this exact minute. It's as though Tucker was brought into my life at this time to pull them out of me.

He hums over my breasts and lowers his head to my stomach, making me hyper aware of what he'll do next. The feel of his scruff along my sensitive skin heightens my senses, acting as an electric bolt through my veins, turning the lights on deep within me. I never realized that up until this moment, sex had been an insignificant shadow, a passionless burning only Tucker Jameson could ignite.

"You taste like sweet honey," he murmurs, working his way farther south. "Fuck, why did I wait so long for this? *For you?*" Gliding his hands down my stomach, he moves them past my hips to my thighs where he spreads them wide to accommodate for his broad shoulders. I'm completely exposed to him, in one of the most raw ways possible, and I feel nothing but comfort. Ready.

His jaw deliciously scratches its way down to just above

my pubic bone. He rests his chin on the center of my legs and leisurely runs his tongue back and forth over the sensitive skin a few inches below my belly button. I squirm relentlessly beneath him, just a few more inches . . .

"Has anyone every fucked you with their tongue, Emma?"

My mind feels like fog, his voice heavy in my heart but not registering as I'm clouded with anticipation. "What?" I ask, my breath heavy with each pass through my lungs.

He moves farther down, his face directly between my legs. With two fingers, he parts my slit and leans forward while looking up at me with those devastatingly smoldering blue-green eyes. "Has anyone ever"—he lowers his head. My heart starts to beat out of my chest, my entire body tingling with numbness. His tongue peeks out of his mouth and very lightly, almost as if he doesn't touch me, licks the length of my slit—"tongue fucked you?"

My eyes are sealed shut, unable to bare the pleasure that waits for me. Above me, my fists grip onto the pillow my head rests on and I shake my head.

"I want to hear it from your beautiful lips. Tell me no one has ever tongue fucked you. Tell me I'm the first."

Finding my voice, I weakly say, "You're the first, Tucker. You're the first man to tongue fuck me."

He sighs and then shakes his head, his scruff rubbing against my inner thighs. I want more of that. "How is that even fucking possible?" He kisses me gently on my inner thighs, getting so close, that one swipe of his tongue gives me nothing and only makes me more frustrated. "Fun fact, Emma, I like eating pussy." My legs clench from his confession, which makes him lightly chuckle. "But you're going to have to show me those peepers of yours before I taste you. Open your eyes, Emma."

In so much need, I do as he says, connecting with him in one of the most intimate ways possible.

"That's it, baby. Keep those eyes on mine this whole time. Do not close them. I want to see you fall apart while I fuck you with my tongue. Got it, beautiful girl?"

I nod, feeling tears stinging the backs of my eyes for an unknown reason. Everything is heightened in me right now. I blame the threatening tears on that, not on the way Tucker seems to look straight into my soul.

"Good."

He kisses me a few more times on my inner thighs until he moves his mouth over my center and flattens his tongue. His eyes trained on me, he presses his tongue against my clit and moves it upward applying just enough pressure to make me scream out his name.

"Tucker." I moan, my head falling back from my impending release, which I know will come sooner than expected.

My legs fall farther apart and when I situate myself for the ride of my lifetime, Tucker's tongue ceases to move. What? Is he teasing again? Please, I can't take any more of this.

When I look down at him, he smiles. "That's it, baby. Keep those eyes on me."

Crap.

Eyes.

Focus.

Bracing myself with my elbows, I lift up so I can completely focus on the way his tongue lusciously swipes along my slit. I've never felt anything like it. I've never SEEN anything like it. A man, so desperately happy to be resting between my thighs, eyes fixated on mine while his mouth works magic on me, kissing, nibbling . . . sucking. It's too much.

My legs feel like they're floating on clouds, my body lifeless, the only feeling coursing through my body is a light prickling sensation screaming through my veins, preparing me for my fall. The buildup is strong, heady, overwhelming. My breathing erratic with each swipe, with each pull on my clit, with every hum from his mouth.

I'm climbing, reaching, vibrating with release, on the edge.

"Yes," I whisper. My stomach drops, my clit pounds against his tongue. "Yes." I get louder. My body starts to shake. "Yes!" Tunnel vision collapses around me, the only thing in my sight is Tucker staring up at me. He winks and then rapidly flicks his tongue over my clit, pushing me off the edge into a downward spiral of unrelenting pleasure. Sparks fly in my head, my stomach bottoms out, and I scream, "YESSSS!"

I try to keep my eyes open. I try not to pass out from the onslaught of my orgasm, from the white-hot pleasure taking me under, blacking me out from the world around us. But I fail as I collapse onto the bed while Tucker casually continues to lick me, his strokes becoming slower and slower with each pass until he finally lifts off the mattress and stands on the side of the bed.

He keeps his eyes on me, his hair more of a mess than before . . . did I do that? I can't even remember. His voice is husky when he speaks. "That was the fucking sexiest thing I've ever seen." His hands go to his jeans where there is an unmistakable bulge. "But I can't give you much time to recover, baby. I need inside you. Now." There is no question in his sentence, just a statement, as if there is no other option for him.

With the energy left inside me, I roll to my side, push my hair out of my face and say, "How do you want me?"

I'm not imagining it. I know I'm not, but his eyes get darker, more sexy, as if I just said the very thing he was hoping to hear. One hand on his jeans, he assesses me with a tilt of his head. He's gorgeous, standing tall, his abs contracting, his strong forearm flexing as he rubs his jaw, his tanned and toned body silhouetted by the stairway light. He's positively sinister.

"I would say on your stomach so I can dig my fingers into your ass while I'm buried inside of you but I need to see your face. I want to know the exact moment you feel me bottoming out inside of you."

Oh God, can someone orgasm just from words? Because I'm pretty sure I just did.

"Stay where you are, I'll move you how I want you." He winks and then pulls his jeans off his body, leaving him with only a pair of black briefs and a straining erection. The sex-er-gizer bunny inside me wants to hoot and holler at him to take it all off, but I bite my tongue and wait for him to give me a show. "You're killing me with your looks, Emma."

"What looks?"

"Like you want to wrap those luscious lips around my cock." He sticks his hand in his briefs and cups himself.

Fuck. Me.

He nods at his nightstand and says, "Grab a condom for me, Emma, and open it."

Oh God, this is really happening. I mean, I know this is happening. He's already had his head buried between my thighs, we are by far past the line of friendship here, but this next step, this is a big one. This will really change everything and for the life of me, I can't seem to stop myself from moving forward.

I reach over into his nightstand, find a condom, and when I look back up at him, his eyes are fixed on my body, his briefs are tossed to the side, and he's casually stroking his massive erection.

*Nine inches deep.*

He was not exaggerating.

"Shit, babe, that innocent look on your face is splitting me in half. Put the condom on the mattress and lie back down."

Not able to take my eyes off his cock, wondering how it's going to feel inside me, I lie down and wait. I watch impatiently as he breaks open the foil wrapper and sheathes himself. For a second, he stands next to me, giving my body a once-over as he cups his balls. His cock stands to attention, tempting me to stroke it, but before I can get the courage to do so, he's kneeling on the bed and hovering over me.

"Spread your legs, Emma." The tone of his voice is low, gravelly, strained almost.

"Do I still have to hold my hands above my head?" I ask as I spread my legs, hoping he says no.

He shakes his head. "I want to feel your hands on my body when I come inside of you."

Before I can answer, his mouth is on mine and his body is pressing against me, his erection rubbing along my leg is starting up that burning need once again. Knowing I can have a little bit of control of my own, I cup his face and really revel in this moment, in the way Tucker kisses like he means it, leaving everything on the table, not shying away from making his intentions known. *He wants me.*

His lips move against mine seamlessly, his tongue pressing, tangling, smoothing along mine, his teeth occasionally pulling on my bottom lip until I gasp, only for him to soothe the area with his tongue. It's so damn sensual that I feel dizzy; my mind turns to mud, shutting down all my other senses. My soul focus is on him and the way he makes me feel.

Which is absolutely incredible, like I'm the greatest gift he's ever received.

"Need inside you," he murmurs along my lips just before he pulls away and sits up. He grips his cock, looks down at my entrance and leans forward, planting one hand on the mattress as he slowly rubs the tip of his cock along my wet slit.

"Oh yes," I moan, wiggling forward, encouraging him to keep moving, to finally make that connection I've been dying for.

His eyes fall to mine just as he starts to enter me. He's thicker than any man I've ever been with so he feels like he's stretching me to full capacity. My mouth falls open from his girth, from the slow pace he's going, and when he asks if he's hurting me, all I can do is shake my head and answer, "More." He grunts and pushes deeper until he's fully inside me.

I have to take deep breaths as I allow myself to adjust, to let his length settle in. I can't help it, the words fall from my lips before I can stop them. "You're so big, Tucker. I don't know if I can take it."

"Shhh," he coos in my ear as he lowers himself. "Just relax, baby, take deep breaths."

"I'm just so full."

He peppers kisses along my jaw, loosening the tension building inside me. As he makes his way up and down my neck with his mouth, I let my hands wander over his body from his strong shoulders, to his corded back. It's never been like this for me. I've never known sex to feel this . . . this fulfilled. *Taken.* I've never had such a strong, capable, sweet, and sexy man to hold on to, and to dote on me.

And now that I have it, I don't know if I'll ever be able to let go.

"You feel so fucking good, Emma." His hips start to move, pumping his cock in and out of me. He's slow at first, giving me a chance to accommodate his thrusts, but once he finds I've relaxed, that my legs have spread wider for him, he picks up his pace and pushes against the mattress, holding his body above mine.

I can't help but glance at our connection, at the way Tucker's abs contract with each thrust, at his ripped arms and pecs flexing and straining. I've never needed to *watch* during sex, but this is beyond hot and it spurs me on.

"Need more," he grunts. So he picks up my leg and drapes it over his shoulder causing my body to twist just slightly and giving him a better angle. That's when he hits that spot and my eyes shoot wide open as well as my mouth.

"Oh fuck." He starts to pound into me, knowing exactly how he's bringing me so close to the edge. "Oh, Tucker, right there. Oh my God."

My entire body starts to tingle, hum, and burn with awareness. One of his hands grips my leg that's slung over his shoulder, the other is braced on my hip as he continues to thrust. Every muscle in his chest strains, flexes, and works to bring us both pleasure. *He's so beautiful. I want him to be mine.*

"Christ." He quickens his pace. I welcome the force and open wider for him. I have nothing to grip since he's propped up, so I press my hands against the headboard and push against him when he pushes into me.

That does it.

My vision goes black, my walls tighten around him, and pure pleasure shoots through me, the kind of pleasure I've never felt before. Everything is different with this man. The way he touches me, the way he talks to me . . . the way he looks at me. *The way he feels inside my body.* It's all so intoxicating. I'm drowning in his presence.

"Fuck, I'm going to come, baby," Tucker calls out right before he stills and grunts out one of the sexiest sounds I've ever heard. His expression is soaked in pleasure, his eyes tight for a second before they open and spot me as he takes a deep breath and smiles.

Oh God. Right there. That's the reason he could break my

heart and shatter it to pieces. That one boyish look . . . it guts me.

I catch my breath as Tucker cleans up, but I don't get much time to think because he's quickly hopping back in bed, putting us both under the covers, and bringing me into his chest where my head rests. He strokes my hair as I snuggle into him.

We are silent for a second, unsure of what to say after having such a momentous event, but Tucker doesn't take long to come up with something, to solidify this man forever in my heart.

"I never knew the girl who used to scold me for peeing off a back porch would be the girl who would flip my world upside down." He lets out a long breath. "Fuck, Emma, you're so goddamn perfect. That was perfect. We were perfect. " *He's absolutely correct.*

I dance my fingers across his chest and kiss his jaw. "It was perfect."

"There is one thing I need to bring up though."

My stomach twists in a knot, wondering if I did something wrong. Wondering if he's going to mention *her*. "Uh, what's that?"

He clears his throat and says, "You owe me a new gallon of ice cream, because that cookie dough is melted to shit right about now."

I giggle into his chest and nod with a sigh of relief. "That's fair . . . DJ Hot Cock."

That gets a chuckle out of him. He kisses the top of my head and says, "Very accurate description, huh?"

"Spot on." I smile to myself, loving that even after we crossed the point of no return, we can still be us. Because it's just Tucker and me. That's it, no one else.

But, I still can't help wondering as Tucker starts to drift off into a slumber, was this how he was with her? Light and breezy after sex? Did they cuddle? Did he tell her she was perfect? Did he shatter her world with one night in bed?

Because I think he'll shatter mine, right into a million unfixable pieces.

# Chapter Eighteen

## TUCKER

The ringing of my alarm pulls me out of my deep slumber. I quickly turn it off before it can be more obnoxious than it already is.

Not wanting to wake Emma, I carefully slip from under her grasp and slide out of bed, making sure to line up my pillow for her to snuggle against. It does the trick as she readjusts and makes a cute little humming sound as she nuzzles her head.

I take a moment to observe her. Her chestnut-brown hair is a mess from my hands, her breathing is steady—an even rhythm that soothes me—and her mouth is slightly open, reminding me of just how deliciously dirty her mouth was last night.

I run my hand over my face and shake my head. I fucked Emma Marks. Not just once, but three times. Three fucking times.

I tug on my hair and go to my closet where I grab my running clothes and shoes. Naked, I tiptoe downstairs, dress, and lace up my shoes.

I need to clear my head. I need to process everything from last night.

I strap my phone to my arm, press shuffle on my running

playlist, and take off when I've shut the side door to the house. I don't bother with a warm-up; I get straight into my pace and turn toward Port Dickson Community Park.

*Coldplay's* "The Scientist" streams through my earbuds, providing a thoughtful melody for me to run to, maybe a little too thoughtful as the lyrics immediately start to speak to me.

"Nobody said it was easy, it's such a shame for us to part . . ."

My feet pound against the pavement, my knees absorbing little shock from the vibrations, jolting my body more than usual. I'm stiff, confused, fucking terrified. I slept with another woman, a woman that wasn't Sadie.

"Take me back to the start . . ." The song hits me square in the fucking heart where it rests heavy with . . . fuck, I don't know what's weighing it down. Regret? No, I don't regret last night. There is no way I could ever regret the connection I shared with Emma or the way she so effortlessly gave me her body. Nor how much I loved taking her body.

So if it's not regret, then why do I feel like I'm sitting in a choke hold, the ability to breathe becoming less and less with each step forward?

I had sex with another woman. That thought is on replay in my head. I kissed Emma, ran my tongue along every part of her body, buried myself deep within her, fucked her, and came in her while her name slipped off my tongue. And when we passed out, I held on to her, tightly, as if I let go, she would disappear just like Sadie did.

Christ.

I pick up my pace, straining my muscles in the chilly morning air.

Last night was the first night in over a year that I felt . . . at peace. It was even better than the other two nights I've slept with Emma in my arms, but for once, there was no doubt. Unease.

There weren't any questions in my mind of what I could have done better, of how I could have saved my relationship, how I could have possibly helped Sadie during the miscarriage. I never once thought about the baby we created, if it was a boy or a girl. The nursery didn't call my name; it didn't sit like an anvil of *what ifs* on my chest. And I didn't have an urge to bolt out of the house I bought for Sadie, to flee from the giant reminder of what I lost. Instead, I spent my night tangled next to an exquisite woman who graced me with her beautiful heart and showered me with her irresistible cuteness in those goddamn pajamas.

Fuck, I like those things. I like her. I like her a lot, and I think that's what terrifies me. For the first time in so long, I'm not pining for the girl I always thought I'd marry. *The woman of my past.*

I pause and run my hands through my hair.

*Emma.* I want to be with her. I want to hold her, make dinner with her, listen to fucking *One Direction* while she giggles in my arms. I want to wear matching lobster oven mitts and high five over shitty soup. I want her for her quirks, her smile, her beautiful brain, and her loving and caring heart.

"Shit," I mutter, turning back toward the house.

"Here Comes the Sun" by The Beatles plays on my phone, acting almost as an epiphany as I sprint-run back to the house with one thought on my mind: Emma.

*Little darling, it's been a long cold lonely winter. Little darling, it feels like years since it's been here . . .*

*Here comes the sun . . .*

• • •

I slam the side door shut, tear off my phone strap and toss it on the counter along with my earbuds, and head toward the stairs when I see Emma's light on in her bedroom. She's not a morning

235

person, why is she up?

I open the door to her bedroom, startling her in place. She's wearing her pajama top and thong, and that's it. Her hair is a mess like always in the morning, which makes me smile until I see her red-rimmed eyes and tear-stained face.

"Hey, what's wrong?" I start toward her, but she puts up her hand.

"Please just leave me alone, Tucker."

"Like hell I will." Not allowing her any space, I come up in front of her, grip her cheeks, and wipe away the tears on her face. "What's wrong, Emma?"

She shakes her head and presses her hands on my sweat-soaked shirt. "I don't need your pity, Tucker."

"Pity? What the fuck are you talking about?"

She takes a look at me, actually takes me all in and bites on her bottom lip for a second. "You . . . you went for a run?"

"Yeah. I run every morning. What the hell is going on?" Her face flushes and I slowly start to connect the dots. *Surely she wouldn't think . . .*

"Did you think I just got up and left?"

She looks away, clearly embarrassed. "Maybe."

I can't stop the chuckle that pops out of me. Outraged from the humor I find in the situation, she shoves my chest and says, "It's not funny. What am I supposed to think? I woke up and you were gone. I came downstairs to see if you were making eggs and you weren't here. I assumed you regretted everything and tried to get the hell out of here." She points to the open suitcase on the bed and adds, "I was going to start packing to make it less awkward."

"Yeah, and where were you going to go with that little suitcase of yours?" I wrap my arms around her waist and pull her into my body.

236

Trying to save face, she lifts her chin and says, "Logan's. He would have taken me in."

That doesn't sit well with me. "Like hell you would go there."

She sighs heavily. "He doesn't—"

"He sure as fuck does. He's just waiting to make his move. He needs to know you're off limits."

"You don't own me."

I laugh and tip her chin. "That's cute, Emma." I lean forward and kiss along her jaw until I reach her ear. "Pretty sure last night I owned every last inch of you."

She tilts her head to the side and lets out a long breath. "That means nothing." *Nothing? I don't think so.*

I bite on her earlobe and palm her ass at the same time. "It means everything, baby. Now come take a shower with me."

Not giving her a chance to protest, I link her hand with mine and take her into the bathroom. I tear my shirt off over my head and lean into the shower and turn it on, letting the water heat up. When I turn back to Emma, she seems nervous by the way she's fidgeting her hands in front of her.

"What's wrong?"

She shrugs and fidgets with the waistband of my briefs that are peeking past my running pants. "The lights are on. You're going to see all of me."

"So? My tongue was all over your body last night, are you really going to be shy now?"

"It was dark, you couldn't see any, you know, weird lumps and whatnot." *Does the girl not know how fucking gorgeous she is?*

"Babe, I can guarantee there are no weird lumps. Now stop being ridiculous and take a shower with me." She still looks uncertain, shy, which is so odd to me given what we did last night. "Emma, it's me. There is nothing you should be shy about."

"I know, but it is *you*, Tucker. I never in a million years would have thought you and I would have shared a night like last night."

I tilt my head to the side. "Are you having second thoughts about last night?" My gut churns from the thought of her regretting everything we did. Call me a dick, but it never crossed my mind that Emma would feel remorse about what we did. Seeing her with tears in her eyes, thinking I had left her, actually gives me confidence. She wants us. *How could she think I didn't want her to stay?*

She shakes her head, easing the twisting in my stomach. "No, I don't have any regrets."

I cup her face and press a light kiss against her lips. "Good, because neither do I. In fact, I want a repeat." My hands go to her shirt where I start to unbutton it. She assists me as well, starting from the bottom and once we have them all undone, I shove the fabric off her shoulders and watch it float to the floor before I take her all in.

I run my hand over my jaw, standing there in her red thong that does nothing to cover her up. Her breasts are marked from my scruff, beard burn trails over her body from where my mouth was last night, and lucky for me, her nipples are already puckered, ready to be sucked into my mouth.

"You're gorgeous, Emma. Why you're nervous I have no clue. You're so fucking sexy." Just from the sight of her, I'm hard and I want to prove it to her. I take her hand and place it on my erection. Her eyes go wide as they find mine. "See what you do to me, baby? You make me so fucking hard, just standing there. So don't you ever for one moment feel self-conscious around me. Okay?"

She nods and then a wicked gleam flashes in her eyes. Hand still on my cock, she lightly squeezes. Oh fuck, it feels like my eyes roll in the back of my head just from the small touch. She literally has no idea what she does to me.

"Careful what you start, Emma, if you don't plan on finishing it," I breathe out.

Stepping away, she drops her thong to the floor and then slips her hand past the shower curtain to test the water. Clearly pleased with the temperature, she slips in but not before she says, "Joining me?"

Hell yeah.

I strip down in two seconds and slip past the shower curtain where I'm greeted by a very wet Emma. Her head moves slowly under the shower as water runs down her body. I follow the rivulets tumble past her breasts, to her flat stomach and all the way down her legs.

Hell . . .

"Are you trying to torture me?"

She pops her eyes open and smiles. When she looks down, she sees my cock straining for her touch. She glances up at me, almost like she's asking for permission, before she steps out of the water and reaches for my erection. She strokes me, lightly, curving her hand up and over the tip. I watch her small hand work me, loving how she has a rhythm, a reason for everything she's doing. When her other hand cups my balls, I groan louder than expected as pleasure shoots up my spine.

"Babe, slow down."

She doesn't listen. No, her strokes become tighter, harder, longer.

"Fuck, Emma . . ." My breathing becomes labored, my legs start to shake, and with every squeeze of my balls, I can feel my impending orgasm.

"I want to see you come," she says. "I want to see how I make you feel."

I had other plans for us in this shower, but I can't deny her request, not when she looks at me with those passion-filled eyes.

Shit. I'll have to revert to plan B.

I place one hand against the tiled wall to steady myself and lace the other through her hair as I say, "Then make me come."

Pleased, her grip grows tighter, making me pop up on my toes with each stroke. I grind my teeth together, loving the pull she has on me, the way I feel in her hands. Fuck, she's so damn good at this. When she rolls my balls in the palm of her hand and squeezes the tip of my dick, my legs almost give out on me as everything turns black. I climb so high that when I fall over the edge with one final stroke, I come so hard in her hand that I feel like I'm about to fall to the tiled floor.

A roar rips from me, her hand a vise on my balls, my hips pumping feverously as I expel every last ounce inside me. The water washes away my cum, but when I open my eyes to look at Emma, I can see she's completely and utterly satisfied. *Magnificent.*

Leisurely, she moves her hand over my dick as the other presses against my beating heart. "One touch from you, Tucker, and I'll be coming on your hand. That was so hot. I need you to take care of the ache you've put between my legs." *No way in hell I could deny that request. Not from this girl.*

Catching my breath, I watch her wiggle next to me, searching release. "How wet are you?"

"So wet. So ready. Fuck me, Tucker."

I raise an eyebrow at her. "This coming from the girl who, only a short while ago, was afraid to be naked with me in the daylight."

She shrugs and runs her finger over my jaw, her nail trailing along the scruff. "You make me feel beautiful."

I cup her face and look her in the eyes. "You are beautiful,

Emma."

With that, I push her under the water and then against the wall. The shower sprays off my back as I raise both of her hands above her head and clasp them against the wall with one of mine. She smiles brightly, knowing what's coming next.

"Spread your legs." She does as she's told so I finger the outside of her pussy. "You want relief, right here?"

She nods. "Yes." Her voice is but a whisper. "I need it, Tucker."

"Tell me, Emma"—I move my mouth over her cheeks, down her jaw, to her neck, and then nip at her nipples—"Is your clit hard for me?"

I clamp down on one of her nipples just as she says, "God, yes."

Knowing I don't have all morning, I move my hand down to her pussy where she groans from the contact and start rubbing her clit with my thumb as I insert two fingers inside her. She gasps from the insertion, pauses momentarily, but then relaxes and lets me work my hand as I play with her nipple in my mouth.

Her hips rotate against my hand and as the hot water pelts me, and I take in the moment when her pussy clenches around my fingers and she pants my name while her orgasm eclipses her stunning face. I love how vocal she is. It's sexy as hell.

She starts to fall from the clouds as she goes limp against the wall. I scoop her up and bring her under the water to warm her body. She rests her head against my chest and hugs my waist as the shower splashes around us. It's a personal and intimate moment, one I've never experienced. It's *us. Emma and Tucker.* Honestly? I want to soak it all in because this right here, this makes me happy. *My beautiful, incredible Emma makes me happy.*

• • •

"Why are you smiling?"

I point to my chest. "I'm not smiling, you're smiling."

Emma sits on the counter, her wet hair tied in a bun, an oversized shirt covering her otherwise naked body, and a cup of coffee in her hands. She's smiling like a fool as she watches me make the eggs she requested when we were drying off after our shower. Unlike her, I need to get to work so fucking Julius doesn't go off on one of his egotistical rants.

"I'm not smiling," she lies as she tries to hide her smirk behind her coffee cup, her *Monday* coffee cup.

I set the spatula down on the stove, fuck spoon rests, and saunter over to her. I situate myself between her legs and place my hands on her thighs.

"You're smiling and I can guess two reasons why." I hold up my fingers as I count them off. "Sex in the shower and me eating you out on the sink." I couldn't help it; I needed to taste her one more time before I left her.

"Did anyone ever tell you you're a cocky son of a bitch?" She puts her coffee cup on the counter and runs her hands over my shoulders.

"Thick dicks are usually cocky, babe," I tease, garnering an eye-roll from her and a chuckle from me.

"Oh my God, I hate you."

"Nah, you don't hate me. You like my dick way too much."

"Eh." She shrugs and then says, "Now your tongue, that I can keep around."

"Hey"—my brows knit together—"you're going to give my dick a complex."

She pats my crotch gently. "He'll just have to prove himself tonight. Show me he's the better muscle." She rubs her hands together. "Tongue versus dick, I wonder who's going to win."

I laugh and rub her thighs. "Sounds like you're the winner in

242

the end."

She gives me an adorable smile. "Yeah, pretty much."

I shake my head and kiss her quickly on the forehead before going back to the eggs. "You're sex-crazed."

"This coming from the man who had to lick me one more time before he went to work."

I glance over my shoulder at her and say, "Wanted to make sure you tasted the same, see if you were as good as I remembered."

"And the verdict?"

"You tasted better." I wink and grab two plates for our eggs. I dish out our breakfast and take the plates to our little card table in the dining room. Emma follows behind me with silverware and our coffee. We work seamlessly together and it feels so . . . natural. I've never experienced this either.

She takes her first bite of the eggs and moans with her eyes closed. I watch her mouth chew and swallow which only causes me to have to readjust myself in my chair. When she takes another bite and moans, I clear my throat and say, "All right, no more egg moaning."

"Egg moaning?" She looks genuinely confused.

I point my fork at her. "When you eat, keep your happy-stomach moans to yourself. You're making me hard."

"You're getting hard watching me eat eggs?"

"No," I adjust again. "I'm getting hard hearing you moan, which just so happens to be the same sound you make when I rub my nose along your inner thigh. So cut it out."

She crosses her arms over her chest and studies me for a second, trying to tell if I'm serious. I am, I am so fucking serious. No egg moaning. "Fine," she answers. "If I can't moan while eating eggs, you can't wear those clothes."

"What?" I look down at my white Henley and work jeans. "What's wrong with my work clothes?"

"There's nothing wrong with them, they're just . . . too tight. They make your chest look massive and heaven forbid I don't see your abs poking through, trying to say hello. Every time you move, some kind of muscle bulges. Have you ever heard of the size up? Honestly," she huffs.

I look down at my shirt; it's not too tight. It fits perfectly. "It's an extra large, that's what I wear. It fits fine."

She motions to my biceps. "Those pythons are trying to reach out and bite me."

A rip of laughter pops out of me from her terminology. "Pythons?"

"You know what I mean. It's just not fair. So if I can't egg moan, you can't wear those shirts."

"Okay," I answer, agreeing easily.

"Okay." She nods, happy with herself. As she scoops up more eggs, I reach behind me and pull my shirt over my head where I toss it on the back of my chair. When I turn back around to face her, her mouth is open, eggs still on the fork, staring at my chest. "What are you doing?"

I look down at my bare chest and then back up at her. "You said you didn't want me to wear that shirt around you, so I took care of the problem."

She drops the fork of eggs on her plate and leans back in her chair while crossing her arms over her chest. "You don't play fair, Jameson."

I wink at her. "Never said I did, baby."

She mumbles something under her breath and then cocks an eyebrow at me. "Fine." Before I can respond, she grabs the hem of her shirt and pulls it over her head, dropping the garment to the floor and revealing her delicious naked body. With a wicked and smarmy smile, she picks up her fork and starts eating her eggs again . . . while moaning.

Tou-fucking-ché. *With emphasis on the fucking . . .*

# Chapter Nineteen

## EMMA

*Tucker: I can't decide what to have for dinner tonight. I'm torn.*

*Emma: Is this one of those interludes where you say something like you can't choose between chicken wings or what I'm serving between my legs?*

*Tucker: Awfully full of ourselves, wouldn't you say?*

*Emma: . . .*

*Tucker: I was going to suggest soup and sandwiches or beef tips in gravy.*

*Emma: Is beef tips and gravy some kind of code for your dick and my juice?*

*Tucker: Christ, Emma. LOL. NO! I actually like beef tips.*

*Emma: So you weren't alluding to eating me out or having sex at any point during this texting conversation.*

*Tucker: No.*

*Emma: Tucker . . .*

*Tucker: EMMA . . .*

*Emma: TUCKER JAMESON!*

*Tucker: Fine, I originally was going to say either spaghetti or your pussy. Happy?*

*Emma: Completely satisfied.*

*Tucker: Is it weird that I want to kiss you so fucking bad right now?*

My heart floats in my chest as I read his text over and over again. The smile that graces my lips is a permanent fixture these days. No matter how hard I try, I can't seem to shake it.

"You're in a good mood," Logan says, pulling my head away from my phone and back to the books in front of me.

"Huh?"

He points his pencil at me. "Your smile. Did someone tell you that you'll never have to stick another person with a needle again?"

"Am I?" I try to make my face normal, less smiley, but it's almost impossible. Tucker makes me happy. It's been a month since we first slept together and since then, it's been every night, every morning, and anytime we're near each other. He's insatiable. Hell, so am I. I can't keep myself away from him or out of his bed, or out of his arms, or away from his demanding lips. And I don't want to.

"Yeah. I haven't seen you in days and now your head is buried in your phone rather than your books, and you can't stop grinning like a fool. What's going on?"

Confession. I haven't told Logan about Tucker. Adalyn knows, she knew the second she saw me after Tucker and I had sex. I think her exact words were, "You boned him, didn't you?" It's hard to hide anything from Adalyn. But Logan is less perceptive, or maybe my avoidance helped out a bit. I've just felt awkward around him ever since Tucker suggested Logan wants me. I don't think it's true, but then again, sometimes when I catch him looking at me, I do wonder.

"Nothing really," I answer, pulling on the ends of my hair, unable to make eye contact.

"Not buying it." He tilts my chin up with his pencil and says, "Tell me."

Why is this so awkward? He's my friend, so I should be able to tell him anything. Just peel the Band-Aid off, get it over with. I take a deep breath and say, "Uh, Tucker and I started seeing each other."

"Tucker, your roommate?"

Is there really any other Tucker? I don't say that, but come on, Logan. "Yeah, that Tucker."

His eyebrows pull together, and I'm a little surprised by his reaction. I thought they got along. "Huh, I didn't think you were interested in him. I thought he's your best friend's ex-boyfriend. Isn't that against girl code or something?"

Well, there's the splash of ice-cold water I DIDN'T need to wipe the happy smile off my face.

I don't know what to say. How does one really react to another person blatantly calling them out? So I just shrug and sift through my book. All the words blend together, forming one giant sentence that makes no sense.

*Isn't that against girl code or something?*

Stupid Logan and his logic. I've been so caught up in Tucker that I haven't even thought of the outside world, of the people around us, of the repercussions of our coupling.

"I don't mean to upset you." Yeah, right! "I guess I was just caught off guard, that's all," Logan says, placing his hand over mine. As has been his habit, his thumb caresses my skin in what I've always considered a *reassuring* way.

"You didn't upset me." I try to think of how to respond and instead just go with honesty. "I really didn't think about anyone else besides us. It just happened so fast, and I guess I haven't sat back to think about what it all means."

"Is it serious?"

To me it is. To Tucker, I really have no idea.

"We haven't really had that conversation. We've just been, you know, seeing where it all goes."

Logan nods and puts his pencil down in the crevice of book. "Well, it seems like he makes you happy. It's hard not to notice the change in your demeanor."

"He does make me happy."

"And what about him? Does he feel the same way about you?"

I don't like Logan's questioning. "What kind of questions are these?" He's making me question Tucker's intent, and I really don't care for it. *Is that Logan's intent? To make me doubt Tucker?* I don't want to think about *us* because the minute I start thinking about how Tucker feels inside, my gut starts to churn. As long as I've known Tucker, his heart has been Sadie's. It's always been Sadie, and the thought of him still harboring feelings for her literally tears me in half, makes me feel physically ill. I can't think about it. I won't think about it. I refuse to. *Didn't he say he needed to work through that before we slept together? Did we rush that? Did he simply give in to me because he was horny?*

"I'm just concerned about you. I don't want you to start something that's going to break you later on."

"Why do you think he's going to break me? You barely know him and you haven't seen us together, so you don't see how he treats me."

"That's true, but what I do know about him scares me. You've told me about his ex, about how he's felt about her, how he bought that house for her. And then there's that room, the room he won't let you in. And don't forget about . . . what is it? Rule number six? Don't talk about Sadie?" He strokes my hand again, concern in his eyes. "Come on, Emma, it doesn't seem like he's over her and instead of dealing with his baggage, he's covering it up with you as a distraction."

*Ouch.* That hurts and what hurts even more is that his comment seems to ring too close to the truth for my liking.

"Don't be mad at me, Emma," Logan says, tugging on my hand. "I'm just looking out for you."

"I know." I nod. "I, uh, I have to get going, though. I have somewhere I have to be." I start to pack up my things as quickly as possible.

"Emma, don't go. I'm sorry. I just don't want you to get hurt."

I try to catch my breath as I pack. "I know and I appreciate that. I just have to go."

Logan stands and stops me from putting a book in my backpack. "Don't just run away. Talk to me, Emma."

Irritation overwhelms me, and I snap at him. "Talk to you? I just told you how happy I am and you throw a wet blanket over it. Why would I want to talk to you when you make me feel like crap?"

His face registers shock, and I feel slightly bad for lashing out. "I'm sorry, Emma. I really was just looking out for you. I don't trust him and his intentions." *Yeah, Logan. That much is obvious.*

I snag my book from him, stuff it in my backpack, and zip it up. I toss the bag over my back and say, "Well, I'm a big girl, Logan, and I know what I'm doing. I appreciate your concern but please just stay out of it."

With that, I take off toward my car while I check my phone. There's a text form Tucker.

**Tucker: When are you getting home? Racer is here and I want an excuse to kick him out.**

I sigh and tuck my phone into my pocket. *Home.* That's exactly what it has felt like. Returning home. To Tucker. Damn Logan. He's the reason it feels a lot less exciting now.

Logan succinctly brought all my fears to the forefront of my mind and I'm not ready. Not ready to wonder if my life with Tucker is transient. Not ready for him to ask me nicely to leave with a "Thank you very much, Emma, but my heart will never be yours." Not ready to have my heart shatter and wonder if I'll ever be whole again.

*I'm not ready to be let go, and I'm not sure I ever will be.*

• • •

When I pull up to the house, there are blinding lights blasting in the living room, making the whole house look like it's harboring the sun. Confused, I grab my bag and head in. I drop my stuff onto the kitchen counter and make my way to the living room where there's music playing—*One Direction*, ha!—and lamps pointing toward the fireplace where two bare-chested men wearing tool belts and rocking the fireplace kneel on the floor. Tucker has a pencil tucked behind his ear, his hair all askew as if he's been running his hand through it, and Racer is sporting a backward baseball cap.

Both men rival each other in the muscle department, their chests bronze despite the winter months, their backs rippling as they place a very light colored rock on the fireplace. The room has also been painted a pale grey, making it feel light and airy. How long was I studying that they could get all of this work done?

"Just put the mortar on the damn thing and give it to me," Tucker says, holding his hand out.

"You've gotten to put all the rocks on, I should get to do some too."

"Stop being a little bitch and hand me the rock. I want to get this done before Emma gets home."

"I'm not being a little bitch." Racer sits back on his heels and points to his tightly flexed chest. "You're being the little bitch and not sharing. Sharing is caring, Tucker."

"You put them on crooked."

"The fuck I do. They call me the fireplace master back at the job site. You're lucky I'm here helping you without charge. I could be invoicing you one hell of a bill if I wanted to."

"The amount of pizza and beer you shoved down your throat while painting will cover that bullshit invoice. Now hand me the damn rock."

"No." Racer seems to put his foot down.

"For fuck's sake, Racer." Tucker pulls on his hair in frustration. I was right, he has been yanking on those beautiful strands, and I can guess the reason why.

I decide to step in.

"Just let him put the rock on," I say, turning the music off at the same time, startling both of the six-foot-three men right out of their construction boots.

"Fucking hell," Racer says, dropping the mortar-covered rock right on the hardwood floor.

"Jesus, Racer." Tucker picks it up and yells, "Quick, wipe that shit off my floors."

Tucker places the rock on the fireplace and then stands, wiping his hands on his low-slung jeans. Despite the anguish I'm feeling, which is making my stomach do all different kinds of flips, I can't *help but* take Tucker in. He looks just like that meme that floats around the Internet of the man standing on the bed, shirtless, fixing a light. The meme reads, "I don't know what he's fixing, but mine just broke."

When he starts toward me, all I can think is, yes, mine broke too, whatever the hell it is and I want him to fix it.

With purpose in every step he takes toward me, his muscles shift and flex, giving me one hell of a show. "You're home early, babe. I thought you would be studying later."

So did I.

Feeling a little off-ish—thank you, Logan—I say, "Yeah, we ended early tonight." I scan the room and nod. "Looks good in here." I lean to the side and say, "Hey, Racer."

He scrubs the floor and then pulls up the rag and waves it at me. "Hey, Emma." Then he tosses the rag at Tucker and says, "Your precious floor is fine, dickhead."

Tucker ignores him and takes a step forward, but I step back, unsure of how I'm feeling right now. He doesn't seem to like my retreat from the way he narrows his eyes at me.

"Uh, I'm tired. I'm going to get ready for bed, call it an early night. Don't worry about making noise or anything. Nice seeing you, Racer."

"Have a good night," he calls out as he starts laying rock on the fireplace, unsupervised. From here, he seems to be doing a fine job.

I turn back to Tucker and meekly smile at him. "Night."

His face turns in disapproval, but before he can say anything, I go back in the kitchen, snag my bag, and go to my bedroom where I quietly shut the door.

*He's covering it up with you as a distraction . . .*

Logan's words repeatedly sting as they play on repeat in my head. It's like he reached inside my brain, pulled out the fears I've been trying to keep hidden since Tucker and I kissed, and laid them out before me. I hate that my fears are making me insecure and causing me to question everything that's happened between Tucker and me. Has anything we've done together meant anything to him? Or have I been a temporary escape for him from his pain? *Enabling him to forget.* Does he make comparisons between Sadie and me and believe he's *settling* for second best?

I feel so sick to my stomach. Not in the mood to do anything but lie in my bed, I change into a set of pajamas and crawl under my covers. I turn toward my nightstand, set up my iPad, and go to my Netflix app. I just need some mindless binging. As I'm searching through the TV shows, my door cracks open. Tucker sticks his head in, sees me in bed and invites himself in, shutting the door tightly behind him.

He's still shirtless and in his jeans, but now he's without his boots and tool belt. His bare feet pad across the hardwood floors until he reaches my bed. He sits down and pulls the sheets that are covering my shoulders and takes in my taco-covered pajama set.

"Are you okay, Emma?" he asks after studying me for a few seconds.

"Yeah." Do not cry. For the love of God, do not cry, he will think you're crazy. "Just tired."

His hand caresses my cheek. "No, there's something bothering you. What aren't you telling me?"

Ah, why does he know me so well already?

I shake my head. "Long day."

I can tell he's not buying it, but he lets it go as he says, "Okay, I'll get rid of Racer, clean up, and then I'll wrap you up in my arms. Give me half an hour to finish everything."

"Don't worry about it. You do your thing. I can catch you in the morning."

He lifts an eyebrow at me. "You'll catch me in the morning?"

"For breakfast?" I ask as a question. I'm really not good at this lying thing.

"So after a month of spending every night together, of not only having sex, but talking, laughing, and enjoying one another, you're just going to *catch me in the morning*?"

This isn't going as planned. Why can't I be more coy about

things? I wear my emotions on my face, unmasked and for everyone to see, especially Tucker who's so adamant about studying my every move.

He takes my silence as his answer and nods his head. He stands from the bed and walks out of the bedroom without another word. Shit.

Shit. Shit. Shit.

I bury my head in my pillow and try to drown out the negative thoughts in my head, but I'm having a difficult time.

*If he cared,* he wouldn't have just walked away.

*If I wasn't a distraction*, he would still be in this room.

*If he wasn't still hung up on Sadie*, he would have pulled the covers off me and snuggled up against me.

But none of that happened. Instead, he left, and I feel cold, unwanted, and sick to my stomach. This night isn't going anywhere, so I turn off my nightstand lamp and turn away from my door. Tears fall down my cheeks as I try to comprehend how I'm going to handle the morning.

I should just end it. I should just thank him for the mind-blowing sex, shake his hand as a peace offering, and be done with it. *Easier said than done.* But how does one go about doing that when their heart is already invested?

More tears fall, soaking the pillow beneath me. I take in a deep breath. My door opens again and then quickly shuts. I hold my breath as I try to act as still as possible. There's no movement and I wonder if he entered the room or was just checking my door for squeaky hinges. But I have my answer when I hear him pad across the floor.

He steps to my bed, and I wait for his next move. I feel so nervous. Are we about to get into a huge fight? I still as he pulls the covers down and when I think he's going to turn me over, instead, he climbs into bed behind me and wraps his arm around my waist, burying his head into my hair. He holds me tightly and the feel of his arm around me breaks me apart.

*He came back.*

*Does that mean I'm not just a distraction?*

A sob escapes me as I cry into my pillow. Every fear and emotion I've been holding back since Logan tore my little bubble apart comes flying out.

"Shh," he coos into my ear. The arm that's wrapped around my waist falls to the hem of my shirt and he snakes his hand under the fabric, and I instantly feel comforted from the skin-on-skin contact. There is nothing sexual about his touch, he doesn't try to touch my breasts; he just holds me tight.

"I'm s-sorry," I slightly stutter.

"Don't be sorry, Emma. Just talk to me."

"Is Racer still here?"

"Yes. He's finishing up the fireplace and then taking off."

I shift so I'm on my back and can see Tucker's face. "Oh, you should go finish with him. I don't want you to be rude."

"Racer's a big boy. He can handle finishing up on his own. You, on the other hand, I want to know what the hell is depriving me of your beautiful smile."

My lips purse as I try to hold back more tears. He's so sweet, and it's confusing. Is he being nice because I'm his friend, or is there something else? I want to believe there is something else. I feel like there is, but then again, I also feel a slight resistance in Tucker, as if he hasn't fully given himself over to me. When I really consider *us*, that's what's concerning, because it all just circles back around to what Logan pointed out.

"Emma, please," he whispers as his forehead presses against my cheek. "If it's something I did, I'm sorry. If it's because of Racer being here, I was only trying to get the living room fixed up to surprise you. I wanted to make it warm and inviting, a place where you can study instead of being locked in your room or at the library all the time. I even bought a coffee table. Fuck, I'll never have Racer come over again."

Oh this sweet, sweet man.

"It's not Racer," I breathe out.

"Then what is it?" He pulls me in tighter. It's as if he's worried that if he lets go, he'll lose me forever. "Please talk to me, Emma."

I bite down on my lip for a second and come to the realization that I'm just going to have to talk to him. Be honest. Jesus, be a grown-up.

"I told Logan about us." The mention of Logan's name has Tucker sitting up and looking down at me, his hand still around my waist.

"What did he fucking say to you? Did he touch you? I swear to God, I will drop him to the floor so fucking fast."

I press my hand against Tucker's chest to calm him down. "He didn't touch me, Tucker. We're just friends."

"Yeah, then what the fuck did he say to you? Because clearly whatever he said is why you're so upset."

"He was just nervous about your intentions, that's all." Okay, he might have said a little more than that, but I'm not ready to speak about Sadie, and I know Tucker isn't as well, hence rule number six.

"About my intentions?" he roars. Oh boy, he's mad. Maybe this wasn't such a good idea. Tucker has never liked Logan and now I know he's never, ever going to like him. "Where does this dickhead come off questioning my relationship with you? He doesn't even know me; he doesn't know us."

"He was just concerned, that's all." I try to rub the tension in Tucker's chest, but he doesn't budge. His muscles are firing up and he's raking his hand through his hair. He hops out of bed and that's when I realize he's only wearing a pair of boxer briefs. He paces the room, anger in every step. Quite frankly, I'm beginning to feel concerned for Logan's welfare. Shit, I never should have said anything. I can kiss goodbye study sessions over here with Logan, as there's no way Tucker will allow him in this house.

"He doesn't need to be concerned because it's none of his goddamn business." Tucker turns toward me, one hand on his hip, the other pulling on the back of his neck. Frustration courses through his body and you can visibly see it in how his body flexes with fury, like he's about to spin around and punch the living shit out of my wall. "So what did he say? Did he tell you to break up with me? To move in with him so he can take care of you because I'm some fucking monster?"

"No, nothing like that."

"Then what did he say?" Tucker asks, anger pouring off him.

Think, Emma. Diffuse this situation. Make it better, because right now it seems like Tucker is about to have an aneurism.

I sit up on the bed and push my back against the wall. "Can you please sit down? You're making me nervous."

His face relaxes and instantly turns into concern with a slice of regret. "Shit," he mutters and sits down next to me. He pulls me onto his lap so I'm facing him, and he places his hands on my hips. "I'm sorry, I didn't mean to make you nervous. I'm just . . . fuck. I'm irritated. I don't like that whatever he said upset you. What we have is between us, Emma, and no one else. "

"What do we have, Tucker?" I ask softly, wanting desperately to hear that he feels the same about me as I do for him.

He lifts my chin and looks me in the eyes. "We have something fucking special. Something that makes me happy. You make me happy, Emma. Everything about you from your smile to your laughter, to your healing touch, I can't get enough of you."

I swallow hard. "But don't you think there are some things

between us that are holding us back?"

"Like what?"

*Sadie.*

Isn't it obvious? And what about the room I'm not allowed in? But instead of bringing up my best friend, I say, "Your mom, you don't ever want to talk about her."

"I don't," Tucker agrees. "She's a vile woman who deserves what's been handed to her."

"Don't you think you should talk about it though? For healing?" I'm totally alluding to something else. Hint, hint, Sadie, but he doesn't take the bait.

"There is nothing to talk about, babe."

"Then why is she on the rules of not to talk about?" HINT, HINT!

He runs both hands over his face and blows out a long breath. "Because, she's not worth the words. She was a terrible mom. When my dad wasn't around, she didn't care that she had a child. There were days where I only had a meal to eat because I scrounged it up from school or friends helped me out. And when my dad passed, it was all downhill from there. I had to fend for myself. The only good thing that came from my mom was her signing off on me working for Julius at such a young age. Granted, I caught her when she was high as shit, but I got her signature and from there on out, I was self-sufficient. She's a piece of crap, Emma, not worth talking about."

I cup his face, my heart breaking for the boy I knew so many years ago. I was either naïve, or totally oblivious to real life, but I never really got the impression that Tucker was fighting to provide for himself as a kid. "I'm so sorry I wasn't there for you when you needed it."

"You didn't know. Not many people did. I didn't wave around my dirty laundry, asking for help. I got it where I needed it."

Aka, Sadie.

My heart rips apart.

It stings.

How I now wish I was the one who helped him back then, the one who took him in and took care of him, not Sadie.

"Still. I wasn't a good friend."

"You've always been a good friend, Emma." He brings his lips to my forehead and kisses me softly. "You're better than anything I deserve." He sighs and says, "I'm sorry Logan made you question what we have. I don't want you worrying, Emma. We're solid, babe. There is nothing for you to worry about, okay?"

*We're solid, babe.*

*Nothing to worry about.*

His answers seem so simple, and yet, it feels entirely way too complicated.

He brings his mouth close to mine and repeats, "Okay?"

I stare into his soulful eyes. *They* speak of his intentions, the intentions Logan so blatantly said are ill warranted. But from my point of view, from where I can see it, he's genuine. And I might regret this, but I nod. "Okay."

"Are we going to be okay?" His eyes search mine. "Because I'm addicted, Emma. I'm addicted to you, and I don't want anything to stand between us."

*Are we going to be okay?*

Can he truly be so oblivious? There is one giant elephant standing between us. *How can he not see that? Or is it not an issue because I'll never . . .*

"I know."

"So we're good?"

I swallow hard and nod. "We're good, Tucker."

He lets out a long breath and then sinks us down on the

mattress. He lays me on top of him and strokes my hair with one hand as the other holds me close to his body. His warmth wraps around me and eases some of the building anxiety. There might be some unanswered questions on my end, but right now, lying here in Tucker's arm, I know one thing: I'm addicted to him as well and I'm pretty sure he now holds my heart in his hands. What he does with it is up to him.

*I just hope I don't break.*

# Chapter Twenty

## TUCKER

"Help me with this," I ask Racer as I try to position the plush cream rug I bought for the living room. The other day I went to Olum's Furniture and dipped into my savings. I purchased some things for our house, hoping to surprise Emma. *Again.*

"I came to finish up this mantel, not decorate with you," Racer replies while leaning against the wall, arms crossed.

"Just fucking help me. Christ, dude."

Racer huffs and walks over to the other side of the rug and helps me position it. "You should do it at an angle, offset the furniture. Gives the room a fun yet cozy feeling." I lift an eyebrow at him and he shrugs. "Nate Berkus was on Rachel Ray the other day, and he has some good pointers."

Racer's celebrity crush is Rachel Ray. He loves her.

"I think straight is fine."

"Have it your way."

He helps me move the couch back into position, and then adds the navy blue armchairs I purchased for either side of the rug. Across from the couch, I lined up the new oak buffet that matches the coffee table, and doubles as a TV stand. I brought my TV down from my room and set it up so Emma and I can snuggle on the couch and watch movies, instead of always having to watch things on her computer screen, or in my bed. *Although, that had its advantages . . .*

And then there's the dining room. Instead of our card table, which holds some good memories, I purchased a bar-height seven-piece dining room set that takes up the space perfectly and fits in with the rest of the furniture in the house. I topped everything off with a few bunches of fresh peonies around the house because they're Emma's favorite. They were a bitch to find. I had to go to a florist.

"I think that does it." I wipe my forehead and look around the space. Shit, it looks really good in here. "The fireplace came out great, man. Thanks for the help."

Racer dusts off his fingers on his bare chest and says, "Told you I was the fireplace master."

He is. He took a dreary brick fireplace and turned it into something slightly rustic with the wood-top mantelpiece. A nice centerpiece for the comfortable living room.

"Are you going to put those somewhere?" Racer points to a few picture frames currently placed on the new dining room table.

"Shit, I almost forgot." I take the frames to the mantel and line them up, making sure my favorite picture of me kissing Emma's cheek in Skaneateles is in the middle. That smile; fuck, she's looks so damn happy. I'm a fucking lucky bastard.

Racer takes it all in and nods. "Yeah, those will score you some brownie points." He clears his throat and adds, "You like her, like really like her."

I nod. "Yeah, I fucking do."

Thoughtfully, Racer runs his hand over his jaw. "Does this mean you can move past Sadie, and redo the nursery?"

Never skipping a beat, Racer gets straight to the point. I don't blame him though. He's watched me for over a year try to deal with the backlash. I'm sure *he's* ready for me to move on.

"Small steps, man," I answer, feeling the weight of the nursery now hanging on my shoulders. Last time I was in that room was when I showed it to Sadie. I'm not ready to return, although now, I'm not as sure why. Sadie's gone. There is no baby . . .

"Okay, but don't you—?" Lights shine in the windows indicating Emma's return home.

"Shit, you're not supposed to be here." I scramble to gather Racer's tools and his shirt and toss them at him. "I don't want you acting like a dickhead when she sees it all for the first time."

"You mean I don't get to be a part of the grand reveal? After everything I did to help? That's fucked up, man."

"You'll live. I'll tell you about it tomorrow. Now fucking move."

I push him toward the side door just as Emma walks in. She's wearing a pair of yoga pants and a green Binghamton University sweatshirt. Her hair cascades over her shoulders and her blue eyes are highlighted with just a hint of mascara. God, she's so beautiful.

She takes us both in and carefully sets her backpack on the counter. With a pop to her hip she points at both of us and says, "It's a little concerning that I keep coming home to you two without your shirts on. Is this something I should be worried about?"

"Ha, Tucker wishes." Racer pushes me, and I push him back.

"We were just doing some work," I answer.

"Yeah, and Prince Charming over here won't turn the heat down while we're working because he doesn't want you to be cold when you get home."

Emma sweetly smiles at me, stands on her toes and gives me

a light kiss on the lips. "Thank you."

Racer rolls his eyes as I wrap my arm around Emma's waist. "All right, I'm out. See you tomorrow, dude. Bring the Oatmeal Pies, you owe me."

I do owe him. We say our goodbyes and when the side door shuts, I grip Emma's hands and say, "I have something to show you, but you have to close your eyes."

She closes them and says, "Am I going to open my eyes and see you standing there with your pants down? You don't have to go to such great lengths to have sex you know, you can just ask."

"It's not sex." I chuckle and guide her into the living room. I angle her in the corner so when she opens her eyes she can take in both the living room and the dining room. I hold her shoulders and take a deep breath; I really hope she likes it.

I lean over her shoulder and whisper in her ear, "Okay, open your eyes, baby."

"Oh my gosh, Tucker." She turns to me and then looks around again. "It looks like a magazine in here. Did you do this all by yourself?"

"Racer helped." I swallow hard. "Do you like it?"

"Do I like it? Are you kidding? It's gorgeous. It's so beautiful in here." She looks around, her fingers caress the armchairs and she leans over and smells the flowers I placed around the two rooms. When she turns back to me, she shakes her head in disbelief. "This is incredible, Tucker."

I start to walk toward her when her eyes look behind me and they start to fill with tears. I follow her line of sight and see that she spotted the pictures I framed of us for the mantel. She walks over to them and I follow closely behind, wrapping my arms around her waist.

She caresses the frames gently, taking her time looking at them.

"I thought it would be nice to have some pictures of us on display."

She shakes her head and says, "I can't believe you did all of this."

"I did it for you," I whisper. "I want you to be comfortable here. I want a comfortable place for you to study, especially with finals lurking. I want a place where we can snuggle and watch movies together. I want us to have a proper table to eat dinner at, not something that can fold up and fit between a slot between the fridge and the wall."

"Tucker, from the moment I walked in this house, I've been comfortable. I love living here."

"You do?"

She nods. "I do. I didn't want you to furnish the house for me. I wanted you to be the one who felt comfortable in this house, to make it your own. Your home."

I grip her waist and say, "I made it *ours*. *Our* home." And fuck if that isn't the truth. It's not a cold, lonely house. It's a warm, welcoming home. *Because of her.* I lean down and press a kiss against her lips, loving how her hand instinctively grips the back of my neck to deepen the connection. When I pull away, I drag my thumb over her bottom lip. "I always want you to be happy, Emma. Always."

"I am happy, Tucker."

"Good." I kiss her forehead and say, "Promise me if you're ever unhappy, you'll tell me. No hiding things like that convo with Logan, all right? I want you to come to me, okay?"

"Promise."

• • •

"Seriously, hands down, Tom Hanks is the best actor of all time." Emma lifts off my chest and fidgets with her hair. "He's so versatile."

I glance at the TV and then at Emma again. "You're making that statement after watching *The Burbs*?"

"I am." She holds her chin high.

"You know he's had way better performances, right?"

"I felt like he was so earthy in this film."

"Earthy?" I chuckle. "Where the hell do you get earthy from?"

She shrugs. "Just seemed like the proper term."

"It's not."

"You don't know."

"I do." I snag her waist and plop her on my lap. The candles in the room are slowly starting to burn out, and the family sized bag of peanut M&M's we decided to share is almost gone. I couldn't have picked a better way to spend my night with Emma. In my arms, in the new living room, watching a movie, and breathing in her fresh, flowery scent.

Goddamn, I like her so much. For so long, I never thought I'd have this. *Her.*

"I'm so glad you're here, Em."

She looks up at me, probably sees the serious intent in my unexpected comment, and smiles. "Me too, Tucker."

Because I can't not touch her, I stroke her cheek with the back of my hand. They're builder's hands. Rough. Overused. Often cracked from the cold. Yet she never flinches when I touch her silky soft skin. I'm not good with words, so I don't really know how to communicate how much it means to me that she's here. That she seems just as glad to be home as I am to welcome her. All I can do is touch her, and hope she knows. *Hope she knows I'd feel empty and lifeless without her.*

"What do you have planned for the rest of the evening?" she asks, shifting on my lap with a smile. *And there it is. The smile that is both sweet and wicked.* By the gleam in her eyes, she can feel my hard-on. It's that easy with her. She just touches me and I get hard.

"I was hoping you had something planned for me."

"Is that right?"

"Yeah. I think it's time we break in this couch."

"I was hoping you were going to say that." She stands from my lap and pulls her pajama shirt over hear head, revealing a purple lace bra that barely covers her luscious tits, followed by taking her pants down, showing off a matching thong that's so thin I'm not sure it should even be considered underwear. Her long brown hair sways over her shoulders as she pushes it to the side to show off her little outfit.

"You had that under your pajamas the whole time and never said anything?" I ask, so fucking turned on.

"I did."

"And here I had to watch the movie the entire time with my shirt off. How is that fair?"

She starts to play with the straps of her thong as she answers, "It's not my fault you're a terrible negotiator."

"I didn't even know we were negotiating."

"And whose problem is that?" She reaches down to my jeans, unbuckles them, and pulls my pants off with a little assistance from me, leaving me in nothing but a pair of boxer briefs.

She pouts for a second and says, "I thought you would be wearing those grandpa panties I like so much."

She straddles my lap and presses her hands against my chest while her hips start to slowly move over my erection. Fuck yes, that feels good.

"They're not grandpa panties. They're just regular briefs."

"Yes, they are. They're gramp-ties."

"Is this your idea of foreplay?"

She rubs her thong-clad ass over my lap. "I don't know, you

tell me. Seems like it's working."

"Only because you look so fucking hot."

"You like this outfit?" She continues to maneuver on my lap, my cock hard as a fucking rock, and I'm certainly enjoying the view.

"If that's what you want to call it." I nod at her chest. "Take your bra off, babe."

A wicked smile appears across her face. "Make me."

"You really want to play that game? You know I'm significantly bigger than you, right?"

"Size means nothing."

I thrust up into her, causing a little moan to pop out of her mouth. "It should matter."

Her hands fall to my chest as she braces herself against me. "Maybe it does a little."

I reach behind her and pop off her bra, watching it fall down her shoulders and exposing her gorgeous breasts. Wasting no time, I bring her chest forward and lower my head so I can suck one of her nipples into my mouth.

"God, yes," she moans.

*God, yes* is fucking right. Everything about her is so damn right. *Every. Fucking. Time.*

• • •

Slap.

"Ouch, that hurt." I shake my hand and then hold it to my chest.

Emma points her wooden spoon at me and says, "Stop eating all the croutons out of the salad or else there'll be none left for our guests."

There is a knock at the side door. I go to answer it as I say, "You can ask nicely; you don't have to go whacking me."

She wiggles her eyebrows at me. "I thought you liked a good whacking."

Fucking sassy woman.

I open the door to find Adalyn, Smalls, and Racer waiting. Emma cutely asked me the other night if we could have a little dinner party to break in the new dining room table and honestly, I can't deny that woman anything, so I agreed. And it didn't seem like that bad of an idea, although I was nervous about Emma inviting Logan, but since she didn't mention his name on the attending guests list, I assumed she didn't ask him to come over. Smart move, because I don't know how long I could fake being nice to that douche.

"We're here," Racer says, shaking a bottle of wine in my face. "Wine is from me."

Smalls smacks Racer on the back of the head. "Wine's from me, asshat. Is that why you offered to carry it in?"

"Of course." Racer hands me the wine and then says, "We picked up this little lady in the driveway as well. I'm assuming she belongs to Emma, either that or we found a lurker and invited her to dinner."

"Hi, Adalyn. Glad you could come." I step aside for her to enter with the boys. I slug Racer in the shoulder as he passes and say, "Don't call Emma's friends lurkers."

Racer rubs his arm. "Damn, did everyone's sense of humor take a trip to the shit pit? Or are we supposed to act all proper because we're having a dinner party?"

"Little class, man," Smalls mumbles as we step into the kitchen. Emma and Adalyn are already hugging when I finish closing the door.

Adalyn pulls away and gestures to Smalls and Racer. "Going to be honest, I'll be staring at those two all night." She turns to the guys and continues, "Listen up, boys. I'm not going to be sad if you eat with your shirts off. Just a suggestion, take it or leave it."

Racer pats Smalls on the back. "Trust me, sweetheart, you don't want this guy taking his shirt off. His pancake nipples will scare you for weeks. I still have yet to put a flapjack in my mouth, too scared I might be eating Smalls's nipple." He nudges Smalls in the side with his elbow. "Talk about nipple confusion."

Smalls shakes his head. "You're fucking twisted, man." Smalls takes off into the dining and living area and from the kitchen you can hear him say, "Damn, it looks nice in here."

Emma nudges me with her elbow and kisses my jaw before turning back to the cheddar broccoli soup she's been working on. "Should be done soon. Table is set, Tucker, so if you want to pour wine for everyone, that would be great."

I cringe. "Want me to pour it into the day-of-the-week mugs? We really don't have any glasses besides two."

"You don't have wine glasses?"

"Babe, I had two mugs when you moved in. Do you really think I have wine glasses stored away somewhere?" The boys normally bring beer.

She chuckles and shakes her head. "Dumb question. Well, mugs will have to do."

"Aw, you two are so cute," Adalyn coos. "Can I help with anything?"

"I think we're all set," Emma answers as she stirs the soup.

"Good, because that was just a polite offer."

Racer snorts and puts his arm around Adalyn. "I like this girl. Why don't we go enjoy some wine in a coffee mug while trying to stare through Smalls's shirt to see his pancake nips?"

"Sounds like a fetching idea."

They walk into the living area with the mugs and wine in hand, leaving me a little worried about what might be blossoming between those two.

"That can't be good."

"I'm not worried." Emma takes a sip of the soup and makes a cute little noise of approval.

"Why aren't you worried?"

"Racer isn't Adalyn's type. If anything, they'll become best friends."

"Why isn't he her type?" I ask, feeling slightly defensive for my friend.

"They're too similar." She points to the bowls on the opposite counter. "Can you bring those over here please?"

"Nothing wrong with being similar." I place the bowls next to the stove where she starts filling them with her soup that I'm looking forward to trying.

"Not at all, but Adalyn needs someone broody, a challenge. Racer is too easygoing for her. Don't get me wrong; if they ended up having sex, I wouldn't be surprised. But a relationship? Never going to happen."

"Well there goes double-dating," I tease as I wrap my arms around her and kiss the side of her neck. "Smells fucking fantastic, babe."

"Tastes even better."

I lightly nibble and lick the skin along her neck. "I couldn't agree more."

She turns in my grasp once she's done filling up the bowls and says, "Do not get a boner right now. I wanted to have a nice dinner party. No boners allowed."

"Yeah, no boners allowed, dude." Smalls walks in with a mug of wine.

Emma startles and steps away from me as if we were just caught by her parents. I don't let her get very far and pull her back into my chest. "Do you need something?" Emma asks, trying to be the polite hostess.

Smalls tilts the mug in our direction to show us the wine. "This shit is fucking nasty. Apparently I'm polite, but can't choose a wine to save my own ass. Got beer, man?"

"In the fridge on the top shelf. Help yourself and grab one for me too."

"You're not going to drink the wine he brought?" Emma asks. "You don't want to be rude, Tucker."

I lower my hand to her ass, lean forward and press a light kiss on her lips as I squeeze her behind. "And I also don't want to drink the sludge he brought, so being rude doesn't faze me."

Smalls hands me a beer. "If it was Racer who brought the wine, Tucker would be drinking it because we both know Racer would bitch and complain about it until the bottle was gone."

"True fact." We bump our bottles together and Smalls takes off into the living room again.

Looking around the corner to see if he disappeared, Emma whispers, "Do you think I have to drink it?"

"I think you're going to have to bite the bullet, babe."

Gripping the beer around the neck of the bottle, she brings my drink to her lips and says, "If I have to drink the crap wine, so do you."

Taking down half the bottle, she places it on the counter and then starts bringing the bowls of soup into the dining room.

Damn.

Funny thing is, if Emma asked me to drink the crap wine, I would, because it seems I'd do anything for this girl. She has quickly become everything to me. She makes me feel real, justified, like everything I've done in my life leading up to this moment was meant to be. That I walked through hell and finally came out on the other end slightly burnt but fucking happy.

Funny thing about true happiness, though. You never know it's inside you until someone pulls it out.

# Chapter Twenty-One

## EMMA

"I really appreciate you driving me home, Sadie. Adalyn forgot she had to babysit her sister's kids so she left me stranded at school."

"Not a problem at all. Andrew has a late night of studying planned, and I'm all booked out, so driving you home gave me the opportunity to get out of that stingy library."

I buckle up and set my bag and books on the floor in front of me as I let out a long breath. "Why does this feel like the longest semester ever?"

"Probably because it's your last before you go out into the workforce. I'm sure you're itching to be done with all the studying. When do you take your exam for your license?"

"The NCLEX? Two days after graduation. I wanted to get it over with."

"I would too. Are you nervous?"

I look out the window at the freshly budding trees and shake my head. "No, I think my head has been buried in books for four years, and I feel prepared. But the next month is going to be hell when it comes to studying."

Hopefully Tucker will understand less time will be spent

with him and more with my books, but maybe if I'm lucky, he'll want to help me study. Who am I kidding? There is no doubt in my mind that he will want to, he's always asking if I need to be quizzed.

"There's no question about it, you will pass." Sadie stops at a stop light and turns to me. "I really am proud of you, Emma. You've always known what you want to do and you went out and accomplished it."

"Thanks," I reply, shyly. The praise coming from Sadie feels weird. Maybe because in the back of my mind, I keep thinking about how I feel like I'm betraying our friendship.

"So what's the next step after you take the exam? Are you looking for jobs?"

"Yeah." I fiddle with my shirt as I think about the jobs I've started applying to as a Registered Nurse Applicant. "I've been talking to a few different hospitals."

"Really? So you're not just applying around here? I heard Lourdes is a really good hospital to work for, if you can get in."

"Yeah, I've been in contact."

"Where else?"

"Syracuse, Scranton," I swallow hard, "Boston, and Burlington."

"Oh wow." Sadie is silent for a second. "I didn't know you were thinking out of state. I just assumed you would stay here. Gosh, you can't move." She laughs, but I know it's a nervous one. "What are we going to do without our sweet and caring Emma? It's not going to be the same without you."

"It's not like I'm moving there tomorrow. Just trying to keep my options open, you know?"

"I guess so." She takes a deep breath and says, "Ugh, we need to spend more time together, especially if you might be moving." When she stops, she points her finger at me, "You've been a busy lady lately, it's hard to get ahold of you." Maybe because all of my time has been spent in Tucker's bed. I start to sweat from the thought of it. "Makes me believe you're in a relationship. It's how I was when I first met Andrew, blocked off the rest of the world." I cringe and then quickly turn my face. It's true; I'm acting just like Sadie when she first met Andrew. "Emma?" The tone of her voice makes the hair on the back of my neck stand to attention."

"Mmm?" I reply, eyes still focused out the window.

"Are you in a relationship, and you haven't told me? And don't say no. Your ears are bright red and so is your face."

Crap! Damn you, ears and face, for giving me away. I really don't want to have this conversation with Sadie right now, especially since we're about to pull up to the house. She'll also know if I deny it, I'll be lying. Therefore, I go for the evasive answer.

"Uh, sort of—"

"I knew it." She slaps the steering wheel. "I told Andrew the other day that I thought you were in a relationship, but he said I was just hoping everyone was in a relationship, because I'm in one and I'm happy so I want everyone to be happy. Frankly, it was a boost to his own ego, but I knew I was right. Is it that Logan guy you spend all your time with? Did you finally fall in love?"

"No." I shake my head. Boy, Tucker would not like that assumption. "Logan and I are just friends, that's it." How many times am I going to have to reiterate that to people?

Although, I'm not sure where my friendship with Logan stands right now. We haven't really spoken since he told me his opinion of Tucker. For all I know, that friendship could be dissolved.

*I hope it's not.*

"Okay, so it's not Logan. Is it another nursing student? What's his name? Is he hot? Of course he's hot. I mean, look at you. Does Smilly know him? I swear if you told Smilly and not me, I'm going to knock your nipples off your boobs."

"Smilly doesn't know. No one really does."

"Not even Tucker? I mean, you are roommates, so I'd assume he would see your new boyfriend."

Oh Christ. I didn't know palms could drip with sweat but here I am, wiping my hands on my pants, praying for her to drive faster.

"You know, since it's so new, I really don't want to talk about it. Superstitious and all." I cross my fingers and hold them up to Sadie, which garners an eye-roll.

"You're still superstitious about things? Please don't tell me you continue to wear pink underwear on Tuesdays and Thursdays in hopes you will one day marry Chris Pine."

I chuckle at my ridiculousness. "My Chris Pine-ing days are over unfortunately."

"So unfortunate." We pull into the driveway, Sadie puts the car in park, and turns to me, hands in her lap. "At least promise me when you're ready to talk about the new boy you'll tell me all about him."

I nod and gather my things, unable to formulate words. "Thanks for the lift, Sadie."

"Any time. Have fun finishing up your studying and say hi to Tucker for me."

Yeah, that's not going to happen. "Sure. See ya."

I rush from her car and quickly make my way into the house. It's quiet when I shut the door, but I know I'm not alone. Tucker's truck is parked out front and his wallet and keys are on the counter. The man is around here somewhere.

"Hello?" I call out.

There is a crash in the dining room that pulls my attention. I set my things down and rush to where I heard the sound. Tucker is standing in the dining room, his hand in his hair, his work clothes still on, and a potted plant shattered on the floor.

"Oh no, are you okay?"

He puts his hand out to stop me. "Don't come closer, babe. I don't want you to step on any glass."

"What happened?"

Hand still in his hair, he looks up at me through his lashes and says on a chuckle, "You startled me."

"I startled you?" I laugh.

"Yeah. I was trying to get this little herb garden I made into the kitchen before you came home, since you suggested the other day that we should grow our own herbs."

Freaking melt my heart.

"Aw, Tucker, that's so sweet."

"Yeah, well it's a fucking mess now. Do me a favor, babe? Go into the basement. In the back far right corner, under some blankets, there is a shop vac. Can you grab it? It will be the easiest way to clean this mess up."

"Sure, not a problem."

I go to the basement, which is through the kitchen by the side door and hold on to the rail as I make my way down the rickety stairs. I don't ever go in the basement, so navigating my way around is proving to be difficult.

"Lights, where are the lights?" I feel around for a light switch but there are no walls for a light switch. I'm about to turn around when my head skims across something dangling from the ceiling. For a second I freak out thinking it's a spider trying to spindle my hair into a web when I realize it's a pull cord for a light.

"Oh, thank God," I mutter, turning the light on.

From above, I can hear Tucker moving around toward the

front door. Hopefully he's not tracking dirt everywhere because that will be a nightmare to clean up.

I look around toward the corners but don't see a shop vac. I look under the blankets like Tucker said but see nothing. "Where the hell are you, shop vac?" I call out, hoping the machinery will make itself known. I take a few minutes to look around but Tucker really doesn't have much in the basement besides some random tools, painting supplies, and wood. Makes sense since he works in construction.

"Hmm . . ." I tap my chin, take one more look and then head back upstairs. When I reach the kitchen, I hear voices coming from the living room.

"Wow, it looks amazing in here." *Sadie?* She came inside?

"Thanks," Tucker gruffs out. "I, uh, thought I would make it not look so sterile."

"You did an amazing job. It truly looks like a warm and inviting home in here, Tucker."

"That's how I envisioned it." For some reason, his answer makes me feel ill. It's how *he* envisioned it. What does *that* mean? Did he mean when he bought the house for Sadie? Or did he envision it this way when trying to make it comfortable for me? This shouldn't matter, I shouldn't care, but with Sadie in the next room, walking through the house that was supposed to be hers—*theirs*—I have a sinking feeling it is the former.

I walk toward the dining room and peek around the wall, observing them for a second. Sadie is holding one of my nursing books—shit, I must have left it in the car in my haste to get the hell away from her probing questions—and Tucker stands a few feet away, hands in his pockets, his eyes trained on her. His body language doesn't read stiff like I expected it to be. It's more natural, almost leaning in her direction.

"This is a little awkward." Sadie laughs, which causes Tucker to laugh as well and then grab the back of his neck.

With a tilted head, he smiles at her and says, "It's good to see you, though."

My stomach sinks to the floor and my throat starts to clamp up. It's not the words, but the way he spoke them, with a rich, velvety tone that almost sounds grateful of her presence. Embarrassment and humility crashes into me like a wave of big, fat regret. Was I just dreaming these last few months? Was I living in the clouds, thinking that maybe, just maybe Tucker would actually get over Sadie, and find comfort and love with me? Did I even stand a chance?

I clamp my arms around my stomach and shift my feet, trying not to feel sick. When I shift, the floor creaks, drawing their attention. Sadie makes eye contact with me and smiles. "Hey, girl. You left your book in my car. Thought you might need it."

Putting on a bright smile and avoiding all eye contact with Tucker, I walk up to Sadie and take the book while saying thank you. "Yeah, I would have missed this one tonight."

"Oh, I'm glad I brought it back tonight instead of trying to find you tomorrow." Sadie folds her hands together and looks around one last time. "I better get . . . oh, look, these are cute." She walks up to the fireplace and I squeeze my eyes shut. Shit, the picture frames. "Wh—" Sadie whips around toward me and whispers behind her hand. "You're with Tucker?"

Crap. I could say no, but the picture of Tucker kissing me on the cheek is a dead giveaway. Instead of lying, I nod my head.

"You two are dating?" This time Sadie turns to Tucker who is still pulling on the back of his neck, but with more force now.

"I mean, we're kind of just having fun," Tucker answers, avoiding all kinds of eye contact.

*Excuse me?*

*Just having fun?*

This time I look at Tucker. He glances at me, regret in his eyes. Yeah, you better regret that little statement. *Or maybe he won't. Maybe he wants me to know this about us.*

Angry, frustrated, and hurt, I squeeze my book to my chest and say, "Yeah, just having fun. Nothing to worry about, Sadie. I would love to hash this out with you, but I really should get to studying." I turn away when I realize I should probably apologize. "I'm sorry for not telling you earlier and stepping over my best-friend boundaries. I should have thought about the repercussions before entering into something so casual." That last jab was for Tucker. A part of me really hopes it hurts him but from the way he's looking at Sadie . . .

*He still loves her.*

*He's not over her.*

From the look on his face, it probably didn't have the impact I wish it did. *We're kind of just having fun.* "Thanks for returning my book."

I give her a small wave and go straight to my room, making sure to dodge the broken pot on the ground.

Once my door is shut, I sink to the floor and put my head in my hands as tears start to fall from my eyes, a waterfall of pain and regret cascading past my fingers. What was I thinking, starting something with Tucker? A great pair of abs, a gentle heart, and a caring soul swept me up into his arms, took me for an unforgettable ride, and when I thought everything was going to work out for the long haul, I'm reminded of my rose-colored glasses. Rose-colored glasses that have blinded me to the truth.

Sadie. It's always been Sadie. And I'm not mad at her; I don't blame her for anything. They have history. So much history that of course, it would be impossible for Tucker to overcome that pull. *No one will come between that for him.* I should have seen it from the beginning, but I had too much hope for what could be between us.

Logan was right. And as I sit here feeling my heart ripping into thousands of pieces, I despise having to admit that.

*I'll never be Tucker Jameson's girl.*

*That door is closed.*

# Chapter Twenty-Two

"What the hell are you doing, Tucker?"

I stare off at Emma's room, a sinking feeling in my bones, the kind of feeling that's lighting up warning signs in my head, telling me that I just fucked up everything with Emma.

*We're just having fun.* Fuck, why the hell did I say that? My initial thought was to protect Emma, to save her relationship with Sadie. I thought if I made what we have between us seem casual, Sadie wouldn't be as mad, but it had the reverse effect. Instead, I hurt Emma.

"Tucker, go after her," Sadie says.

I rake my hand through my hair, my heart pulling in Emma's direction, but my head fucking with me. "Why did you come here?" I ask, malice in my voice.

Sadie takes a step back from my unwarranted anger. "Emma left her book in my car, and I wanted to make sure she had it. Why are you angry at me?"

"Because," I snap while I start to pace the room. "Because you're the one thing that could fuck up this whole thing."

"Me?" Sadie points to herself. "How could I possibly be the reason to fuck up anything between you and Emma? First of all, I had no clue anything was even going on between you two. Second of all, I've moved on, Tucker, so Emma should have nothing to worry about in that department, unless . . ."

The way she trails off her sentence grates on my nerves. "Unless what?"

She takes a step forward and I take a step back. She sighs and continues, "Unless you haven't moved on."

"I have," I answer quickly. There is doubt in my mind that I have. I don't look at Sadie and wish she were still mine. I can't. I feel like my heart has moved on but not my head. Isn't it usually the reverse? Isn't it the heart that takes longer to heal? If that's the case, then why am I still all caught up in my head, like there's a giant roadblock there, stopping me from making any goddamn progress?

"If you have, then there shouldn't be any worry in Emma's eyes." Sadie gestures to the pictures on the mantel and then around the living room. "This seems like a hell of a lot more than just having fun. And from the way Emma has been MIA lately, I'm going to assume what's going on between you two means a lot more to her than the casual fling you portrayed."

"It means more to me too," I say softly and pull on my hair. "Fuck."

"Does she know that?"

Frustrated and angry at myself, I direct that anger at Sadie. "I really don't need a fucking counseling session from you right now, Sadie."

Not taking my shit, she steps forward and pokes me in the chest. "It sure as hell seems like it. Tell me, if I went into the second bedroom, would a crib still be in there?"

My eyes snap to hers, rage blasting behind my lids. "Go ahead, Sadie, fucking talk about the baby we lost, see where that gets you."

"You can't keep living in the past, Tucker."

"I was doing fine before you showed up."

"Were you? Or were you just pretending you were fine? How can you ever be fine, Tucker, if you still have the past resting in a bedroom a few short feet away from Emma's room? Does she even know what's behind that door?"

I shake my head, hating myself, hating how fucked up I am, hating how Sadie's miscarriage still hollows me out into a shell of nothing every time I think about it. Every time I think about her.

"How do you think she feels then? You devalued what you two have in front of me, the person she's probably most terrified of when it comes to you because of our history, and you still have things hidden from her?"

Not to mention fucking rule number six. Shit. I've fucked this all up.

"Fuck," I mumble and take a seat in one of the armchairs. Sadie sits across from me on the couch and places her hand on my knee.

"Tucker, I care about you, and all I want is for you to find peace and be happy. It seems like Emma is your happy, but the peace, that's within you. You need to find acceptance and move on, until you can do that, you can't fully be with Emma. And I love that girl. *She* doesn't deserve to be strung along, only being handed half of you."

She's right; I hate that she's fucking right. But something I desperately wanted was taken away from me. How do I just become okay with that? Find *peace* in that?

"How did you do it?" I ask, Sadie, my eyes trained on the floor in front of me.

"How did I do what?"

"How did you get over the loss of our baby? How did you

move on?"

"I don't ever think you get over it, Tucker. Our baby is a piece of you that will always rest in your heart. Sometimes you have to look at it in a different light. We weren't ready and our relationship wasn't healthy. Maybe there was some powerful cosmic force that saw we weren't prepared mentally. It wasn't our time, and that's what we have to focus on."

"I was ready," I say on a whisper. "I was ready to be an amazing fucking dad." My throat closes up just thinking about how I had it all planned out in my head. How I was going to get up in the middle of the night and help with feedings, how I was going to be master diaper changer, how I was committed to giving our baby a healthy and loving home.

*I was going to be better than her.*

I was going to be so much better than her . . . my mother.

I was going to prove that bad parenting isn't hereditary, that you can break from what's expected of you, rise above it all, and be the antithesis of neglect and hate.

"You still are going to be a great dad, Tucker. You're young and have a lifetime ahead of you to show the world the thoughtful, genuine, and caring man you've become despite the home you grew up in. Be sad about the baby we lost, but don't let it dictate the rest of your life."

Her words ring true in my head. That's what I've been doing. But how? How do I prevent that from happening? The loss of my dad dictated both my physical and emotional poverty. The loss of a mother's nurturing hand in my life forced me into a job I love and am damn good at. The loss of Sadie meant I lost my best friend and many past connections.

*That* loss allowed my soul to meet my Emma.

Losses aren't all bad. In fact, losses can bring about good. Different but good.

*Be sad about the baby we lost, but don't let it dictate the rest of your life.* That's what Sadie's done. I need to accept what we lost. To focus on my future. No, not *my* future. If there is one thing that is abundantly clear now, it's *our* future I want. The one I want with Emma. The one I hope I can rectify with Emma. I want *us*.

Because there is one thing I know for certain. Losing Sadie and the baby crippled me for a time, but losing Emma will destroy me.

• • •

Sadie left a little while ago. I took my time cleaning up the broken pot and locking up the house before I went to Emma. I needed to get my head on straight before I talked to her, before I apologized for being a total ass.

There isn't a light shining under the crack of her door so I look at the time on my phone. Past ten, shit. Unsure if I should knock, I waver between what to do. If she's sleeping, will she want to wake up and have a conversation? But if I wait until the morning, will that be too late? I'm thinking the latter is not the way I want to go so I knock. When I don't hear her answer, I open the door a few inches and peek inside.

I was right, she doesn't have a light turned on and over on her bed, she's in a curled-up ball, her back facing me.

Needing to make things right, I walk over to her bed and sit on the side, pressing my hand on her hip. She startles for a second but then doesn't make a move after that.

"Emma," I whisper, hoping not to scare her too much.

"What, Tucker?" she replies, her voice groggy.

"I'm sorry if I woke you up, but I really want to talk to you about tonight."

She turns in the bed and sits up. From the light pouring in

from the moon, I can see her eyes are puffy from crying. Bitter pain runs down my spine. I did this to her. I'm constantly doing this to her, upsetting her when she's done absolutely nothing but love on me.

She wipes her cheeks and then pulls her legs into her chest, a defensive position I don't care for. "There is nothing to really talk about, Tucker."

"Like hell there isn't. I was an ass back there. I shouldn't have said what I did."

"Oh, that we are just having fun?" I cringe from her sarcastic tone. "Because isn't that what this is? Just fun? There isn't any emotional connection behind what we have as it's just been sex, right?"

"No—"

"Well, it was for me." She jabs me in the gut. "Just a little fun before I graduated. Isn't that what you wanted, Tucker? Rule number one, let loose? Well, I did. I let loose, I had some fun, and now it's time for me to focus on graduating, taking my exams, and moving on and moving out."

I grind my teeth together from hearing her say those two words. *Move out.* Just hearing those words causes a deep-rooted ache within me. Move out, fuck, that terrifies me. I don't want her to leave. She can't fucking leave.

I try to take her hand, but she doesn't let me, so I run my hand over my face, my frustration over this situation growing exponentially and my inability to voice my thoughts that are clogging my throat. "It wasn't just fun for me, Emma. You mean something to me."

"Yeah?" She nods. "Good to know." Fuck I hate this. This is not *my* Emma.

"Are you going to say what we have doesn't mean anything to you?"

Her response isn't quick. It's more calculated as she chews on her bottom lip, her eyes falling to her knees, trying to figure out how to break my fucking heart. I can see it in her posture, in the way she's shutting down. For once, she's saving herself before I can do any more damage.

When she looks back up at me, I can see the finality in her eyes. This is over for her. Too bad it's not fucking over for me.

"You're my friend, Tucker, so of course you mean something to me. But what we've had, it was just temporary, not long-term. I think it would be best to end everything and stay as friends, so at least we have that."

"Stay as friends." I nod, anger vibrating off me.

"Yeah, I think it's for the best. Plus with everything changing in a month, who knows where I'll be? Best to end it now."

"Where you'll be, what the hell is that supposed to mean?"

"I've been applying for jobs, Tucker. Some are out of state."

"What?" I stand, my anger blinding me now. "You've applied to jobs out of state? When in the hell were you going to tell me this?"

"I didn't think it was necessary . . . since we were only having fun." She hits me with those regretful words again, but I call bullshit.

I lean forward and plant my hands on either side of the wall behind her, trapping her, forcing her to look me in the eyes. I speak low, deliberately. "You can dick around all you want, Emma, but you and I both know we weren't just having fun. Was I scared about admitting my feelings to you in front of Sadie? Yeah. Did I want to protect your relationship with Sadie by minimalizing what we have? Fuck, I did. Did I mean any of it? No. Because what we have between us is different. It's solid. It's fucking beautiful. I might have fucked this up between us tonight, but moving forward, I won't be doing that again because you mean everything to me, Emma. Fucking everything."

I push off the wall and walk to her door just as she calls out, her voice shaky, "It's over, Tucker."

"Not if I can fucking help it."

I slam her door shut and retreat to my room, my heart heavy, and a whirlwind of emotions swirling through my head. *I can't lose her. Why the fuck did I say something so stupid? Things were so good. You're a stupid asshole, Jameson.*

She's the best thing in my life.

*My everything.*

She's not moving. This is not over. That woman down there, she's meant to be mine, and I'll be damned if I let her walk away from me. She doesn't need to protect her heart from me. She holds mine in her hands, and I'll never take it back. Emma Marks is mine.

# Chapter Twenty-Three

## EMMA

Have you ever tried studying when all you can think about is the broken heart that beats regardless within your chest? It's pretty much impossible. I haven't retained anything in three weeks, which is proving to be detrimental to my studying schedule. Graduation is in two weeks, my exam is two days after that and all I can think about is Tucker.

*Not if I can fucking help it.*

His parting words to me. Since that night, I haven't heard from him. Not a phone call, not a text, not even a little morning hello. The only thing I've received from him was a note on the counter two days after our fight saying he's been sent to Pittsburgh for another training project. He wasn't sure when he would be back. He asked me to water the plants and be sure to eat my daily amount of vegetables.

That was it.

Since then, nothing.

I know I ended everything, but after his parting words, I thought maybe there was some hope, maybe he could get past his demons and fully embrace me. *Us.* But three weeks of radio silence has tamped down that hope, straight into the grave that is Tucker and Emma.

"Uh hello, earth to Emma." Adalyn snaps her fingers in my face. "Are you going to say hi?"

"What?" I look away from the sentence I've highlighted five times to see Logan standing at the end of our table. "Oh, uh, hey, Logan."

"Hey." He looks to Adalyn and then back to me. "Think I can borrow you for a second?"

Since I have yet to actually retain what I'm reading, I'm thinking a little break in the monotony of studying might do me some good.

"Yeah, sure."

"Want to go get some coffee at the kiosk?" he asks.

"Sure. Adalyn, do you want anything?"

"Caffeine dripped from the coffee bean's teat. Ask if they have an IV."

"I take that as a dark roast, black." She nods and focuses all her attention on the books in front of her. That should be me. Single focused.

*Should.*

As we walk to the kiosk, we're both silent, making this outing a little awkward. We order our drinks and while we wait, Logan finally breaks the ice by knocking his foot playfully against mine. "I don't think we've ever been this quiet around each other."

"I don't think so either." I nervously laugh and then sigh. "Listen, Logan, I'm sorry for getting so defensive—"

"No, I'm sorry. I shouldn't have been so bold in my assumptions. You were right, I didn't know you two as a couple, and I never should have said anything. I'm sorry."

"It's okay." Our order is called out and instead of going back to the library, we sit on the bench. Adalyn's coffee is piping hot so we have some time to spare.

"So, how's it going with you two?"

My eyes sting as I hold back the tears that have wanted to fall every second of every day whenever I think of Tucker. "It's not going," I answer, my throat choking up on me.

"What do you mean? Did you break up?" I nod. "Oh shit." Logan wraps his arm around me and pulls me in close. "I'm sorry, Emma. Please tell me it's not from what I said."

I shake my head. "No, I think what you said actually held some weight."

"Really?" He doesn't sound happy, more sad than anything. *What the?*

"Yeah. I don't think he was ready to really hand his heart over. I don't think he was using me as a distraction. I do think he cared for me, but I could tell he wasn't ready, and honestly, I don't think I'm strong enough to wait around for him to love me."

"Do you love him?"

I lean my head against Logan's shoulder as a stray tear falls down my cheek. "Yeah, I do. I don't think there was any choice in the matter for me. My soul connected with his and I fell for him." *I fell hard.* "Despite knowing the whole time there was a roadblock between us. I just thought we'd be able to get over it. But I was wrong."

"Did you break up with him?" I nod. "Were you protecting yourself?" I nod again. "So where does he stand in all of this? What did he say? Did he accept the breakup and move on? Or did he put up a fight?"

That night has been on replay in my head for weeks. I can see it playing out so easily, remember everything said. The sound of his voice as he shut my door, the hope I felt . . . The hope then squashed by his silence.

"It seemed like he was putting up a fight. I didn't think he'd accept my decision, but I haven't heard from him in weeks."

"What do you mean? Don't you share a house?"

"He's been in Pittsburg training for three weeks." My voice hiccups on me.

"Oh." Logan is silent, taking a moment to process what I said. He brings his coffee to his lips and takes a drink before saying, "But he sounded like he wasn't giving up?"

"That's how it seemed when I broke things off. But I haven't heard from him. I think it's over." And admitting that hurts more than when I was trying to save my heart.

"You don't know that for sure."

"Logan. I'm not going to be wishful here. If he cared, he would have contacted me by now. I'm done." *It hurts to hope.* I stand and brush my bottom off before turning to him. "Ready? Adalyn is going to be pissed if her coffee is cold."

"Yeah." He holds his coffee and Adalyn's as he puts his hand on the small of my back for a brief second, guiding me toward the library. "I don't think you should throw in the towel just yet."

"You're sweet, Logan, but I'm not holding on to any hope."

"I think you should."

"Why are you pushing this? According to Tucker, you want to fuck me, and he would have sworn you would have swooped in by now," I tease, but I'm also curious to hear his answer.

"He thought that, did he?" Logan asks, a smile to his face as he takes a drink of his coffee. "Then I did my job."

"Did what job?"

"Made him feel threatened. Jealous. That right there tells me there is still hope, Emma. If he didn't care about you, he wouldn't have cared about me. But he cares."

"You made him jealous on purpose?"

He loops an arm around my shoulder and kisses the top of my head. It's funny how with Logan, when he does that, I feel cared for by an older brother. When Tucker kisses me like that, I feel treasured. No. *I felt treasured.* "I have to make sure my girl is taken care of. You're my best friend, Emma, and only the best man deserves you. So if I have to act territorial to see if he's willing to piss a circle around you, then I will do just that."

"Oh my God," I laugh. "You're such an ass."

"A caring ass." He winks over his coffee cup. "I expect the same kind of treatment from you."

I poke him in the side, putting a little distance between us. "Just you wait. Once you meet the girl for you, I'm going to make sure your life is a living nightmare."

"Come on, it wasn't that bad."

"He got defensive about you." That causes Logan to throw his head back and laugh. "It's not funny. He was really convinced you wanted to sleep with me."

He continues to laugh, drawing the attention from others around us. "Oh that's great. Man, Emma, he really fucking likes you because I wasn't even that bad."

I huff as I walk into the library. "I can't believe that's something guys do."

"Only the smart ones looking out for their girls. Now, tell me in detail everything he said about me."

I point my finger at him. "You're a dick."

"Come on, just give me a little something."

"No." We get to the table where Adalyn is studying and sit down. Logan hands her the coffee, and she breathes it in before taking a long swig.

"Oh, that's good." She glances between the both of us. "Why are you laughing, did I miss something?"

"Logan was pretending to like me in front of Tucker to piss him off."

She takes another sip. "Oh, I know." She fist-bumps Logan.

"Well-played. You really got the old jealousy bug ticking in his bones."

"You knew?" I shout and am quickly hushed by people around us so I whisper, "You knew?"

"Of course." She shrugs her knowledge off. "Classic best-friend move made by a guy. He couldn't have executed it any better." They laugh at my expense.

"I hate you both." I cross my arms over my chest and try not to pout. "Not like it helped anyway."

"He still hasn't talked to you?" Adalyn asks, confused. "Not even a text?"

"Nothing." I bite the inside of my cheek, willing away the tears that threaten to fall.

The silence is killing me. I miss him. I miss his rough, sleep-ridden voice in the mornings, his work clothes that cling to every last inch of muscle on his body. I miss his kisses, his strong arms wrapped around me, the way he would whisper in my ear, igniting my entire body. And mostly, I miss his heart that *seemed* to care deeply for me.

I shrug, putting on a brave face. "Maybe it's for the better. I may have a job panning out in Boston. Maybe a new city is just what I need."

A fresh beginning, something far away from the place I've recently called home.

# Chapter Twenty-Four

"Fucking pizza," I mutter, pushing the box to the side. Four fucking nights in a row of the stale shit. Who ever said you can't get sick of pizza is wrong. I'm all cheesed out. Three weeks living off hotel breakfast, soggy sandwiches, and pizza at night has left me more irritated than when I was told I had to report to Pittsburgh for some bullshit management training. Honestly, I think Julius is required to go to these courses for his business but sends me instead to complete his dirty work.

And what makes it even worse? I'm too fucking far away from Emma.

I had everything planned out on how to fix this shit between us, but my quick departure screwed everything up and the last thing I want to do is try to fix this over the phone. So instead, I've taken this time to journal.

I know . . . *journal.*

I've never picked up a pen and thought about writing down my feelings, but that's what I've been doing, every night. Writing it all out, bleeding my emotions through my pen and onto the paper. And do you know what I've come to realize since I've started journaling? The emotional attachment I have to Sadie has a lot to do with how she took care of me when I needed someone to love me, to watch over me, and not with the love we once shared. Funny how long it took me to realize that.

The baby, well, my need to travel down the opposite path my mother paved for me is overwhelming. The baby gave me an opportunity to love something other than myself, to show the world that despite my upbringing, I can be a man, a provider, a responsible and loving parent. But Sadie helped me. We weren't ready, and maybe this time I've spent building my career will help make me an even better father when another opportunity presents itself.

The silence between Emma and me has also been for her benefit. I needed to get my head on straight. I want to be the man she deserves, the man who will provide for her, the man who gives her all of his heart without anything standing in the way. Because I know with one hundred percent certainty. That's what I want. *Her*.

My phone rings, pulling me away from Hayden's hockey game that's on the small flat-screen TV in front of me.

*Racer.*

"What's up, man?"

"I missssssss you!" he cries like a dickhead in the phone. "I need an Oatmeal Creme Pie in my mouth."

"You know you can buy them yourself, right?"

"I would but I'm saving my money."

"You're such a cheap fuck."

He laughs on the other end of the phone. "I fucking know it and wear that title with pride."

"Please tell me you've at least stopped taking toilet paper from the porta-potties."

"Why the hell would I do that? If I have to go in there to take a piss, I'm at least going to get something out of it." He laughs as if he just thought of something. "Oh shit, Julius went into one of the shit boxes today and came out raging in red, pants unbuckled, yelling about there never being toilet paper. I fucking fell over laughing. Smalls got it on his Snapchat. Did you see it?"

"I don't do social media, you know that."

"Fuck, you're such a grandpa."

"Is there a reason for this phone call, or did you call just to dick with me?" I put my phone on speaker and lay it against my chest as I put both my hands behind my head and watch the muted game play out.

"Didn't know I had to have a reason to talk to my best friend."

"Best friend, huh? Laying it on thick. What do you want, man?"

"I don't want anything, but there is something I need to talk to you about."

"I knew it." I chuckle into the phone. "What is it? Did you fuck up another fireplace? Slam your head through a wall? Slide down another fucking banister only to pop the railing off?"

"First of all, I slid down a banister once and learned my fucking lesson. Second of all, I don't fuck up fireplaces and you know it, so stop being a little bitch about my stone-laying abilities. And this has nothing to do about work. It's about Emma."

I sit straight up, the hairs on the back of my neck rising to attention as nerves take up residence inside my stomach. "What about Emma? What's wrong? Is she okay?"

Fuck, I should have called her. I should have been talking to her. What if something happened to her and I never found out? I would never forgive myself.

"She's fine. I actually got a call from Adalyn today."

"Adalyn? How does she have your number?"

"We exchanged numbers at the dinner party." Christ. "She

was worried about what's going on between you two and concerned that Emma might do something irrational."

"What are you talking about?" I start pacing the hotel room, unsure of what to do with this built-up tension.

"Adalyn said she's thinking about moving to Boston for a job."

*What the hell?*

"Boston?" I run my hand over my face. "Fuck. Fuck!"

"Dude, I thought you were going to fix things with her. Did that change? Adalyn said you haven't talked to Emma in three weeks. What the fuck? Are you trying to lose her forever?"

"No. I was just trying to get my head straight. Figure my shit out before I went after her."

"That's great and all, but not talking to her at all is hurting you *and her* more than you realize. You have to do some major damage control. When are you supposed to come back?"

"Not for another two damn weeks."

"Jesus, what the hell are they making you do out there?"

"Learn how to speak nicely to employees," I deadpan, thinking about the idiotic classes I've taken so far. "How the hell am I supposed to do this when I'm so far away? Talking on the phone doesn't seem like enough, it almost seems like a cop-out."

"Yeah, but it's better than nothing."

"Nothing isn't an option anymore, and the phone isn't what she deserves. I need something more."

Racer chuckles in the phone. "The determination in your voice is making my heart flutter with romance."

"Shut the fuck up," I mumble, still pacing the floor. How can I fix this? She can't fucking run off to Boston and out of my life forever.

I think back to our earlier conversations, about how she based a man off their first kiss, how she had to be swept off her feet with one single press against the lips. Well, since I'm not there to do that, I'm going to have to think of other ways to sweep her off her feet.

"I'm going to need your help, man," I say into the phone as ideas start to formulate in my mind.

"It's going to cost you."

I know he's kidding. The dickhead would do anything for me, but I still ask, "How many boxes are we talking?"

"I've missed that curly-headed broad. I'm thinking ten boxes of Oatmeal Creme Pies, five Nutty Bars, five Zebra Cakes, and two Cosmic Brownies, because let's not go too overboard."

"Yeah, not too overboard," I reply sarcastically. "Should I include a toothbrush for you to avoid cavities with all that sugar?"

"Might not be a bad idea. Get me some floss too. Gums need love too, Tucker. Gums need love too."

I laugh, a little bit of tension easing out of my chest, but not much. "Thanks, dude."

"So what do you have planned?" He's serious now and I can just picture him, pen in hand ready to write down the plan.

"I need to put some things together. I'll be sending you a package tomorrow. Call me when you get it, because I'm going to be very specific as to how we make this happen."

"Sounds complicated. I might need ten boxes of Nutty Bars."

"You're lucky you're going to get five; don't push it, man."

"Sorry, but who's helping who here?" Racer teases.

"I have no problem asking Smalls . . ."

"No," Racer yells into the phone. "I want to do it. I'm involved now, you can't take that away from me."

I roll my eyes and shake my head. "Do me a favor, man, reach between your legs and check for your balls. They still there?"

"Oh . . . are we getting kinky now? I'm not prepared for phone sex. Give me a second." He clears his voice and talks in a deep, rich tone, "How you doing, baby? Want me to stroke my gonads for you?"

I hang up and chuckle, not giving him a chance to further whatever fucking disastrous conversation that would have been. With a renewed sense of direction, I grab my wallet, stuff it in my back pocket, and head to my car in the parking garage just as I get a text message.

**Racer: *It's offensive to me that you would hang up just as I start to stroke my penis.***

Fucking idiot.

**Tucker: *Thin ice, man. Smalls is on speed dial.***

**Racer: *Don't you fucking dare! This reconciliation is in my hands . . . that and my penis.***

**Tucker: *I must be a total moron to have gotten you involved.***

**Racer: *Moron or genius? We will just have to wait and see.***

I guess we will.

# Chapter Twenty-Five

EMMA

I put my car in park and look at the dark house in front of me. Empty, that's how it feels. Empty, cold, and not like home. It's become a place to lay my head. Despite Tucker's attempts at making it seem like a home, it really isn't one without him living in it, without his eggs and bacon waking me up in the morning, or without that rough, yet sexy voice of his bouncing off the walls, joking and teasing.

It just isn't the same at all.

I can't wait to get out of here. There's no point for me to move out since graduation is right around the corner, so I just have to grin and bear it.

Sighing, I exit my car, sling my backpack over my shoulder, and enter the house. I lock up before entering the kitchen and don't even bother turning on the light. I ate at the student union with Logan and Adalyn, just like every other night for the past few nights. Eating by myself has been rather depressing, so I try to avoid it as much as I can.

I turn the lights on in my bedroom and startle for a second. It's empty. Everything is gone, the only thing in the room is a vase of peonies with a card on the ground. Is this how he tells me to move out? With the dreaded thank-you note I predicted and some flowers as a last hurrah? What the hell, Tucker? But he said he would fight for me, and I know him.

*He does fight for those he cares about.*

My heart switches from terrified to twisting and turning from the possibility of Tucker being here. I drop my bag and sit on the ground. I smell the peonies, which draw a smile on my face and pick up the card. Written in familiar handwriting is the word "Baby." Butterflies float around in my stomach and my throat starts to grow tight.

Excited and nervous, I open the card. On the front is a picture of Niall from *One Direction* that makes me laugh out loud. Inside there is a long note with a few folded papers. I decide to read the note first.

*Hey baby,*

*When I said I wasn't giving up, I meant it, but first I have a few things to apologize about. (I wanted to do this in person, but work has gotten in the way, so please bear with me as I try to make this work for us)*

*Apologies:*

*I'm sorry it's taken me this long to contact you. Just because I haven't talked to you doesn't mean I haven't thought about you every second of every goddamn day we've been apart. You consume every moment of my day, Emma, and it's the reason why I've taken this time to get my head straight. I've had some challenges in my life and without addressing them, without truly finding acceptance, I wouldn't be mentally healthy enough to give you all of me. And that's what I want. I want you to own every ounce of me, Emma.*

*I'm sorry if I ever made you question the way I feel about you, if you ever felt second best to Sadie, or if you ever thought you weren't good enough for me, if I merely was just using you for fun. Nothing could be further from the truth. Since the moment you moved into my house, our home, I've felt light again, free, like the world around me is suddenly full of color. You, baby, are the best thing to ever happen in my life and nothing can ever change that.*

*I'm sorry I put a roadblock between us, a rule that ended up hurting us more than helping us. At the time, I was still struggling with finding a way to deal with the pain that consumed me. I didn't want to be reminded of all that I lost. And then you came along and lit up a bright future for me. So rule number six is off the table . . . which brings me to . . .*

*Hopefully you haven't already looked at the papers folded in the card. If you haven't, open them up, take a look, and then come back to this card.*

Tears in my eyes, I unfold the papers and find journal entries in Tucker's handwriting, dated the day he left up until two days ago. The entries are not even the slightest bit pretty; they're scribbled, crossed out, almost angry in nature. But as I start to flip through them, the anger seems to become less and less as the days go on. I take a moment to read them, going through the same emotional roller coaster Tucker did writing about Sadie, why she was important to him, the baby and why he was so attached, and at the end, our break up and why *that* demolished him.

I'm having a hard time catching my breath as his last sentence sticks out above the rest.

*I don't want to let go. I can't let go. She's my forever.*

A single tear falls on the journal entries, and I quickly wipe at my eyes to avoid ruining the beautiful words below me. With my breathing evening out, I turn back to Tucker's letter and pick up where I left off.

*I mean it, Emma. You're my forever.*

*I know I fucked up, big time, but I plan on making it up to you, and it starts now. I might not be there with you right now to brush a kiss across those beautiful lips of yours before you go to bed, so I want to give you the next best thing . . . well, the next best thing I could think of.*

*You might be wondering where all your stuff is, right? Since you're who I want, you're the girl of my dreams, I want you to be sleeping where I dreamt of you for so many nights before I finally claimed those lips. Go upstairs.*

Gathering the card, journal entries, and flowers, I go upstairs making sure to turn on the stairway light. When I reach the top step, I'm floored. Tucker's room is a combination of both of us. His bed, my dresser. His nightstands, my lights. My rug decorates his floor and my throw pillows decorate the armchair in the corner. And on the bed, there is a brand new white comforter and light grey sheets that make the bed look like a cloud floating in the middle of the room. On every surface, there are pictures of us together, some from when we were young, some taken recently, and of course, there are peonies all around the room.

I can't believe he did this.

On the bed is another card, and I waste no time opening.

*Welcome home, Emma.*

*This home, it's ours. No more separate rooms, no more separate beds. We live here together, as one. Racer decorated for me so he better have followed my specific directions and if he touched your underwear in any way, I will make sure to handle him when I get home.*

There is a side note written in a different handwriting that says, *"I didn't touch your underwear, but I did peek. Can't blame a fella. I really liked the yellow lace bra. Hot, Emma. Love, Racer."*

I laugh out loud and cover my mouth. I wondered how Tucker

did all of this. I guess I owe Racer a thank you.

I go back to the note.

*I hope you like the room. When I get home, we can change anything you want, paint it, or hang things. Whatever you want, baby, I will make happen. Until then, rest easy and know that I'm dreaming about you.*

*Yours forever,*

*Tucker*

I read the note a few more times before reaching for my phone, my heart full, and the urge to jump and scream in happiness filling me up. I dial Tucker's number and hold my breath, waiting to hear his rich voice over the phone. But after five rings, his voicemail picks up.

"Hey, you've reached Tucker. If this is Emma, be patient, baby. I'll be in touch soon. Until then, dream of me. If this is Racer, I swear I will tell everyone about your Taco Tuesday mishap if you give me shit for this message." The robot comes on the phone and I hang up as I laugh out loud. I want to talk to him . . . badly, but it seems he has a plan I need to wait out.

Sighing, I look around *OUR* room and sink into the bed.

It isn't over.

It's far from over.

• • •

"Sorry. Hey, watch it, there are people behind you, you know. No, I won't be quiet. What kind of fucking maze is this? Yes, I go here. What kind of question is that? What am I majoring in? I'm majoring in go fuck yourself . . ."

I look up from my books as I hear a familiar voice grow louder and louder.

"Go ahead, touch me again, see where that gets you. I'm just looking for someone. No, I'm not a lurker. If you would just let me . . . EMMA!" My name is shouted through the entire library, sending a wave of embarrassment down my spine.

I hop up from my seat to find Racer with a bouquet of flowers in his hand, a small bag, and a coffee, struggling against Garrett, one of the library assistants. Racer easily towers over Garrett, but Garrett is feisty and is poking Racer in any way he can, making him spin in circles. It's quite the scene.

Going to his rescue, I say, "Garrett, it's okay, he's with me."

Racer sighs in relief when he sees me approach. Giving Garrett a poke back, he says, "Told you I wasn't lurking. Christ, man." Racer pushes past Garrett and looks over his shoulder briefly before turning to me. "Your library watchdog is a real douche." Racer turns around again while walking backward. "Learn some self-defense. Yeah, you better run away."

"Stop it," I hush him. "You're going to get me kicked out."

I guide him back to my table. "The guy is a tool bag."

"He's just doing his job." I sit at my table and nod at the chair next to me. "What are you doing here?"

He holds up his goods. "Isn't it obvious? I'm Tucker's little bitch tonight."

A snort pops out of me as I cover my mouth. He raises his eyebrow at me as I apologize. "Sorry, you're very sweet for helping out."

"Yeah, well, he sent me a shit ton of Little Debbie snacks so I'm indebted to him right now." He hands me the flowers and coffee and sets the bag on the table. "Did you like the room?"

"I love it. It's perfect. Thank you for working hard on it."

He waves me off. "Had a little help from Smalls. With the current job finished and Tucker away, we need to fill our days with something. No big deal. Tucker had everything laid out, and we just had to follow his blueprint. As he bought everything online, I just picked it up at the store."

"Wow." I take a sip of the coffee, letting the warm liquid stretch down my throat. "He really planned everything out, didn't he?"

"You have no idea. That dick face has it bad for you." Racer leans forward and whispers, "Make sure you make him sweat it out a bit. Don't give in too easily." He winks and then pulls away. He stands and pushes the bag toward me. "That's from Prince Charming. I've got to get going, early morning tomorrow. See ya, Emma."

"Bye. Thanks, Racer."

He salutes me and takes off, keeping an eye on Garrett the entire time.

I have a bouquet of peonies in hand, my favorite coffee in front of me, and a gift bag ready to be opened. I giggle from Racer's attempt to make it look pretty with tissue paper and open it. Another card.

*Hey baby,*

*Fuck, I miss you. I miss your smile, your laugh, the way you can so easily make me feel at ease. I miss everything and can't wait to get home to hold you in my arms once again. Until then, here's a little care package to get you through these long nights of studying.*

*Get at it, babe, hit those books hard. I'm thinking of you . . . always.*

*Forever yours,*

*Tucker*

If he's trying to get me to fall for him, he doesn't need to try any longer. I'm there. I am so freaking there.

When I reach into the bag, the first thing I pull out is a box of Swiss Cake Rolls with a note on them.

*Snack it up, babe. And just because they're phallic shaped doesn't mean I'm alluding to anything. But am I picturing you eating these? Fuck yes. P.S. Don't give any to Racer.*

I shake my head and reach into the bag again, pulling out a pack of pencils.

*Do you use pencils? I don't know. But saw them and thought, my girl can't run out of pencils. So here you go.*

*My girl.* Those two words ring happiness into my heart.

The next thing in the bag I pull out is a T-shirt. Tucker's T-shirt. I take a sniff of it before reading the note. It smells just like him and makes my heart ache.

*In case you were missing me. I hope you are. Wear it to bed, dream of me, baby.*

I'm missing him terribly.

The last thing is a gift card to Starbucks in a giant coffee mug with a picture of him smiling like a lunatic on the front. I laugh out loud, disrupting the silence in the library.

*For your growing collection of mugs. Knowing you have to put your lips on my face every time you drink out of this mug makes these days a little easier. Also, get some coffee; you're going to need it for your late nights.*

He's thought of everything. I so desperately want to wrap my arms around him and thank him, to show him that I miss him, that I want nothing more than to be curled up against his chest right now.

Needing to hear his voice, I call him, making sure to be quiet. When his voicemail picks up again, I sigh in frustration.

"Hey, you've reached Tucker. If this is Emma, keep hanging in there, baby. Take this time to study, get ready for the end of the year. When you get home, be sure to look under your pillow. There's a gift card to Macy's. Get yourself a graduation dress. You deserve it. If this is Racer, thanks for the help. Your second payment of Little Debbie Snacks is on its way. Stop bitching about it." The robot comes on again and I laugh, but this time, with a heavy heart. I want him home.

I want him home now.

• • •

Two days until graduation. No more clinicals, no more classes, no more mind-numbing lectures. I should be happy. I should be overjoyed, excited, shouting from the rooftops like Adalyn and Logan who are still at the bar celebrating. But instead, I sit in the driveway of an empty house, aching for the one person I want to celebrate with. The one person who still isn't home.

I turn off my car and once again, walk into an empty house. When I step into the kitchen, a giant sign on a poster board greets me. In glitter paint—*oh, Racer*—it reads, Congratulations, Emma! You're done!

A soft smile plays over my lips from the gesture. Tucker hasn't missed a beat since he first switched our rooms around. Whether it was ordering pizza for me one night, leaving notes around the house just so I can be connected to him, or sending a gift card to take out Logan and Adalyn for dinner to celebrate. He's been there every step of the way, and yet, he hasn't. I understand he has to be gone for work, but I just want him back. This distance is really taking a toll on my aching heart.

At the bottom of the poster, there's an arrow pointing me in the direction of the hallway. I follow it to another arrow that points me toward the bathroom. When I get to the bathroom, one more arrow greets me and points me in the direction of the spare bedroom. The bedroom I'm not allowed to go into.

My heart rate picks up as I spot a card taped to the door. With a shaky and unsteady hand, I reach for it and read the front.

**Open me.**

I twist the card around, stick my finger in the envelope and tear it open. There is no card, just a letter written on hotel paper.

Leaning against the wall, I sink down to the floor, needing some support, and read the letter.

*Hey baby,*

*Congratulations on finishing up classes, you must be so proud of yourself. I know I am. If I haven't said it before, I admire you, and I'm damn fucking proud of you. Your soul was made to take care of people, and the world of medicine is lucky to have you. Just a few more days and it will all be over. Your hard work will finally pay off.*

*As for me, I wanted to wait until you were done with school to open up to you one last time. What's behind this door is a painful past, something that's taken me a long time to understand, something that's taken me even longer to accept.*

*But I'm ready. So when you are, open the door and take it all in.*

*Forever yours,*

*Tucker*

With the letter close to my chest, I look over at the unopened door and wonder what's behind it. I guess there's only one way to find out.

Regretful that Tucker isn't here to do this with me, I think about saving this moment until he's home but change my mind. He laid this all out for me, he has a plan, and I should follow it. On shaky legs, I take a deep breath and open the door. It's almost pitch black, so I feel around the wall for a light and when I hit a switch, my eyes adjust to the brightness, taking a second to observe what I'm seeing.

The walls are painted a pretty, neutral yellow, the floors are waxed and glistening under the single light in the room, and in the middle of it all is a vintage white crib. My heart seizes in my chest, the beat slowing to a snail's pace, as an aching feeling turns me numb from the inside out.

A nursery.

He's been hiding a nursery this entire time. Tears fall down my face, staining my cheeks as I walk over to the crib where another card rests. This one I open immediately while I sit on the ground, my legs feeling too weak to hold me up.

*Hey baby,*

*Thank you for being brave and walking into this room without me. I'm sorry I can't be there with you while you take this in, but I thought it was important for you to know all of me.*

*This is it. The last thing I've been holding back.*

*When I found out Sadie was pregnant, I tried to grasp anything to resurrect our failing relationship, so I bought this house with the hope of starting a family here. I spent a day painting this room and building this crib as a surprise. Unfortunately, I never got to show her when she was pregnant. As you know, we lost the baby, and we lost ourselves.*

*I can't tell you the excitement I had in my bones to be a dad. I was so fucking thrilled. I was going to do it right, I told myself. I was going to bring this baby into a loving home. I was going to take care of it and give it the childhood I wish I had.*

*I was going to do everything right.*

*And then everything went wrong. I couldn't understand why I would lose my baby and Sadie at the same time, but after a lot of reflection, I've come to realize the home I wanted to bring that baby into wasn't ready. And the love between Sadie and me was embellished in my head from many years of relying on her.*

*By the time she went to college, we weren't in love but were just latching on to what we'd had in the past. I'm not sure how much of a loving home we could have provided for that baby given our doomed relationship.*

*Would we have made it work? Yes, but sometimes bad things happen for a reason.*

*There isn't a day that goes by that I don't think of the baby, but I have to be grateful because from a horrific event came light.*

*I will always wonder about him or her. The baby will forever be in my heart, but I'm ready to move past the pain and be the man you deserve, because with great tragedy came an unexpected blessing: you.*

*I miss you. Wear my shirt tonight, dream of me.*

*Forever yours,*

*Tucker*

The letter slips through my hands as I cry an ugly amount of tears. This man . . . this soulful, passionate, sincere man. His heartache is my heartache, and I'm feeling it all the way to my toes. This is what he has hidden from the world. From me. This is why his soul hadn't completely healed. I get it.

*I get* you*, Tucker.*

Desperate, I call him. "Please pick up, please pick up," I mutter, rocking back and forth on the floor.

When his voicemail comes on the line, *again,* I lean back on the floor, more tears pouring out of me.

"Hey, it's Tucker. If this is Emma, please know I want nothing more than to be holding you right now, kissing your forehead, and chasing your heartache away. Just know, baby, I'm happy and you make me happy. If this is Racer, I'm not reimbursing you for the glitter paint, so don't ask again."

This time, I don't laugh. Instead, I'm numb, lying on the ground, wishing for some kind of miracle that Tucker will soon be home, because I'm not sure I can go many more days without him.

• • •

"We did it!" Adalyn shouts, hands in the air as she runs in place in excitement.

"Does this mean you can take my pulse and be accurate?" Racer asks as he looks between Adalyn, Logan, and me.

Adalyn stops mid run and gives Racer a pointed look. "If you can't take your own pulse you shouldn't be a functioning member of society."

"I get nervous that I won't be able to find one. I don't want to be dead."

Logan grips Racer on the shoulder. "If you're able to feel around for a pulse, you're not dead, man."

Unable to concentrate on the banter, I look around the sea of people, trying to spot any semblance of the man I desperately want to see. For some reason, I thought maybe, just maybe, he would show up for my graduation. But since he's not with Racer, my hope is quickly vanishing.

My parents have already left for their car so they aren't stuck in traffic forever. We have plans to go to dinner later. But before they left, we took our pictures, they kissed me on the cheek, and my dad slipped a check in my pocket. Classic Dad.

Sadie and Andrew sent me a huge bouquet of flowers, which brought tears to my eyes.

*Sadie*.

Before I received that first note from Tucker, while I was still feeling so confused, lost, and bereft, Sadie visited me. She told me she understood why I'd felt I couldn't tell her about our relationship. There was no anger, no malice, just a hint of sadness. But not for herself. For me. For Tucker.

She also said something very surprising. When she had looked at that picture of the two of us on the mantel, she had nearly cried. Not because she still loved and wanted Tucker, but because she saw Andrew in Tucker's expression. She'd been shocked, naturally, but she'd also felt relief. She'd never seen that look on Tucker's face before, and that was when she knew he was finally on his road to recovery. That was when she knew he was going to be okay. She held me as I cried for what seemed like hours. When she left, she told me to not lose hope. *"Emma, there is no doubt in my mind that Tucker is in love with you. When he used to look at me, his expression was always one of neediness."* Picking up my favorite photo she said, *"This man hugging you? I haven't met this man. But I saw the potential in the boy with the sad eyes. I saw that despite the horrendous shit he'd been handed in life, he fought. He fought to hold on to me, because that is the faithful, adoring man inside him. He fought to be brilliant in his job, because he takes pride in everything he does. He's been preparing all his life to be the best at everything he does, and you, my beautiful friend, will be the one who benefits from the hard knocks he's experienced. He will give you his soul, his heart, his love."*

Now, after the weeks of focused Tucker loving, I know those words are true, but standing here feeling excited about my achievement, I can't help feeling desperately sad as well. I have his soul, his heart, and his love, which for this moment, might need to be enough.

Racer must notice my searching because he comes up next to me and pulls a card out of his back pocket. "Sorry, Emma. He wanted to be here."

That's when my heart falls.

He's not coming.

Resigned, I give Racer the best smile I can muster and take the card. While Adalyn takes pictures with Logan, I open the card. At least I'll have his words today. I don't know how he's managed to get them all to me via Racer, especially the incredible timing. The effort that's gone into it, the time. And

315

for Racer to also be so invested . . . Tucker's so incredible. How I wish I could hold him and tell him *thank you. And I love you.*

When I open it, it's completely blank. I turn the card around, look in the envelope for anything I may have missed, but when I don't see anything, I turn to Racer to see if he gave me the wrong card. I know he wouldn't do it on purpose, but he's had to do so much in the last few weeks.

That's when I see a giant bouquet of peonies coming toward me and right behind them is the man of my dreams.

# Chapter Twenty-Six

## TUCKER

She's so beautiful. Standing there in her green graduation gown, unzipped so I get a glimpse of her white, form-fitting dress underneath, I can't help but think how goddamn lucky I am.

A few feet away stands the woman who captured my heart when I least expected it. She came back into my life as a friend and burrowed her soul into mine, making it almost impossible to breathe without her.

Over the past few weeks, I've had Racer and Adalyn keep tabs on Emma's emotional state for me. I needed to feel her out, to make sure my plan was working, because showing up today wouldn't go well if she isn't feeling the same way I am.

Thankfully, from what Racer has said, Emma wants me back, and fuck if I couldn't get home quick enough.

I spent last night at Racer's and this morning, I spoke with Julius. I demanded another raise for the bullshit he's put me through, and if he didn't match what I was asking for, I would walk away.

With heavier pockets, I'm now ready to get my girl back.

I watch Racer hand her the card and hate when her face falls flat. I knew she would expect me to show up today. It was an obvious time to surprise her, but I couldn't help it. This is the start of a new chapter in her life and I want to be a big part of it.

She flips the card around looking for any kind of note. There isn't supposed to be one. When she looks up, I know the minute she spots me because her eyes fill with tears and her hand goes to her mouth.

Knowing it's my cue to move, I walk toward her, loving the way she is so overjoyed with emotion that she can't control the tears that fall from her beautiful eyes.

When I reach her, I hand her the bouquet of peonies I bought from a local florist that knows me by first name now.

"Hey, baby."

"Tucker," she says on a whisper. "You came."

I reach up and wipe away her tears with my thumbs. God, I've missed her. "I wouldn't have missed it for anything." I take her in and smile brightly at her. "You look beautiful, Emma. Is that dress new?"

She nods. "It's from you."

"It's perfect."

She stands there, silent for a second before she turns to Adalyn and hands her the bouquet. With her hands now free, she walks up to me and without taking a second to think, she wraps her arms around my waist, her hands threading under my leather jacket. I return the embrace and prop my cheek on the top of her head.

*I'm home.*

Her lithe body shakes beneath me so I squeeze her tighter, letting her know I have her. When she pulls back to look at me, she says, "I missed you so much."

"I missed you more, Emma." I tilt my head toward a concrete wall. "Can we talk for a second?"

She nods and then tells the group we'll be back. When I turn to look at our friends, they're all standing in a line together, smiling brightly, even Logan. Maybe that guy isn't as bad as I thought he was . . . maybe.

With her hand in mine, I guide her to the half wall and lift her up on it. I position myself between her legs so we're looking each other in the eyes. I stroke her cheek, wiping away her tears, and she presses her hands on my shoulders.

"I can't believe you're here. When Racer handed me the card, I really thought I was going to break in half. I just wanted you home."

"I wanted to be home, believe me." I rub my hands on her thighs gently and say, "I'm sorry—"

She presses her finger against my lips. "No more apologizing, no more explaining. You have done enough of both." She cups my cheek. "Tucker, you wrote that you admire me, well, the feeling is mutual. You've been to hell and back again, and yet you stand here on your own two feet, able to listen, to provide for yourself, for me, and to open your heart once again." Her thumb strokes over my cheek. "You have taught me about perseverance, about the strength a human possesses, and that despite your upbringing and influences, you rose above it all and became the most beautifully broken man I've ever met." She leans forward and presses her forehead against mine. "I love you, Tucker. And I want to be yours forever."

I squeeze my eyes shut for a second, trying to comprehend her words and the impact they have on my soul.

She loves me.

*Emma. Marks. Loves. Me.*

I'm where I belong, in her arms, in the only place that's felt like home to me.

I press a kiss against her lips and say, "I love you, Emma. This right here, this feeling of being in your arms, it's home. It's as if I've waited so damn long to love someone as much as I love you. You're it for me, Emma. My love, my soul, my home."

She presses her hand against my chest, right over my heart and says, "You're where you belong."

And she couldn't be closer to the truth.

I grew up believing the love I felt for Sadie was as good as it gets. Life is funny, and right when you think you have it all figured out, it throws you for a loop. Some of the darkest days bring the lightest of life-changing moments. I know this is true because Emma *is* my light.

Who would have thought that the night I saw Emma at the bar would be the moment to completely redirect my future?

I hated being at my house alone. I hated every second of its emptiness, of what it represented. It felt like a glaring reminder of my failure.

And then there was Emma. Bright, beautiful, and sassy-mouthed Emma Marks.

She didn't just transform the empty walls of my house into a home; she transformed me. Her light. Her love. Her brightness changed me from being a mere shadow. A desperately despondent and aimless man.

I'm not reliant on her love to hold me up. That was the old me.

With a home that feels like home, a gorgeous woman in my forever, I'm a man fulfilled. I'm a man with hope. I'm a man with love.

I'm DJ Hot Cock, a fucking lucky bastard, ready to make music with my DJ Jazzy Nurse Tits.

Forever.

# Epilogue

## TUCKER

"I swear to God, Racer, if you don't stop poking me I'm going to kick you in the dick."

He puts his hands down and hops in place. "I'm just so excited. How can you not be excited?"

Maybe because I'm fucking terrified. We spent the entire day during one of Emma's twelve-hour shifts fixing up the deck in the backyard and making it into a little oasis for Emma to enjoy when she wants to relax with an old-fashioned after a long day on her feet.

We woke up really fucking early, stained the deck, built the furniture I purchased, including a coffee table fire pit, and hung bulb lights across the entire deck. There is a log ready to be burned, s'mores ready to be consumed, and a question on the tip of my tongue ready to be asked.

"You know, you can go around the corner and wait with everyone else. You don't have to stand here."

"But then you would be by yourself. Plus I enjoy seeing you sweat." He tickles my cheek with his finger that I swat away.

"Get the fuck out of here." The sound of a car door shutting rings through the night. Eyes wide, I turn to Racer and whisper,

"Go, now!"

"Fine." He holds up his hands and then pulls me into a bear hug. "Ugh, my little man is all grown-up."

"Christ." I push him off me and straighten my polo. "I'm seriously calling on Smalls whenever I need help now."

"Lies, so many fucking lies."

Racer takes off before I can respond and hides next to garage with everyone else.

My stomach is flipping a mile a minute and my entire body feels shaky, so I stuff my hands in my dark jeans and try to calm my racing nerves.

I hear the kitchen door shut and I know she's seeing the sign to meet me out back. Since the door to the deck is right off the kitchen, it's going to be hard to miss the new lights illuminating the backyard, but hopefully she won't see everything from the kitchen window.

I see her in the window and my heart rate picks up. She opens the door and peeks out first, a giant smile on that gorgeous face. "What did you do?" she asks as she steps out onto the deck and takes it all in.

Damn, she looks so cute in her scrubs.

"I wanted to give you a little place to relax after your long days," I reply while walking up to her and linking our hands together.

"Tucker, you've given me an entire house to relax in. You didn't have to do this."

"I know I didn't, I wanted to." I kiss the top of her head and spin her around to the light music that's playing in the background. "What do you think?"

I hold her close to me as we slow dance on the deck; her eyes trail over the lights, the moonlit sky above us. When she meets my eyes, she says, "It's perfect."

"Almost perfect."

I spin her around one last time before dropping to my knee. I hold on to her hand as the other goes to her mouth. "Tucker . . ." she whispers as I pull a ring box out of my pocket.

Taking a deep breath, I look her in the eyes and say, "Emma, you came back into my life when all I could see was darkness surrounding me. You moved into our house when I wasn't sure if I even wanted to still live there myself. You helped me see the beauty in the place we call home. You brightened every ounce of my life with your smile, your teasing, and your weird random purchases that still continue to boggle my mind." She giggles as tears fall from her eyes. "You've shown me how to love again, how to live again, and how to see this world in full color. I can't imagine a day without you in my life, in my arms." I let go of her hand and pop open the ring box. She cries even harder. "Emma, will you please do me the honor of marrying me?"

She shakes her head yes, happy tears streaming down her cheeks. I stand, a weight of happiness lifting me up as I place the ring on her finger and then cup her face. "I love you so much, Emma, so fucking much."

"I love you too," she squeaks out before looping her hand around the back of my neck and pulling me into one of the best pair of lips I've ever had the privilege of kissing.

From behind us, a wave of cheers erupts as our friends start clapping and coming in for hugs. Racer is the first one to wrap his arms around us. He's screaming in excitement and jumping up and down.

"I knew she would say yes." He shakes us to the point that I'm forced to push him away, but not before he grabs my cheeks and lays a huge kiss on my lips.

I wipe my mouth and say, "What the fuck, man?"

Both Emma and Racer are laughing at my expense as Smalls

wraps me in a hug and does the same exact thing. "Lucky girl," Smalls replies as he pats my cheek.

When Andrew, Sadie's boyfriend approaches me, arms wide, lips puckered, I stiff-arm him and say, "Don't even think about it."

It's taken me a bit to get used to hanging out with Sadie again, but in all honesty, it feels good to have her around as a friend. And Andrew, shit, it's hard not to like the guy. He's so damn charismatic. We might get along a little too much which freaks Emma and Sadie out of course.

"Aw, come on, man, just a little lipper." Andrew points to his lips and I push him away.

"Get the fuck out of here." I laugh.

Emma is showing off her ring to Sadie, Adalyn, and our good friend Smilly from Whitney Point. They are cooing over the diamond as Emma looks up at me, her eyes sparkling with so much love that I don't know if I could ever feel so much for one single person.

That girl, the one with the long brown hair and bright blue eyes, the one who wears a matching pajama set to bed every night, the one who used to fawn over our drunk asses as kids, and the one who wakes up with the craziest morning hair I've ever seen, she's perfect. She's mine, and I will forever be hers.


The End

Made in the USA
Las Vegas, NV
19 February 2023